QUO VADIS?

QUO VADIS?

HENRYK SIENKIEWICZ

In a New American Translation by
Stanley F. Conrad

HIPPOCRENE BOOKS
New York

Library of Congress Cataloging-in-Publication Data
Sienkiewicz, Henryk, 1846-1916.
[Quo vadis? English]
Quo vadis? / Henryk Sienkiewicz; in a new American translation
by Stanley F. Conrad.
ISBN 0-7818-0010-1
I. Conrad, Stanley F. II. Title.
PG7158.S4Q43   1992
891.8'536—dc20   92-28651
CIP

For information, address:
HIPPOCRENE BOOKS, INC.
171 Madison Avenue
New York, NY 10016

Printed in the United States of America.

QUO VADIS?

CHAPTER I

IT was already noon when Petronius awoke from sleep and, as usual, felt very tired. The day before he had attended Nero's feast which lasted far into the night. For some time his health had been failing. He himself admitted that when he awoke he felt numb and was unable to think properly. However, the morning bath and the expert massaging of his body by his trained slaves gradually accelerated the flow of his sluggish blood, roused him, restored his spirits and his strength so much so that he left the bath with eyes sparkling with joy. He felt rejuvenated, invigorated and so unsurpassed in elegance that Otho himself could not compare with him. He looked indeed the embodiment of the name attributed to him: "Master of Elegance."

He rarely visited the public baths except when an orator whose fame was extolled in the city happened to be there or when there were combats of exceptional interest near the baths. Anyway, he had his own private baths. The famous builder Celer, with the help of his partner Severus of equal fame, had worked on them with such great taste that Emperor Nero himself had to admit their superiority over those which he possessed, even though the imperial baths were more varied and extensive and furbished with much greater luxury.

During last night's feast Petronius was bored by the clowning of Vatinius. Together with Nero, Lucan and Seneca, he took part in the dispute concerning whether a woman has a soul. Now, rising late as usual, he partook of the baths. Two powerful slaves laid him on a cypress table covered with a large white Egyptian towel. With hands dipped in perfumed oil they began to massage his well-formed body.

He shut his eyes waiting for the heat of the room and the warmth of their hands to work on his body and ease the tiredness. After a while he opened his eyes and inquired about the weather. He also asked about the gems which the jeweler had promised to send him that day for inspection. It appeared that the weather was fine with a light breeze from the Alban hills and the gems had not been delivered yet. Petronius had closed his eyes again and given an order to be carried to the *tepidarium,* when from behind a curtain the *nomenclator* brought notice that young Marcus Vinitius who recently returned from Asia Minor had come to visit him.

Petronius gave orders to admit his guest to the *tepidarium* to which he himself was carried. Marcus Vinitius was the son of his elder sister who years before had married Marcus Vinitius the Elder, a man high in government under Tiberius Caesar. Young Marcus had served under the great Corbulo in the war against the Parthians and at the close of the war had returned to the city. Petronius liked and admired young Marcus very much and for a two-fold reason. First, because Marcus was a handsome and athletic man. The other, because his nephew had the decency not to engross himself in vice and corruption which was so rampant everywhere. This, Petronius prized very highly.

"Greetings to you, Petronius," said Marcus as he briskly entered the *tepidarium.* "May all the gods bestow success upon you, especially Asklepios and Kypris for under their dual protection nothing evil can befall you."

"Welcome to Rome and may your rest be serene and peaceful after the war," replied Petronius, extending his hand from the folds of the soft cloth in which he was wrapped. "What's new in Armenia or, since you were in Asia Minor, did you linger a while in Bythynia?"

Petronius had at one time been governor of Bythynia and in addition had ruled that country with vigor and justice. This contrasted strangely with the present character of the man who was noted for preferring the soft life of luxury. Therefore he gladly recalled those times since they were proof of what he had been and of what he might have become had it pleased him.

"Yes, I happened to visit Heraklea," answered Vinitius. "Corbulo sent me there at one time with orders for reinforcements."

"Ah, Heraklea! I once met a young lady there for whom I would have given all the divorced women of this city not excluding Poppaea. But, that's old history. Tell me rather about the Parthians and their barbarian allies who, as Arulenus claims, walk on all fours at home and pretend to be members of the human race only when they come in contact with us. The people of Rome speak much of them now perhaps because it is dangerous to speak of anything else."

"The war is going badly and, if it were not for Corbulo, it might have turned into defeat."

"Corbulo...by Bacchus! A real god of war...a man of Mars, a great leader though quick tempered, honest and stupid. I like the man perhaps for the sole reason that Nero is afraid of him."

"Corbulo is not a stupid man."

"Perhaps you are right...no matter. As Pyrrho says, stupidity is no worse than wisdom and there is not much difference between the two."

Vinitius began to talk about the war but when Petronius closed his eyes the young man noticed how tired his uncle looked, a weariness which the baths could not hide. He therefore changed the subject and with great concern asked about his health.

Petronius opened his eyes. Health? No, he did not feel well. However, thank goodness, he had not reached that sorry state of young Sisenna who had lost all feeling in his limbs to such a degree that when he was carried to his bath in the morning, he asked his slaves, "Am I sitting or am I standing?" But it is true. He does not feel well. Vinitius had indeed committed him to the care of Asklepios and Kypris. It was not known however whose son Asklepios was—the son of Arsinoe or Coronis; and if the mother was not sure what could be said of the father? Who can be absolutely sure of his father these days?

At this Petronius began to laugh, then spoke again, "As a matter of fact two years ago I offered to the gods three dozen live blackbirds and a cup filled with gold but do you know why? I said to myself, 'It may or may not help me but what's the harm?' If people still offer to the gods, they feel the same as I do about it. Perhaps the only exceptions are the mule drivers whom the travelers hire at the Capena gate. As to Asklepios, well...I had dealings with his offspring too. When I had a bit of trouble with my bladder last year I allowed them to chant incantations over me. I was sure they were fakes but I said to myself, 'What's the harm?' The world is full of deceit, life is full of illusion. Belief in the soul is an illusion also. The main thing is to know the difference between pleasant and boring illusions. I tell my slaves to burn cedar wood mixed with amber because I prefer perfumes to stenches. Since you have commended me also to the care of the goddess Kypris, I can tell you that I have known her protection over me to the extent that I have twinges in my right foot. Even so she is a good goddess. I suppose that you yourself will soon offer white doves at her altar."

"How right you are!" exclaimed Vinitius. "Parthian arrows missed me in the war but love's dart has struck me without warning, and just a short distance from the heart of Rome."

"By the white knees of the Graces! Tell me all about it when it's convenient for you."

"It is precisely about this matter that I wish to get some advice from you."

While the slaves were busy attending Petronius, the latter invited his nephew to enjoy a swim in the lukewarm water. Vinitius did so. Petronius admired his young and muscular body with an eye of an artist. "Hercules did not have a better formed body than you have," he remarked.

The young man, pleased at the compliment, began to swim about with great vigor. Soon he joined Petronius who had ordered a lector, with a bronze tube at his breast and rolls of paper in the tube, to read to him as was his custom.

"Do you wish to listen?" asked Petronius.

"If it is your own composition, gladly," answered the young tribune. "If not, I would prefer to talk to you. Nowadays all kinds of poets harangue people on practically every street corner."

"They surely do! You can't pass a basilica, a bath, a library or a bookshop without seeing a poet gesticulating like a monkey. Agrippa, when he returned from the east, mistook them for madmen. Such are our times. Nero writes verses and all follow his example. Only one should not write better verses than Caesar and that is why I'm concerned about Lucan. But, thank goodness, I write prose and when I do, I certainly don't praise myself or others. What the lector intended to read is about poor Fabricius Veiento."

"Why poor?"

"Because he was told to journey into exile and not to come back to Rome till ordered to do so. This odyssey will be easier for him than for Ulysses, for believe me, his wife is no Penelope. Of course, it was a rash act on the part of the powers that be but it seems that they don't act any other way these days. The book itself is rather dull but it gained popularity only because the author got himself exiled. Now all you hear is, 'Scandal...shame.... ' It could be that the author used his imagination in some cases but I tell you that I know the city and its people quite well and I can assure you that many of his accusations are less severe than are the facts themselves. Everyone is searching the book in fear to see whether there is mention of himself in it. However one is pleased when he finds the names of his friends or acquaintances. At one bookshop alone there are at least a hundred copyists of the book and its success is assured."

"Is there any mention of you in the book?"

"There is but the author presented me in a better light than I deserve. You see, we here have lost all sense of right and wrong although Seneca and some others pretend that they know the difference. To me it's all the same. By Hercules! I say what I think. At least I know what is ugly and what is beautiful and that is what our revered, red-bearded poet Nero is unable to understand."

"I am sorry however for Fabricius.... He was a good companion."

"His own vanity was his undoing. He was only suspected of being the author but he just could not keep quiet. He began confiding in so many people that he was finally trapped. Did you hear the story about Rufinus?"

"No."

"Then come with me to the *tepidarium* and I'll tell you."

They passed on to the cooling room in the center of which was a beautiful fountain of bright cerise color. From it wafted the smell of violets. They seated themselves in velvet-covered niches ideal for cooling off. After sitting in silence for a few minutes Vinitius looked about the room and noticed a statue of a bronze faun who, holding a nymph in his arms, was eagerly attempting to kiss her. "That one knows what is best in life," he remarked.

"Perhaps, but you also love war which I detest because there is not much chance of keeping clean and well groomed in war tents. Each man to his own preference. Nero loves singing...especially his own. Old Scaurus loves his Corinthian vase which stands near his bed and which he kisses when he is unable to sleep. He has almost kissed the edges off. Tell me, do you write verse?"

"No. Can't compose at all."

"Do you play on the lute and sing?"

"No."

"And do you indulge in chariot racing?"

"I tried once at Antioch but with little success."

"Then I am at ease concerning your welfare. And, to what party do you belong in the hippodrome?"

"To the Greens."

"Now I'm definitely not worried about you. Yes, you have large possessions but you are not as rich as Pallas or Seneca. You see, for us these days it is well to write verses, to sing, to recite poetry and to compete in the circus, but it is much better, and especially safer, not to write verses, not to play or sing and not to compete in the races. It is useful to show admiration and hope that our red-bearded emperor shows it at the same time. You are a handsome young man so you should be careful that Poppaea does not fall in love with you. There is danger in that. But surely, she is too experienced for that. She had enough of love with her two previous husbands; now she wants something else. Do you know that Otho still loves her madly? He wanders over the cliffs of Spain and sighs. He forgets about his former habits and it takes him nearly three hours a day to do his grooming. Who would have expected this of Otho?"

"I understand that," said Vinitius, "but if I were in his place I would do something else."

"What's that?"

"I would enroll faithful legions of mountaineers of that country. They are good soldiers, those Iberians."

"Vinitius...Vinitius...I dare say that you would not do that. Things like that are done, it is true, but no one would dare mention it, even conditionally. You know what I would do if I were

Otho? I would laugh at Poppaea, I would laugh at Nero and I would form legions—yes—not of Iberian men but of Iberian women. Moreover, I would write epigrams but I would not read them to anyone, not like that poor Rufinus."

"You were about to tell me his story."

"Come. I will tell you that in the *unctorium* (anointing room)."

But in the anointing room Vinitius was distracted by the beautiful women slaves who were awaiting them. Two of them, Africans resembling statues of ebony, began to anoint their bodies with exotic perfumes from Arabia; others, Phrygians skilled in hair dressing, held in their amazingly supple hands, combs and mirrors made of polished steel; two others, Grecian maidens from the island of Cos who resembled goddesses in their beauty, waited for their turn to approach and fold the togas of their master and his guest.

"By Zeus, your choice of bodies is exceptional!"

"I prefer quality to quantity," answered Petronius. "My entire household in Rome does not exceed four hundred, and I judge that for personal attendance, only upstarts need a greater number of slaves."

"Even Nero does not possess such beautiful bodies!" exclaimed Vinitius.

Pleased at this remark from his nephew, Petronius turned to him and said, "Well, you know, I am neither as unobliging as Bassus or as pedantic as Aulus Plautius."

When he heard this last name, Vinitius put aside his admiration for the beauty of the maidens from Cos for a moment and turning to Petronius asked in astonishment, "Why did you mention the name of Aulus Plautius? Did you know that my horse threw me just as I was about to enter Rome and I had to spend several days nursing a broken arm in the house of Aulus which happened to be close by? One of his slaves, Merion, attended me until I got better. Actually, it's about my stay there that I wanted to talk to you."

"Why? Is it because you fell in love with his wife Pomponia? If so, then I'm sorry for you because she is not young and moreover she is virtuous. I can't imagine a worse combination."

"No, not with Pomponia. Alas, I really don't know for sure who the girl is. Her name is either Ligia or Callina. They call her Ligia, I suppose because she comes from the Ligian nation, but she has her own barbarian name, Callina. I found that house a strange one indeed. Although there are many people in it, it is quiet at times and peaceful as it is in the groves of Subiacum. For several days I did not realize that a divinity lived in that house. I accidently glimpsed her bathing at the garden fountain, and I swear to you by the mist from which Aphrodite appeared that the early sun's rays passed right through her body. I was sure that she would vanish any moment, she was so beautiful and unreal. After that scene I managed to see her only twice more and I tell you, Petronius, that I find neither rest nor peace since. I don't want anything the city can give me; I want neither women nor gold, neither wine nor feasts. I want Ligia. I yearn for her day and night.

"Why don't you buy her from Plautius if she is a slave?"

"She is not a slave."

"What is she then, one of his freedwomen?"

"Never having been a slave, she could not be a freedwoman."

"Well, who is she then?"

"I heard that she is a daughter of a barbarian king or ruler."

"I must say, Vinitius, you arouse my curiosity."

"If you wish to hear me out, I will try to satisfy your curiosity. The story is not long. You must remember the exiled king Vannius who spent some time here in Rome. He was noted for his expert play at dice and his chariot racing. Well, if you recall, Emperor Drusus placed him back on his original throne as king of the Suevi. At first he ruled well and with success but soon reverted to his tyrranical ways, whereupon his own nephews determined to depose him once more."

"Yes," said Petronius, "I remember. That all happened during the recent Claudian times."

"Right," Vinitius continued, "war broke out in that country. Vannius summoned to his aid the Yazygi; his nephews called in the Ligians who, hearing of the riches of Vannius and enticed by the hope of booty, came in such numbers that Caesar Claudius himself began to fear for the safety of the bounty. He did not wish to interfere in a war among the barbarians but he wrote to Atelius Hister who commanded the legions of the Danube to keep a watchful eye on the course of the war and not to permit them to disturb the peace of Rome. Whereupon Hister demanded a promise of the Ligians not to cross the boundary. To this they not only agreed but also gave hostages among whom were the wife and daughter of their leader. The custom of the barbarians, as is known to you, is to take their wives and children on their war expeditions. Well, the result of all this is that Ligia happens to be the daughter of that Ligian king."

"How do you know all this?"

"Aulus Plautius told me all this himself. The fact is that according to their agreement the Ligians did not cross the boundary, but as you know barbarians come and go like a storm. The Ligians did the same. After defeating their enemy they vanished with their war booty and with their wild ox-horns on their heads. The hostages remained with Hister. The mother died soon after and Hister, not knowing what to do with the daughter, sent her to Pomponius, the governor of all Germany. Hister, after returning to Rome for his triumphal march, gave her to his sister Pomponia Graecina, the wife of Aulus Plautius. In his house where everything is virtuous, Ligia grew up to be as virtuous as Graecina herself and so beautiful that even Poppaea cannot compare with her."

"And so?"

"So I repeat to you that from the moment when I saw how the sun's rays at the fountain passed through her body, I fell madly in love with her."

"So she is transparent as a lamprey eel or a baby sardine."

"Please, I beg you, Petronius, do not jest about this. Perhaps I do not speak strongly enough of my desires. Bright garments frequently cover up deep wounds. I have to tell you this too. While returning from Asia, I spent one night in the temple of Mopsus and he did appear to me in a dream and assured me that a great change would take place in my life through love."

"Pliny claims that he does not believe in the gods but he believes in dreams and perhaps he is right. My jests do not prevent me from thinking that truly there is only one deity and she is the eternal, creative, all-powerful Venus Genetrix. She brings souls together; she unites bodies and all things. Eros formed the world out of chaos. Whether he did the right thing is another question, but since he did so, we should acclaim his might even though we do not have to like it."

"Alas, Petronius, it is easier for you to philosophize than to give me advice."

"Well, tell me what do you really want?"

"I want Ligia. I want these arms of mine to embrace her and keep her close to me. I want to breathe with her breath. If she were a slave I would give for her a hundred maidens with their feet painted white to show that they were put on sale for the first time. I want to have her in my house till my head is as white as Mount Soracte in winter."

"She is not a slave, nevertheless she does belong to Plautius. Perhaps he would be willing to give her up."

"Evidently you do not know Pomponia Graecina. Anyway, they have both become attached to her as if she were their own daughter."

"Pomponia...yes you are right; she is as stalwart and unflexible as a cypress tree. If she were not the wife of Aulus, she might very well be hired as a mourner. She still wears black clothes, mourning the death of Julia. Even though she is alive, she resembles the asphodel, the flower of the dead. Moreover, she is a one-man woman so that makes her rather unique among our divorced ladies of Rome, almost as unbelievable a sight as the sight of a phoenix which, according to what is said, appears only once in about five centuries. There is in fact a rumor that one has appeared recently in Egypt, have you heard?"

"Petronius...Petronius...let us discuss the phoenix some other time."

"What can I say, Marcus? I know Aulus Plautius. Even though he does not condone my way of living, yet perhaps, he may like and respect me a little more than he does some others. He knows that I have never been an informer like Domitius Afer, Tigellinus and the whole bunch of Nero's companions. Without pretending to be a Stoic I have often been outraged at Nero's actions even though people like Seneca and Burrus overlook them. However, if you think that I can do something with Aulus, then I am at your service."

"I think you can. I believe that he can be swayed, especially by a person of your caliber and intelligence. Please, talk to him."

"You give me more credit than I deserve but if it is only a matter of talking to him then I will do so when they return to Rome."

"They got back two days ago."

"In that case let us go to the dining room where dinner is about ready. After that we will visit Aulus Plautius."

"You have always been kind to me," exclaimed Vinitius. "As soon as I get back home I'm going to order my sculptor to erect a statue of you before which I will place offerings as to a god. As beautiful a statue as the one you have here." And Vinitius pointed to a statue of Petronius as Hermes with a staff in his hand. He added, "By the light of Helios...if the divine Alexander resembled you, I do not wonder at Helen."

There was as much sincerity as flattery in his remark. Petronius indeed, though older and less muscular than Vinitius, was more handsome. The women of Rome admired not only his intellect and good taste which gained for him the title of Master of Elegance but also his graceful body. This admiration was also evident on the faces of the two maidens from Cos who were arranging the folds of his toga. One of these two, Eunice by name, was secretly in love with him and she showed that love in her eyes which were full of submission and rapture. But Petronius did not pay the slightest heed to this and turning to Vinitius he quoted Seneca's opinion of women, "Woman is fickle..." Then, escorting Vinitius, he led him out of the room.

After they had left, the two Grecian maidens and the other slaves began putting away the vessels with perfumes when a sound was heard beyond the curtains. The men were signaling the women to come. All the girls vanished quickly, all except Eunice who, after a moment's pause, listening to the voices and laughter of the men and women slaves, picked up a richly inlaid stool on which Petronius had just been sitting, and put it carefully before his statue. The room was full of sunlight and the hues came from the many-colored marbles with which the wall was covered. Eunice stood up on the stool and finding herself at the level of the statue, she threw her arms around its neck. Then, throwing back her golden hair and pressing her warm body to the white marble, she pressed her lips with ecstasy to the cold lips of Petronius.

CHAPTER II

AT a time when ordinary mortals were past their midday meal, they ate breakfast, after which Petronius proposed a nap. According to him it was too early for visiting people.... "There are those who go about visiting people even at sunrise, but I think it's a barbarous custom, not Roman. The afternoon hours are the best, not earlier than at the time when the sun passes to the side of Jove's temple and begins to look askance at the Forum. In autumn it is still warm and people prefer to sleep after eating. After a stroll of the prescribed thousand steps, it is pleasant to relax and doze a little to the hum of the fountain in a room shaded from the afternoon sun." Vinitius judged this to be sensible and the two men began to walk, speaking casually about events occurring on the Palatine, in the city, and even philosophizing a little on life in general. After the walk they slept but not for long, barely a half hour. Petronius, after rubbing his hands and temples with verbena, a perfume he much preferred, remarked, "You can't imagine how this perfume invigorates and refreshes me. Now I'm ready. Let's go."

The litter that was to carry them had been awaiting them for some time so Petronius gave the command to be carried to the house of Aulus. The residence of Petronius was on the southern slope of the Palatine hill; the shortest route therefore was by way of the Forum. Petronius gave orders to stop first at the jewelers which was on the way.

Muscular slaves carried the litter without much effort. These were preceded by other slaves who walked before the litter paving the way when necessary. Petronius, raising his perfumed hands to his nostrils from time to time, seemed to be deliberating something in his mind.

"It occurs to me," he said after a while, "that if your beautiful goddess is not a slave, she might very well leave the house of Plautius and move to yours. You would surround her with love and shower her with wealth as I do my adored Chrysothemis, of whom, speaking between us, I have just about had enough as she of me."

Marcus shook his head.

"No?" asked Petronius. "Perhaps the decision can be left up to Caesar, and then, thanks to my influence, our red-bearded emperor would be on our side."

"You don't know Ligia," replied Vinitius.

"Then permit me to ask you, do you know her? Did you speak to her? Have you confessed your love to her?"

"I first saw her at the fountain. After that I saw her only twice more. Remember that during my recovery I stayed at a separate villa set aside for guests and, having a broken arm, I could not join them at meals. Only on the eve of the day when I was to leave did I meet Ligia at supper but I could not say a word to her. I had to listen to Aulus and his account of his victorious expedition in Britain and then about the fall of the small states in Italy which Licinius tried to prevent. I doubt if Aulus can talk about anything else and I doubt if we will be able to prevent hearing his story of the war unless you want to hear him talk about the loose morals of our times. They have pheasants on their preserves but they do not eat them believing that every pheasant that is eaten brings nearer the end of Roman power. I met her a second time at the pool in the garden. She had a branch in her hand and was sprinkling the irises with it. I stood before her confused and unable to utter a word."

Petronius glanced at him with a bit of envy on his face. "Lucky man," he said. "Though everything in life were to change for the worst, one thing will always remain the same: eternal youth."

After a while he asked, "And did you speak to her?"

"When I had recovered a bit, I told her that I broke my arm falling from my horse but the suffering I had endured in this house was preferable to me to any delight elsewhere. Sickness was better here than health anywhere else. She became confused listening to my words, then she began drawing something with the branch on

the sand nearby. She then raised her eyes and looked down again at
the marks she had drawn on the sand. Then she ran away from me
without a word."

"She must have beautiful eyes."

"As beautiful as the blue sea and I was drowned in their beauty.
Believe me the Archipelago is less blue. At that moment the young
son of Plautius ran up to me with a question but my mind was so
engrossed with Ligia that I did not know what he was saying."

"O goddess Athene!" exclaimed Petronius. "Remove from the
eyes of this youth the bandage with which Eros has bound them....
If not, he will break his head against the temple of Venus." Then
turning to Vinitius he said, "O spring bud on the tree of life...O
first green shoot of the vine.... Instead of taking you to Plautius I
ought to take you to the house of Gelecius where there is a school
for youths who wish to learn something about life."

"What do you mean by that?"

"What did the young lady write on the sand? Was it not the
name of Amor, or a heart pierced with his dart or something like
it so as to tell you that her heart understands love and its secrets?
Didn't you notice anything on the sand?"

"I wear this toga of a man longer than you think," replied
Vinitius. "Before little Aulus ran up to me I did look at her
markings because I know that frequently maidens in Greece and in
Rome draw on the sand a confession which their lips will not utter.
But, guess what she drew."

"If it's something other than I supposed, I cannot guess."

"A fish!"

"What did you say?"

"I said a fish. Now tell me what did that mean? Is it because cool
blood was up till now flowing in her veins? I don't know. But you,
Petronius, you who just called me a spring bud on the tree of life,
you certainly would know what that sign means."

"My dear boy, you better ask Pliny about fish. If old Apitus were
alive he could also tell you something about them. In his lifetime
he ate more fish than you can find in the bay of Naples."

Further conversation was impossible on account of the noisy
rabble in the streets. However they soon turned into the Roman
Forum where, on clear days before sunset, crowds of people assembled to stroll among the columns, to relate and listen to news, to

watch many important personages borne in their litters and also to wander in and out of the many jewelry and bookshops and places where money was changed. There were also stores where silks, bronzes and many other articles were sold, especially at the side facing the Capitol.

Half of the Forum was already buried in shade but some of the temples erected on higher ground were still bathed in sunshine. Those built on a lower level had already cast their shadows on marble slabs. All kinds of columns were in abundance everywhere you looked. Some towered above others, some extended to the right, some to the left; some looked as if they were reaching for the heights; others seemed to be reaching for the walls of the Capitol; still others resembled tree trunks in various colors like flowers with Ionic tips or Doric quadrangles.

Above that forest gleamed colored ornaments, the various gods sculptured on their pedestals; there were a few bronze chariots interspersed which gave the impression that they were about to fly into space. Through the middle of the market and along the edges of it flowed a river of people; crowds were sitting on the steps of the temple of Castor and Pollux or walking around the temple of Vesta. From above, they all resembled swarms of many-colored ants or beetles. There were others ascending or descending the immense steps which led to the temple dedicated to Jupiter. Others stood in groups listening to orators standing on pedestals. There were still all kinds of noises: shouts of vendors selling fruit, wine or water mixed with fig juice; sounds of different jugglers trying to get attention, yells of sellers of different kinds of medicines; there were soothsayers and interpreters of dreams clamoring for attention. Here and there amid all the shouting could be heard musical sounds played on Egyptian and Grecian instruments. The sick, the pious, the afflicted could be seen bearing offerings to the temples.

In the midst of all the people on the flagstones, flocks of doves gathered eager for the grain that was thrown to them. Agitated, they would rise in flight only to settle down again for more food. From time to time the crowds would move aside in order to allow the various litters to pass. These held many people of note, such as senators, officials and notorious women of Rome. Their faces were usually haggard from lack of sleep caused by dissolute ways of living. The many-tongued populace yelled out their names as they

recognized them, adding to each either praise or ridicule. There
were also soldiers marching with measured tread, looking about
solemnly making sure order prevailed. Everywhere the Greek language could be heard as often as the Latin.

Vinitius, who had been away from the city a long time, looked
with much curiosity upon that swarm of humanity and on the
famous Roman Forum which, he reflected, dominated the sea of
the world but which was in turn flooded by it. As a matter of fact
the local gentry was almost lost in that crowd composed of all races
and nations. One could see black Ethiopians, light-haired inhabitants of the distant north, Britains, Gauls, Germans, slant-eyed
people from the Far East, some from the Euphrates and from the
Indus with beards dyed brick red, Syrians from the banks of the
Oriontes with black but mild eyes; also dried-up dwellers of the
deserts of Arabia; Jews, Egyptians, Numidians and Africans;
Greeks from Hellas who, with the Romans, dominated the city.
(Their influence however was by means of science, art, wisdom and
also deceit.) There were Greeks from the Islands, from Asia Minor,
from Egypt, from Italy and from Gaul. Among the throng one
could also see slaves who had become freedmen, still showing the
pierced ears of slaves. All in all, an idle population waiting to be
amused, supported and even clothed by Caesar. There was also no
lack of visitors whom the ease of life and the prospects of fortune
enticed to the great city. There were priests of Serapis with palm
branches in their hands; priests of Isis, to whose altar more offerings were brought than to the temple of Jove; priests of Cybele
bearing in their hands golden clusters of rice... priests of many
divinities; dancers of the East with bright headdresses, dealers in
amulets, snake charmers and Chaldean fortunetellers; and finally
people without any occupation whatever, who applied every week
for grain at the different storehouses by the Tiber and who fought
for lottery tickets to the circus and spent their nights in rickety
houses in the poor district across the Tiber, and sunny and warm
days under covered porticoes or in the smelly eating houses of the
Subura on the Milvain bridge or before the rich mansions where
from time to time remnants from tables of slaves were thrown out
to them.

Petronius was well known to these crowds. Many times Vinitius
could hear the cry, *"Hic est!"* (Here he is!). They loved him for his

generosity and his popularity had increased especially from the time when they found out that he had declared himself before Caesar as opposed to the sentence of death issued against the whole *familia* (household), against all the slaves of the prefect Pedanius Secundus, without distinction of sex and age, because one of them had killed that tyrannical monster in a moment of despair. Petronius indeed mentioned in public that the only reason why he spoke up to Caesar was because he was the Master of Elegance whose esthetic taste was offended by a slaughter befitting barbarians but not Romans. Nevertheless, people who were indignant about the perpetrated massacre loved Petronius from that time on. But he did not care for their love. He was aware that this same crowd of people also loved Britannicus who was poisoned by Nero and Octavia too who was smothered in hot steam after her veins were opened. There was Rubellius Plautus banished by Nero and Thrasea to whom they may bring a death sentence any day now. All these the mob loved. Their love could well be considered as an ill omen. Petronius had contempt for the multitude because he considered himself above them as an aristocrat and as Master of Elegance. And, certainly they had no part in elegant living. People with the smell of roasted beans which they carried about them and who were always hoarse and sweating from playing *mora* on street corners or amid various columns did not deserve in his eyes the name "human."

Without taking notice therefore of the applause or even of the kisses thrown him from the lips of some women, he began to relate the tale of Pedanius, reviling meanwhile the fickleness of that rabble which the morning after that terrible butchery applauded Nero on his way to the temple Jupiter.

When they arrived at the bookshop of Avirunus he called a halt, descended from the litter and upon entering the bookshop purchased an ornamented manuscript which he in turn presented to Vinitius.

"Here is a gift for you," said he.

"Thanks," answered Vinitius. Then, noticing the title asked, "*Satyricon?* Is it one of the latest works? Whose is it?"

"Mine. But I don't intend to imitate Rufinus whose history I was about to tell you a while back. That is why no one knows who the author is. And, please don't tell anyone about it."

After looking through the manuscript Vinitius ventured the remark, "You mentioned that you did not write verses but I see here many of them interwoven with the prose."

"When you read it notice especially the scene of the feast of Trimalchio. As to writing verses, well, ever since Nero decided to take up writing verses I find writing them distasteful. Vitellius, when he wishes to relieve himself, uses ivory fingers thrust down his throat; others use flamingo feathers steeped in olive oil or a mixture of wild thyme. Me, I read Nero's verses and the result is the same. I can always praise his poetry with a clean stomach if not with a clear conscience."

After that remark he had the litter stop before the goldsmith's shop where he settled the affair of the gems. This done he ordered that he be taken to the mansion of Aulus. On the way there he said to Vinitius, "I'll tell you the story of Rufinus. You will see what an author's vanity can lead to."

But before he started on it they found themselves in front of the dwelling of Aulus. A young and sturdy doorman led them into the antechamber before which a caged magpie greeted them noisily with the word *"Salve."* On the way from the antechamber to the main living quarters Vinitius remarked to his uncle, "Did you notice that the doorman here is without chains?"

"An unusual house," answered Petronius in an undertone. "Did you know that Aulus' wife Pomponia was accused of taking part in a superstition brought from the East which honors a certain Chrestos? She was accused by our notorious Crispinilla who evidently cannot forgive Pomponia because one husband has sufficed her for a lifetime. A one-man woman! Today in Rome it is easier to get that rare delicacy a plate of mushrooms than to find such a woman. They tried her before a domestic court but found her not guilty."

"You are right; this is indeed an unusual house. I'll tell you later what I saw and heard in it." ·

Meanwhile they were ushered into the main living quarters and the slaves brought chairs and stools to rest their feet. Petronius who had never visited this house before, thinking that he would only see sadness and austerity there, looked around in astonishment and surprise. There was an air of brightness and cheerfulness about him everywhere he looked. The sun's rays fell upon the fountain in a quadrangular basin called the impluvium placed there to catch the rain from the opening in the ceiling. There were flowers around the fountain, especially lilies and ferns—lilies in extreme abundance. There were whole clumps of them both red and white. Irises, of beautiful sapphiric blue, had delicate leaves, silvery from the spray of the fountain. Among the dewy masses in which the lily pots were hidden, were little bronze statues representing children and water-birds. In one corner a bronze faun, as if wishing to drink, was inclining his greenish head grizzled by dampness. The floor was of mosaic, the walls partly marble, partly wood upon which colorful paintings of fish, birds and griffins attracted the eye. From the door to the side chamber they were ornamented with tortoise shell and ivory. At the corners were statues of some of the ancestors of Aulus. Peaceful affluence, noble and assured, although far from excess, was evident all around.

Petronius, who lived with much greater ostentation and elegance, could find nothing which offended his taste. He turned toward Vinitius with the intention of telling him so, when a slave pushed aside a curtain and they could see the hurrying figure of Aulus Plautius.

He was a man nearing the evening of life and although his hair was gray, his face was full of energy, fully alive and eagle-like in appearance. Now, however, there appeared a look of astonishment and a bit of alarm at the sight of Petronius who was well known as Nero's companion and counselor.

Petronius, being shrewd and a man of the world, noticed this immediately and so, after the first greetings, speaking with eloquence and ease, made known to Plautius that he was here only to thank him for the care given to his nephew and that gratitude alone was the cause of this visit to which, moreover, he was emboldened by his old acquaintance with Aulus.

Aulus assured him that he was a welcome guest and as to gratitude he was himself grateful to Petronius although perhaps Petronius could not guess why. Petronius truly could not. In vain he raised his hazel eyes endeavouring to remember the least service rendered to Aulus or to anyone. He recalled none. If it was done, it was done involuntarily on his part.

"I love and esteem Vespasian whose life you saved when he had the misfortune to fall asleep while listening to Nero's verses," remarked Aulus.

"He was indeed fortunate in that he did not hear them," replied Petronius. "I will not deny the fact that the matter might have ended with misfortune. Nero was about to send a centurion with the friendly advice to open his veins."

"But you laughed him out of it."

"That is true or rather it is not exactly true. I merely told Nero that if Orpheus put wild beasts to sleep with song, Nero's triumph was the same since he was able to put Vespasian to sleep. Our red-bearded emperor can be chided only if and when you mix a great flattery with a little criticism. Our gracious Empress Poppaea understands this perfectly."

"Alas, such are the times," answered Aulus. "I lack two front teeth which were knocked out by a stone from the hand of a Briton so I speak with a lisp. Still my happiest days were spent in Britain."

"Because they were victorious," added Vinitius.

Petronius, alarmed lest the old general launch upon the history of his former wars, changed the subject. He began to tell about the finding of a young dead wolf having two heads by some people in the vicinity of Preneste. This happened during the time of a lightning storm in which a bolt of lightning struck the temple of Luna which was very unusual because it happened in late autumn. As a result of all this the priests of that temple prophesied the fall of the city of Rome or perhaps the ruin of one of its noble families. This ruin they said could be averted only by more offerings to the temple.

Aulus, when he heard the story, expressed the opinion that such clear signs should not be overlooked. The gods were no doubt angered by the excess of wickedness and so expiatory sacrifices to the gods were certainly in order.

"Your home, Plautius, is not large," remarked Petronius, "even though a great man lives in it. Mine is indeed too large for such a person as I, although in comparison to others it is also small. But even if it were a question of the ruin of a great house such as for instance the Domus Transitoria would it be necessarily worth our while to bring offerings to avert the ruin?"

Plautius did not answer. Evidently he feared to express his opinion on the matter in front of Petronius. This undue fear irked the latter somewhat for Petronius, with all his inability to sense the difference between good and evil, had never been an informer and one could converse with him about anything in perfect safety. However he changed the subject again and began to praise the home of Aulus, the peace and serenity that prevailed therein.

"It is an old residence," said Plautius "in which nothing has been changed since I inherited it."

After the curtain was pushed aside which divided the entrance from the interior, the hall was visible. The living room and the garden shone brightly beyond. From the garden could be heard joyous laughter.

"General," said Petronius, "let's get closer to such sincere laughter which these days is much too rare."

"Gladly," answered Plautius. "That happens to be my son Aulus and Ligia playing ball. Though as to laughter it seems to me, Petronius, your whole life is a joyful laughter."

"Life is worthy of laughter so I laugh at it," answered Petronius, "but here laughter has a different sound."

"Anyway, Petronius does not laugh in the daytime, only at night," put in Vinitius.

While thus conversing, they passed the length of the house and reached the garden where Ligia and little Aulus together with some slaves were enjoying themselves at playing ball. Petronius cast a quick glance at Ligia. Little Aulus ran up to greet Vinitius who approached Ligia. She gazed at him a little out of breath, flushed, with her hair a bit windblown but very beautiful.

In the garden, shaded by ivy, grapes and woodbine, sat Pomponia Graecina. Hence they all went to greet her. She was known to Petronius even though he had never visited Plautius before. He had formerly seen her at the house of Antistis and also at the residence of Seneca and Polion. He always admired her for her poise, dignity and serenity which could be seen in her movements and in her words. Pomponia disturbed his understanding of women to such a degree that he, self-confident as perhaps no one else in all Rome, not only felt for her a kind of esteem but even lost his usual self-confidence. And so, thanking her for the care of Vinitius, he could not help but address her as "Lady" which never occurred to him when speaking, for example, to Calvia Crispinilla, Scribonia, Valeria Selina and other women of high society. After greeting her and thanking her he mentioned that he was sorry to see her so rarely. She neither attended the circus nor the amphitheater. To this she answered calmly, as she affectionately placed her hand on the hand of her husband, "We are both growing old and appreciate our domestic quiet."

Petronius was about to deny this when Aulus added in his somewhat lisping voice, "And we also feel more and more out of tune with people who give Greek names to our Roman gods."

"The gods have been for some time figures of speech," replied Petronius laconically. "Since we were taught rhetoric by Greeks, it is therefore easier for me for instance to say Hera than Juno." Saying this he turned to Pomponia as if to signify that in her presence no other gods could come to mind. Then he began to contradict her remark about getting old.

"Some people, it's true, grow old quickly. There are others however about whose faces Saturn seems to forget." He was sincere in saying this because Pomponia, although middle-aged, still preserved a youthful appearance, her beautiful and delicate features giving an impression of a woman much younger than she actually was even despite her dark robes and solemn mien.

Meanwhile little Aulus, who had become quite friendly with Vinitius during his former stay in the house, came up to him with Ligia at his side and begged him to join them in playing ball. Petronius now had a chance to observe Ligia a little better than before. Under the climbing ivy with the light quivering on her face she seemed to Petronius more beautiful than at first glance, truly a nymph in disguise. As he had not spoken thus far, he rose, inclined his head and, instead of the usual expressions of greeting, quoted the words with which Ulysses greeted Nausikaa: "I beseech you, O Queen, are you a goddess or a mortal? If you are one of the daughters of men who dwell on earth, thrice blessed are your father and mother and thrice blessed your brethren."

Such a compliment from a man of the world like Petronius was flattering indeed. Pomponia herself was pleased. As to Ligia, she listened, confused and flushed, not daring to raise her eyes. But an impish smile began to appear at the corners of her lips and on her face a struggle was evident between the timidity of a maiden and the desire to respond. The latter evidently got the upper hand because, looking quickly at Petronius, she answered him with the same words that Nausikaa answered Ulysses, quoting them quickly as if out of breath: "Stranger, you seem no ordinary man and a wise one." Then she turned and ran out gaily as a bird.

This time Petronius was astonished for he had not expected to hear verses of Homer from the lips of a maiden of whose barbarian extraction he had previously heard from Vinitius. Hence he looked with an enquiring glance at Pomponia who at the moment did not give him an immediate answer for she was looking with a smile at the pride reflected on the face of her husband.

Aulus was not able to conceal that pride. First, he had become attached to Ligia as to his own daughter and second, in spite of his old Roman prejudices which caused him to rant against everything Greek, he nevertheless considered the knowledge of Greek as the summit of social polish. He himself had never been able to learn it well which he was sorry to admit. Therefore he was very pleased that an answer was given in the language of Homer to this elegant man of fashion and letters who was ready to consider his house as barbarian.

"We have a Greek teacher," he said to Petronius, "who teaches our boy and the girl joins him in the lessons. She is a bit flighty but she is dear to both of us and we have grown attached to her."

Petronius gazed through the branches of the woodbine into the garden and at the three who were playing ball. Vinitius had thrown aside his toga and wearing only his tunic was striking the ball which Ligia, standing opposite with raised hands, was trying to catch. At first the maiden did not make a great impression on him; she seemed too slender, but from the moment when he saw her closer, he thought to himself that the goddess Aurora might look like her. There was something about her that was indeed unusual and wonderful.

He considered and evaluated everything about her: her face rosy and clear, her beautiful lips, her eyes as beautiful as the sea, the alabaster whiteness of her forehead, the wealth of her dark hair with a touch of Corinthian bronze gleaming in its folds, her slender neck, the beautiful slope of her shoulders, the whole pos-ture...flexible, young with the youth of May and budding flowers. The artist in him was aroused and the worshiper of beauty. He felt that beneath a statue of this girl one might write "Spring." Sud-denly he remembered his own Chrysothemis and he wanted to laugh. At this moment Chrysothemis with her golden powder on her hair and darkened brows seemed to him a bit jaded, like a yellowed rose tree shedding its leaves. Yet all of Rome envied him because he possessed Chrysothemis. The Empress Poppaea came to mind and in comparison to Ligia she also seemed to him a soulless, waxen mask, even though she was famous for her beauty. In this girl there was not only spring but a radiant soul which shone through her beautiful body as a flame radiated from a lamp.

"Vinitius is right and my Chrysothemis is old, as old as Troy," he reflected. Then he turned to Pomponia Graecina and, pointing to the garden said, "I understand now, my lady, why you and your husband prefer this house to the circus and to feasts on the Palatine."

"Yes," she answered turning her eyes in the direction of little Aulus and Ligia.

The old general began to relate the history of the girl and what he had heard years before from Atelius Hister about the Ligian people who lived in the dark forests of the north.

Vinitius, Ligia and little Aulus finished playing ball and began now to walk along the sand of the garden appearing against the dark background of myrtles and cypresses like three white statues. Ligia held little Aulus by the hand. After they had walked a while they sat down on a bench near the fishpond. Soon the boy ran off to throw stones in the fishpond. Vinitius continued the conversation begun during the walk.

"Yes," he said in a low intense voice. "Barely had I cast aside the *praetexta* (garment worn by youths), when I was sent to the legions in Asia. I had not known the city nor life nor love. I know a little Anacreon by heart, a little of Horace, but I cannot, like Petronius, quote verses when my mind is numb from admiration and unable to find suitable words. As a youth I studied under Musonius who taught me that happiness consists of desiring those things that the gods desire, therefore it depends on our own will. However it seems to me that there is nothing greater and more precious than that which love can give. The gods themselves seek that happiness, hence I, O Ligia, who have not known love thus far follow in their footsteps. I also seek her who can give me happiness...."

He paused and for a while there was nothing to be heard save the light splash of the water into which little Aulus was throwing pebbles. After a few moments he began again, his voice a little softer and more emotional.

"You surely know Vespasian's son Titus? They say that he had scarcely ceased to be a youth when he fell in love so deeply with Bernice that being away from her caused him so much grief that it nearly drew the life out of him. So could I too love, O Ligia! Riches, glory, power...are nothing by comparison. The rich will find one richer than himself; greater glory of another will eclipse one who is famous; a strong man will be overcome by someone stronger. But, can Caesar himself...can any god even, experience greater delight and be happier than a simple mortal at the moment when at his side reposes his beloved...and when he kisses her lips? Hence, love makes us equal to the gods, O Ligia."

She listened to him with unease and astonishment. It seemed to her that she was listening to a beautiful sound of a Grecian flute. Vinitius was singing a kind of song, a wonderful song which made her pulse beat faster in her veins and her heart was filled with a sort of faintness, fearful but at the same time delightful, mysterious. It seemed to her that he was talking about things which up till now were latent inside of her but which began to rouse as if from slumber and which began to take a more definite form...more pleasing...more beautiful.

Meanwhile the sun had already passed the Tiber and had sunk low over the gardens of the Janiculum. On the motionless cypresses there appeared a ruddy light and the whole atmosphere was filled with it. Ligia raised her eyes as if awakened from sleep. He appeared to her more handsome and noble than all men, than all Greek and Roman gods whose statues she had seen on the facades of temples. With his fingers he clasped her arm lightly just above the wrist and asked, "Do you guess what I'm trying to say to you, Ligia?"

"No," she whispered in answer in a voice so soft that Vinitius was barely able to hear.

He did not believe her and drawing her hand toward him he would have placed it on his heart, which under the influence of desire, roused by the beautiful girl, was beating like a hammer. He would have expressed burning words of his love had not Plautius appeared on the path set in a frame of myrtles, speaking to them while approaching.

"The sun is setting; beware of the evening coolness and do not trifle with the goddess Libitina."

"I did not feel the coolness; that is why I did not put on my toga," replied Vinitius.

"You can barely see half of the sun out there beyond the hills. Oh, if only we had the climate of Sicily where people gather in the square at sunset to bid farewell to the disappearing sun with singing."

And, forgetting that a moment ago he had warned them about catching cold he began to talk about Sicily where he had large cultivated fields which he loved. He mentioned that he had in mind one day to move out there and spend the rest of his life in peace and quiet. "One has enough of winter frost when these same winters have indeed whitened his hair. The leaves have yet to fall from the trees, and over the city the sky is still serene, but when the grapevines turn yellow, when snow falls on the Alban hills and the gods visit the countryside with piercing wind, who knows that I may move my entire household to my quiet countryseat in Sicily."

"Do you wish to leave Rome?" asked Vinitius with alarm.

"I have wished to do so for a long time for it is quieter in Sicily and safer." And again he began to reminisce about his gardens, his herds, his house amid the trees, the hills grown over with thyme and mint among which were swarms of buzzing bees.

Vinitius paid little attention to all this. His fear was predominently of losing Ligia if she were to go away. Thinking only of this he involuntarily glanced toward Petronius who sat with Pomponia, in the hope perhaps that he, Petronius, would help him out somehow.

Petronius meanwhile was admiring the view of the setting sun, observing the whole garden and the people standing near the fishpond. The white garments gleamed like gold from the evening rays of the setting sun. In the sky the evening light had begun to assume purple hues of an opal. A strip of the sky became lily-colored. The dark silhouettes of the cypresses grew still more pronounced than during the daylight. In the people, in the trees, in the whole garden reigned an evening calm.

Petronius felt strongly this sense of calm, especially in the people. In the faces of Pomponia, Aulus, their son and Ligia there was something which he was not aware of and which he did not see in the faces which surrounded him every day or rather every night. Here was light, repose and serenity due to the mode of life these people lived. The thought came to him, a bewildering thought, that there might exist such beauty and serenity which he who craved these things did not even imagine existed. At this thought he turned to Pomponia and said, "I've been thinking how different this world of yours is from the world our Nero rules."

She raised her delicate face toward the evening light and said with simplicity, "Not Nero, but God rules the world."

A moment of silence followed. Soon they heard the footsteps of the old general, Vinitius, Ligia and little Aulus. Before they arrived, however, Petronius asked, "Do you then believe in the gods?"

"I believe in God Who is One, just and all-powerful," answered the wife of Aulus Plautius.

CHAPTER III

"SHE believes in God Who is One, all-powerful and just," said Petronius when he and Vinitius were being carried in the litter from the house of Aulus. "If her God is all-powerful, He controls life and death and if He is just, He sends death justly. Why then does Pomponia wear mourning clothes after the death of Julia? Mourning Julia, she blames her God. I must repeat this reasoning to our red-bearded monkey, Nero. In dialectics I consider myself no worse than Socrates. As to women...I maintain that each woman has three or four souls but not one that can reason. Let Pomponia ponder the question of their great logos with Seneca or Cornutus. Let them summon the shades of Xenophon, Parmenides, Zeno and Plato who are out of place in these dark Cimmerian regions as a finch would be in a cage. I wanted to speak to her and to her husband about something else. If I had told them outright why we came, no doubt their virtue would have made as much noise as a bronze shield by a blow of a club. And I dared not. Will you believe me, Vinitius, I did not dare. Peacocks are beautiful birds but they have too shrill a cry. I feared an outcry. But, I must praise your choice. A true rose-fingered Aurora. And do you know what she reminds me of? Spring.... Not our spring out here in Italy where an apple tree puts out its blossom only here and there and olive groves turn gray, but the spring which I once saw in Helvetia, young, fresh and beautiful green. By that pale moon overhead, Marcus, I'm not surprised at you for loving such a beauty, like the goddess Diana. However I want to tell you this: If you tear her away from Aulus and Pomponia, they will try to tear you to pieces as the dogs once tore Acteon.

Vinitius remained silent for a while, then he began to speak with a voice broken with passion, "I desired her before. I desire her much more now. When I held her arm flame engulfed me. I must have her. If I were Zeus I would surround her with a cloud as he surrounded Io. I would kiss her lips and hold her close to me until she would cry out in my arms. I will not sleep. I will order one of my slaves to be flogged and listen to his screams...."

"Calm yourself," said Petronius. "Your cravings are the cravings of a carpenter from the dens of Subura."

"No matter.... I must have her. If you can't do anything I'll find a way myself. Aulus considers Ligia as a daughter; why should I look on her as a slave? Since there is no other way, let her annoint the door of my house with wolf fat and let her sit at my hearth as my wife."

"Calm yourself!" repeated Petronius. "We do not capture barbarians in order to make wives of their daughters. Beware of such a step. We will consider other methods. Chrysothemis seemed to me a daughter of Jove and yet I did not marry her just as Nero did not marry Acte, although she was the daughter of King Attalus. Calm yourself! Know that if she wants to leave Aulus of her own free will, he has no right to stop her. Know this also: you are not the only one who is burning with love. Eros has aroused a flame in her also. Believe me.... I noticed. Have patience. There is a way to do everything right, but today I have done enough thinking and this tires me. But tomorrow I promise that I will think of your problem and I assure you that Petronius is not Petronius if he will fail to find some solution."

They were both silent again. Finally Vinitius spoke, "I thank you. May fortune be bountiful to you."

"Be patient."

"Where did you give orders for the litter to take us?"

"To Chrysothemis."

"You are lucky to possess her whom you love."

"I? Do you know why she still amuses me? She is playing around with my freedman Theokles and she thinks that I do not know about it. Yes, I loved her once but now she amuses me with her lying and her stupidity. If she should begin to flirt with you, know that I'm not jealous."

All at once Petronius paused and turning to Vinitius exclaimed, "I think I may have a plan for you."

"May all the gods reward you!"

"Yes, I believe it will work. In a few days the divine Ligia will be yours."

"You are greater than Caesar!" exclaimed Vinitius.

CHAPTER IV

PETRONIUS kept his promise. He slept all day following his visit to Chrysothemis but in the evening he gave command to be carried to the Palatine where he had a confidential talk with Nero. As a result of this, on the following day a centurion and several soldiers appeared before the house of Aulus Plautius.

While Nero reigned as emperor, times were uncertain and fraught with danger for many. Messengers of this kind were frequently heralds of death. So, when the centurion struck the door of the house of Aulus Plautius, fear spread throughout. The family surrounded the old general, assuming that he was in danger of some kind. Pomponia, embracing his neck with her arms, clung to him with all her strength and her pale lips moved quickly, uttering whispered words. Ligia, pale as a linen sheet, kissed his hand. Little Aulus clung to his toga. From the whole house crowds of slaves began to emerge with cries of fear on their lips. Some women began weeping and wailing.

The old general, accustomed for many years to facing death, remained calm; only his face became hard as if chiseled in stone. After a while, when he silenced the outcries and commanded the attendants to leave, he said, "Let me go, Pomponia. If my time has come we'll have time to take leave."

He then pushed her aside gently, but she said, "God grant that your fate will be mine as well, O Aulus." Then, falling on her knees she began to pray with a force which fear alone for some dear one can give.

Aulus went toward the centurion who was waiting for him. It

was old Caius Hasta, his former subordinate and companion during the wars in Britain. "Greetings to you, General," said he. "I bring you the emperor's greeting and order. Here are the tablets and the signet, proof that I come in his name."

"I am thankful to Caesar for the greeting and I shall obey his command," answered Aulus. "Be welcome, Hasta, and tell me what orders you have brought me from Caesar?"

"Caesar has learned that the daughter of the king of the Ligians lives in your house. This king gave her to Rome as hostage with the pledge that the boundaries of the empire will never be violated by the Ligian people. The divine Nero is grateful to you, O General, for the hospitality which you have provided for this maiden; but now, not wishing to burden you any longer and realizing that as hostage this girl should be under the protection of Caesar himself, he commands you to relinquish her to him immediately."

Aulus was too much a soldier to permit any act of anger or displeasure or words of complaint. However, he could not hide altogether a sudden look of anger on his face. In times past, the legions in Britain quaked in fear before that look and even now there was a momentary sign of fear evident on the face of Hasta. In view of the order, however, Aulus felt defenseless. He glanced briefly again at the tablets and signet, then raising his eyes to the old centurion, he replied in a calm voice, "Wait here, Hasta. The hostage will be delivered to you." After these words he passed to the other end of the house where Pomponia, Ligia and little Aulus were waiting in fear and alarm.

"Death threatens no one nor banishment to distant lands," said he. "Still, Caesar's messenger is a bearer of misfortune. It pertains to you, Ligia."

"Ligia?" asked Pomponia with astonishment.

"Yes," answered Aulus.

Turning to the girl he spoke thus: "Ligia, you were brought into our house as a child. Pomponia and I love you as our own daughter. But you also know that you are not our daughter. You are a hostage given by your people to Rome and guardianship over you belongs to Caesar. Now, Caesar takes you from our house."

The general spoke calmly but in his voice there was a strange, strained tone hardly audible. Ligia listened without fully understanding what it was all about. Pomponia became white as a sheet. Outside in the corridors, the slaves began to gather again.

"Caesar's orders must be obeyed," said Aulus.

"Ah!" exclaimed Pomponia, embracing the girl as if wishing to protect her. "Aulus, it would be better for her to die than go there."

Ligia, nestling in her arms began to sob and repeat, "Mother...Mother."

On the face of Aulus anger and pain were reflected once more. "If I were alone in the world," said he bitterly, "I would not surrender her alive and my kinsmen would offer gifts to Jupiter the Liberator in memory of this day. But I haven't the right to place in jeopardy your life nor the life of our son who may live to see happier times. I will go to Caesar this day and implore him to give Ligia back to us. Whether he will listen to me I know not. Meanwhile, farewell, Ligia, and know that both Pomponia and I bless the day when you entered our lives."

Thus speaking he placed his hand on her head. Even though he tried to preserve his calm, when Ligia turned to him with her eyes filled with tears and seizing his hand pressed it to her lips, his voice was filled with deep fatherly sorrow. "Farewell, our joy and the light of our eyes," said he.

Meanwhile Pomponia, when she had conducted Ligia to her room, began to comfort, console and encourage her, uttering words which sounded strange in a house where there still was in use the custom of offering gifts to the gods of Rome.

"Now the hour of trial had come. In his time Virginius had pierced the heart of his own daughter to save her from the hands of Appius. There was also Lucretia who had preferred to take her own life instead of being committed to a life of shame. The house of Caesar is a den of iniquity; it is evil and many a crime is committed therein. But we, Ligia, know why we do not have the right to take our own lives. Yes, we have a greater law, the law of our God and whoever emerges from the corruption that is rampant in that house and remains pure and spotless has the greater merit. Life is short.... We believe in resurrection after death into eternal life. There, neither Nero nor any other tyrant has any power. There, instead of pain, will be delight; instead of tears, rejoicing."

Then, she began to speak about herself. Although she tried to appear calm, there was much pain in her heart because Aulus, her dear husband, had not yet embraced Christ. Her son was not permitted to be taught the truth. Therefore, when she pondered that it might be thus to the end of her life and that for them the moment of separation might come which would be a hundred times more grievous and terrible than the temporary one over which they were both suffering then, she could not understand how she might be happy even in heaven without them. She had wept many a night and had passed many nights in prayer imploring God for mercy and grace. She offered her suffering to God and waited and trusted.... Now, when a new blow struck her, when the tyrant's command took from her a dear one, the one whom Aulus called the light of their eyes, she trusted still, believing firmly that there was a power greater than Nero's and a mercy mightier than the tyrant's anger.

She pressed Ligia's head to her bosom still more firmly. The girl dropped to her knees after a while and covering her eyes in the folds of Pomponia's dress she remained thus a long time in silence. When she stood up again, some degree of calm returned to her face.

"I grieve for you, Mother, and for father and also my brother, but I know that resistance is useless and would destroy all of us. I promise you that in the house of Caesar I will not forget your words."

Once more she threw her arms around Pomponia and they both left her room. She then said farewell to little Aulus, the old Greek, their teacher, her maids and all the slaves. One of these, a tall and broad-shouldered Ligian named Ursus, who was among those permitted by the Romans to accompany the hostages, stepped forward. He fell at the feet of Pomponia saying, "Oh lady, permit me to go with her and watch over her in the house of Caesar."

"You are not our servant but Ligia's," answered Pomponia. "But how will you be able to protect her in the house of Caesar?"

"I know not, lady. All I know is that iron crumbles in my hands as if it were wood."

Aulus approached them at this moment and, finding out about the request of Ursus, not only did he not oppose his wish but declared that he, Aulus, did not have the right to detain him. Ligia, as a king's daughter, must have her retinue even though a hostage in the house of Caesar. Here he whispered to Pomponia that under the guise of an escort she could add as many slaves as she thought proper. The centurion could not refuse to receive them.

There was a certain comfort for Ligia in this. Pomponia was pleased that she could surround her with servants of her own choice. Therefore, besides Ursus she appointed Ligia's handmaiden, two girls from Cypress who were well skilled in hair dressing and two German girls for the bath. Her choice fell exclusively on adherents of the new faith. Ursus too had professed it for a number of years. Pomponia could count on the faithfulness of these servants and at the same time was consoled with the idea that soon the grains of truth would permeate even Caesar's house.

She even had time to write a note to Acte who was Nero's freedwoman, committing Ligia to her care. Pomponia, it is true, had not seen her at the gatherings of confessors of the new faith but she had heard from them that Acte had never refused them a service and that she eagerly read the letters of Paul of Tarsus. It was also known to her that Acte was a woman different from the women of Nero's house and that in general she was considered a good influence in the palace.

Hasta felt that it was only right that a king's daughter should have her own retinue and had no objections to taking the servants along with Ligia. He was surprised only how few they were. He asked however for the favor not to tarry too long for fear Nero would be displeased at the delay. At the parting Pomponia and Ligia began to cry again and hold each other tenderly. Aulus in turn placed once more his hand on the head of the girl. After a while the soldiers, followed by the cries of little Aulus who in defense of his sister threatened the centurion with his little fists, conducted Ligia to Caesar's house.

The old general gave orders to prepare his litter at once. Meanwhile he spoke to Pomponia, "Listen to me, Pomponia. I will go to Caesar though I fear that my visit will be useless and even though the word of Seneca means little with Nero at present, I will also go to Seneca. Today, Sopronius, Tigellinus, Petronius or Vatinius have more influence with him. I'll wager that Nero had not even heard of the Ligians nor of Ligia being a hostage in Rome and if he did so now, he was persuaded by someone and it is easy to guess who it was."

She raised her eyes to him quickly, "You mean Petronius?"

"That's right."

A moment of silence followed; then the general continued, "You see what it is to admit over our threshold any of these people without conscience or honor. Cursed be the moment when Vinitius entered our house for he brought Petronius here. Woe to Ligia. They are not seeking a hostage; what they want is a concubine," and his speech became more harsh and lisping on account of the helpless rage and sorrow that he felt for his adopted daughter. He had to struggle within himself and only his clenched fists showed how severe was the struggle.

"I have revered the gods up to now, but at this moment I think that it is not they who rule the world but one mad, malicious monster named Nero."

"Aulus," said Pomponia, "Nero is only a handful of dust in comparison to God."

Aulus began to pace nervously. In his life there had been great deeds but no great sorrows, hence he was unused to them. The old soldier had grown attached to Ligia more than he himself had been aware. Besides, he felt humiliated. A hand which he despised was weighing on him heavily and he felt powerless before it. At last, when he managed to compose himself somewhat, he said, "I believe that Petronius did not intend her for Caesar because he would not want to offend Poppaea. He wanted her for himself or for Vinitius. Today, I will find out."

Soon the litter bore him in the direction of the Palatine. Pomponia went to console little Aulus who wept for his dear sister while threatening Caesar.

CHAPTER V

AULUS correctly surmised that he would not be admitted to see Nero. They told him that Nero was busy with singing and playing the lute and furthermore he did not receive those whom he himself had not summoned. In other words, Aulus must not attempt to see him in the future.

Seneca, though ill with fever, received the old general with due honor but when he found out why Aulus came to see him, he laughed bitterly and said, "I can render you one service, noble Plautius, but don't let Caesar know that I have compassion for you and that I would like to help you. If Caesar knew this, he would not grant your wish even if it were only to spite me."

It would be of no use, he advised him, to see such men as Tigellinus, Vatinius or Vitelius. Possibly they might, for money, do something to undermine the influence of Petronius but on the other hand they would, most likely, disclose to Nero how dear Ligia is to you and Nero would all the more resolve not to relinquish her to you. Here, the old sage began to speak with biting irony about himself, "You have been silent, Plautius...you have been silent for a long time and Caesar does not like those who are silent. Why did you not acclaim his virtues, his singing, his divinity, his chariot racing and his verses? Why did you not glorify the death of Britannicus whom he murdered? Why did you not praise the slayer of his mother Octavia? You are lacking in foresight, Aulus, which we who live happily at his court possess in proper measure."

Thus speaking, he raised a goblet which he carried at his belt, drew water from the fountain, freshened his burning lips and continued... "Ah...Nero has a grateful heart. He loves you because you served Rome and glorified her name to the ends of the earth. He loves me because I was his teacher during his youth. So you see, this water that I drink, I know is not poisoned and I drink it. Wine would be less reliable. If you are thirsty, drink this water. The aqueducts draw it in from the Alban hills and anyone wishing to poison it would have to poison every fountain of Rome. So, you see, it is still possible to be safe and live to a ripe old age. I am sick, it is true, but my sickness is not of the body."

This was true. Seneca lacked the strength of soul which, for example, Cornutus and Thrasea possessed; hence his life was a series of concessions to crime. He realized that as an adherent to the principles of Zeno, the Stoic, he should pursue other ways of life. Knowing this, he suffered more than from the fear of death.

The general interrupted these sad reflections of Seneca. "Noble Annaeus, I know how Caesar rewarded you for the care with which you surrounded his youthful twenty-one years. But, the one who caused all this to happen to Ligia is Petronius. Show me a method against him, indicate to me the influence to which he yields, and use, if you can, all your noble eloquence with him in my behalf."

"Petronius and I," answered Seneca, "are persons of opposite camps. I know of no methods to sway him; he yields to no man's influence. Perhaps, even with all his corruption he is better than those scoundrels with whom Nero surrounds himself at present. To show him that he has done an evil deed is a waste of time. He has long since lost the faculty which distinguishes good from evil. But, show him that his act is ugly, then you will shame him. When I see him I will tell him that his act is worthy of a freedman. If that won't help, nothing will."

"Thank you even for that," answered the general.

Then he ordered his litter bearers to carry him to the house of Vinitius. He found the latter practicing fencing. He was angered at the sight...that at a time like this Vinitius could calmly go about his leisure with sword play. As soon as he found himself alone with Vinitius he voiced his bitterness in a torrent of reproaches and invectives.

When Vinitius learned that Ligia had been carried away to Caesar's house, he grew deathly pale. So great an emotion showed in his face that Aulus could not for a minute suspect him of sharing in the deed. The young man's forehead became covered with beads of perspiration; the blood, which had rushed to his heart, now returned with full force to his face with a burning wave; his eyes began to emit sparks; his mouth to hurl disconnected questions. Jealousy and rage in turn engulfed him. It seemed to him that Ligia, once she crossed the threshold of Caesar's palace, was lost to him forever. When Aulus mentioned the name of Petronius, he was filled with suspicion and was sure that Petronius wanted to make fun of him or that he wanted to curry Nero's favor by giving Ligia to him, or even perhaps to keep her for himself. That anyone who once saw her did not desire her was not possible to his way of thinking. He was impetuous by nature but now he did not know what to do. Finally, he spoke to Aulus, his voice choking in his throat, "General, return home and wait for me. Know that if Petronius were my own father I would avenge this wrong done to Ligia. Return home and wait for me. Neither Petronius nor Caesar will have her." And, turning to one of the corners of the room wherein the statues of his revered gods stood, he exclaimed with clenched fists, "By these gods I will kill her and myself first." After uttering these words he left, tossing over his shoulder once more the admonition to Aulus: "Wait for me!"

Outside he sped directly to the house of Petronius.

Aulus returned home a bit encouraged. He felt that if Petronius had persuaded Caesar to take Ligia and give her to Vinitius then the latter would return her to him. Furthermore, he was consoled by the thought that should Ligia not be rescued, she would be avenged. He believed that Vinitius would do everything that he had vowed. He saw his rage and implacable determination. He himself, although he loved Ligia as his own daughter, would rather kill her than give her up to Caesar. Were it not for the safety of his wife and only child, he would doubtless have done so. Aulus was a soldier; he knew little of the Stoics but in character he had much in common with them. To him death was more acceptable than disgrace.

When he returned home, he tried to console Pomponia with the news that he had acquired and both of them began to impatiently await news from Vinitius. Time passed. And when evening came they heard the gong at the gate; soon a slave approached them and handed a letter to Aulus. The old general began to read with a trembling hand. Suddenly his face darkened with anger and passing the letter to Pomponia, he said, "Read."

Pomponia took the letter and read as follows: "Marcus Vinitius to Aulus Plautius.... Greetings. What has happened, has happened by the will of Caesar before which bow your heads as I and Petronius incline ours."

A long silence followed.

CHAPTER VI

PETRONIUS was at home. The doorkeeper did not dare to stop Vinitius who burst into the house like a tornado. Learning that the master of the house was in the library, he rushed there. Finding Petronius writing, he snatched the quill from his hand, broke it, then threw it on the floor. Grabbing Petronius by the shoulders and looking into his eyes, he shouted hoarsely, "What have you done with her? Where is she?"

Suddenly an amazing thing happened. That seemingly weak and effeminate Petronius seized the arms of the youthful and strong athlete and grasping both in his one hand with a grip of steel said, "I'm weak only in the morning. In the evening I regain my former strength. Try to escape. A weaver must have taught you gymnastics and a blacksmith your manners."

His face did not even betray any strong emotion but if one looked closely into his eyes he would see in them a reflection of energy and daring. After a while he released Vinitius' hands. The latter stood before him shamefaced and at the same time enraged.

"You have hands of steel," he said, "but if you have betrayed me, I swear by all the gods that I will thrust a knife into your body even if it were in the chambers of Caesar."

"Let us talk calmly," said Petronius. "Steel as you see is mightier than iron, hence even though one of your arms would make two of mine, yet I don't have to fear you. However I am sad at your rude manners and if ingratitude would still astonish me, I would be astonished at your ingratitude."

"Where is Ligia?"

45

"In a brothel...that is in the house of Caesar."

"Petronius!"

"Calm yourself and sit down. I asked Caesar for two things which he promised to grant me. First, to take Ligia from the house of Aulus Plautius and second to give her to you. Now...have you a knife in the folds of your toga? Would you like to kill me? If you still do, my advice would be to wait two or three days because if you kill me they would put you in prison and in the meantime Ligia would be lonely in your house by herself."

Silence followed. Vinitius looked with eyes full of astonishment at Petronius. Finally he spoke. "Please forgive me. I love her so much and love is making me act thus."

"Look at me, Marcus. I spoke to Caesar in the following manner: 'My sister's son has fallen in love with a skinny little girl who happens to be in the house of Aulus. He loves her and sighs over her so much that his own house is turned into a steam bath from his sighs. Neither you, Caesar nor I, who both can evaluate real beauty, would give a thousand sesterces for her, but that son of my sister has always been as dull as a tripod and now he has taken leave of all wisdom in his love for this girl.'"

"Petronius!"

"If you can't guess that I merely spoke thus in order to ensure the safety of Ligia then I am ready to believe that I may have spoken the truth about you to Caesar. I talked him into thinking that the girl is not pretty and Nero who nowadays trusts in my judgment will not consider her beautiful and so will not desire her for himself. This was necessary to make sure that our red-bearded monkey will follow our wishes. Not he but Poppaea will evaluate her and I'm sure, seeing her beauty and fearful about her own influence, she will try to get rid of her as soon as possible. I spoke to Nero in this manner: 'Take Ligia and give her to Vinitius. You certainly have a right to do so. Besides, in doing so, you will irritate Aulus, the Stoic, and you don't care for Stoics.' And...so he agreed to my suggestion. Why shouldn't he? This will give him an opportunity to annoy decent people. You yourself will be made official guardian of the hostage and the Ligian treasure will be yours. So, as a friend of the valiant Ligians and as a faithful servant of Caesar, you will not waste this gift but, on the contrary, will try to increase the benefits. In order to preserve appearances, Caesar will detain her in his house for a few days but after that he will send her to you. Lucky man!"

"Is this true? Nothing threatens her in Caesar's house?"

"If she were to remain permanently there, then there would be danger, not from Caesar but from Poppaea who would certainly strive to get rid of her anyway at all. Even by killing her. However, nothing will harm her being there just for a few days. You know, in Nero's palace there are about ten thousand individuals. Nero will not notice her, all the more so because he left everything to me and I know that she is in the care of Acte. As you must know, Acte is a good soul. Evidently Pomponia is of the same opinion because she too got in touch with Acte. Tomorrow, Nero is giving a feast. I have requested that you will repose beside Ligia at the feast."

"Please pardon my impulsiveness, Caius. I thought that you had given orders to take her for yourself or for Caesar."

"I can forgive your impulsiveness but it is more difficult for me to forgive your rudeness, your rude gestures and loud voice which might remind me of those who play the game of *mora*. That I don't like, Marcus, and do guard against it. You should know that Tigellinus is Caesar's pimp, not I. Besides, if I wanted the girl for myself, I would look you straight in the eye and say to you, 'Vinitius, I'm going to take Ligia and keep her until I tire of her.'" And in his eyes the young man found a cold and insolent stare which confused him all the more.

"The fault is mine," said he. "You are kind and generous and I thank you from the bottom of my heart. Permit me though but one question. Why did you not make arrangements to send Ligia directly to my house?"

"Because Caesar wants to preserve appearances. People in Rome will talk about this...that we removed Ligia as a hostage. While they are talking she will remain in Caesar's palace. Afterward she will be moved quietly to your house and that will be the end of it. Nero is a coward. Even though he knows that his power is unlimited, he still tries to maintain some kind of appearances for his mad acts. If you have recovered somewhat, permit me to philosophize with you. I have thought about this more than once: Why does crime, even by a powerful Caesar, seek to be justified? Why does it wish to appear as a virtue such as justice and truth? Why bother to justify itself even if it has might on its side? To murder a brother, mother, wife...is a thing worthy of some Asiatic tyrant not of a Roman Caesar. If that happened to me, I would not write letters to the Senate justifying my deeds. But Nero writes to the Senate trying to justify all his actions. Why does he do this? Because he is a coward. And yet...Tiberius Caesar was not a coward but he did the same thing. The answer must be that evil must pay homage to virtue. And you know why? Because crime is ugly and virtue is beautiful. Therefore a truly elegant man is also virtuous; therefore I am also virtuous. Today I must pour out some wine in honor of the sophist gods such as Protagoras, Prodicus and Gorgias. Sophistry too can be of service sometime. Hear me further, Vinitius. I took Ligia away from Aulus in order to give her to you. She and you will make a beautiful couple. Therefore, my act is beautiful and being beautiful it cannot be bad. Marcus, here you have in front of you virtue personified. If Aristides were living today, he would have to come and offer me a reward for a fine treatise on virtue."

Vinitius, concerned more with reality than treatises on virtue, replied, "Tomorrow I shall see Ligia and after that I will possess her in my house and have her until I die."

"You will have Ligia and I will have Aulus on my head. He will summon vengeance of all the infernal gods against me. If he were only able to talk without his lisping. No doubt he will blame me for everything."

"Aulus has been at my house. I promised him some news of Ligia."

"Write him that the will of Caesar is law and that your first son will bear the name Aulus. The old man should have some consolation. I may even ask Nero to have him present at tomorrow's feast. Let him see you there next to Ligia."

"Don't do that. I'm sorry for them, especially for Pomponia."

And...he sat down to write that letter which saddened Aulus so much.

CHAPTER VII

THERE was a time when Acte, the former favorite of Nero, was held in high esteem by even the most influential of Rome. However, she never took advantage of her high position and of her influence over the young ruler. If it did happen, it was only to plead someone's case before Nero. Quiet and unassuming, she won the gratitude of many and made no one her enemy. Even Octavia did not hate her. To those who envied her, she seemed harmless. It was a sad truth that she continued to love Nero with a love that lived not in hope but only in memories of the time when Nero was not only younger and loving but also better. She could not get that love back she knew, so she expected nothing and, since there was no real fear that Nero would return to her at this stage, she was considered harmless and so was left in peace, even by Poppaea herself.

But because Caesar had loved her once and put her aside in a friendly manner, there was a certain respect shown her by all. Nero let her live in the palace with beautiful apartments and some servants for her needs. And, as in their time, Pallas and Narcissus, though freedmen of Claudius, not only sat at feasts with the emperor but also had places of honor as powerful ministers, so too Acte was invited at times to Caesar's table. This was done perhaps because her beauty and charm were real ornaments to any feast. And, anyway, Caesar had long since ceased to care about anyone's opinions of his choices as partakers of his feasts. These were varied indeed. Some were senators who, in order to please Nero, sometimes played the role of jesters. Some were patricians, old and young, eager for luxury, excess and enjoyment. Some women had great and famous family names yet these did not hesitate to put on yellow wigs for an evening and seek adventure on dark streets. Some were high officials, some high priests who at full goblets were willing to jeer at their own gods. There was a mixture of every sort: singers, imitators, musicians, dancers, poets who while reciting their poetry, thought only of the amount of money that might fall to them and so they praised Caesar's verses with enthusiasm. Some were philosophers who, being always hungry, followed with eager eyes the different dishes which were brought around. There were also noted charioteers, tricksters, magicians, fortunetellers, jesters and different adventurers of fashion or folly brought together for a moment's notoriety. Among the diverse medley of humanity, one could even distinguish former slaves by their pierced ears which they tried to cover with long hair.

The most noted reclined at the tables and while eating and drinking were amused by the various entertainers brought for the occasion. These awaited the moment in which the servants would permit them to rush at the remnants of food and drink. This sort of talent for amusement was furnished by Tigellinus, Vatinius and Vitelius who had to provide for them suitable clothing befitting the chambers of Caesar who liked to have them present. Luxury and opulence were in evidence. The glitter of gold shone everywhere. The high and the low, descendants of great families and the poor of the city, artists and riffraff, all thronged to the palace to sate their dazzled eyes by a pomp and splendor of such magnitude as to almost surpass human amazement and estimate. So they approached this giver of every favor, wealth and property with fear and trepidation because they knew that a single glance of this tyrant may devour them, it is true, but it might also exalt them beyond measure.

It was such a feast that Ligia was to take part in that day. Fear and uncertainty plagued her. She was still dazed at the turn of events. She was in fear of Nero, the people in the palace and the noise and confusion that she encountered there. She had heard many times before from Aulus, Pomponia and others about these feasts of Nero, the shamelessness and debauchery that were usually present at these gatherings. Though young, she was not unaware of the evil practices rampant in Nero's Rome. She was sure that nothing good would come from her being present at this feast. However she had promised Pomponia that she would resist the evil temptations to the best of her ability and keep faith with the new religion which she embraced totally with her pure soul. She loved her Divine Teacher for the sweetness of His doctrine, the bitterness of His death and the glory of His resurrection.

She was also aware now that neither Aulus nor Pomponia would be answerable for her actions. Having such thoughts in mind, she wondered whether it would be better to resist and not to go to the feast. Fear and alarm tormented her on the one hand; on the other she wanted to show that she was ready to suffer and die for her faith if by refusing Nero she would then incur his wrath. The Divine Teacher had commanded her to act thus against corruption and evil. Pomponia had told her that the most zealous among the members of the new faith wished for themselves a test, even if it meant suffering death to prove their worth and imitate Him who suffered for them. In the past she herself had these thoughts and desired to die for Christ if the time came. She visualized herself as a martyr with wounds on her feet and hands, her soul as pure as the angels borne by them to the throne of heaven after martyrdom. Of course there was much childish imagination in such dreams and childish pleasure. This, Pomponia tried to curb in her. Now, when opposition to Caesar's will might result in some terrible punishment and the martyrdom scene of her imagination might become a reality, her fear was mixed with a kind of curiosity as to how they would torture her. Her mind and soul were thus torn between curiosity and fear.

When Acte became aware of Ligia's thoughts, she looked at the girl with astonishment as if she were out of her mind. To oppose Caesar and expose herself to his anger would be the height of folly. Furthermore, Ligia was abandoned by her own people, the Ligians. Who then would intercede in her behalf? No law protected her since she was not a citizen of Rome. Besides, Caesar was powerful enough to trample on any law in a moment of anger. She must obey Caesar's will. There was none other on earth.

"These are the facts of life, Ligia. I too have read the letters of Paul of Tarsus and I believe that there is a God in heaven and the Son of God Who rose from the dead, but on earth there is only Caesar. Think of this too, Ligia. I know that your belief does not permit you to be what I was and, when it becomes a choice between ignominy and death, you are to choose death. But, can you say for sure that either one or the other awaits you here? Moreover, choosing death might not keep you from the disgrace and ignominy which might confront you before you die, just as the daughter of Sejanus, a maiden who had to undergo the crime of rape before death under Emperor Tiberius. Ligia...Ligia, do not irritate Caesar. If the moment does come when you will have to choose, then you will act as your faith commands, but do not seek death for no reason at all and do not provoke this earthly and cruel god."

Acte spoke with compassion but also with some emotion and, being shortsighted, she closely scrutinized the effect of her words upon Ligia.

Ligia suddenly embraced Acte as a child would her mother with complete trust and said, "Acte, you are very good."

Acte, pleased with the praise and confidence, pressed her to her heart. After a moment she replied, "My happiness has passed and my joy is gone but I am not entirely wicked." Her eyes filled with tears as she walked back and forth and began speaking in a despairing voice. "No, neither was he wicked then. He wanted to do good deeds, I know that. He changed when he stopped loving. Others made him what he is...yes others and Poppaea."

"Are you sorry for him, Acte?"

"Yes, I'm sorry for him," she answered in a low voice.

"Do you still love him?"

"I love him."

After a while she added, "No one loves him but me."

Silence followed during which Acte tried to recover her composure. When her face once again reflected the look of inner calm, she said, "Let us talk about you, Ligia. Don't think for a moment of opposing Caesar. That would be madness. Don't be afraid. I know this palace quite well and I'm certain that from Caesar nothing threatens you. If Nero wanted you for himself I'm sure that he would not have you brought here to the Palatine where Poppaea reigns. Nero, since she bore him a daughter, is more than ever under her influence. No doubt he commanded you to be brought here and to be at the feast through anger at Aulus and Pomponia. Petronius wrote and asked me to take care of you as you know. Pomponia also wrote to me so perhaps they had an understanding. Maybe he did that at her request and if so that is added proof that nothing threatens you here. He may even persuade Nero to give you back to Aulus. I don't know whether Nero loves him more than others but I do know that he rarely has the courage to act contrary to his opinion."

"Oh, Acte!" answered Ligia. "Petronius paid us a visit before I was taken and my mother was convinced that Nero took me at his request."

"That would be bad," said Acte. But after a brief pause she remarked, "Perhaps Petronius mentioned your name while he was with Nero, that you are a hostage of Rome and Nero who is jealous of his power wanted you here because all hostages belong to Caesar. He does not like Aulus and Pomponia. That is certain but I seriously doubt that Petronius would take such a step in order to take you for himself. I don't know whether he is better than the others but he is different from them. Perhaps there is someone else who may be able to intercede for you. Do you know of any one?"

"I know Vespasian and Titus."

"Caesar does not like them."

"And Seneca."

"If Seneca advised something, that would be enough to make Nero act just the opposite from his advice."

"And Vinitius?"

"I don't know him."

"He is a relative of Petronius. He returned from Armenia not so long ago."

"Do you think Nero likes him?"

"Everyone likes Vinitius."

"And would he intercede for you?"

"He would."

Acte smiled tenderly and said, "Then you will no doubt see him at the feast. You will be there because you must. Only such an innocent child as you could think otherwise. Besides, if you wish to return to Pomponia you will have a good opportunity to ask Petronius and Vinitius to use their influence for your return. Both of them will tell you that it is madness to resist the will of Caesar. There would be no hope for you if you did. Come, Ligia, don't you hear the commotion outside? The guests are already arriving."

"You are right," answered Ligia, "and I will follow your advice."

In this resolve to follow the advice of Acte, Ligia did not herself realize how much she wanted to see Vinitius again and how much womanly curiosity there was to see the pomp and splendor of one of Caesar's feasts about which she had heard so much...to see Nero's court, the renowned Poppaea and the other notorious women. But also, she did feel in her heart that the advice of Acte was correct and so she decided to attend the feast.

Acte conducted her to her own rooms to dress her for the feast. Though there was no lack of slaves in Caesar's house and Acte had enough for her own use, still through sympathy for the girl whose innocence and beauty had captured her heart, she decided to dress her up herself. It soon became clear that in the young Grecian, in spite of her sadness and the impact on her of the letters of Paul of Tarsus, there was still in her much of that Hellenic spirit which admired physical beauty above everything else on earth. When she had undressed Ligia she could not restrain an exclamation of wonder at the sight of her beautiful body, slender yet full, created as it were from pearl and roses. Stepping back a few paces, she looked with delight on the matchless beauty of early spring.

"Ligia!" she exclaimed finally. "You are a hundred times more beautiful than Poppaea."

But, reared in the strict house of Pomponia where modesty was observed even when women were by themselves, the maiden, as wonderful as a dream, a work of art and a song of beauty, stood blushing from modesty, with knees pressed together, and her hands on her bosom with downcast eyes. Then with a sudden movement of her hands she removed the pins which held her hair and with a shake of her head she covered herself with her abundant locks as with a mantle.

Acte, approaching her and touching her dark tresses said, "Oh what beautiful hair you have! I will sprinkle it but lightly with powder. It gleams of itself in the light. The curls are natural too. Everything is beautiful about you. Your Ligian country must be wonderful to have such maidens."

"I do not remember it," answered Ligia, "but Ursus told me that my country abounds in forestland."

"Flowers bloom in those forests," said Acte, dipping her hand in a vase filled with verbena and moistening Ligia's hair with it. When she had finished this work, Acte anointed her body lightly with perfumes from Arabia and then dressed her in a soft gold-colored tunic without sleeves over which the outer dress of pure white would be put on later. The hair dressing was completed with the help of two of Acte's slaves. Two others took care of the sandals on her feet with golden lacings drawn crosswise. After the outer dress was put on, Acte fastened some pearls on her neck.

They were both ready soon and when the first litters began to appear before the main gate, both entered the side portico from which the chief entrance to the courtyard and the surrounding columns of Numidian marble was visible.

Gradually people passed in greater and greater numbers under the lofty arch over which the splendid chariot of Lysias seemed to bear Apollo and Diana into space. Ligia's eyes took in all that magnificence below of which the modest house of Aulus could not have given her the slightest idea. It was sunset; the last rays of sun were falling on the yellow Numidian marble of the columns and shone like gold. Among the many columns depicting gods or heroes, the crowd of people flowed past, men and women. They were dressed in togas and robes falling gracefully toward the ground in soft folds touched by the rays of the setting sun. A huge statue of Hercules could be seen above the crowd. Acte pointed out to Ligia the different personages passing by: senators in wide-bordered togas and colored tunics; men of noble rank and famed artists. She pointed out the Roman ladies, many of them dressed in Grecian and oriental fashion, especially in different styles of headdress. Acte named many of them whom she knew, adding their histories which filled Ligia with amazement, wonder and fear. For her, this was a strange world whose beauty was pleasant to her eyes yet whose ugly background filled her with dread. She could not grasp the contrast. It seemed to her that with all that beauty around all these people, they should live the lives of demi-gods free from care and worry. Meanwhile the low voice of Acte disclosed from time to time the wicked secrets of the palace and the people entering it.

"See there in the distance is the colored portico on whose columns and floor are still visible the red stains from the blood with which Caligula sprinkled the white marble when he fell beneath the knife of Cassius Chaerea; there his wife was slain; there his child was dashed against a stone; under that wing is the dungeon in which the younger Drusus gnawed his hands from hunger; there the older was poisoned; there Gemellus shook in terror and Claudius in convulsions; there Germanicus was terrorized....Everywhere those walls had heard the groans and death rattle of the dying. These people that you see now hurrying to the feast in colorful togas bedecked with flowers and jewels may be condemned to die tomorrow. On more than one face, if you look closely, you will observe terror and alarm and uncertainty of what the next day will bring. These seemingly demi-gods who appear free from care and worry may be full of greed and envy."

Ligia's thoughts could not keep up with Acte's words and her heart became full of dread at all this splendor. She yearned to be back in the peace and quiet and the calm of the house of Aulus with Pomponia where love not hate and crime held sway.

Meanwhile new waves of guests were flowing in from the Vicus Apollinus. There was much more noise now from the different people. The courtyard and the colonnades were swarming with Caesar's slaves of both sexes and with Praetorian soldiers who kept guard in the palace. Here and there could be seen the dark face of a Numidian in a feathered helmet and with large rings in his ears. There were slaves bearing lutes and lyres, hand lamps of gold, silver and bronze; also bunches of flowers grown and cultivated artificially despite the late autumn season. The sounds of conversation were mingled with the splashing of the fountain, the rosy streams of which fell from above onto the marble.

Acte had ceased speaking. Ligia was still gazing at the throng as if looking for someone. Suddenly her face lighted up; she saw among the columns the approaching forms of Vinitius and Petronius. They passed inside, handsome like white gods in their togas. When she saw them, it seemed to Ligia that a great weight was taken from her shoulders and in her heart she was glad, especially upon seeing Vinitius. She felt less alone. That terrible yearning for Pomponia and the house of Aulus was less painful now. The desire to see Vinitius and to talk with him drowned out the fearful voices in her soul. Despite the words of Acte and the warnings of Pomponia about the evils of Caesar's palace, she now desired to be at the feast with Vinitius. At the thought that she soon would hear that dear voice which had spoken of love and of happiness to her like a song in her ears, pure delight seized her innermost being.

Upon reflection, however, she began to fear this prompting of her thoughts and feelings. Would not she be false to the teaching of her faith? False to Pomponia and to herself too? It is one thing to be compelled to go by Caesar; it is another thing to delight in being there. Whereupon she felt guilty about her desire to be with Vinitius; she felt unworthy of her faith. Had she been alone, she would have fallen on her knees to beg forgiveness of her Divine Savior for those sinful thoughts. Amid this turmoil of her inner feelings, she felt herself being guided by Acte to the grand dining room, the place of the feast. Her eyes were clouded with emotion and the beating of her heart almost took her breath away. As in a dream she saw thousands of lamps gleaming on the tables and on the walls; as in a dream she heard shouts with which the guests greeted Caesar. The shouts deafened her, the glitter dazzled her, and she was barely able to follow Acte who seated her at the table next to her. After a while she heard a known and low voice at the other side.

"Greetings to you, most beautiful of maidens on earth and of the stars of heaven. Greeting, O divine Callina."

Ligia, having recovered somewhat, looked up. At her side was Vinitius. He was without his toga for it was the custom, for convenience sake, to put aside the toga at the time of feasts. He was covered only with a sleeveless, scarlet tunic embroidered with silver designs. His bare arms were ornamented, according to fashion from the East, with two broad golden bands fastened above the elbows. His arms were smooth but muscular, true arms of a professional soldier seemingly fashioned for the sword and shield. On his head was a garland of roses. His brows were prominent, eyes dark as was his complexion. He was handsome indeed with the added picture of youth and strength. To Ligia he looked so handsome that she was barely able to respond with, "A greeting to you, Marcus."

"Happy are my eyes which see you, happy my ears which hear your voice which is dearer to me than the sounds of lutes and lyres. If I were to be given a choice as to who would rest here by my side at this feast, you or Venus herself, I would choose you... O divine one." And he looked at the girl with burning eyes full of adoration. His glance fell from her face to her neck and her bare arms and the shapely outlines of her figure, admiring her and at the same time devouring her with his eyes. Yet, besides desire, there was a great mixture of happiness and joy.

"I knew that I would see you here," he continued, "but even so, when I beheld you here, such a delight shook my soul as never before."

Ligia, having recovered herself and feeling that in this throng and in this house he was the only person who was near to her, began to tell him of her fears and to ask him about everything that she did not understand. How is it that he knew that he would find her here? Why was she here? Why did Caesar take her away from Pomponia? She is afraid to be here and she has great hope that he and Petronius would intercede for her before Caesar.

Vinitius, in an off-handed manner, tried to explain that he himself had heard from Aulus that she had been taken. Why she is here he knows not. Caesar gives account to no one. But, let her not fear. He, Vinitius, is close at hand and will remain near her. He would rather lose his eyes than not to see her. He would rather lose his life than forsake her. She is his soul and therefore he will guard her as his own soul. In his own house he will erect in her honor an altar as to a divinity and he will offer myrrh and aloes, and in the spring, saffron and apple blossoms. Besides, since she is fearful of Caesar's house, he promises her here and now that she will not remain in here for long.

And even though he spoke evasively, there was truth in his voice because his feelings were true. His pity for her was sincere and her words touched him so deeply that when she began to assure him that Pomponia would esteem him for his goodness and that she herself would be grateful to him all her life...he could not master his emotions. It was clear to him that he would never be able to deny her requests. His heart began to melt within him. Her beauty intoxicated his senses and he desired her but at the same time he felt that she would always be dear to him and truthfully that he would be able to do homage to her as a divinity. He felt an irresistible need to speak of her beauty and charms. As the noise of the revelers increased, he drew closer to her and began whispering kind, sweet words which flowed from the depth of his soul, words as resonant as music and intoxicating as wine.

She was swayed by his ardent words. Among the strange people around her, he alone seemed close, known to her and more and more liked by her. His evident devotion to her made him seem dear to her. He began to reassure her of her safety; he himself would take her away from Caesar's house; he would not forsake her; he would serve her always. At Aulus' house he merely touched upon a love that he felt for her, now he admitted his love openly. She was indeed most dear and most precious to him.

Ligia heard such words from a man's lips for the first time in her life, and as she listened it seemed to her that something in her was awakening from sleep; a sweet sense of joy and happiness engulfed her in a feeling of delight which was mixed, however, with some alarm. Her cheeks began to burn, her heart to beat faster, her mouth open slightly as if in wonder. She was seized with fear because she was listening to such things, yet she would not miss one word for all the world. Briefly lowering her eyes, she would again raise them in full brilliance toward him as if to say, "Speak on." The sound of the music, the smell of the flowers and perfume began to entrance her. In Rome it was the custom to recline at banquets but at home Ligia occupied a seat between Pomponia and little Aulus. Now, Vinitius was reclining by her side, youthful enthusiasm in his voice, burning love in his eyes and she, feeling the ardor that flowed from his very being, felt great delight. A kind of pleasant sweetness, a forgetfulness seized her, a sort of sweet drowsiness enveloped her.

Her nearness to him began to act on Vinitius also. His nostrils began to dilate like that of a thoroughbred steed. His heart beat faster under his scarlet tunic. His breathing grew short and his words began to falter. This was the first time that he was so close to her. His thoughts became fuzzy. In his veins he felt a flame which he tried, in vain, to quench with wine. Not wine but her beautiful face, her bare arms, her maiden breast heaving under the golden tunic, and her shapely figure hidden in the white folds of her dress, intoxicated him more and more. Finally, he seized her arm above the wrist and drawing her toward himself, whispered with trembling lips, "I love you, Callina, my divine one!"

"Let me go, Marcus," said Ligia.

Misty-eyed he continued on, "Love me, my goddess!"

Right then he heard the voice of Acte who reclined on the other side of Ligia.

"Caesar is looking at both of you."

Vinitius was suddenly angry at Caesar and at Acte. Her words had broken his moment of enchantment. He thought that she purposely wanted to interrupt his talk with Ligia. So, raising his head and looking over the shoulder of Ligia at the young freed-woman, with a bit of malice in his voice, he said: "The time has passed, Acte, when you reclined at Caesar's side and they say that blindness threatens you, so how can you see him now?"

She answered sadly, "I see him though, and he, being short sighted is looking at you through an emerald.

Everything that Nero did aroused attention even in those nearest him, hence Vinitius was alarmed. However, he soon regained his self control and began to glance imperceptibly toward Caesar. Ligia, whose earlier view of Caesar was vague due to her confusion, now looked at him with fear.

Acte was right. Nero, bending over the table with one eye closed and holding before the other a round polished emerald which served him as a magnifying glass, was looking at them. For a moment his glance met Ligia's and her heart was filled with terror. When still a child on Aulus' Sicilian estate, an old Egyptian slave told her of a dragon which occupied dens in the mountains. Now it seemed to her that the greenish eye of such a monster was looking at her. She grasped the hand of Vinitius as a frightened child would. Thoughts ran through her mind.... Is this he...the all-powerful? Somehow her imagination of him as the all-powerful and wicked emperor was different from what she saw now. She had imagined some kind of a horrible and wicked face, but now she saw a huge head on a thick neck. Ugly, it is true, but at the same time comical and a bit childish in appearance. A purple tunic, the color forbidden to ordinary mortals, cast a bluish tinge on his short but broad face. He had no beard because he had sacrificed it recently to Jove, for which all Rome gave him thanks, though people whispered to each other that he had sacrificed it because his beard, like that of other male members of his family, was red. Only his forehead had a bit of Olympic power in it. In his contracted brows the knowledge of supreme power was evident, but under that forehead of a demi-god was the face of a monkey, a drunkard and a clown, vain, full of changing desires, swollen with fat despite his youth. Moreover, it was sickly and foul. To Ligia he seemed wicked but above all repulsive.

After a while Nero ceased to look at her and laid down the emerald. Then she was aware of his protruding eyes, blinking due to the excessive light, glassy, without thought, resembling the eyes of the dead.

Nero, turning to Petronius at his side, said to him, "Is that the hostage with whom Vinitius is in love?"

"That is she," answered Petronius.

"What are her people called?"

"The Ligians."

"Does Vinitius think her beautiful?"

"Array a rotten olive trunk in the gown of a woman and Vinitius will declare it beautiful. But on your countenance, incomparable judge, I read her sentence already. You need not pronounce it. The sentence is true; she is too slight, too thin, a mere blossom on a slender stalk; and you, o divine judge of beauty, esteem the stalk itself in a woman. You are absolutely right. The face alone does not count. I have learned much in your company but even now I have not the same perfect cast of eye as you have. I am ready to lay a wager with Tullius Senecio regarding his mistress that, at a feast when all are reclining, even though it is difficult to judge the entire figure your verdict now is:'Too narrow in the hips.'"

"Too narrow in the hips," answered Nero blinking.

A barely perceptible smile appeared on the lips of Petronius. Tullius Senecio, who till that moment was busy conversing with Vestinus or rather ridiculing him and his belief in dreams, turned to Petronius and even though he had no idea what they were talking about said, "You are mistaken.... I hold with Caesar."

"Very well," answered Petronius, "I have just maintained that you possess a minimum of brains but Caesar insists that you are an ass pure and simple."

"Habet!" (Let him have it!) said Caesar, turning his thumb down as was done in the circus when the life of a gladiator was not spared.

Vestinus, thinking that the conversation was about dreams, exclaimed, "I believe in dreams and Seneca told me one time that he does also."

"Last night I dreamed that I had become a Vestal Virgin," said Calvia Crispinilla, bending over the table.

At this Nero began clapping his hands; others followed and soon the clapping of hands was heard all around. Crispinilla had been divorced a number of times and was known throughout Rome for her dissolute life.

But she, not disconcerted in the least, said, "So what! They are all old and ugly. Only Rubria isn't too bad but even she gets freckles in the summer."

Petronius replied, "Admit though, purest Calvia, that you could become a Vestal Virgin only in your dreams."

"But if Caesar ordered it to be so?"

"I should then believe," replied Petronius, "that even the most impossible dreams do come true."

"They do come true!" exclaimed Vestinus. "I can understand those who do not believe in the gods but how is it possible not to believe in dreams?"

"What of prophecies?" inquired Nero. "It was once prophesied to me that Rome would cease to exist and that I would rule the East."

"Prophecies and dreams are related," said Vestinus. "Once a certain proconsul, who was a great disbeliever, sent a slave to the temple of Mopsus with a sealed letter which he would not allow anyone to open. He wanted an answer to the question written in the sealed letter. The slave slept a night in the temple in order to have a prophetic dream. Next morning he spoke thus of his dream:'I saw a youth in my dream; he was as bright as the sun and he uttered only one word, Black. The proconsul, when he heard this grew pale and turning to his guests, all disbelievers like himself, said, 'Do you know what was in that letter?'" At this Vestinus paused and raising his goblet with wine, began to drink.

"What was in the letter?" asked Senecio.

"In the letter was the question: What is the color of the bull which I am to sacrifice, white or black?"

The interest aroused by this narrative was interrupted by Vitelius who, already drunk when he came to the feast, burst out suddenly in senseless laughter.

"What is that barrel of fat laughing at?" asked Nero.

"Laughter distinguishes men from animals," said Petronius, "and that is the only reason he is not a wild pig."

Vitelius suddenly stopped laughing and began looking around him with astonishment, his mouth open and lips moist, as if for the first time he noticed the others about him. Then he raised his two ugly and fat arms and said in a hoarse voice, "My knightly ring has fallen from my finger; it was inherited from my father."

"Who was a tailor," added Nero.

At this Vitelius again burst out with laughter and began to search frantically for his ring in the folds of the dress of Calvia Crispinilla.

Vestinus began imitating cries of a frightened woman. Nigidia, a friend of Calvia who was a young widow with the face of a maiden and the eyes of a harlot, said aloud, "He's looking for something which he did not lose."

"And which will be useless to him if he finds it," added Lucan.

The feast grew more lively. Slaves brought more courses of food and more wine. They ate and drank greedily while petals of flowers fell from the ceiling.

Petronius begged Nero to dignify the feast with his singing before the guests drank too much. A chorus of voices supported his request, but Nero at first refused. It was not a question of courage alone, he said, though that failed him always. The gods knew what a struggle every success cost him. He did not avoid the struggle however, for it was necessary to do something for art's sake. Besides, if Apollo gifted him with a good voice, it was not right that such a divine gift be wasted. In fact it was a duty to the state that such a great gift be not wasted. But today, he was really hoarse. Last night he placed leaden weights on his chest but that did not help. A trip to Antium to breathe the sea air may help.

Lucan, however, implored him in the name of humanity. All knew that the divine poet and singer had composed a new hymn to Venus, compared with which the hymn of Lucretius was merely a sound of a yearling wolf. Let the feast be a real feast. So noble a ruler should not cause such tortures to his subjects. "Be not cruel, O Caesar!"

"Be not cruel!" repeated all who were sitting near.

Nero spread his hands in resignation, whereupon all faces assumed an expression of gratitude and all eyes turned to him. He first sent a slave to Poppaea saying that he would sing. He informed those present that she had not come to the feast because she did not feel well but since no medicine gave her such relief as his singing, he would be sorry to deprive her of this opportunity.

Poppaea soon appeared. Till now she had ruled Nero as if he had been her subject, but she knew that when his vanity as a singer, a charioteer or a poet was involved, there was danger in provoking it. She came in, beautiful as a goddess, dressed like Nero in robes of purple and wearing a necklace of large pearls...beautiful, golden haired and though divorced from two husbands, she had a face and look of a virgin. She was greeted with shouts of "Divine Augusta!"

Ligia had never seen anyone so beautiful and she could not believe her own eyes for she knew that Poppaea Sabina was one of the vilest women on earth. She learned from Pomponia that Poppaea had talked Caesar into murdering his own mother and his wife. She knew from accounts given her from different guests of Aulus and also from the servants. She had heard that statues erected in her honor were overthrown and broken almost each night all over the city. She had heard of the names written about her on the city walls. The perpetrators, if caught, were condemned to the severest punishments. Yet at the sight of this notorious woman, considered by the followers of Christ as evil incarnate, it seemed to her that the angels in heaven would have such beauty. Involuntarily she asked the question, "Ah, Marcus, can this be possible?"

But he, incited by the amount of wine he had drunk and irritated because so many things took her attention from him and his words, said to her, "Yes, she is beautiful but you are a hundred times more beautiful. You don't realize that. If you did, you would be in love with yourself just like Narcissus was. She bathes in the milk of donkeys but Venus herself bathed you in her own. Do not look at her. Turn your eyes on me, my love. Touch this goblet of wine with your lips and I will put mine on the same place."

He began to get closer and closer to her and she moved closer to Acte. But at that moment there was a demand for silence because Caesar had risen. The singer Diodor had given him a lute of the kind called delta. Another singer, named Terpnos, who had to accompany him in playing, approached with an instrument called nablium. Nero, resting the lute on the table, raised his eyes and for a moment there was total silence broken only by a rustle as roses fell from the ceiling.

Then he began to chant, or rather to declaim rhythmically to the accompaniment of the two lutes, his own hymn to Venus. Neither the voice, though somewhat broken, nor the verses were bad so that reproaches of conscience took possesion of Ligia. The hymn, though glorifying the impure pagan Venus, seemed to her beautiful and Caesar himself, with a laurel crown on his head and uplifted eyes, seemed nobler and much less terrible and less repulsive than at the beginning of the feast.

The guests gave him a thunderous applause when he finished. Cries of "O heavenly voice!" were heard round about; some women raised their hands as if in ecstasy; others wiped their tears in joyous praise. The entire room was filled with acclamations of praise of one kind or another. Poppaea, bending her golden-haired head, raised Nero's hand to her lips. Pythagoras, a young Greek of amazing beauty, the same one whom later the half-insane Nero ordered to marry him, knelt now at his feet.

Nero, however, turned to Petronius from whom, above all others, he desired praise. Petronius indeed did not fail him. "If it is a question of music," he said, "Orpheus must be at this moment as yellow from envy as is Lucan here. As for the verses, I am sorry that they are not worse because if they were, I might find proper words to praise them."

Lucan did not take offense at this. On the contrary, he looked at Petronius with gratitude and, assuming ill-humor, began to mumble. "Cursed be fate which commanded me to live contemporary with such a poet. I could have been famous but I am merely a candle in comparison to our divine sun."

Petronius, who had an amazing memory, began to repeat extracts from the hymn and praise and analyze the more beautiful expressions. Lucan joined him in his praise. Nero's face reflected extreme delight and utmost vanity almost to the point of stupidity. He threw out verses of his own at them which he considered more beautiful. He then began to console Lucan and tell him not to lose heart; a man is what he is and should not tempt Jove and other divinities. Thereupon, he turned to escort Poppaea, who truly did not feel well and asked to be excused, out of the room. However, he commanded the guests to remain and enjoy themselves and he would return soon. He did return shortly and began to gaze at further spectacles which he, Petronius and Tigellinus had prepared for the feast.

There were other verses read and sung and different dances, especially the one performed by the famous Paris who imitated the adventures of Io, the daughter of Inachus. To the guests and especially to Ligia, who was unaccustomed to such scenes, it seemed enchanting. Paris, with motions of hands and body, was able to express most intimately the ecstasy of a young woman in love, shaken by spasms of delight. That was clearly a picture not merely a dance, a very expressive picture, bewitching and shameless. Other dances followed, even more shameless. It seemed to Ligia that living fire was burning her and that lightning should strike this house and the roof fall in upon these scenes. But from the golden net fastened to the ceiling only roses fell. Vinitius himself, almost drunk now, spoke thusly, "I saw you at the fountain in Aulus' house. It was daylight and you were not aware of it but I saw you. I see you now as I saw you then. Take your dress off like Crispinilla. Gods and men seek love. There is nothing in the world but love. Put your head on my breast and close your eyes."

Her pulse beat wildly; she had the feeling that she was falling into some deep abyss. A voice inside of her kept repeating, "Ligia, save yourself." But that voice was getting fainter and fainter. Momentarily, she was sure that it was too late for one whom inward fire had engulfed as it did her and who was so enthralled by such loving words as she had heard from the lips of Vinitius. Perhaps, she thought, she was lost forever. She grew weak and felt she was about to faint and wondered what would happen then? She wanted to rise and leave but she knew that under the penalty of Caesar's anger, no one could leave before Caesar did. But even if she could, she had no strength to do so.

Meanwhile the end of the feast was not yet in sight. Slaves brought in new courses of food and filled the empty goblets with wine. In the center platform appeared two athletes to show their prowess in wrestling. They began as they wrestled to heave their powerful bodies shining from olive oil into one huge mass. Bones cracked in their powerful arms and from their set jaws came an ominous gritting of teeth. Their feet gave off dull thumps as they moved about and then remained motionless each embracing the other in their fierce test of strength. Roman eyes followed these movements of powerful arms and bodies with delight. The struggle however did not last long. One of them was Croto, a master and founder of the school of gladiators, whose reputation as the strongest man in the Empire was not in vain. He soon had his opponent at his mercy...a death rattle was heard and his opponent fell with his back broken.

Shouts and applause greeted the outcome. Croto, resting his foot on the body of his fallen foe, crossed his huge arms on his chest and cast his eyes triumphantly about the hall.

Next appeared men who imitated the sounds of different animals and clowns of all kinds. Only a few people watched them however. The quantities of wine which had been consumed began to have effect and most people were drunk. Gradually the feast turned into an orgy. The Syrian girls who first appeared in the Bacchic dance now mingled with the guests. The music changed into a wild outburst of noise. The air became stifling from overheated bodies; lamps burned with dimmed flame; wreaths fell askew on the heads of the guests; faces grew pale and covered with sweat.

Vitelius rolled under the table. Nigidia, stripping herself, dropped her drunken head on Lucan's chest; he also, drunk like the others, began blowing the golden powder from her hair, raising his eyes in delight. Vestinus, with a drunkard's stubbornness repeated for the tenth time the answer of Mopsus regarding the sealed letter of the proconsul. Tullius, who reviled the gods, yelled out, "If Xenophon is as round as a ball, he could be pushed around like a barrel."

But Domitius Afer, an old robber and an informer, took offense at this, spilling his wine on his tunic in the process. He had always believed in gods. People say that Rome will perish and there are some who contend that it is perishing already. If that should come about, it would be because the youth are without faith, and without faith there can be no virtue. People have also abandoned the former days of strict habits and it never occurs to them that Epicureans will not stand against the barbarian hordes. As for him, he is sorry that he has to live in such times and that he must seek in pleasures a refuge against grief which would soon kill him if he didn't.

Saying this, he drew a Syrian dancer to himself and began kissing her neck with his toothless mouth. Seeing this, the consul Memmius Regulus laughed and raising his bald head with wreath awry, exclaimed, "Who says Rome is perishing? Nonsense! I am a consul and I know better. Thirty legions of troops are guarding our Roman peace."

Here, he placed his finger on his forehead and began yelling, "Thirty legions of troops...thirty legions...from Britain to the boundaries of Partha." Suddenly he paused, "By Jove, there are thirty-two!" Then he rolled under the table and began to vomit flamingo tongues, chilled mushrooms, locusts in honey, fish, meat and everything which he had eaten or drunk.

The number of legions guarding Roman peace did not pacify Domitius. "No, No. Rome must perish. Faith in the gods is gone and without it there are no strict habits of life. Rome must perish. Such a pity! Life was pleasant. Caesar was gracious. Wine was good. What a pity!" And, lowering his head on the bosom of a Syrian dancer, he burst into tears.

Lucan had blown all the gold powder from Nigidia's hair and she, being drunk, had fallen asleep. Next, he took wreathes of ivy from the vase before him, put them on the sleeping woman and looked about him delightedly. "See...I am not a man.... I am a faun!"

Petronius was not drunk. Nero who drank little at first out of regard for his heavenly voice emptied goblet after goblet at the end and became drunk. He even wanted to sing more verses, this time in Greek, but he had forgotten them and instead sang an ode to Anacreon. The lutists at first accompanied him but failing to keep time, they stopped. Nero was enchanted with the beauty of Pythagoras and fell to kissing his hands in ecstasy. "Such beautiful hands I have seen only once before. Whose were they?" Then, placing his palm on his moist forehead, he tried to remember. After a while, fear was reflected on his face.... "Ah! My mother's...Agrippina's!" And he began to shake with fear. "They say that she wanders at the seaside by moonlight. All she does is walk as if looking for something. When she comes near a boat, she looks at it and moves away but the fisherman on whom she gazes soon dies."

"Not a bad theme," said Petronius.

Vestinus, stretching forth, whispered mysteriously, "I do not believe in gods but I believe in spirits."

Nero did not pay any attention to what was said and followed his own thoughts. "After all, I honored her memory by gifts. I have no wish to see her. This is the fifth year. I had to condemn her because she sent assassins against me and I had no choice. You would not be listening to my songs now if I did not."

"Thanks be to Caesar in the name of the city and the world!" yelled Domitius.

"Wine. Strike up the music."

The uproar began anew. Lucan, all in ivy, shouted above the noise, "I am not a man. I am a faun and I dwell in the forest. Eeee...Hoooo!"

Caesar got drunk. Most guests were drunk, Vinitius no less than others. Whenever he did, he became quarrelsome. His dark face became pale and his tongue slurred when he spoke now in a commanding and loud voice, "Give me your lips! Today...tomorrow...what's the difference. Caesar took you away from Aulus in order to give you to me, you understand? Tomorrow at dusk I am to send for you. Caesar promised me that. You are now mine. Give me your lips now, I don't want to wait till tomorrow." He moved closer to embrace Ligia. Acte tried to come to her help. Ligia too tried to ward him off with the remnants of strength she possessed. She now realized that she had to fight against him with all her might. She also tried to beg him not to act in such a manner and to have pity on her, but incensed with wine he pulled her closer and closer to him. To Ligia, he was no longer a kind and thoughtful Vinitius, dear to her. No, he was rather a drunken, wicked satyr who filled her with revulsion and terror. In vain she tried to avoid his kisses, her strength ebbing rapidly.

As he rose to take her in his arms and hold her close, it seemed to him that a tremendous power removed his arms from her neck with as much ease as if they had been arms of a mere child and pushed him aside like a dried limb or a withered leaf. "What is this?" Vinitius rubbed his astonished eyes and saw before him the huge body of the Ligian called Ursus whom he had previously seen in the house of Aulus.

Ursus stood quietly but looked at Vinitius with his blue eyes in such a way that the blood seemed to freeze in the tribune's whole being. Then the giant took his queen in his arms and carried her out of the hall slowly, followed by Acte.

Vinitius sat down petrified with fear; finally he tried to stand up and run after them, crying in a broken voice, "Ligia, Ligia!" But insane rage and also the wine cut his legs from under him. He staggered about and seeing the naked arm of one of the dancers, grasped it and began asking, "What happened?"

"Drink!" she answered. He drank from her goblet and fell to the floor.

Most of the guests were already prone drunk; some were tottering to leave and some were sleeping on the couches at the table, snoring or giving forth the excesses of wine.

Meanwhile, from the golden network above, roses kept dropping on those drunken consuls, senators, nobles, philosophers, poets...on drunken dancers and patrician ladies, on all this social sphere which although still dominant and powerful yet with the soul beginning to depart from it; this society, although garlanded yet perishing.

Outside the dawn was breaking.

CHAPTER VIII

NO one attempted to stop Ursus. No one even asked what he was doing. Those who saw a giant slave carrying his drunken mistress away made nothing of it. Furthermore, Acte accompanied them and her presence removed any suspicion.

In this way they entered one of the adjoining chambers and thence to Acte's apartments. Ligia's strength deserted her completely and she clung to Ursus for dear life, but when the cool, clean morning air hit her she opened her eyes. It was growing light outside. Passing some columns, they turned into a side portico, coming out, not in the courtyard, but, in the palace gardens where the tops of the pines and the cypresses were beginning to glow in the morning sunshine. That part of the building was empty but the echoes of the music and sounds of the feast still could be heard but indistinctly.

It seemed to Ligia that she had just been rescued from hell and brought out to God's world outside. There was then something else than that disgusting festival hall. There was the sky, the dawn, light and peace. Sudden weeping seized the girl and sheltering her head in the huge arms of Ursus she cried, "Let's go home, Ursus, home to the house of Aulus."

"We will go!" answered Ursus.

They found themselves now at the entrance of Acte's apartment. Ursus placed Ligia on a marble bench close to the fountain. Acte tried to reassure her. She urged her to go to sleep, telling her that for the moment there was no danger. After the feast the drunken guests would sleep till evening but for a long time Ligia could not

calm herself and, pressing her temples with both hands, she repeated the words, "Ursus, let's go home to the house of Aulus."

Ursus was ready. It's true that the Praetorian guards stood at the
gates, but he knew that he could pass them safely. Furthermore, the
soldiers would not stop the people who were leaving. The palace
entrance was crowded with litters. Guests were beginning to leave
in droves. No, no one would detain them. They would pass with
the crowds and then go home. Anyway, what does it matter? His
queen commands it, so it has to be. He will carry out her orders.

"Yes, Ursus. Let us go," said Ligia.

However, Acte had to dissuade them from this foolish move.
They would gain exit, it's true. No one would stop them. But don't
they both realize that they are not allowed to flee from the house
of Caesar? Whoever does this offends Caesar. Yes, they may go but
in the evening a centurion with his soldiers will bring a death
sentence to Aulus and Pomponia. Then they will seize Ligia again
and then there will be no rescue for her. Should Aulus and Pomponia receive her under their roof, death surely awaits them.

Ligia felt crushed. There was no hope. She must not bring ruin
on Aulus and his house. At the feast she had hoped that she would
be returned to them by Vinitius and Petronius but now she realized
that it was through them that she was brought here. So, there was
no help from them for her. Only a miracle could save her, a miracle
from God's omnipotence.

"Acte," she spoke in despair, "did you not hear from the lips of
Vinitius that Caesar had given me to him and that he will send his
slaves for me this night?"

"I did," answered Acte. She noted the deep despair in Ligia's
voice but she did not understand the cause for it. She herself had
been Nero's favorite paramour. Even though she was not corrupt in
her morals, she still could not find shame in such a relationship.
Being a former slave, she was used to the laws of slavery. Besides,
she still loved Nero. If he wanted her back, she would return to him
happily. Knowing that Ligia must become the mistress of the
youthful and handsome Vinitius or otherwise to expose Aulus and
Pomponia to grave danger, she could not understand how the girl
could hesitate one instant.

"Because," she added after a while, "it would certainly be much
safer for you with Vinitius than in Caesar's house." And at that

moment it did not occur to her that what she meant was: "Be resigned to your fate. Become the concubine of Vinitius."

Ligia, who still felt the burning, brutal lips of Vinitius full of animal desire on her own, felt now the flush of shame rush to her face.

"Never!" she cried out. "I won't go to him nor will I remain here."

"But," asked Acte, "is he so hateful to you?"

Ligia could not answer her right away because she was overcome with bitter tears. Acte took the poor girl in her arms and tried to console her. Ursus, breathing heavily, opened and closed his giant fists. Loving his queen with a blind devotion of a faithful servant, he could not bear the sight of her tears. In his still half-wild Ligian heart was the wish to return to the festive hall, throttle Vinitius and even Caesar himself, but he feared that acting thus he would displease his queen and furthermore, by acting thus, he wasn't altogether sure that he wouldn't also displease the Crucified Lamb whose true disciple he wanted to become.

Acte, while calming Ligia, asked again, "Is Vinitius so hateful to you?"

"No," said Ligia. "I do not hate him. I am a Christian and it is not permitted for us to hate."

"I know, Ligia. I also know from the letters of Paul of Tarsus that it is not permitted for Christians to defile themselves in immorality; not to fear death more than sin. But, tell me, does your teaching permit one person to cause the death of another?"

"No."

"Then how can you bring down Caesar's vengeance on Aulus and his family?"

A moment of silence followed this question, a question which caused Ligia to see the bottomless pit before her.

"I ask you," continued Acte, "because I feel sorry for you and I have compassion also for the good Pomponia and Aulus and their child. I've been here in Caesar's house quite some time and I know what Caesar's anger can do. You cannot flee from here. Beg Vinitius to return you to Pomponia."

But Ligia dropped to her knees to beg someone else. Ursus knelt down also and they both began to pray earnestly. Acte looked at them in wonder. Ligia with her head turned heavenward seemed to

implore rescue. The morning sunshine, casting light on her dark
hair and white dress, shown in her eyes and she seemed to glow in
the light. A kind of superhuman exaltation was evident in that pale
face, those parted lips, in those raised hands and eyes. Acte now
realized why Ligia could not become the concubine of any man. A
different world was opening before her eyes, a world which she was
not accustomed to seeing. Such a prayer from the pure maiden
before her, in that palace of crime and infamy, filled her with
amazement and wonder. A moment ago it seemed to her that there
was no help for Ligia but to be taken to Vinitius, but now she
expected some kind of miracle, some aid to the stricken girl,
something which Caesar himself was powerless to resist. Perhaps
some kind of winged army would descend from the sky to help her.

Finally, Ligia got up with a face now serene with hope. Ursus
rose also and looked at his queen, waiting her command. Her eyes
filled with tears but she spoke in a strong voice, "No, I cannot
bring ruin upon them, Acte. May God bless Aulus, Pomponia and
little Aulus, but I must not see them again." Turning to Ursus, she
told him that he alone remained to her in the world, that he must
be her protector and father. They can no longer seek refuge in the
house of Aulus for fear of Caesar's anger, but she cannot go to
Vinitius nor can she remain here. Let Ursus conduct her out of the
city, let him conceal her some place where neither Vinitius nor his
servants will find her. She would go with Ursus even beyond the
sea, even beyond the mountains, to the barbarians where the power
of Caesar cannot reach her. Let him take her and save her for he
alone remained to her.

The Ligian was ready and, as a sign of obedience, he bent down
at her feet to show his willingness. But on the face of Acte, who
had been expecting a miracle of some kind, there was surprise and
even disenchantment. Had Ligia's prayer effected only this much?
To flee from the house of Caesar is to commit an offense which
must be avenged and even if Ligia succeeded in hiding, Caesar
would avenge himself on the family of Aulus. If she wanted to
escape, let her try to escape from the house of Vinitius. Then,
Caesar, who does not like to concern himself with the affairs of
others, may not wish to aid Vinitius in the pursuit. In any case, it
will not be a crime against Caesar.

To Ligia, however, the safety of the house of Aulus was uppermost in her mind. They could not be blamed at all if they did not know of her whereabouts and could testify to this with honesty. Therefore, she determined that they would not flee from the house of Vinitius, but on the way to it. Vinitius, in his drunken stupor, told her that he would send his slaves for her in the evening. Had he been sober, he undoubtedly would not have divulged this information. Evidently, he or Petronius had won from Caesar the promise to give her to him on the following evening and if not this evening then surely the next. But, Ursus will save her. He will come and rescue her and take her to a safe place. No one can resist the strength of Ursus, not even that strong athlete who wrestled at the feast. However, in case Vinitius sends a large number of slaves, Ursus will go at once to Bishop Linus for aid and counsel. The bishop will take compassion on her; he will command the Christians to go with Ursus in order to rescue her. They will help Ursus who will then take her out of the city and hide her away from the power of Caesar. As she spoke thusly, Ligia felt a measure of assurance in the success of her escape. Turning to Acte she asked, "You will not betray us, will you Acte?"

"By the memory of my mother, I will not! But, pray to your God that you will be able to escape."

The gentle and kind eyes of the Ligian giant gleamed with satisfaction. He himself was not able to form a successful plan but this he certainly could do. He would go to the bishop for the bishop could read in the heavens what is necessary to be done. He would himself assemble enough Christians to help him. Is he not aware of how many Christians there really are in Rome? Yes, even among the gladiators? He could even summon a thousand if he wanted that many. He will then rescue his queen and take her outside the city. They will go to the ends of the earth if need be.

Here, he began to see in his mind's eye the great forest of his childhood days. "To the forest...to the forest...yes," he mused to himself. But he soon shook himself as if from a dream and began preparations to go to the bishop. In the evening he will be ready. Neither the slaves of the patrician nor even the Praetorian guards will stop him and his group of Christians. Let him beware who will fall under his fists, even if he is in full armor. Iron itself will crumple in his hands.

Ligia raised her finger to him and with childlike seriousness spoke, "Ursus, do not kill!"

Ursus put his huge fist behind him and began to mumble, trying to explain, "He must rescue the light of his eyes, his queen. She herself had said that it was up to him now. He will do his best not to kill but if it's not possible and he must kill, he will repent and ask the Innocent Lamb to have mercy on him. He has no wish to offend the Lamb, but his hands are so heavy and so strong."

There was tenderness and love in the expression of the giant man but he tried to hide it by adding quickly, "I will go to the bishop."

Acte, in turn, put her arms around Ligia's neck and began to weep. Once again the freedwoman understood that there was a world in which greater happiness existed, even in suffering, than in all the excesses and luxuries of Nero. Once again a kind of door to the light was opened a little more before her but she felt that she was unworthy to pass through it yet.

CHAPTER IX

LIGIA no longer despaired even though she knew she had to give up Pomponia whom she dearly loved as her own mother and also the entire family of Aulus. She was consoled at the thought that now she would be able to sacrifice something she loved for her faith because she would be on her own from now on. Perhaps there was a bit of childish curiosity in wondering what her future life would be like wandering about, even among wild beasts and barbarians, but at the same time there was no doubt of her trusting faith and the knowledge that she was acting in accord with the commandments of the Divine Lord and from now on only He would watch over her as His own obedient and faithful child. Then, she asked herself, what harm could befall her. If suffering came, she would endure it in His name. If sudden death, He will take her to heaven where in time she would be reunited with Pomponia and her family for all eternity. More than once when she was in the house of Aulus, she pondered why she, a Christian, could not do more for the Crucified Lord of whom Ursus spoke with such tenderness. Now, however, the time had come and Ligia spoke of this opportunity to Acte who could not understand her.

To leave everything, to leave wealth, comfort; to leave the city, the gardens, temples and everything that is beautiful, to leave a sunny land and friends...for what?...To hide from the love of a handsome nobleman...this and more could not be understood by Acte. At times she felt that Ligia's action was right; that there must be some mysterious happiness in it, but she could not yet fully understand it. Moreover, all this would certainly come to no good end and there was great danger to Ligia. Acte was timid by nature and she wondered with fear in her heart about the coming night and what would happen to Ligia. She did not mention her fears to Ligia however. She prevailed upon her though to take her rest, especially after spending a sleepless night. Ligia agreed and the two of them entered the bedrooms which were furnished with luxury, due to Acte's former relationship with Nero. But, in spite of her weariness, Acte could not sleep. She had been sad for a long time but now she was seized with a kind of uneasiness she had not felt before. Life for her had seemed meaningless, but now she had a strange feeling of being stained somewhat by Nero and his surroundings and she felt as if she were leading a dishonorable life.

There were mixed thoughts in her head...again a certain opening to some light seemed close to her but it faded gradually. In that moment of light, however, she was so dazzled that she could not perceive anything clearly. She felt that in that light there was a kind of happiness, even a great happiness, such that in its presence everything seemed small and unimportant. Even if Nero set aside Poppaea and called her back to him, it would be as nothing to this new happiness. The thought came to her also that if Nero took her back, it would not be the same any more. Nero now took the form, not of a demigod, but of a being as pitiful as any slave, and that palace which to her was so splendid up to now was merely a heap of stones.

All these feelings and thoughts began to cause her torment and she could not sleep. Wondering if Ligia too was tormented with uneasy feelings, she turned to her in order to console her about her future plight, but to her surprise, she found that Ligia was asleep like a child in peaceful repose. Into the curtained bedroom some light penetrated and by this light Acte was able to see Ligia sleeping without trouble.

"She sleeps. Yes, she is still a child so she is able to sleep," thought Acte. Yet, it came to her mind that this child chose to flee rather than to live with Vinitius, to prefer deprivation to a life of shame, to wander about rather than be in a splendid house with robes and jewels, feasts and the sounds of lutes and music. Why?

She gazed upon Ligia as if to find the answer to her question. She saw Ligia's noble features, her calm forehead and beautiful arch of her brows. Her dark hair, parted lips and her maidenly bosom moving with her regular breathing. Then she thought again, "How different she is from me and the other women of the palace." At this moment Ligia was more beautiful than all the flowers of Caesar's gardens, more than all the statues in his palace.

She thought of the dangers which threatened the girl and a great sense of pity seized her. A motherly protective feeling rose up in her; Ligia was to her now not only a beautiful girl but also a very dear child and she felt a great compassion for her. Feeling thusly she bent down and kissed her dark hair.

Ligia slept on as if she were with Pomponia and there was no danger. She slept on and on. Midday passed and she finally opened her blue eyes and looked about her in astonishment, wondering why she was not in the house of Aulus.

"Is it you, Acte?" she asked seeing the Greek woman near by.

"Yes, it is I."

"Is it evening?"

"No, child, but noon has passed quite some time ago."

"Has Ursus not returned yet?"

"Ursus did not say that he will return here. He will be watching out for your litter with the Christians in the evening."

"Yes, you are right."

They then left the bedrooms and went to the baths where they both bathed, then to breakfast and afterward to the gardens of the palace where no danger was expected since Caesar and his court were still sleeping. For the first time in her life Ligia looked upon those magnificent gardens full of pines, oaks, olive trees and myrtles, among which many statues were interspersed. The ponds gleamed in the waning sun; there were beds of roses blooming, watered by the sprays of fountains; grottoes covered with ivy and woodbine; silver-colored swans swimming in the ponds. Amidst statues and trees wandered tame gazelles from the deserts of Africa. Many colored birds of every variety and from many countries of the world flew about or perched in the trees.

The gardens were empty except for the slaves who were working as gardeners; some of them sang softly while they worked. Others were resting from their labors, sitting in the shade or watering flowers, mostly roses and crocuses.

Acte and Ligia toured the gardens. Ligia, despite her fears of future events, enjoyed seeing all the beauty around her and could not resist the pleasure, curiosity and wonder of all that she saw. It even occurred to her that if Caesar were good, he might indeed be happy in such a place amid such splendid gardens.

After walking around, they grew a bit tired and sat down on a bench hidden amid cypresses, and began to talk of the things which weighed on their minds and hearts, that is, Ligia's escape. Acte felt less secure about the success of the venture than Ligia herself. At times, she thought it was an act of madness which could not succeed. She felt a growing pity for Ligia. She again was convinced that it was a hundred times better to prevail upon Vinitius to allow her to return to her former home. After a while she asked Ligia how long she had known him and whether she did not think that he could be persuaded to have her returned.

Ligia shook her head sadly. "No. In Aulus' house Vinitius had been different. He had been very kind but since yesterday's feast, I'm afraid of him and I'd rather flee from him to the Ligians."

"But in Aulus' house he was dear to you, was he not?" inquired Acte.

"He was," answered Ligia, bowing her head.

After a moment's thought, Acte said, "Ligia, you are not a slave like I was. Vinitius could marry you. You are a hostage, it's true, but you are a daughter of a king. Aulus and Pomponia love you as their child. I'm sure that they would be willing to adopt you. Vinitius might then marry you."

Ligia answered quietly but with more sadness, "I would rather go to the Ligians."

"Ligia, do you want me to go right away to Vinitius, arouse him if he is still sleeping and tell him what I'm telling you now? I would speak to him thus: 'Vinitius, this is a king's daughter and a dear child of the famous Aulus Plautius. If you love her, return her to them and take her as your wife from their home.'"

The girl answered with a voice so low that Acte was barely able to hear her, "I would rather flee." And there were great tears in her eyes.

Further conversation was interrupted by the rustle of approaching steps and before Acte had time to see who was coming, Poppaea Sabina appeared in front of the bench followed by a small retinue of slave women. Two of them held over her head bunches of ostrich feathers secured by golden wires. With these they fanned her lightly and at the same time protected her from the autumn sun which could still cause sunburn. A woman from Egypt, black as ebony and with her breasts swollen with milk, bore in her arms an infant wrapped in purple with golden fringes. Acte and Ligia rose thinking that Poppaea would pass the bench without stopping, but she halted before them and said, "Acte, the bells on the doll which you had given as a present were badly fastened. The child tore one of them off and put it in her mouth. Luckily, Lillith saw it in time."

"I'm sorry, divinity," answered Acte, crossing her arms on her breast and inclining her head.

Poppaea began to look at Ligia. "What slave is this?"

"She is not a slave, divine Augusta, but a foster child of Pomponia Graecina and a daughter of the Ligian king given by him as hostage to Rome."

"And she has come to visit you?"

"No, Augusta. She is dwelling in the palace since the day before yesterday."

"Was she at the feast last night?"

"She was, Augusta."

"At whose command?"

"At Caesar's command."

Poppaea looked more closely at Ligia who stood with bowed head. Suddenly a frown appeared on her face. Jealous of her own beauty and power, she lived in constant fear lest she be replaced by a more fortunate rival just as she herself replaced and ruined Octavia. Hence every beautiful face in the palace aroused her suspicion. With critical eye she began to appraise this maiden before her. She took in every part of Ligia's form, estimated every detail of her face and she became frightened. "This is really a nymph in disguise," she thought. "Venus herself gave her birth." And she had to admit to herself that she was growing older and it had begun to show on her. She was consumed by wounded vanity and alarmed at the realization of what might happen if Nero would really evaluate the beauty of such a one as this girl before her. Nero evidently had not yet seen this girl or, seeing her through the emerald, had not really appreciated her beauty. But what would happen if Nero would meet her in the daytime, in the sunlight? Moreover, she is not a slave but a king's daughter. Immortal gods!

She is more beautiful than I and much younger. Her frown increased and her eyes began to gleam with cold hatred.

"Have you spoken with Caesar?" she aked Ligia.

"No, Augusta."

"Why do you choose to be here rather than in the house of Aulus Plautius?"

"I did not wish it, gracious lady. Petronius persuaded Caesar to take me from Pomponia. I'm here against my will."

"And you would like to return to Pomponia?" This question Poppaea asked with a softer and milder tone and Ligia felt sudden hope.

"Lady," she said, extending her hand toward her, "Caesar promised to give me as a slave to Vinitius but please intercede for me and have me returned to Pomponia."

"Then Petronius persuaded Caesar to take you away from Aulus and give you as a slave to Vinitius?"

"That is true, lady. Vinitius is to send for me today but you are good so please have compassion on me." Saying this she bent down and took the hem of Poppaea's dress as in supplication and began to wait her reply with a beating heart.

Poppaea looked upon her for a moment and an evil smile appeared upon her face. "Then, I promise you that this day you will become a slave of Vinitius," she said and walked away as if an evil vision. To the ears of Ligia and Acte came the wail of the child who for some reason began to cry loudly.

Ligia's eyes filled with tears and taking Acte's hand said, "Let us return. Help can only come from God."

They returned to Acte's apartment and stayed there until evening. When darkness came and the slaves brought in lighted tapers, both women became pale. They stopped conversing and waited in silence. Ligia was thinking about Ursus and the Christians. Were they waiting to rescue her? Will it be successful? Her breathing became quicker from emotion and anticipation. Acte feverishly collected some jewels and fastened them on the hem of Ligia's dress, imploring her at the same time not to reject this gift which would aid her in escaping. They both waited with bated breath. Soon it will come whatever it may be.

Suddenly the curtain at the entrance moved aside without noise and there stood a tall, dark man, his face marked with the ravages of a former sickness of smallpox. Ligia recognized him. He was Atacinus, a freedman of Vinitius whom she had previously seen at the house of Aulus.

Acte stood up in alarm. Atacinus bent his head in greeting and spoke, "A greeting from Marcus Vinitius who awaits you, divine Ligia, with a feast in his house which is bedecked in garlands in your honor."

The lips of the maiden grew pale. "I go," she said.

Then she threw her arms around Acte in tearful farewell.

CHAPTER X

THE house of Vinitius was indeed decorated in myrtle and ivy which hung on the walls and over the doors. The columns were encircled with grapevines and flowers. The entrance hall was lit up brightly with eight- and twelve-branched candelabra. There were other lamps of all sizes and shapes. There were lamps made in the shape of vessels, trees, animals, birds and statues. There were cups of perfumed oils, lamps of alabaster, marble and gilded Corinthian bronze, not as beautiful as Nero's famed candlestick which he robbed from the temple of Apollo, but beautiful nevertheless and made by famous artisans. Some of the lamps were shaded by Alexandrian glass or transparent material from the Indus, of red, blue, yellow or violet colors so that the whole entrance hall shone with many-colored rays of light.

There was the fragrance of nard to which Vinitius had become accustomed and to like when he was in the East. The rest of the house, in which many male and female slave figures could be seen moving about, was also lit up brightly.

In the dining room a table for four persons was laid out. Petronius and his Chrysothemis together with Vinitius and Ligia were to be the only participants at the feast. Petronius advised Vinitius not to go for Ligia himself but to send for her by his trusted Atacinus and thus to receive her in his house as if with honor.

"You were drunk yesterday," said he. "I saw you. You treated her rather roughly, like a stonecutter from the Alban hills might act. I advise you, be not overly insistent and remember that one should drink good wine slowly. Know also that it is indeed a pleasant thing to desire a loved one but it is more pleasant to be desired by her."

Chrysothemis had her own and somewhat different opinion on this point but Petronius, calling her his Vestal and his dove, began to explain the difference which must exist between a trained charioteer of the circus and a youth who takes up the reigns of a chariot for the first time. Then, turning to Vinitius, he continued, "Win her confidence, make her joyful, be gracious and magnanimous. I have no wish to see a gloomy feast. Swear to her by Hades that you will even return her to Pomponia and it will be to your advantage when tomorrow she will prefer to remain with you."

Then, turning to Chrysothemis, he added, "For five years I have acted thus, more or less, with this fickle dove and I cannot complain about her response."

"I did resist you at first, you satyr!" replied Chrysothemis, striking him playfully with her fan.

"Out of consideration for my predecessor."

"But were you not at my feet?"

"Yes, but only to put rings on your toes."

She momentarily looked at her toes which were indeed adorned with beautiful rings, and she and Petronius began to laugh. But Vinitius paid little attention to their light banterings. His heart was beating anxiously about Ligia. "They must have left the palace now," he said as if to himself.

"They must have," answered Petronius. "In the meantime, let me tell you the story of Apollonius or perhaps of Rufinus whose story I failed to finish. I know not why."

Vinitius, however, cared to hear the story of Rufinus as little as of Apollonius. His mind was on Ligia and though he agreed that it was more appropriate to receive her in his house than to go for her personally, he was sorry he did not go because he would all that much sooner have been able to see her.

The slaves brought in an ornamented tripod which held bronze dishes with burning coals on them. They then sprinkled some myrrh and nard on the coals.

"Now they are turning toward the Carinae," said Vinitius.

"He won't wait. He'll run out to meet them and most likely miss them in the darkness," exclaimed Chrysothemis.

At this Vinitius smiled and said, "Oh, I'll wait. I'll wait." But his face still showed concern and anxiety. Seeing this, Petronius said, "I doubt if I ever will be able to make a true philosopher out of this true son of Mars."

"They are now in the Carinae."

As a matter of fact, they were. Atacinus and his group were at that moment turning into the section of Rome called the Carinae. Slaves with lighted lamps were in front and other slaves were at both sides of the litter. They moved slowly however. The streets were dimly lighted in that area and now it seemed to Atacinus that the streets were becoming unusually crowded. People were spilling out from the alleys and pushing against his slaves. Others appeared to stagger around as if they were drunk and increasingly stumbled into the litter bearers.

"Make way for the noble Tribune Marcus Vinitius," shouted the bearers and slaves by the litter.

Ligia became aware of these dark forms about the litter and her heart beat with alarm mingled with hope. "It is he! It is Ursus and the Christians." Her lips trembled in anticipation. "Oh Christ, help them please. Lord, help us now."

Atacinus himself became alarmed at the unusual crowd around him. This was very strange and uncalled for. His slaves shouted louder. "Make way for the noble Marcus Vinitius!" But the crowd became more numerous. Atacinus had ordered his slaves to use their clubs to pave the way, when suddenly a cry arose and almost at once all the lamps were extinguished by the crowd around them. There was a struggle around the litter. Atacinus realized then that it was an attack upon him and the litter, and was horrified because he knew that sometimes Caesar himself headed these nightly ventures for his amusement. This was well known in the city as was the fact that out of these escapades he himself sometimes came back with bruises upon his body. But, those who defended themselves were put to the sword and slain even though they were senators. During such attacks by Nero, the Roman guards were ordered to stay put and not to patrol the city.

Meanwhile the noise around the litter grew still louder, as people fought and trampled one another. The thought uppermost in the mind of Atacinus was to save Ligia and himself and leave the rest to chance. So, drawing her out of the litter, he took her in his arms and tried to escape in the darkness, but Ligia called out loudly, "Ursus, Ursus!"

She was dressed in white so it was not difficult to recognize her. Atacinus was hastily trying to wrap a mantle around her when a mighty grip encircled his neck and a huge, crushing weight fell on his head with the weight of a massive rock.

He fell down as if pole-axed, dead even before he hit the ground.

The slaves of Vinitius were all mostly on the ground, either killed or wounded. Some were scattered about fearing for their lives. The litter was broken to bits. Ursus bore Ligia away in his arms accompanied by his helpers who gradually dispersed along the way.

Those of the slaves of Vinitius who were still alive now assembled together and took counsel. They did not dare to go back empty-handed. After a short deliberation they returned to the place of the conflict where they found a few corpses and among them Atacinus. There were some wounded who could not move and had to be carried away. They all slowly returned to Vinitius' house, but they did not dare enter. They debated among themselves how to divulge to their master what had happened. "Let Gulo tell him," they whispered. "Blood flows from his wounds. The master loves him and it will be safer for him than for any of us."

Gulo, an old slave who had nursed Vinitius and was given to Vinitius after the death of his mother, the sister of Petronius, said, "All right, I will tell him. But all of you come with me so that his anger will not fall on me alone."

Meanwhile, Vinitius in his impatience was walking back and forth muttering to himself. "They should have been here already." Petronius and Chrysothemis laughed at his antics.

Suddenly they heard steps in the entrance hall and mutterings of voices. Then the slaves rushed in, raising their voices and began to wail.

Vinitius sprang toward them. "Where is Ligia?" he cried with a harsh voice.

"Aaaaaaa...Master."

Then Gulo pushed himself forward with his bloody face and entreating arms. He exclaimed in anguish, "See, Master, our blood. We fought. See our blood."

He barely finished when Vinitius in complete rage grabbed a
bronze lamp and with one blow shattered the skull of the slave.
Then, seizing his own head with both hands, he drove his fingers
in his hair and wailed bitterly, *"Me miserum...me miserum!"* His face
became livid, his eyes wild and a hoarse cry came out. "Bring the
whips."

"Master, have pity," groaned the slaves.

Petronius stood up with a look of disgust on his face. "Come,
Chrysothemis. If you want to look upon raw flesh, we might as
well go to the butcher's stall." And they walked out.

Throughout the house decked in ivy and prepared for a feast,
there were heard cries mingled with groans and the whistling of
whips which continued until morning.

CHAPTER XI

VINITIUS did not sleep that night. After the departure of Petronius when the yells and moans of his flogged slaves could not satisfy his rage or his pain, he gathered a group of his slaves and rushed out with them in order to find Ligia. They roamed the different districts of Rome: the Esquiline, the Subura, the Vicus Sceleratus and all the adjoining alleyways. They passed the Capitol and over the bridge of Fabricius and next they searched the section called the Trans-Tiber. All for naught. Vinitius had little hope that he would find her but he had to do something to fill the great void that he now felt. They had to return finally at daybreak when the carts of the dealers in vegetables began to appear in the city and the bakers were opening their shops.

On returning he gave command to put away Gulo's body which no one dared to touch. He also gave orders to send those slaves from whom Ligia had been taken to the terrible rural prisons. This punishment was considered more horrible than death by most of the slaves and they all dreaded it. Finally, he threw himself on a couch, not to sleep, but with confused thoughts began to shape and form plans to find Ligia. It seemed to him that to lose her, not to see her again, was out of the question. For the first time in his life he met with resistance to his imperious nature of a commanding officer. He could not understand this and would not accept it. How could anyone dare to go contrary to his wishes? He would rather see the city sunk in ruins than his desires thwarted. Hence, it now seemed to him that what had happened to him should demand divine and human vengeance.

For the first time in his life he was unable to reconcile himself to fate. Never had he desired anything as much as Ligia. He felt that he would not be able to live without her. He asked himself what he was to do without her in the days which would follow. Then again he would rage against her. He would find her and punish her severely. But such thoughts were few. He wished more than anything else to hold her in his arms, to hear her voice, see her eyes and her body. At these thoughts, he called to her, holding his head in his hands. He wanted to think calmly but that was impossible. Finally a thought struck him: Aulus and Pomponia would surely know about Ligia's whereabouts...and he sprang from the couch and hurried to their house.

On his way down, he pondered darkly the possible refusal of Aulus of his demands. If they would not return her to him, he would take his revenge upon the whole household. Yes, it is true that they nursed him when he was sick but this was different. He would be avenged. Petronius would assist him in bringing the decrees of death to Aulus and his whole family. He knew that Nero very seldom denied anything to his favorites, the Augustians.

Suddenly a terrible thought struck him like a blow.... "What if Caesar himself had taken Ligia?" Everyone in Rome knew that Nero, to avoid boredom, sometimes took part in night attacks upon citizens of Rome in order to fish for, as he expressed it, a pearl among the populace. On these nightly excursions he would sometimes capture a pretty girl whom he would take to his palace. Thinking thusly, Vinitius was filled with foreboding and doom. Certainly, Nero, seeing Ligia at the feast, would consider her most beautiful and desirable. He, therefore would want her for himself. How could it be otherwise? It is true that Ligia had been in Nero's house on the Palatine and he might have openly taken her...but...as Petronius put it, Nero did not dare to act openly in his criminal acts, being a coward at heart. Even though he had the power to act openly, he chose almost always to act in secrecy in the performance of his many crimes. This time, fear of Poppaea may have inclined him to act in secret. Surely, Aulus Plautius, being a former general, would not have dared to go contrary to the wishes of Caesar. Who other would dare? That giant of a blue-eyed Ligian? The one who carried her in his arms from the feast? No. A slave would not dare. Hence no one had done this deed but Caesar.

At this conviction, sudden darkness grew in his eyes and drops of sweat covered his forehead. In that case Ligia was lost to him forever. It was possible to take her away from the hands of anyone else but not from the hands of Caesar. He now repeated with greater fear and anguish, *"Vae misero mihi."* He pictured her in Nero's arms and for the first time in his life he knew of thoughts which a man cannot endure. Now especially he realized the extent of his love for Ligia. In his mind's eye he was able to picture her and to hear her every word. How he saw her first at the fountain in the house of Aulus. At the feast he felt her closeness, the fragrance of her hair and her whole body, the delight of the kisses which he forced upon her. She now seemed to him a hundred times sweeter and more desirable and more beautiful than ever before. When he thought that she would be possessed by Nero, a great ache seized him, a pain so enormous that he now stood still wanting to beat his head against the wall. He felt that he was going mad and only vengeance on Caesar would prevent that madness. Yes. He would be avenged. This thought calmed him a bit. Thinking of revenge he spoke out loud, "I will be your Cassius Chaerea!" (He alluded to the assassin of Caligula.) Saying this he took some earth from one of the vases and made a vow to the gods of vengeance, Erebus and Hecate.

Then he felt a little better. Now he had something to live for, something to occupy his days and nights. Changing his mind about going to Aulus, he ordered his litter bearers to take him to the Palatine. Along the way he pondered the possibility that he would not be allowed to see Nero.... That would surely be proof that Nero was the guilty one. He also wanted to see Acte, hoping to find out something from her about Ligia. Acte surely would be the most logical person to see.

Convinced of this, he commanded the slaves to hasten. He had heard of Egyptian priests of the goddess Pacht who could bring diseases on whomever they wished; he determined to learn the means of doing so. In the East, they had told him too that Jews have certain invocations by which they cover their enemies' bodies with sores. He had a number of slaves who were Jews. He would then, upon his return home, try to get these secrets from them. Mostly he thought of his short Roman sword with which a thrust could spill much blood, such as was used when Caligula was assassinated. The result of that tragic episode was still evident in the stains of blood upon the columns of the portico. For vengeance, he was ready to exterminate all of Rome and if the vengeful gods would decree that all people should die except for him and Ligia, he would go along with that wholeheartedly.

When he reached Caesar's palace, he regained his presence of mind and thought. "If the guards give me any difficulty, then I will know she is within the palace gates." But the centurion of the guards came up to him with a smile on his face and said, "A greeting, noble tribune. If you come to visit with Caesar, you come at a very inopportune time. I'm afraid that you will not be able to see him."

"What happened?" asked Vinitius.

"The infant Augusta fell suddenly ill yesterday; Caesar and the Lady Poppaea are attending her with physicians whom they had summoned from the city."

This was very important news to Vinitius. When a daughter was born to him, Nero went simply wild with joy. He commanded the Senate to solemnize the event, to commit the womb of Poppaea to the gods. A votive offering was made at Antium where the delivery of the baby took place. Various games to honor this event were scheduled and also a temple was erected in commemoration. Nero, unable to be moderate in anything, showed love for the child beyond measure. To Poppaea, the child was dear also, if for no other reason than that it strengthened her position with Nero and made him unable to resist her whims and fancies.

In answer to the news of the centurion, Vinitius merely remarked, "I only want to see Acte." The fate of the child held little concern for him in the present state of his mind.

Acte, however, was also occupied at the bedside of the child and he had to wait a long time for her return. When she did, she paled at the sight of him.

"Acte!" cried Vinitius, seizing her hand and drawing her close to him. "Where is Ligia?"

She looked into his eyes and said, "I wanted to ask you the same thing."

"She is gone! They have taken her away from me," he wailed in agony.

After a moment, he regained some composure and spoke. "Acte, if life is dear to you, if you don't want misfortune to fall on you such as you cannot imagine, tell me truthfully did Caesar take her?"

"Caesar did not leave the palace at all yesterday."

"By the shades of your mother, by all the gods...is she not in the palace?"

"Nero did not take her on the way to you. Since yesterday when the infant Augusta got sick, he has not left her cradle."

Vinitius drew a sigh of relief. What he feared the most did not occur.

"Well then," he reasoned, "Aulus Plautius must have done it. Woe to him."

"Aulus Plautius was here to see me this morning. I could not see him because I was busy with the sick child but I know that he too asked of the whereabouts of Ligia. He said that he would return to see me."

"He wanted to turn suspicion from himself, no doubt," said Vinitius.

"He left a few words on a tablet for me. I'll show them to you and from them you will see for yourself that he does not know where she is either. First, he went to your house and then he came here." She then went and got the tablet and showed it to him.

Vinitius read the tablet and was silent. Acte seemed to read his thoughts because she remarked after a while, "No, Marcus. Whatever happened was because Ligia herself wished it to happen thus."

"Did you know that she wanted to escape?"

"I know that she does not wish to be your concubine." And she looked at him with misty but stern eyes.

"And you...what have you been all your life?"

"I was a slave at first."

Vinitius began to rage to himself and to Acte. Caesar had given her to him, so she was his. Yes, he will find her even if she was buried in the catacombs. Why shouldn't she be his concubine? She would be his slave too. He would flog her and do whatever he wished. He'd find her all right.

He grew more and more excited as he raged on. Acte knew that he spoke through anger and bitterness and pain so she did not take much stock in his wild raving. She finally asked him why he came to see her.

Vinitius did not answer her directly. He came because he wanted to. He thought that she would have some information for him, but if not, he would go to Caesar and get his help in order to find the girl quickly. By fleeing, she opposed the will of Nero, hence he will aid him in his search. Petronius too will support him in asking Caesar's help.

Acte answered him in solemn words, "Vinitius, take care that acting thus you will lose her forever."

"What do you mean?"

"Listen to me, Marcus. Yesterday, Ligia and I were in the gardens and we met Poppaea with the infant Augusta. In the evening the child fell ill and her nurse insists that she was bewitched; that the foreign woman whom they met in the garden bewitched her. Should the child recover all will be forgotten, but if the child dies, Ligia will be accused of witchcraft and there will be no hope for her."

After a pause Vinitius said, "Maybe she did bewitch her. Maybe she bewitched me also."

"Lilith, the child's nurse, told Caesar that the child began to cry hard after leaving us in the garden. Most likely the child was already sick when they decided to take it for a walk in the garden. Marcus, seek Ligia by yourself if you so wish, but please do not speak of her to Caesar until his child recovers. Otherwise, his and Poppaea's vengeance will fall on Ligia and perhaps also on you. Her eyes have wept enough because of you already and may all the gods protect her."

"Do you love her, Acte?"

"Yes. I love her," she spoke with tears in her eyes. "She loved you too, you blind man, but you spoiled it all!"

Vinitius sprang up at these words of Acte. "It is not true!" he cried. "How could you know that?...How could Acte know such a thing? What kind of love is it that prefers to go away from him?...to live in poverty?...uncertain of tomorrow...than the riches and pleasures that he could give her?...It cannot be true!" He would shower Ligia with everything which he possessed, but she chose to flee.... What kind of love is that? Who can understand this? He would sink a sword in his breast right now if it wasn't for the hope of finding her soon. Moreover, what kind of love is it that wishes to flee rather than to surrender? No.... She does not love him now nor had she loved him before. On the contrary, she had hated him then as she hates him now....

Acte, who was usually mild and timid, now burst forth with indignation. How had he tried to win the poor girl? Instead of asking Pomponia and Aulus for her hand in marriage, he chose to take her away from them by force. He wanted her not as a wife but as a concubine...her, a foster daughter of the great former general Aulus Plautius and a true daughter of a Ligian king. He had her brought through Caesar to this palace of infamy. He defiled her innocent eyes with the sight of a shameful feast. How did he treat her at the feast? Did he not know that she was brought up by Pomponia? Had he not enough sense to realize that there are women different from Nigidia and Calvia Crispinilla or even Poppaea herself? Does he not understand now that Ligia is a pure virgin who prefers death to infamy? Does he not know that there are other gods than Venus or Isis who are worshiped by the profligate women of Rome? "No, Ligia did not confess her love for you to me but she did tell me that she had placed such great hopes in you to rescue her from here and that you would surely take her back to Pomponia. And speaking thus, she blushed like a maiden who loves and trusts." Yes, Ligia's heart beat for him but he, Vinitius, had terrified and offended her, had made her indignant. Sure he can seek her now with the aid of Caesar's soldiers, but her destruction is final if Caesar's child dies.

Through his anger and pain a new emotion began slowly emerging in the soul Vinitius. The information that he was loved by Ligia shook him to the depths of his being. He recalled the scene in the garden of Aulus when she listened to his words with a blush on her face. At this, a great feeling of joy permeated his whole being. Now he began to realize that he could have won her gradually. She would have wreathed his door front, rubbed it with wolf's fat and then sat as his wife by his hearth on the sheepskin. He would have heard from her lips the ceremonial words: "Where you are, Caius, there I, Caia, am also." And, she would have been his forever. Why on earth did he not act thus? As it is she is gone and it may be impossible to find her. Now his anger turned toward Petronius. Yes, Petronius was to blame for everything. Had it not been for this insane counsel of his, she would not have to wander now perhaps in distant lands. Instead she would be his. Now it is too late.

"Too late!" It now seemed that a great gulf was widening at his feet.

Acte repeated his words: "Too late!" This sounded so final coming from her lips that he was unable to speak further. Wrapping himself mechanically in his toga, he was about to take his leave when suddenly the curtain separating the entrance from the room was pushed aside and he saw before him the grieving face of Pomponia Graecina.

Evidently she too had heard of the disappearance of Ligia and judging that she could see Acte more easily than Aulus, she had now come for news. Seeing Vinitius, she turned pale and said after a pause, "Marcus, may God forgive you what you have done to Ligia."

At these words he stood silently for a moment not understanding them and full of amazement. Then, he took his leave, not knowing what to answer.

In the court and under the gallery were crowds of people mingling with the slaves of the palace. Senators and high military people were there, all trying to find out about the health of the infant and at the same time making a show of themselves in the palace and exhibiting proof of their anxiety even in the presence of Nero's slaves. News of the illness of Nero's child had spread quickly and more and more people began to appear in the palace. Some of the new arrivals, seeing Vinitius emerging from the palace interior, bombarded him for some news, but he hurried on without answering their questions until Petronius himself, who also came for some news, stopped him.

Undoubtedly Vinitius would have been enraged at the sight of Petronius whom he now blamed for what happened to Ligia, but he felt so crushed in spirit, so tired and listless, that for the moment his innate irascibility was gone. He only pushed Petronius aside in order to pass.

"How is the divine infant?" asked Petronius.

At this question, anger in full force arose in him and he replied viciously, "May Hades swallow her and this whole house!"

"Quiet, fool!" cried Petronius, and looking around to see if anyone had heard the outburst, continued. "If you want to know something of Ligia, come with me. I will say nothing more here. Come and I will talk with you in the litter." And, putting his arm around the young tribune, he conducted him from the palace as quickly as possible. He had no news but he wished to get Vinitius out of there quickly. He also felt sorry for him and he felt a bit responsible for what had happened.

When they entered the litter, he said, "I have given command to my slaves to watch every gate of the city. They have an accurate description of the girl and the giant who guards her. I'm sure now that it was he who came to her rescue. Listen to me, Marcus. Perhaps Aulus and Pomponia wish to hide her on some estate of theirs; in that case we shall learn the direction in which they took her. If, on the other hand, my slaves do not see them at the gates, we shall know for sure that she is still in the city and then we will begin to search for her more thoroughly all over Rome."

"Aulus does not know where she is," answered Vinitius.

"Are you sure?"

"I saw Pomponia in the palace. They are also looking for her."

"They could not have left the city yesterday; the gates are closed at night. Two of my people are watching each gate. One is to follow Ligia and the giant, the other is to return at once to me with the news. If she is in the city we shall find her because the huge Ligian can be easily recognized by his size and the width of his shoulders. You are lucky indeed that it was not Caesar who took her; of that I am certain because there are no secrets from me in the Palatine."

In a voice broken with emotion, Vinitius now told Petronius all that he had heard and seen in his talk with Acte and of the new dangers that threatened Ligia due to the accusation of witchcraft. If Ligia is to be found by them, she would have to be hidden from Poppaea and her anger and revenge. Then he began to reproach Petronius bitterly for his counsel. Had it not been for that everything would have gone differently. Ligia would have been in the house of Aulus and he, Vinitius, would be able to see her every day and he would have been happier than Caesar himself. Speaking thus, tears of sorrow and anguish began to fall from his eyes.

Petronius, who was astonished to see this great emotion of love on the part of the young man, cried out in wonder. "Oh Venus...Goddess of Love...you mighty lady of Cyprass, you alone are the ruler of men and gods."

CHAPTER XII

WHEN they reached the house of Petronius they were informed that of the slaves sent out to the gates of the city, none had returned as yet. New orders together with food provisions were sent out to them. They were ordered to watch carefully all who left, and they would be punished severely if they failed in this duty.

"You see," said Petronius, "they are still in Rome. We will find them. Give orders to your own people to look for them at the gates also, especially those slaves who were present at her capture. They will, no doubt, recognize her sooner than any other slaves."

"I have given orders to send those slaves to the rural prisons, but I can remand the order and send them to the gates." And, writing a few words on a wax-covered tablet, he handed the message to Petronius who in turn gave orders to have it sent at once to the house of Vinitius. They then passed into the interior of the house, sat down and began to talk. The golden-haired Eunice and Iras pushed bronze footstools under their feet and poured wine out of pitchers exquisitely wrought by famous artisans.

"Among your slaves do you have any who happen to know the giant Ligian?" asked Petronius.

"Atacinus and Gulo knew him but Atacinus fell by the litter and, as for Gulo, I killed him myself."

"That's too bad. I'm sorry for Gulo; he used to carry me in his arms when I was a child...and you too."

"I even intended to give him his freedom," said Vinitius, "but no matter, let's talk of Ligia. Rome is an immense sea."

"Yes, and there are pearls found in the sea. Of course, we won't find her today or tomorrow but we will surely find her, never fear. You, yourself, have accused me of giving you bad advice in this matter of Ligia, but I want you to know that the advice in itself was good; unfortunate events alone made it turn out badly. By the way, I suppose you know that Aulus Plautius had intended to take his family to Sicily. If so, then the girl would have been far from you anyway."

"If he did, I would have followed them into Sicily. Moreover, she would have been out of danger. Now, if Nero's child dies, she will certainly be hounded by the emperor's wrath. Poppaea would see to that."

"That is true and that's what alarms me. But, perhaps the young one will recover. If she dies...well, we will think of something then."

Here Petronius thought a while and added, "They say that Poppaea believes in the religion of the Jews and also in evil spirits. Caesar is superstitious. If we spread the word that evil spirits have indeed spirited her away, most likely it will be believed, especially as neither Caesar nor Aulus Plautius have taken her. Her escape was really mysterious. The Ligian could not have done it alone; he must have had help and where could one slave find so many people in one day to help him?"

"Slaves help one another in Rome."

"Yes, and that is why one day blood will flow in Rome. It is true. They do support one another but it is also true that they do not fight one another for fear of grave punishment. I'll wager that if you mention to your slaves that evil spirits have been the cause of this abduction of Ligia, they would eagerly concur since this would justify their inability to fight off the abductors. Ask one of them, as a test, if he didn't see spirits taking off with Ligia and he will swear at once by Zeus that he saw them."

Vinitius suddenly looked at Petronius with fear in his eyes. "If Ursus could not have men to help him and was not able to take her alone...well, who could have done so if not spirits?"

Petronius began to laugh. "See," said he, "they all will believe it since you yourself almost believe it. We ridicule the gods, yet we are superstitious. Yes, Marcus, we will be able to hide Ligia from the people when we do find her, and all the people will believe that evil spirits have taken her away. We will be able to hide her in one of your villas or mine."

"Then, who could have helped her?"

"Her co-religionists."

"Who are they? What deity do they worship?"

"Almost every woman in Rome honors a different deity. No doubt Pomponia reared her in the religion of the deity which she herself worships. Which one she worships, I do not know. One thing is certain: No one sees her offering gifts to one of the many temple gods of Rome. I recall that once she was accused of being a Christian, but that is impossible because they say that Christians worship a donkey's head and are enemies of the human race. Furthermore, a domestic court cleared her of this charge. Pomponia could not possibly be an enemy of the human race; she treats her slaves kindly and is a virtuous person as anyone can attest."

Vinitius added, "Yes, it is true. At no house are slaves treated more kindly. I myself have witnessed that."

"So you see, Pomponia herself mentioned some god to me who, she said, was one powerful and merciful. Where she has put all the other gods.... that's her affair. Her powerful god though could not be so powerful if he had just two adherents. They, therefore, are the ones who helped Ursus."

"Her god also forgives. When I met her at Acte's she said to me, 'May God forgive you, Marcus, the evil you have caused Ligia and us.'"

"Evidently their god is some sort of cure-all who is also forgiving. Ha...let him forgive you and as a sign of forgiveness, let him return Ligia to you."

"I would offer him a hecatomb tomorrow! I have no desire for food nor bath nor sleep. I will take a lantern and wander through the city. Perhaps I will find her. I really don't feel well."

Petronius looked at him with concern. There were dark shadows under his eyes which were shining as if with fever; he was unshaven, his hair in disorder and really looked sick. The two beautiful female slaves, Iras and the golden-haired Eunice, gazed upon him in sympathy, but he and Petronius took no notice of them whatever, just as if they were mere pet animals.

Petronius said, "Fever is tormenting you."

"Yes, I think so."

"Then listen to me, Marcus. I don't know what a doctor would prescribe for you but I know how I would act in your place. Until this lost one is found, I would seek in another the pleasure that I cannot have with the one that is lost. I have seen many female bodies and many of them are beautiful in your house. No, don't deny it. I also know what love is and I know that no other can fully take the place of the one loved...yet some kind of distraction can surely be found in another."

"No, I don't want any other!"

Petronius, who really felt sorry for his nephew and who wished to soften his pain, began to ponder how he might do so. Looking at the beautiful bodies of Eunice and Iras whose duty was to fold the togas of their master and his visitor, he spoke thus: "Perhaps your slaves do not have the same charm or novelty," and placing his hand on one of the girls, Eunice, added, "Look at this one! Fontius the younger offered me three beautiful young girls for her. Look at her beautiful figure and face. I, myself, don't know why I have remained indifferent to her. Surely thoughts of Chrysothemis should not have restrained me. Well, Marcus, I now make you an offer of her. Take her with you."

When the golden-haired Eunice heard this, she grew deathly pale and looked upon Vinitius with frightened eyes and hardly dared to breathe.

However, Vinitius sprang up suddenly and, pressing his hands to his temples, cried out like a man tortured. "No. No. I don't want her.... I want no other. I thank you but I don't want her. I will go out to roam the streets in a dark cloak. I will go beyond the Tiber...perhaps I will see her there."

And he hurried away. Petronius, seeing that he could not do anything with his nephew, did not try to detain him any longer. Taking the refusal of his gift as a mere temporary dislike for all women save Ligia and not wishing that his generosity go to waste, he turned to Eunice and said, "Eunice, you will bathe and annoint yourself and then you will go to the house of Vinitius for I give you to him." But, she fell at his feet in supplication, imploring him to allow her to remain with him. She cannot go to Vinitius.... she would rather die first.... let him flog her all he wanted but let her remain, please! And, trembling like a leaf with fear and emotion, she stretched her arms to him.

He listened to her in amazement. A slave who disobeyed, who said "I will not...I cannot..." was something unheard of in Rome. Petronius could not believe his own eyes and ears. He frowned. Being too refined to be cruel to his slaves, he strictly insisted on obedience in them. Every whim of their master should be obeyed without question and promptly. He could administer punishment when necessary. Opposition from slaves could not be endured. His face showed no emotion. He looked upon the kneeling girl before him and spoke, "Call Teresias and return with him."

Eunice rose and still trembling, with tears in her eyes, went out to summon the head slave who came from Crete. When they both appeared before him, Petronius said to him, "You will take Eunice and give her twenty-five lashes but be sure that you do not harm the skin."

Saying this, he passed on into the library. He sat down and began to work on his manuscript *The Feast of Trimalchio*. However, Ligia's escape and the illness of the infant Augusta had disturbed him to such a degree that he was unable to concentrate. The illness of Nero's child was above all very important. If Nero really believed that Ligia had cast a spell upon the infant, then would not he himself be blamed for being instrumental in bringing her into the palace? He was fairly certain that he would be able to prove to Caesar the absurdity of the whole idea. Furthermore, he knew that Poppaea was indeed fond of him and might be influenced by him. With these thoughts in mind, he decided to have himself borne to Caesar's palace. After that, he would spend some time with his Chrysothemis. When he was ready to leave his house, he noticed the slender and beautiful form of Eunice. She was standing among other slaves by the wall as he was passing by. He paused when he saw her and frowning a bit wondered why she was still there. Then he remembered that he did not give any other orders concerning her other than the one of flogging her lightly. He called her to him and asked, "Did you not receive the lashes?"

"Oh yes, my lord, I have received them. Oh yes, sir"...and with these words she fell to her knees before him. In her voice Petronius noticed joy, or perhaps gratitude. It was clear to him that she looked on the lashes as a substitute for her removal from the house and now she felt that she could remain after receiving them. Petronius, who understood all this, wondered about it all. He knew human nature quite well and was quite sure that love alone could provide an answer...that only love could provoke this kind of resistance in the girl.

"Do you love anyone in my house?"

She answered very softly, "Yes, sir." With this answer she turned her tearful eyes toward him. With her golden hair thrown back, with fear and hope in her face shining forth, she looked so beautiful, and she looked at him so entreatingly that Petronius who, as a philosopher had proclaimed the might of love and who as an esthete and master of elegance gave homage to all beauty, now felt compassion for this beauty before him.

There was no answer to this question. She merely inclined her head and remained motionless. Petronius looked at the different faces of the slaves; there were many handsome men among them. He then looked at Eunice at his feet, paused in reflection and left. Before entering the litter he paused to ask his head slave about Eunice. "Did Eunice receive the flogging?"

"Yes, sir. You did not want her skin blemished...remember, sir?"

"Did I not give any other command regarding her?"

"No, sir, " answered the slave with alarm.

"That is well. Whom of the slaves does she love?"

Teresias began to speak in a somewhat uncertain voice. "At night Eunice never leaves her bedroom. After she ministers to you with the toga and the baths she never allows herself to be led by the other slaves into the baths but returns to her room. The other slaves laugh at her and call her Diana."

"Enough," said Petronius. "My nephew, Vinitius, to whom I offered her does not wish to accept this gift. Therefore she is to remain here. You may go."

"May I say something else, sir, regarding Eunice?"

"Of course. I told you to tell me all about her."

"Everyone is talking about the flight of the maiden who was to reside with the noble Vinitius. Eunice approached me about knowing someone who could perhaps find her."

"Ah...what kind of man is he?"

"I don't know, sir...but I thought I better inform you of this."

"That is well. Let that man await me and my nephew Vinitius whom you will request to come here tomorrow."

The slave bowed and went into the house. In his litter, Petronius began to think of Eunice. Certainly she wanted Ligia found so she wouldn't have to leave the house of Petronius. It occurred to him also that perhaps the man she spoke of who would see him tomorrow may be her lover. This thought was not pleasing to him somehow. Well...tomorrow he will find out. Thinking also of Chrysothemis, he reflected upon the fact that the other day he noticed some wrinkles under her eyes. Her beauty, which was rumored about Rome, was indeed exaggerated and Fontius who offered him three lovely maidens for Eunice wanted to buy her too cheaply.

CHAPTER XIII

NEXT morning Petronius had barely finished dressing when Vinitius arrived. There was no news from his slaves at the gates. He began to fear that Ursus was able to conduct her out of the city immediately after her seizure and even before the slaves of Petronius had begun their watch at the gates. However, it was true that in autumn when the days grew shorter the gates were closed rather early. Even so, there were many who managed to avoid the gates even at night by climbing over the walls at certain places known only to slaves from all parts of the city. Vinitius had also sent some of his slaves to outlying roads in the country to look for Ursus and Ligia and he had offered a big reward to those who found them. He had doubts about this, however, since he was fearful that there may also be pursuit of Ligia on Caesar's part. He had searched for her himself the previous night but without success. During this search he noticed that the slaves of Aulus Plautius seemed to be seeking something or someone also and that confirmed his belief that it was not Aulus who had taken the girl and that the old general did not know what had happened to her.

When Teresias announced to him then that there was a man who would undertake the job of finding Ligia and who knew how to go about it, he hurried to the house of Petronius and barely had he finished greeting his uncle, when he inquired about the man.

"We shall see him at once. Eunice knows him. She will soon come to arrange the folds of my toga and give us better information about this man."

"Is she the one whom you offered to me yesterday?"

"She is the one whom you rejected. May I say too that I am grateful to you because she is the best *vestiplica* (folder of togas) in the whole city."

Eunice approached them while he was still speaking and taking his toga, folded it gently about the shoulders of Petronius. Her face was calm and peaceful; joy was in her eyes. Petronius looked at her. She seemed to him very beautiful. She began to arrange the folds, bending at times and leaning close to him. He noticed that her arms had a marvelous rosy tone and her shoulders the transparent reflections of pearl or alabaster.

"Eunice, did the man of whom you spoke to Teresias come already?"

"He did, sir."

"What is his name?" he asked. She replied, "Chilo Chilonides."

"Who is he?"

"A doctor I think, but also a sage and a soothsayer who knows how to predict the future and read the fates of people."

"Has he predicted your future also?"

"Yes, sir," and Eunice began to blush charmingly as she admitted it.

"What did he predict to you?"

"That pain will come, followed by happiness."

"Pain came to you at the hands of Teresias yesterday. Happiness should come to you now."

"It has already come to me, sir."

"How?"

"I'm allowed to remain, sir," she said, blushing still more deeply.

Petronius placed his hand upon her golden head. "You have arranged the folds very well today and I am pleased with you."

Under his touch, her eyes became misty with delight and happiness; her bosom rose and fell with emotion.

Petronius and Vinitius passed on into the room where Chilo Chilonides was awaiting them. When he saw them approaching, he bowed profoundly. A smile appeared on the face of Petronius. He recalled his suspicion that this might be Eunice's lover. He now saw that the man before him could not possibly be anyone's lover. In the strange figure of the man before him was something of a mixture between the bizarre and the ridiculous. He was not old but in his dirty beard and curly hair some grey showed here and there.

With his fallen stomach and stoop shoulders he looked somewhat like a hunchback. His head was extremely large, his eyes penetrating, a yellowish complexion was scattered with pimples. It was the face of both the monkey and the fox. His nose was predominant and deep colored veins denoted undue love for the bottle. His soiled outer apparel showed signs of neglect. His dark tunic and mantle with holes in it showed real or simulated poverty. At this unusual sight, Homer's Thersistes came to his mind, so with a slight movement of his hand acknowledging the bow, he spoke the words of Homer: "Greetings, O divine Thersistes! How are the lumps which Ulysses gave you at Troy? What is he himself doing in the Elysian Fields?"

"Noble sir," answered Chilo Chilonides. "Ulysses, the wisest of the dead, sends greetings through me to Petronius, the wisest of the living, with the humble request to cover my lumps with a new mantle."

"By Jove!" exclaimed Petronius. "Such an answer deserves a new mantle."

Further conversation between them was interrupted by the impatient Vinitius who asked, "Do you understand fully what you are about to undertake?"

"When two households of two lordly mansions speak of nothing else and half of Rome repeats the news, it is not difficult to glean the facts. The night before last a maiden named Ligia, or as she is sometimes called Callina, who was reared in the house of Aulus Plautius was abducted on the way to your house, noble Vinitius. I undertake to find her in the city or if she has left the city, which is unlikely, to locate her anywhere she may be hidden."

"That is well," said Vinitius who was pleased with the precise answer of the man. "Do you know the means to find her?"

Chilo smiled cunningly. "You have the means, sir. I have merely the brains and the wit to help you."

At this Petronius smiled. He was now sure that this man would be of help. This one can find the girl, he thought. But Vinitius frowned and spoke between clenched teeth. "Wretch...if you aim to deceive me for money, I will have you flogged to within an inch of your life."

"I am a philosopher, sir, and a philosopher cannot be greedy for money even though a very magnanimous person such as you would offer it."

Petronius inquired, "So you are a philosopher? Eunice told me that you are a doctor and a soothsayer. How do you know her, by the way?"

"She came to me for aid. My fame is well known in Rome."

"So she came to you for aid. What kind?"

"She wanted to be cured of unrequited love."

"And did you cure her?"

"I did more, sir. I gave her an amulet which ensures mutuality. On the island of Cypress there is a temple in which is preserved a girdle of Venus. I gave her a couple of strands enclosed in an almond shell from this girdle."

"And, I suppose, you made her pay well for them."

"One can never pay enough for mutuality in love and I, who lack two fingers on my right hand, am collecting enough money to buy a slave copyist to write down my memoirs and preserve my wisdom for all mankind."

"Of what school are you, divine sage?"

"I am a Cynic because I wear a tattered mantle; I am a stoic because I bear poverty patiently; I am a Peripatetic, a disciple of Aristotle, because, not owning a litter, I go from one wine shop to another and on the way teach those who promise to pay for a pitcher of wine."

"And, at the sight of the pitcher you become an orator."

"Heraclitus declares that everything flows and you cannot deny that wine, being a liquid, flows."

"He also declared that fire is divine; divinity evidently shines from the tip of your nose."

"The divine Diogenes from Apollonia declared that air is the essence of things and that the warmer the air, the more perfect the beings it makes; from the warmest come the souls of sages and since the autumns are cold, a genuine sage should warm his soul with wine. Would you then, sir, begrudge a little heat for the soul, even the minor stuff made in Capua or Telesia?"

"Chilo Chilonides, where is your birthplace?"

"I come from Mesembria."

"Chilo, you are great!"

"And...misunderstood," answered the sage bleakly.

Vinitius fidgeted impatiently. He wanted Chilo to leave immediately and lose no time in his search for Ligia...and this conversation seemed pointless to him.

"When will you begin the search?" he asked Chilo.

"I have already begun," Chilo answered. "While I'm here asking questions I am already searching. Only trust me, noble tribune, and know that if you lose even your sandal strap, I would find it."

"Have you been employed in similar services before?" asked Petronius.

The Greek raised his eyes. "Today, men esteem virtue and wisdom too low for a philosopher not to be forced to seek other means of livelihood."

"What are your means?"

"To know everything and to serve those who need my services."

"And...who also pay for them."

"Ah, sir, I do need that copyist. Otherwise my wisdom will perish with me."

"If by now you haven't collected enough money to buy yourself a decent mantle, your services cannot be very valuable."

"Only modesty prevents me from evaluating them. Remember too, sir, that the benefactors aren't as generous today as they were in previous years. No, my services are not minor but human gratitude is small. When a valued slave escapes, who will succeed in finding him? No one else but the son of my father. When on the walls there are inscriptions against the divine Poppaea, who will indicate the perpetrators to the authorities? At the book stalls, who will discover verses against Caesar? Who is it that knows what is being discussed in the houses of nobles and senators? Who will carry messages which are not entrusted to the slaves? Who listens to news at the barber shops? From whom have wine shops and bakeries no secrets? In whom do slaves put their trust? Who knows every street, every alley and every hiding place in Rome? Who knows what they say at the baths, in the circus, in the market-places, in the fencing schools and even in the arenas?"

"By the gods! Enough, enough, noble sage," cried Petronius. "We drown in your services, your virtues, your wisdom and your eloquence. Enough, I say. We wanted to know who you are and now, by Jove, we know."

Vinitius was glad. He thought that this man, once put on a trail like a hound, would not stop until he found the hiding place. "Good," he said. "What will you need? Do you want any information?"

"No, good sir, I need arms."

"What kind?" asked Vinitius surprised.

The Greek stretched out his hand and made a gesture as if counting money. "Such are the times," he sighed.

"So, you want to be a jackass who intends to storm the fortress with bags of gold?" asked Petronius.

"I am only a poor philosopher. You have the gold."

Vinitius tossed him a bagful of coins, which the Greek caught deftly even though he lacked two fingers on his right hand.

"I already know more than you both think I do. I have not come here empty handed. I know for sure that Aulus Plautius did not take the girl. I have spoken to his slaves. I know that she is not at the Palatine, so Caesar did not seize her. I know that she was helped by one of her servants, a giant of a man named Ursus. He could have found assistance from some people who know them well and were willing to rescue the girl. I think co-religionists would do so...with the danger involved."

"Do you hear this, Vinitius? Did I not say the same thing to you?" broke in Petronius.

"That is an honor to me," said Chilo. Turning back to Vinitius he continued. "The maiden, no doubt, worships some divinity, perhaps the same as the one attributed to Pomponia. I have heard that this was so. Pomponia was tried and exonerated before a domestic tribunal for worshiping some kind of a foreign god but I was unable to find out from her slaves what kind of a god this is or what his worshipers are called. If I could learn that, I would become the most devoted among them and gain their confidence. But...sir...you spent some time at their house.... Do you have some kind of information about this?"

"No, I do not."

"You both have asked me various things, noble sirs, and I did not hesitate to answer your questions. Permit me now to ask you. Have you not seen, noble tribune, any statues, offerings, tokens or amulets on Pomponia or Ligia? Have you seen them making any sign to each other...perhaps only known to them alone?"

"Signs?...Wait.... Yes, I saw Ligia making the form of a fish on the sand once."

"A fish?.... Did she do this once or several times?"

"Only once."

"And, are you certain, sir, that it was a fish which she outlined for you?"

"Yes. Do you guess the meaning of it?"

"Do I?" exclaimed Chilo. And, bowing profoundly he added, "May fortune scatter many wonderful gifts to both of you, worthy sirs."

"Have the slaves give you a new mantle," said Petronius to the departing sage.

"Ulysses gives thanks for your generosity to Tersistes," said Chilo, and again bowing, departed.

"What do you say of this sage?" asked Petronius.

"This: that he will find Ligia but I will say too that if there was a kingdom of rogues, he would be their king."

"You are right. I'll have to get closer acquainted with this Stoic. Meanwhile I'll order my slaves to have this room fumigated."

Chilo Chilonides, wrapping the new mantle about him, felt the weight of the purse given to him by Vinitius and was satisfied with its weight and its jingle. He walked slowly, looking around now and then to see if he was being followed. Seeing that he was not, he turned toward the section called Subura, perhaps the poorest section of Rome.

He began to talk to himself... "I must go to Sporus and pour out a little wine to the goddess Fortune. At last I have found what I was seeking for a long time. He is young and irascible but also generous and ready to give half of his fortune even for that Ligian linnet. Yes, I've been looking for someone like that for a long time. I have to be careful though; that mean wrinkling of his brow bodes no good. Ah, the offspring of wolves lord it over the world today. I would fear Petronius less. O gods! It seems that in these times virtue has no reward and the procurer makes more money than the one practicing virtue. So...she drew a fish in the sand? If I know what that means may I choke myself on a piece of goat cheese. But, I shall know! Fish live under water and searching under water is more difficult than on land, therefore I will have to be paid more for that. Another purse such as this one and I'll cast aside the beggar's role and buy myself a slave. But, what would you say, Chilo, were I to advise you to buy not a male but a female slave? I know you. I know that you would agree. And, if she were as pretty as Eunice, for instance, you yourself would become younger being near her and at the same time have a good and steady income from her. I sold Eunice two threads from my old mantle. She is gullible, but if Petronius would offer her to me I would take her. Yes. Yes, Chilo, son of Chilo. You have lost both father and mother. You are a poor orphan, so why not buy yourself a female slave to console you. She has to live some place, so Vinitius will have to provide a dwelling for me and her. She must dress well, so Vinitius will pay for her clothing. She must eat, so Vinitius will pay for her food. Oh, what a hard life! Where are the times when for a few pennies one could buy enough pork and beans and even a generous portion of blood sausage to satisfy himself amply? But here is Sporus. The wine shops are the best places in which to get information."

Mumbling to himself in this fashion, he entered the wine shop and ordered a pitcher of dark wine. Seeing the skeptical look on the face of the bartender, he dug out a coin from his purse, and putting it on the bar said, "Sporus, I have toiled today with my friend Seneca and this is what he gave me as a reward."

The round eyes of Sporus bulged out still more at the sight of the coin and the wine was soon placed before Chilo who, moistening his finger in it, drew a fish on the bar and asked, "Do you know what that is?"

"Looks to me like a fish...yes...a fish."

"You're not too smart, my friend. You add so much water to your wine that I'm surprised that I do not find a fish swimming in it. This is a symbol which in the language of philosophers means 'smile of fortune.' If you had guessed what it meant, it might have changed your luck too and you would have made some money. Have respect for philosophy and philosophers, I say, or I shall change my wine shop. My friend Petronius has been urging me to do so for a long time."

CHAPTER XIV

CHILO did not show his face for a few days, and Vinitius, who from the moment when he found out from Acte that Ligia loved him was that much more eager to find her, began searching for her once more on his own. He was unwilling to ask the aid of Caesar on account of the ailing infant.

Sacrifices and various offerings in the temples did not help, neither did the help of doctors. After a week of illness, the child died. Mourning fell upon the entire court of Caesar and upon all of Rome. Nero, who at the birth of his child went wild with joy, now fell to depths of despair and, confining himself to his rooms for two days, refused all sustenance and did not want to see anyone. Meanwhile, the Senate assembled in extraordinary session, pronounced the divinity of the child. It ordered the erection of a temple in her honor and a priest to minister at the temple. New sacrifices and offerings were ordered, statues cast in her honor were provided. Her funeral was one immense solemn procession at which everyone was amazed at the undue show of grief by Nero. They wept with him but at the same time stretched out their hands for gifts thrown to them. They secretly, however, amused themselves at the spectacle of the grieving Nero.

Petronius was alarmed when the infant died. Everyone in Rome knew that Poppaea attributed the tragedy to the evil spirits. The doctors supported this belief. In this way they could explain away the fruitlessness of their efforts. The different priests and sorcerers who trembled for their very lives did the same. Petronius was now glad that Ligia had fled. Not wishing any harm to befall the house of Aulus Plautius, but mostly wishing that nothing evil would befall him and Vinitius, he decided to visit the Palatine when the sign of mourning was removed. At the reception of senators and Augustians he wanted to find out how much attention Nero had paid to reports of evil spirits and also to neutralize the results which may come from this belief.

Knowing Nero, he was confident that the emperor did not give credence to evil spirits and spells, but he was also sure that Nero's egoism would feign belief to magnify his own simulated suffering and give him the excuse to take vengeance on someone. Moreover, it would lessen the suspicion in the minds of some that the gods had begun to punish him for his numerous crimes. Nero was not capable of true love for his daughter, though he loved her with exaggerated passion. According to the way Petronius saw it, the result of this was for Nero to exaggerate his suffering. And, he was not mistaken.

Nero listened with a stony face and fixed eyes to the words of nobles and senators. It was evident that even if he suffered he was at the same time curious what impression his suffering would make on others. Every now and then he would exhibit parental sorrow as an actor would portray it on the stage. He would make gestures as if spilling ashes on his head and groaning deeply. Finally...seeing Petronius enter, he cried out in a tragic voice, "Alas! You too are guilty of her death for through you the evil spirit entered these walls and drew the life from her breast. Woe is me! Would that my eyes see no more the light of day!" And, he began to shout despairingly at the top of his voice.

Petronius resolved to gamble everything on one cast of the dice. Stetching out his hand, he seized the silk handkerchief which Nero always wore around his neck, covered with it the mouth of the Emperor and spoke sadly but solemnly, "Sire, Rome and the world are benumbed with sorrow and you may destroy them if you wish, but please, by the gods, preserve to us your divine voice."

All present were amazed. Nero himself was stupefied for a moment. Petronius alone was clearheaded and cool. He knew well what he was doing. He was well aware that Nero's musical accompanists, Terpnos and Diodor, had strict orders to cover Nero's mouth whenever he raised his voice too much and exposed it to danger.

"Oh Caesar," he continued sadly, "we have all suffered an immeasurable loss; may the treasure of your divine voice be allowed to remain with us."

Nero's voice quivered.... Tears came to his eyes. He rested his arms on the shoulders of Petronius and, bowing his head on his breast, began to repeat amidst sobs, "You alone thought of this.... You alone...You alone."

Tigellinus grew yellow with envy, but Petronius continued, "Let us go to Antium. There she came into the world and there also will solace come to you, o divine one. Let the sea air freshen your voice and comfort us all. We, your devoted slaves, will follow you everywhere and you will bring joy to us with your songs."

"True," said Nero sadly, "I will write a hymn in her honor and compose music for it."

"And then we will seek out the warm sun for you in Greece and forgetfulness."

"Yes, sun and forgetfulness in the birthplace of poetry and song." And his gloom began to fade gradually as he thought about it. Conversation which followed was filled with plans for the future regarding the journey, the exhibitions of art and other things pertaining to it.

Tigellinus at one time wished to break in with the matter of evil spirits and Petronius' guilt, but sure now of victory, Petronius took up the challenge. "Tigellinus," he said, "do you believe that evil spirits can harm the gods?"

"Caesar himself had mentioned them."

"Only pain and sorrow uttered them, not Caesar. Our divine Emperor is god and the gods are more powerful than evil spirits.... Do you deny this?"

"No, of course not!"

"Then, why are you trying to deny the divinity to a member of Nero's family, his own daughter?"

"Peractum est!" (It is finished!) muttered Marcellus, standing nearby. The words were those shouted by the populace in the arena when a gladiator received a mortal wound and needed no other to finish him off.

Tigellinus suppressed his anger. Between himself and Petronius there had existed for quite some time a rivalry for the role of Nero's most favorite. For the time being, he had the upper hand only because Nero needed him most. He was the head of the Praetorian Guard and executed all the wants and desires of the mad Emperor. However, as to wit and intellect, he had a shortage of each and Petronius by far superceded him in both.

So now Tigellinus became silent and with hatred in his eyes tried to record in his memory those senators and nobles who, when Petronius withdrew to the inner chamber, surrounded him, supposing that after this encounter with Tigellinus he, Petronius, would surely be Caesar's favorite.

On his way home Petronius stopped off at the house of Vinitius and related the incident. "Not only have I averted grave danger from Aulus and Pomponia, but also from Ligia too. They will not seek her now. I have persuaded that bronze-bearded monkey to go to Antium and then to Naples and Greece. I'm sure that he will go. He has dreamed for a long time of being able to appear publicly in the various theaters. He wants to sing and proclaim in all the important cities of his empire, after which he wants to return to Rome bestowed with all kinds of crowns and triumphal wreaths. During all that time we will be able to seek Ligia unhindered and after we find her, we'll secret her in safety. By the way, has not our noble philosopher shown up yet?"

"Your noble philosopher is a cheat. He hasn't shown up and I doubt if he ever will."

"I think you are wrong. He drew blood from your purse once and I am confident that he will try again."

"Let him beware lest I draw blood from his worthless carcass."

"No, Vinitius! Be patient with him until you are absolutely sure of his deceit. Don't give him any more money but promise him a liberal reward if he succeeds in bringing definite information. Have you done anything on your own?"

"Sixty of my slaves are constantly looking for her in the city. More slaves look for her outside the city, inquiring at every tavern. I myself go out every day and night hoping I may be lucky."

"If you have any definite news send it over to me for I must go to Antium."

"Good."

"And, if you wake up some morning and admit to yourself that it's not worthwhile to torment yourself over the girl, come to us in"

Antium. I can assure you that there will be no lack of amusement and women there."

Vinitius began to pace nervously back and forth. Petronius looked at him for some time and then asked, "Tell me truthfully, and not as one who latches on to one thought and desire and is loath to let go, are you so determined about this girl?"

Vinitius stopped a moment and looked at Petronius as if he had not seen him before. Then he began to pace once more. It was evident that he was restraining an outburst. Then, from a feeling of helplessness, sorrow, anger and yearning, two tears gathered in his eyes. To Petronius these tears were more eloquent than words. Meditating on this for a moment, he said, "It is not true that Atlas carries the world on his shoulders.... It is a woman, and sometimes she plays with it as if it were a toy."

"True," said Vinitius.

They began to take farewell of each other but at that moment a slave announced that Chilo Chilonides was awaiting their pleasure in the antechamber.

Vinitius gave command to admit him immediately, upon which Petronius remarked, "Ha! Did I not tell you? By Hercules, keep calm! Otherwise he will be able to take advantage of you."

"A greeting and honor to you, noble tribune, and also to you, noble sir," said Chilo upon entering. "May your happiness be equal to your fame and may your fame spread to the world from the pillars of Hercules to the boundaries of Arsasides."

"Greetings, O bearer of virtue and wisdom," answered Petronius.

Vinitius , with feigned calmness, asked him, "What news do you have?"

"The first time I came, I brought you hope, sir. Now I bring you the certainty that the maiden will be found."

"That means that you haven't found her yet."

"True, sir, but I have found out what the sign that she made you means. I know who the people are who rescued her and I know the God she worships and that we should seek her among her fellow worshipers."

Vinitius at this news wanted to spring from his chair but Petronius placed a restraining hand on his arm and spoke to Chilo, "Speak on."

Chilo, turning to Vinitius asked, "Are you certain, sir, that it was a fish she drew in the sand?"

"Yes!" exclaimed Vinitius.

"Then she is a Christian and it was the Christians who rescued her."

A moment of silence followed.

"Listen, Chilo," said Petronius. "My nephew promised you a considerable sum of money for finding the girl but also enough rods on your back if you deceive him. In the first case, you will be able to purchase not one but three scribes; in the second, the philosophy of all the seven sages plus your own will not be enough to buy ointment for your back."

"The maiden is a Christian, sir!" cried Chilo.

"Pause a moment, Chilo. You're not a stupid man. We know that Junia Silana and Calvia Crispinilla accused Pomponia Graecina of professing some kind of Christian superstition, but we know too that a domestic court acquitted her. Would you accuse her again? Could you persuade us now that Pomponia and with her Ligia could belong to the enemies of the human race...to the poisoners of wells and fountains? To the worshipers of a donkey's head? To people who murder infants and give themselves to the foulest crimes? Think Chilo. Will this thesis of yours which you are proclaiming to us not rebound as an antithesis on your own back?"

Chilo spread out his arms as if all this was not his fault and said, "Sir, say in Greek the following sentence: 'Jesus Christ, Son of God, Savior.'"

"*Iesous Christos, Theou Uios, Soter....* There, I said it. Now what?"

"Now take the first letters of each of those words and combine them into one word."

"I C H T H U S...Fish!" said Petronius in astonishment.

"There, that is why the fish has become the watchword of the Christians," muttered Chilo proudly.

A moment of silence followed. The revelation of Chilo was so striking that both Petronius and Vinitius were greatly astonished.

Petronius asked, "Vinitius, are you sure that it was a fish she drew?"

"By all the infernal gods!" cried the young man. "If she drew a bird I would have said so."

"Therefore, she is a Christian," repeated Chilo.

"That means," said Petronius, "that Pomponia and Ligia poison wells, murder children and give themselves to debauchery? Utter nonsense! You, Vinitius, have been in their home and I also a little while. Besides, I know Aulus and Pomponia well enough to say that all this is utterly foolish. If indeed a fish is a symbol of Christians, and it is hard to deny this, Christians are not what people think they are."

"You speak like Socrates, sir," said Chilo. "Who has ever examined a Christian? Who has learned the truth about their religion? When I was traveling three years ago from Naples to Rome (Oh, why did I not remain in Naples!), a man joined me. His name was Glaucus, whom people said was a Christian; but in spite of this, he was a good and virtuous man."

"Is it not true that from this virtuous man that you have now found out what the fish means?"

"Alas, sir, on the way someone thrust a knife into that unfortunate and honorable man. His wife and children were sold into slavery. In their defense I lost two fingers from my hand as you can see. But from what I hear, there is no lack of miracles among Christians so I have hopes that new fingers will grow back miraculously on my hand."

"Well now, have you also become a Christian?"

"Since yesterday, sir...since yesterday. It was the fish that did it. Do you see now what power there is in this religion? I shall be the most zealous of their adherents so that they may admit me to all their secrets. Then I shall find out where the maiden is hidden. Perhaps my Christianity will pay me better than my philosophy. I have also made a vow to Mercury that if he helps me in finding the maiden I will sacrifice to him two heifers of the same size and color and even with gilded horns."

"Does your recent Christianity and your older philosophy permit you to believe in the god Mercury?"

"I always believe in that which I have to. And this is my philosophy as of now. This should also please Mercury but unfortunately (You know, sirs, what a suspicious god he is!) he does not trust the promises of blameless philosophers and no doubt prefers his heifers in advance. But he should realize that it is very expensive for me to do this. Not everyone is a Seneca and I cannot afford the sacrifice. However, should the noble Vinitius care to contribute something to that end...well."

"Not a penny, Chilo, not a penny!" said Petronius. "The generosity of Vinitius will surpass your expectations but only when the girl is found...that is, if you will indicate to us her hiding place. Mercury will have to trust you for the future payment of two heifers, although I do understand why he hesitates to do so. In this I do not blame him."

"Listen to me, good sirs. You must admit that my discovery is not small. Even though I have not found the maiden yet, I did find the way through which I must seek her. You both have sent freedmen and slaves all over the city and also around the countryside but have they been successful? Moreover, among your slaves there may be Christians of whom you have no knowledge. It seems that this religion has spread everywhere. These slaves, instead of helping, will betray you. It is unfortunate too that they see me here. Please, noble Petronius and valiant Vinitius, spread word among them that I'm selling ointment for horses which ensures victory in the circus races. I alone will search for the maiden and I will find her myself. Trust me and know that whatever I receive in advance will only encourage me for the future search because I know that at the end of it I will be amply rewarded for my troubles."

After a slight pause, Chilo continued, "As a philosopher I despise money, though Seneca does not, nor even Cornutus. Furthermore, they did not lose any of their fingers in someone's defense so that they are able to write their own memoirs and do not need slaves to write for them. But, aside from the slave whom I intend to buy and besides Mercury to whom I have promised the heifers (and you know how dear is the price of heifers these days), I will need money for the search. Only listen to me patiently. Due to continuous walking in the last few days, my feet ache terribly. I have gone to wine shops to talk to people, to bakeries, to butcher shops, to dealers in olive oil and to fishermen. I have walked through every street and alley way; I have been to different places of runaway slaves; I have lost money...nearly a hundred aces in playing *mora*. I have been in launderies, in drying sheds, in cheap kitchens; I have spoken with mule drivers, with people who cure ailments of the bladder and pull teeth; I have talked with dealers in dried figs; I have even been in cemeteries. And, do you know why? To draw a fish everywhere I went...to look people in the eye and hear what they have to say about the sign."

"For a long time I was unable to learn anything till at last I saw an old slave at a fountain. He was drawing water in a bucket and he was weeping. Coming close I asked why he was weeping. When he had sat down on the steps of the fountain he answered that he had been collecting money for a long time in order to redeem his beloved son from slavery, but his master, a certain Pansa, took the money but refused to deliver his son from slavery. 'And, so I am weeping,' said the old man, 'for though I keep on saying that God's will be done, I can not keep from crying.'"

"Then, sirs, as if struck by a fortunate premonition, I moistened my finger in the water and drew a fish. To this he answered, 'My hope is in Christ too.' I asked him then, 'Did you recognize me by the sign?' 'Yes,' he answered, 'may peace be with you.' Thereupon I began to ply him with questions and he told me all. His master deals in stones brought in by the river to Rome where slaves and hired men unload them from the boats and carry them to buildings in the night time so not to obstruct movement in the streets during the day. Many Christians work among them including his son. But, the work is hard and beyond his son's strength. That is why he wanted to buy his freedom. But Pansa decided to keep the money and the slave. While talking, he began to weep again and I mingled my tears with his. Tears come to me readily because of my kind heart and also the pain in my feet from walking too much."

"I further began to complain that I had come from Naples recently and I did not have sufficient knowledge of the brethren here in Rome and where they assembled for prayer. He wondered why the brethren in Naples did not fortify me with the necessary letters, but I explained that I had letters but that they were stolen from me on the way. Then he told me to come to the river at night and he would introduce me to the brethren who would then conduct me to the various houses of prayer and to the elders who govern the Christian community. When I heard all this I was so delighted that I gave him the sum needed to redeem his son from slavery. I did this in the hope that the noble Vinitius will return it to me twofold."

"Chilo," interrupted Petronius, "lies appear on the surface mingled with truth as does oil mixed with water. I admit that you brought important news and I commend you for it but do not cover the truth with falsehood. What is the name of the man of whom you speak?"

"Euricius, a poor unfortunate old man. He reminded me of Glaucus whom I befriended and defended from murderers."

"I believe you that you befriended Euricius and will be able to make use of him but you have given him no money whatsoever...not even a penny."

"But I helped him to lift his bucket of water and I spoke to him of his son with the greatest sympathy. Yes, sir, indeed, what can be hidden from the penetrating wisdom of Petronius? I did not give him any money, or rather I gave it to him but only in spirit, which should have sufficed if he were but a philosopher, but perhaps real money would be better since it would have been useful in acquiring greater confidence among all the Christians as to my intentions."

"True," said Petronius, "and you should have done it."

"That is why I am here...for the money from the noble Vinitius."

"Give an order to count out five thousand sestertia but only in spirit."

Vinitius replied, "I will give you a man who will take the necessary sum which you will give to Euricius for the payment of his son. Since you have brought important news, you will receive a similar amount for yourself. Come for the man and the money this evening."

"You are indeed a Caesar!" exclaimed Chilo. "Permit me though to go there by myself. It will be better that way. They will be less suspicious if I go by myself, being a Christian as I told them. I will come by tonight for the money. Euricius told me that they have already unloaded everything and are only awaiting more boats which will arrive in a few days. Peace be with you. Thus the Christians take farewell with one another. Peace be with you."

CHAPTER XV

PETRONIUS TO VINITIUS:

This letter is sent to you by a trusted slave and though your hand is more accustomed to the sword than to the pen, I'm sure that you will reply by the same messenger without much delay. When I left you there was good reason to hope that you would soon satisfy your yearnings and the beautiful maiden would be in your arms soon. Perhaps even before the wintry winds blow from the hills of Soracte to the plains of the Campania. May your goddess be the golden Venus whose rays will engulf you and Ligia. At the moment, she may be fleeing from these rays as Aurora the goddess of dawn flees from the sun. Remember too that marble, though precious, is nothing of itself and acquires real value only when the hand of the sculptor turns it into a masterpiece. Be such a sculptor, carissime! To love is not enough, one must know how to love. One must know how to teach the art of love that is true. Though the common plebs and even the animals experience pleasure, the true noble soul makes love a noble art and while admiring it, makes its value divine, thus satisfying not only his body but also his soul. More than once when I think of the emptiness of life, of its uncertainty and its dreariness, it occurs to me that perhaps you have chosen better than what we have here at Caesar's court. War and love...these are worthy goals for which to be born and to live.

You were lucky in war; be also lucky in love. And, if you are curious as to what we do here at Nero's court, then I will inform you from time to time. We are living here in Antium and nursing our heavenly voice. We nourish hatred for Rome and think about betaking ourselves to Naples and to Greece. The Greeks all appreciate us better than the offspring of the wolf which resides on the banks of the Tiber. People will come to us from everywhere to hear our singing and render applause and many crowns as worthy gifts to our bronze-beard.

The memory of the infant Augusta? Yes, we bewail her death still. We sing hymns of our own composition so beautiful that even sirens hide from envy. The dolphins would listen to us were they not prevented by the sound of the sea. No, our suffering is not allayed, hence we will show the world beauty in suffering and wonder if the world notices this beauty. Oh, my dear Vinitius! We shall die as clowns and comedians!

All the Augustians are here, male and female, not counting ten thousand servants and five hundred she-asses in whose milk our Empress Poppaea bathes daily. At times, it is even pleasant. Calvia is growing old. It is rumored that she has asked Poppaea's permission to take her bath after the Empress. Lucan slapped Nigidia because he suspected her of having an affair with a gladiator. Sporus lost his wife in a dice game to Senacio. Torquatus Silanus has offered me for Eunice four chestnut horses which, no doubt, will be victorious in the races this year. I did not accept. I thank you also, by the way, that you did not accept her when I offered her to you. As for Torquatus, the poor man does not know that his end is near. His death has been decided upon. And, do you know what his crime is? Only that he happens to be a distant relative of our divine Emperor. There is no help for him. Such is the world we live in.

As you know, we expected Tridatus here but as yet he has not arrived. Vologeses, however, has written an offensive letter. Because he has conquered Armenia, he asks that it be left to him. If not, he will not yield it in any case. What a farce! So, we have decided on war. Corbulo will receive power such as Pompey once had when he fought the pirates. Nero hesitated for a while giving him so much power. He was afraid of the glory that might be his in case of victory. It was even suggested that the high command be given to Aulus but Poppaea opposed this. Evidently the virtue of Pomponia is like salt in her eye.

Vatinius promised us magnificent gladiator fights which are to take place in Beneventum. Cobblers are indeed on the rise in this empire for Vitelius is merely a descendant of a cobbler but Vatinius is the son of one. Perhaps, he himself drew the thread...who knows? You know the saying: *"Ne sutor supra crepidam!"* (A cobbler is not above his last!) The actor Aliturus had a fine presenta-

tion here yesterday. Being a Jew, I asked him if Christians and
Jews are the same and he answered that the Jews have an ancient
religion but the Christians are a new sect risen recently in
Judea...that in the time of Tiberius the Jews crucified a certain
man called Jesus the Christ and whose adherents increase daily.
They consider him a God. They refuse, it seems, to recognize
other gods...ours especially. I don't know what harm that could do
them.

Tigellinus is openly hostile to me now. So far, I have the better
of him, but in one respect he surpasses me: he is a bigger scoundrel than I and that brings him closer to our bronze-beard. Eventually, they will have an understanding with one another and then
my turn will come. I don't know when, but as things stand the
way they are, it will happen sooner or later. In the meantime life
goes on pleasantly enough and it wouldn't be so bad if it weren't
for Nero. Because of him a man sometimes feels disgusted with
himself. It may be in vain that I consider the struggle for his favor
as some kind of rivalry...as a game in which his vanity is flattered
constantly. Sometimes I think of myself as someone like Chilo
and not much better than he is. By the way, when he ceases to be
useful to you send him over to me. A greeting from me to your divine Christian and beg her not to remain a cold fish where you
are concerned. Inform me of your health and your quest for the
one you love. Know how to love. Teach how to love.

Farewell.

M.C. VINITIUS TO PETRONIUS:

Still no sign of Ligia. Were it not for the hope that I will find
her soon, you would not receive an answer. When life is bitter a
man has no wish to write letters. I wanted to learn whether Chilo
was deceiving me, so the same night in which he came to get the
money assigned for the son of Euricius, I threw on a military mantle and followed him unobserved. When he reached the place, I
watched from a distance hidden behind a pillar and I was convinced that he did not invent Euricius. With my own eyes I saw
what followed. A number of people were unloading stones from a
barge and piling them on the bank. I saw Chilo approach them
and begin to talk with some old man who after a while fell on his
knees. Others surrounded them with shouts of admiration. Before
my eyes I saw Chilo give the money to Euricius, who on receiving
it began to pray with upraised arms. Another person joined him,
evidently his son. Chilo said something which I could not hear

and blessed the two who were kneeling, making some kind of sign as of a cross in the air. All bent their knees at this. A great desire seized me to go among them and promise three times the amount if they would deliver Ligia to me but I feared to spoil Chilo's work and after a while I returned back home.

This occurred about twelve days after your departure. Since then, Chilo has been here a number of times. He keeps repeating that he has gained significance among the Christians in Rome; that if he has no word of Ligia so far it is because Christians in Rome are numerous and as a rule reticent. He gives me assurance, however, that when he reaches the elders who are called presbyters, he will then learn every secret about the Christian community in Rome. He is now inquiring everywhere but in such a way as to not rouse suspicion. Yes, it is hard for me to wait but I feel he is right and so I wait.

He learned too that they have meeting places for prayer outside of the city in empty houses and even in sandpits. There, they worship Christ, sing hymns and break bread together. There are many such places. Chilo thinks that Ligia refrains from visiting these places where Pomponia is apt to be for the reason that in case of trial, Pomponia may truthfully testify that she has no knowledge of her whereabouts and has not seen her at all. It may be that the elders advised this move on the part of Ligia. When Chilo discovers those places of prayer I will go with him and if the gods let me see Ligia, then, I swear to you by Jupiter that she will not escape me again.

I'm constantly thinking of those places of prayer. Chilo advises me not to go with him for the time being but I cannot stay at home. I should recognize her at once even if she were disguised or veiled. They assemble at night but I know that I will recognize her even at night. Her voice and her manner is before me at all times. Chilo is to come tomorrow. This time I will insist on going with him. I will be sufficiently disguised and armed. Some of my slaves have returned from the search of the provinces with no news. However, I am certain that she is still in the city, perhaps even not too far away. I myself have visited many houses under the pretext of renting them. I fear that where she is now is a poor place and then I think she would fare a hundred times better with me than where she is now...perhaps in poverty. I would spare nothing for her sake. You write that I have chosen well; believe me, I have chosen suffering and sorrow. When Chilo comes we will go to the different places of worship here in the city and then beyond the gates. Hope seeks something every morning, otherwise life would be impossible. You tell me that one should know how to love. I knew how to talk of love to Ligia, but now I only yearn and life seems unbearable to me in my own house...Farewell!

CHAPTER XVI

CHILO, however, did not appear for some time and Vinitius did not know what to make of this. In vain he repeated to himself that the search for Ligia of necessity must be slow but sure. His impulsive nature rebelled at such slowness. To do nothing...to wait...to sit with folded arms was so repulsive to him that he could not be reconciled to it at all. To search the alleys of Rome in the guise of a slave was something to do but he knew that it was useless, merely a mask for his own inefficiency. His own freedmen and slaves whom he also ordered to search in the city and elsewhere—all proved less expert than Chilo. There also rose within his breast the feeling and stubborness of a gambler who will not admit defeat and will resolve that he must win in the end. Vinitius had always been this way. From his youth he did what he wanted with a passion of one who never admitted failure. For a time, military discipline controlled his self will but this discipline also convinced him that every command of his to his subordinates must be fulfilled. His prolonged military assignment in the East, among people who were used to slavish obedience to authority, confirmed in him the belief that his every whim should be catered to. Too, his vanity was wounded because he now found resistance and opposition to him in this flight of Ligia. What she did was incomprehensible to him. It was a riddle difficult to unravel; how could anyone act in such a manner toward him. In order to solve this riddle he racked his brain for answers but could find none. He now knew that Acte had told him the truth about Ligia's feeling for him...that she was not indifferent in her affections toward him. But, why then had she preferred to run away from him, from his love, his tenderness and residence in his splendid mansion? To this question he could find no real answer. He only felt now that between him and Ligia, between her beliefs and those of him and of Petronius, there was a gulf as deep as an abyss which nothing could fill or pass over. There came to him at times thoughts that perhaps he hated her as much as he loved her, but even so, he must find her no matter what. Earth could turn upside down but he must find and possess her. By the power of his imagination he saw her as clearly at times as if she were standing before him. He recalled every word she had spoken to him; he felt her presence near to him and his desire for her engulfed him like a living flame.

When he thought that he was loved and that she would have freely been his as his wife, he was seized with great sorrow and a kind of deep tenderness flooded his heart like a mighty wave. But, there were moments too when he grew pale with rage and anger and then he delighted in thoughts of the humiliation and punishment which he would inflict upon her. He wanted to have her, yes, but as a slave to be trampled upon. At the same time he felt if the choice were his to be either her slave or never to see her again, he would, without hesitation, decide to be her slave forever. There were thoughts of the marks which the lash would leave on her beautiful body and at the same time he would be willing to kiss the same marks with love in his heart. Sometimes, he even thought that he would kill her if he found her for all the torment she had caused him.

In all this torture, uncertainty and suffering, he lost his health and his features lost their usual handsomeness. He became a cruel and a very demanding master to his slaves. They and even his freedmen approached him with fear and trembling, and when cruel punishments began to fall on them all, they secretly began to hate him and he, recognizing this feeling in them, began to treat them more cruelly every day. He only restrained himself when he was with Chilo, fearing the latter would cease his search for Ligia. The Greek, noting this, began to gain control over him and grew more and more exacting in his demands. At first, he assured Vinitius at each visit that everything would proceed easily and quickly; now he hegan to find all sorts of difficulties in his path, at the same time assuring the tribune that in the end success will be his but not for a long time yet.

One day he came with his face showing so much sadness and gloom that the young man sprang up quickly and asked him, "Is she not among the Christians?"

"She is, sir, but I also found Glaucus among them."

"What is this to me? Who is this Glaucus?"

"You have evidently forgotten, sir, about me telling you of the old man who journeyed with me from Naples and in whose defense I lost these two fingers, a loss I assure you which prevents me from writing my memoirs. You remember, sir, robbers stabbed him and bore his wife and child into slavery. I left him dying at the inn in Minturna and bewailed his death for a long time. But, I now find him alive and among the Roman Christian community."

Vinitius could not fully understand this. He only felt that somehow this Glaucus stood in the way of finding Ligia, hence he suppressed his anger and asked, "If you defended him, why then should he stand in your way now?"

"Ah, worthy tribune, even gods are not always grateful; what must be the case with mere mortals? True, he should be thankful, but his mind is old and weak. Now he claims that I am the cause of his misfortunes on that road from Naples. This I learned from the Christians. Such is the gratitude that I receive for my lost fingers. He even claims that it was I who conspired with the robbers to kill him and sell his family into slavery. I repeat...what gratitude!"

"Scoundrel! I'm certain that what he claims is true."

"Then you know more than he does, sir. He only surmises that it was so, which still wouldn't prevent him from summoning the Christians and taking revenge on me. He perhaps would have done so but fortunately he does not know my name, and in the house of prayer in which we met, he did not notice me. I, however, recognized him at once and my first reaction was to throw myself at his throat, but wisdom prevailed; also the restraint which I practice to think out everything before taking action. So leaving that particular house of prayer, I asked those who knew him and they told me that he was the man who was betrayed by a companion on his journey from Naples to Rome."

"Why should all this concern me? What I want to hear from you is whether you have seen someone at the house of prayer who will lead us to Ligia."

"It may not concern you, sir, but it definitely concerns me. The health of my skin depends on it and also because I want my teaching to survive me. So, I would rather renounce the reward you have offered me. I do not want to expose my life to danger for mere filthy lucre. The gods themselves will aid me in acquiring philosophy and wisdom."

Vinitius came up close to Chilo, his face angry, ominous.

"How do you know, cur, that death will come to you sooner from Glaucus than from me? How do you know that I won't give orders to bury you in the garden?"

Chilo, who was a coward at heart, looked at Vinitius and clearly understood that one more unguarded word and he was lost beyond redemption.

"I will search for her, sir, and I will find her!" he cried hurriedly. There was a pause broken only by the hard breathing of Vinitius and the far off sounds of slaves singing while working in the gardens. After a while Chilo said, "Death passed me by and I gazed upon it as calmly as Socrates. No, sir, I did not mean to refuse to search for the maiden. I merely want you to know that this search will now be dangerous for me. You yourself doubted me once before until you found out for yourself that Euricius does exist and the only son of my father spoke the truth to you. Now, you may doubt that Glaucus exists. Ah, if only he were a figment of my imagination, then I would go among the Christians without fear, with perfect safety as I did before. Were it so, I would even give up the female slave whom I bought three days ago to care for me in my advanced age and poor condition. But, sir, I repeat that Glaucus does exist and were he to see me again, then you will not see me again and then who will find the maiden?"

Here he paused and began to dry his tears.

"While Glaucus lives," he continued, "how can I search for her? I might meet up with him and then I shall perish and all the fruits of my search up to now will perish with me."

"What do you have in mind; what do you want done now? Speak!"

"Aristotle teaches that lesser things should be sacrificed for the greater and King Priam spoke often of old age as a grievous burden.

Surely, the burden of old age and misfortune weighs heavily on
Glaucus, so heavily in fact that mere death would be a blessing to
him. For, according to Seneca, what is death but a liberation?"

"Stop clowning! You can do that with Petronius, not with me.
Tell me, what do you want?"

"If virtue is folly, then let me be a clown all my life. What I want
is to get rid of Glaucus, get rid of him for good. While he lives, my
life and my search are in danger."

"Then hire men who will beat him to death. I will pay them."

"They will rob you, sir, and then afterward will take advantage
of your generosity and later blackmail you for the crime. There are
many scoundrels in Rome but you will not believe how dear they
come when you try to employ them. No, worthy tribune; suppose
the guards catch them in the act, then they will blurt out the
person's name who hired them and then you would be in trouble.
They won't know me because I won't give them my name. You are
wrong, sir, in not trusting me, for you see my life depends on it,
not to mention the reward which you have promised me."

Vinitius asked him, "How much money do you need?"

"A thousand sestercia, sir. Remember I must find reliable men
who will do the job right and will not leave any trace. For good
work, there must be good pay. Something should be added for me
also to wipe away my tears which I will shed for Glaucus. May the
gods witness how I love him. Now, I will go to find the necessary
men. Furthermore, I have an idea which may prove infallible."

Vinitius gave him the asking amount, at the same time wanting
Chilo to relate to him any progress he might have made till now.
Chilo did not have much to relate. He attended a few houses of
prayer...had been observing everyone carefully, especially the
women, but no luck. The Christians looked upon him with respect
after that generous gift to Euricius. They honor him as a person
who follows the teaching of Christ. He also learned that a certain
Paul of Tarsus, a great teacher among them, is now in Rome. They
are also awaiting the supreme priest of the sect who is to arrive
shortly. He was Christ's disciple to whom Christ enjoined the care
of all the faithful in the whole world. All the Christians here in
Rome are excited about seeing him and hearing his words. I understand that when he comes, most all will try to convene in order to
hear him. When that time comes you may also accompany me to

that meeting. The great crowd and your disguise will make it safe for both of us. Furthermore, Christians are not people who seek revenge. They are on the whole a very peaceful people. Here he began to relate with some show of surprise what he had seen and heard. They never give themselves up to debauchery as was claimed. They do not poison wells and fountains, and they are not enemies of the human race; they do not worship an ass nor eat the flesh of children. No, nothing of that sort at all. Perhaps even among them he might find some people who would kill Glaucus for money, but their religion, as far as he knew, did not incite crime. On the contrary, it urged forgiveness and forgetting of offenses.

Vinitius remembered what Pomponia had told him at Acte's and was glad. At times he felt that this religion of Ligia's may have caused her to hate him but he now felt relieved that it was not so. He was glad that the religion of Pomponia and Ligia was neither criminal nor repulsive. A curious feeling possessed him now, a feeling that this new religion of Christ, unknown and mysterious to him, was the thing which separates Ligia from him. And, with this feeling came fear and also hate for this unknown religion.

CHAPTER XVII

CHILO was sincere in his fear of meeting up with Glaucus and it was important to him to have Glaucus erased. There was considerable truth in what he told Vinitius. He had known Glaucus, had betrayed him, sold his family into slavery and delivered him to be murdered. The memory of all this did not bother Chilo too much especially when he was sure that Glaucus would die. He did not foresee however that Glaucus would come out alive and reach Rome. When he espied him at one of the houses of prayer, he was terrified and decided against further search of Ligia. However, he was more terrified by Vinitius. He understood now that he must choose between the fear of Glaucus and the pursuit and vengeance of a powerful patrician to whom would come in aid one mightier, namely, Petronius. In view of this, Chilo ceased to hesitate. He reasoned that it was safer to have small enemies than great ones and even though his cowardly nature abhorred bloody measures, he now saw the need for the killing of Glaucus by hired men.

Chilo knew that he could find men to kill Glaucus. He met such men, without moral scruples, without honor and conscience, who would even murder their own mothers for money. But he had to be careful whom he picked and make sure he picked those who would not turn on him after completing the contract and demand more money. He thought that he might find some individuals among the Christians, and he would prefer that. They might even do the job through religious devotion and he liked this idea.

Debating this question, he went that evening to Euricius, who with his son were devoted to him. They might assist him in this, he mused. Naturally he did not intend to reveal all of his intentions, but he wanted people who were ready for anything and he thought they might help him in getting such people who would do the job and guard the secret.

Euricius, after redeeming his son from slavery, rented one of those shops which were so numerous in Rome in which he sold olives, beans, unleavened bread, water sweetened with honey and other things. These shops were usually located close to the circus. Chilo met Euricius there making his shop ready for the daily sales. He greeted Chilo with joy and gratitude. Chilo asked if he knew of two or three strong young men among the Christians. He wanted a small favor. He needed these men to ward off danger that was threatening him and he would pay them for their services if they would perform them faithfully and without question.

Euricius and his son Quartus listened to his words with reverence. As their benefactor and also a good disciple of Christ, they were sure that he would not ask anything which was not compatible with the teaching of Christ. They were both ready to do his bidding.

Chilo assured them that it was true and, raising his eyes, seemed to be praying. As a matter of fact he was deliberating whether to take them up on their offer. It would save the thousand sesterces for himself. After a moment of reflection, however, he decided against it. Euricius was old; Quartus, only sixteen years of age. Chilo needed much stronger help. As to the money, he might still save a greater part for himself. So, he refused their offer. He explained that he needed someone with greater strength than they possessed.

"I know the baker, Demas," said Quartus, "in whose mills slaves and hired men are employed. One of these hired men is so strong that he would suffice not for two, but for four men. I myself have seen him lift big boulders which four men could not even budge."

"If he is a God-fearing man who can sacrifice himself for the good of the brethren, please allow me to meet him," said Chilo.

"He is a Christian. Nearly all who work for Demas are Christians. There are both day and night workers and this man who is so strong is on the night shift. If we were to go to the mill now, we would find them at supper and you would be able to speak to him freely. Demas lives near the Emporium."

Chilo consented willingly. The Emporium was at the foot of the Aventine Hill, and not too far from the Circus Maximus. Going by way of the Porticus Aemilia, they would be able to shorten their route considerably.

"I am old," said Chilo on the way. "At times I suffer loss of memory. Our Christ was betrayed by one of the disciples. I cannot remember the name of the traitor. Who was he?"

"Judas, who hanged himself," answered Quartus, wondering how it was possible to forget that name.

"Oh yes, Judas. I thank you," said Chilo.

They went on in silence, and passed the Emporium which was closed, and going around the storehouse from which grain was distributed to the populace, they turned left along the Via Ostiensis and continued on to the Forum Pistorium. They halted before a building from the interior of which came the sound of grinding millstones. Quartus went in, but Chilo remained outside. He was aware that in a crowd he might come across Glaucus and he was careful to avoid crowds.

"I'm curious about this Hercules who works here," he said to himself looking at the brightly shining moon. "If he is a crafty scoundrel, he will cost me something; if he is virtuous but dull, he will do what I want without money."

Further musing was interrupted by the approach of Quartus and another man who was dressed lightly, wearing only a tunic called a exomis, which was cut in a fashion which exposed the right arm and breast. Such garments, since they left freedom of movement, were used mainly by laborers. Chilo, when he looked upon this man, drew a breath of satisfaction. In all his life he never saw such a huge arm and breast.

"Here is the one I told you about," remarked Quartus.

"May the peace of Christ be with you," said Chilo. "Quartus, tell this brother whether I deserve faith and trust and then return in the name of God, for there is no need that your father should be left alone."

"This is the man," said Quartus, "who gave all his money to redeem me from slavery even though I was unknown to him. May Our Savior prepare a reward for him."

The giant bent down and reverently kissed Chilo's hand.

"What is your name, brother?" asked Chilo.

"I received the name of Urban at baptism."

"Urban, my brother, do you have time to talk to me a little?"

"Our work begins at midnight. Now they are preparing our supper so I have time."

"Let us then go by the river and we will talk." They went and sat on the embankment in silence broken only by the sound of millstones and the splash of the flowing river. Chilo looked keenly into the face of the laborer. The face seemed sad but kind and honest.

"This is a good man but dull. He will kill Glaucus for nothing," thought Chilo.

"Urban, do you love Christ?"

"Yes, I love Him very much."

"And your brothers and sisters in Christ. Do you love them also?"

"Yes, I love them also."

"Then, may peace be with you."

"And with you too."

Silence followed. Then Chilo, looking up into the moonlit sky, began to speak about Christ's death. He made his voice sound solemn and impressive. While he spoke of the suffering and crucifixion, Urban wept, and when Chilo began to complain that there was no one to come to the aid of Christ at his time of sorrow and death...to free him from the insults of Roman soldiers and the Jewish priests, the huge fists of the man began to open and close with suppressed rage. The thought of the rabble reviling the Lamb, the soldiers nailing Him to the cross caused his simple soul to cry out for vengeance.

"Urban, do you know who Judas was?"

"I know...but he hanged himself!" exclaimed Urban. In his voice was a kind of sorrow that the traitor was not still alive so that he could go and punish him himself.

"If he were alive, would you not take revenge, Urban?"

"Sure! Who wouldn't?"

"Peace be with you, faithful servant of the Lamb! True, we should forgive wrongs done to ourselves, but who can forgive the wrong done to God? As a serpent breeds a serpent, as malice breeds malice and treason breeds treason...from the poison of Judas another traitor appeared. As the other traitor delivered Christ to the Roman soldiers, so this man who lives among us intends to betray

Christ's sheep to the wolves. If no one will stop him, if no one will crush the head of this serpent in time, then destruction will fall on us all and the honor and work of the Lamb will perish."

Urban looked at Chilo with alarm not fully understanding what he just heard. But the Greek, covering his head with a corner of his mantle, began to speak with a voice as if coming from the bowels of the earth itself.

"Woe to you, servants of the true God! Woe to you, Christian men and women!" Then he fell silent for a moment. In the silence could be heard the noise of the millstones, the song of the millers and the sound of the river.

"Sir," asked the laborer, "who is this traitor?"

Chilo dropped his head. "Who? A son of Judas himself...a son of his poison, a man who pretends to be a Christian but goes about proclaiming that Christians refuse to acknowledge Caesar as god... that they poison fountains, murder children and want to destroy the city so that one stone may not remain upon another. In a few days an order will be given that will throw Christian men and women into prison and then lead them to death just like what happened to the slaves of Pedanius Secundus. All this is being done by this second traitor. If no one punished the first Judas...if no one took vengeance upon him...if no one defended Christ in His hour of torment...who will punish this one? Who will destroy him? Who will protect the brothers and sisters of the faith from him?"

Urban, who had been sitting down, rose suddenly and cried out. "I will!"

Chilo rose also. He looked at the face of the laborer for a while, stretched out his hand to him and said, "Go among the Christians; go to the houses of prayer and ask the brethren of the whereabouts of Glaucus, and when they show him to you, then kill him at once in the name of Christ!"

"Glaucus?" repeated Urban, wanting to remember the name.

"Do you know him?"

"No, I do not. There are thousands of Christians in Rome and they are not all known to one another. Tomorrow, however, I will know. There will be a great gathering at Ostrianum. The first Apostle of Christ has finally arrived and will be there. The brethren will point out Glaucus to me there."

"In Ostrianum?" inquired Chilo. "But that is outside the city gates! All the brothers and sisters? At night? Did you say in Ostrianum?"

"Yes, sir. That is the cemetery between the Via Salaria and Via Nomentana. Did you not know that the great apostle will be there?"

"I have been away for two days, therefore I did not receive his invitation. I don't know where Ostrianum is because I came here not long ago from Corinth where I governed a Christian community. But as you say, at the gathering the brethren will point out Glaucus to you and on the way home you will kill him. For this, your sins will be forgiven. And now, go in peace."

"But, sir."

"Yes, good servant of the Lord?"

There was some doubt showing on the face of Urban. "Not long ago he had killed a man or two. He knows that Christ forbids killing. He had not killed in his own defense or for profit. The bishop himself had given him some brothers to help him but he said not to kill; but he killed. He does not know his own strength. For that he is now doing penance. Others sing while the millstones are grinding but he thinks of his sin, of his offense against the Lord. He has prayed much and wept much. Now he is promising to kill again, but this time it will be a traitor, to protect' others. "But, should not Glaucus be condemned by the elders? By the bishop? By the apostle? It is an easy thing for me to kill due to my strength, and to kill a traitor will be easier still. But suppose Glaucus is innocent? How can I take upon myself a new murder, a new sin, a new offense against the Lord?"

"There is no time for a trial, my son," said Chilo. "The traitor will hurry from Ostrianum to Caesar in Antium. He may even hide in the house of a certain patrician whom he is serving. I will give you something. If you show it to the bishop after the death of Glaucus, he will bless you and your deed." Saying this he took a small coin from his pouch and began to search for a knife at his belt. He finally found it and with its point he made a sign of the cross upon the coin and gave it to the laborer.

"Here is the final sentence and condemnation of Glaucus. It is your sign. If you show this coin with the cross to the bishop after the death of Glaucus, he will forgive you this killing which you do not wish to do."

Urban stretched out his hand for the coin with hesitation. He was not totally convinced that it was right; he had the other killing fresh in his mind.

"Sir, do you then take this deed on your own conscience? Have you heard with your own ears Glaucus betraying his brethren?"

Chilo now realized that he must give proofs, mention names, otherwise doubts will linger in the mind of this poor giant. Suddenly a thought flashed through his head.

"Listen, Urban," said he. "I dwell in Corinth but I came from Cos. Here in Rome I am instructing a certain woman in the faith. She is a slave of Petronius named Eunice. In his house I heard how Glaucus had undertaken to betray all the Christians. Besides, he has promised another favorite of Caesar, Vinitius, to find a certain maiden for him among the Christians."

Here he stopped and looked with amazement at Urban whose eyes suddenly blazed with anger and rage.

"What is the matter with you?" he asked worriedly.

"Nothing, nothing. Tomorrow I will kill Glaucus."

The Greek was silent. After a while he took Urban by the arm, turned him around so that the light of the moon might fall directly on him. He wavered within himself whether to ask further questions or stop with what he suddenly surmised to be a fact. Finally, his usual caution prevailed and breathing easier inquired, "Urban was the name given to you at your baptism, was it not?"

"It was, sir."

"Then peace be with you, Urban."

CHAPTER XVIII

PETRONIUS TO VINITIUS:

My dear Marcus, something is definitely wrong with you. No doubt Venus has obsessed your mind to such a degree that you are not able to think and talk about anything else except your love. Sometime in the future, in your spare time, read for yourself a copy of the last letter you sent me. You will see for yourself that your mind is totally occupied with her and no one else. Your thoughts always come back to her. Your whole being circles above her like a falcon above his prey. By Pollux! Find her quickly before living fire consumes you and you become like the Egyptian sphinx which, it is said, was so in love with the pale Isis, that he grew deaf and indifferent to all things, waiting only for the night so as to gaze with stony eyes at his loved one.

Roam the streets at night in disguise. Go even with the noble philosopher to the houses of prayer of the Christians. Anything that might bring hope and kills time is fine. However let me give you a bit of advice if you do mingle among your Christians looking for Ligia: Ursus, Ligia's slave, is a man of unusual strength. For my sake, take with you for your protection the mighty gladiator Croto. He will ensure your safety. You know how strong Croto is. This will be most prudent I assure you. If Pomponia Graecina and Ligia belong to the Christian faith, knowing them, it is fair to assume that the Christians are evidently not what others say of them. In your desire to rescue someone from their fold, remember they have already given evidence that they can supply plenty of manpower. So, how would you be able to carry your maiden off alone? Chilo will not be able to help you as you well know. Croto, however, will surely give you sufficient help even if

there are ten like this Ursus. You saw the outcome of his match
with the champion of all Africa at the recent feast of Caesar. This,
I repeat, is the best advice I can give you right now.

They have ceased to talk about the infant Augusta here and
also about the evil spirits which caused her death. Poppaea herself
mentions it once in a while but Nero is absorbed with other
things now. Besides, if it is true that she is with child again, then
memory of the other one will soon fade.

We have been in Naples for some time already. The echoes of
our presence here must have reached you for surely Rome does
not speak of anything else. If you were able to think of something
else besides Ligia, then you would know that yourself. Yes, we
traveled to Naples. At first the sad memories of our mother re-
proached our conscience. But do you realize to what depths our
bronze-bearded Emperor has sunk? Even the murder of his own
mother was for him an excuse to write poems and sing tragic
songs as a tragedian on stage. What a clown! Up to now, being a
coward, he had twinges of conscience as to her murder. Now, that
he is convinced that the whole world is at his feet and that no god
will punish him, he only pretends grief as an actor pretends on
stage. He springs up at night sometimes crying that the Furies are
chasing him; he rouses us, assumes postures of tragedian actors,
such as Orestes, and begins to recite Greek verses while at the
same time looking at us all closely to see whether we are admiring
him. And, we do indeed admire him loudly. Instead of telling the
clown to go back to sleep, we take part in his acting and beg the
Furies to go away, to leave in peace so great an artist! By Castor! It
has also come to this: he appeared publicly on stage. The arena
was filled to capacity. Nero saw to that! The stench of the bodies
and of garlic which they eat daily filled the whole arena. Luckily
for me, I was behind the stage with Bronze-beard who asked me
to be with him until the moment he went on stage. And, would
you believe this? He was scared to death! He took my hand and
placed it on his chest and his heart was indeed beating quickly
and his face was white from fear. Yes, he was afraid even though
he knew that the Praetorian guards were dispersed around the
arena with whips in their hands to incite the rabble to mad applause. But there was no need of whips. No monkeys anywhere
howled as much as that mob waved, smiled and even shed tears.
After the performance he regaled us who were behind the stage
with the words: "What triumph can compare with this one?" But
the mob still howled knowing full well that it would ensure them

free theater tickets, gifts, bread, wine and other occasions to witness the clown emperor. Believe me, nothing like this has been done before by Roman rulers. He kept repeating, "Look how the Greeks appreciate me, look at them!" And, it seems to me that from this time on his hatred for Rome increased greatly.

The Senate was notified of this great triumph of Nero by couriers and I suppose they will vote to enshrine this triumph in some way. Everyone is at the feet of Nero, especially the Senate. I have to tell you what happened after the performance of Nero. The theater collapsed, but luckily everyone had already left. Many, even among the Greeks, look upon this as an evil omen that the gods are angry because the dignity of a Caesar was disgraced. Nero, on the contrary, considers it just the opposite since the gods did not allow anyone to be hurt after he had performed...that the people who saw him on the stage were indeed a lucky people. There were offerings and public thanks offered in all the temples here. Nero is encouraged now to make his trip to Greece. But, he still wonders, and he told me this privately, what the Roman populace would say to that. They may not like it; they may even revolt against him, not out of hate but out of love for him, wanting him to be near them in Rome. Between you and me, the Romans want him back but only because of the free bread and circuses that would be theirs upon his return.

We are leaving shortly for Beneventum to gaze upon the splendors promised us by Vatinius, the cobbler's son. After that, we are off to Greece under the protection of the divine brothers of Helen. I have noticed something about myself: that if a man joins the company of madmen, he becomes somewhat mad himself and finds a certain charm in madness. Greece and the journey of a thousand ships, a kind of triumphal advance of Bacchus among the nymphs and bacchants crowned with myrtle, vine and honeysuckle! There will be women dressed in tiger skins harnessed to chariots, flowers, music, poetry and applause for the Greek god Hellas. Yes, all this and something more. We wish to create a kind of oriental empire, an empire of palm trees, sunshine, poetry and reality turned into a dream; reality turned only into life's pleasures. We want to forget Rome. We want to place the center of the empire somewhere between Greece, Asia and Egypt; to live the life not of men, but of gods. To wander in golden galleys under the shadow of purple sails along the archipelago. We want to be Apollo, Osiris and Baal, all in one person; to be rosy with the dawn, golden with the sun and silver with the moon; to com-

mand, to sing, to dream. And, will you believe it? I, who still retain a penny's worth of reason, allow myself to be borne away by
these fantasies which, if they are not realistic, are at least grandiose and rare. Such an empire is indeed only a dream, but what a
dream!

Life is empty in itself except when Venus takes the form of
Ligia or even Eunice. Many times, however, life takes the form of
a monkey. Our bronze-beard will never realize his dream and you
know why? Because in his dreamworld of an empire there is no
place for meanness, treason and death, but in real life there sits a
wretched comedian, a dull charioteer and a frivolous tyrant. We
are now killing people who have displeased us in any way at all.
Poor Torquatus Solanus is now a mere shadow of a man. Soon he
will open his veins and be no more. Laecanius and Licinius are terrified because they know that their end is near. Old Thrasea will
not escape death for the reason that he dares to be honest. Tigellinus is not able as yet to get the better of me. I am still needed
around Nero not only as Arbiter of Elegance but as a man without whose counsel and taste the expedition to Greece might fail.
Sooner or later, though, it has to come to that final act of opening
my veins. When that time comes I want to be sure that our
Bronze-beard should not get my goblet which you saw and admired so much for its exquisite form and beauty. Should you be
close at my death, I will give it to you; if not, I will shatter it to
pieces. Meanwhile, before me yet is the cobbler's treat in Beneventum and also the trip to Greece. Fate alone points out the road to
everyone.

Be well, Marcus, and don't forget to engage Croto as your
helper, otherwise they will snatch Ligia away from you once
again. When Chilo ceases to be needful, send him over to me no
matter where I happen to be. Perhaps I shall make of him a second Vatinius. Maybe consuls and senators will tremble before him
as they now tremble before our noble cobbler. That will be a sight
worth seeing I assure you. When you find Ligia, please let me
know and I will offer up a pair of swans and a pair of doves in the
round temple of Venus which is located here. Once I saw Ligia sitting on your knee seeking your kisses. Try to make that dream a
reality. May there be no clouds in your sky, or if they be, let them
have the color of roses. Be in good health and farewell!"

CHAPTER XIX

BARELY had Vinitius finished reading the letter when Chilo entered quietly into the library where he was sitting. The servants had strict orders to admit him at any hour of the day or night.

"May the divine mother of your generous ancestor Aeneas be as favorable to you as the son of Maia was to me."

"What does that mean?" asked Vinitius with sudden hope flashing in his eyes.

"Eureka!" exclaimed Chilo.

Vinitius was so moved that he was unable to utter a sound for a brief moment. At last he asked, "Have you seen her?"

"No, sir, but I saw Ursus and spoke to him."

"Do you know where she is hidden?"

"Not yet. Another person might have spoiled everything by asking too soon and for his pains he would have received a mighty blow of that mighty fist, after which mere earthly affairs would mean absolutely nothing to him because he would be dead. Another person, sir, might have aroused suspicion in the giant and thereby would cause them to hide the girl in some safe hiding place that very night. I did not act thus. It is enough to know that Ursus works near the Emporium for Demas the miller. Now, all that is necessary is for one of your trusted slaves to follow him from work in the morning and find out where they live because the girl, no doubt, will be at the same house. I only bring you assurance, sir, that since Ursus is here in Rome so also must the girl be in Rome. She will be present without doubt at their gathering tonight in Ostrianum."

"In Ostrianum? Where is that?"

"It is an old cemetery between the Via Salaria and the Via Nomentana. That high priest of the Christians of whom I spoke to you before is to be there to preach and to baptize. They are very careful where they practice their religion. There is no definite edict against them but there are many in Rome who are antagonistic toward them. Ursus told me that most of them will try to be present tonight for this important occasion so that they will be able to see and hear the foremost disciple of Christ. Of the women, Pomponia perhaps may not be able to come since she could not explain satisfactorily to Aulus her absence from her house at night. Aulus, as you know, is still a worshiper of ancient gods. But Ligia, who is under the care of Ursus and the elders, will no doubt be there.

Vinitius lived only in hope of finding Ligia. Now that this hope seemed on the threshold of realization, he felt sudden weakness. Chilo noticed this and made up his mind to take advantage of it.

"The gates are guarded at night by your people, sir, but I'm sure the Christians realize this and must have other means to freely pass. The Tiber too will not be a stumbling block to them. They must have many ways to be able to leave the city at night. I'm sure you will be able to find Ligia at Ostrianum. Ursus promised me that he will be there and kill Glaucus. So please, listen to me. Either you follow Ursus and Ligia to their dwelling place or command your slaves to seize him as a murderer, and having him in your power, demand that he point out Ligia's hiding place. I have done all I could. Another person would have told you that he had to spend much money before he could pry the secret from Ursus. I know that even if I did you would have recompensed me generously. But I did not falsify anything. Once in my life...that is to say...like always in my life, I have been truthful and I have confidence in your generosity. Petronius assured me of that."

Vinitius, who was a soldier, did not allow the momentary weakness to take hold of him for long. He gained control of himself quickly and spoke thus: "You may rely on my generosity but first we must go to Ostrianum...both of us."

"Me too?" Chilo hadn't the slightest desire to go there. "O noble tribune, I only promised you that I would show you how to get Ligia, not to seize her myself. Think, sir, what that Ligian bear of a man would do to me when he finds out about Glaucus being innocent. He would demolish me entirely for inciting him against Glaucus. Remember too, sir, that the greater a philosopher a man is, the more difficult for him to answer the foolish questions of the plebs. If you think that I have deceived you, then pay me only when I point out the house where Ligia lives. Show me, however, even a small amount of your generosity now. If something were to happen to you, the gods forbid, then I at least will be recompensed in part."

Vinitius walked to a small chest, called an arca, standing on a marble pedestal, and drawing out a purse from it, threw it to Chilo.

"These are only minor coins. When Ligia shall be in my house you will get a like amount in gold."

"In gold?" exclaimed Chilo. "You are indeed Jove himself!"

Vinitius frowned and said, "You will receive food here, then you may rest. Do not leave the house until we are ready to go out tonight to Ostrianum."

Fear and hesitation grew on the face of the Greek but he soon calmed down and said, "Who dare oppose you, sir? Your hospitality will fill me with delight and happiness."

Vinitius interrupted him impatiently and asked for details of his conversation with Ursus. It seemed clear to him now after listening to these details that Ligia's hiding place could be discovered tonight or perhaps he would be able to seize her on the way from Ostrianum. Thinking of this he was filled with great joy. Now that he felt reasonably sure that he would find her, all anger toward her vanished. For this moment of happiness he forgave her all. He now felt that he was going to rest after a long journey. He was almost tempted to call his slaves and order the house to be adorned with garlands. He did not feel any animosity even toward Ursus. He was ready to forgive everybody. Even Chilo seemed more sympathetic to him now. The whole house seemed more cheerful and full of sunshine. This reflected on his face, which began to show again his youthful zest for living. He was aware once again how much he loved Ligia and his desire for her awakened him as the earth warmed by the sun awakes in spring. His desire for Ligia was not however as wild and blind as before but more tender and compassionate. He felt his usual energy kindle within him and he was sure that once he found Ligia all the Christians in the world would not take her away from him again. Not even Caesar himself.

Chilo was emboldened by what he saw in Vinitius and he began to give him advice. Vinitius should not think that all is won already, but go ahead with the greatest caution...otherwise everything might be for naught. He begged him not to carry the girl off from Ostrianum. They should go there disguised and their faces hidden in hoods. They would observe everything and everybody only from a distance. When they did see Ligia, it would be safest to follow her at a distance, see what house she entered, surround it the next morning at daybreak and take her out in daylight. Since she was a hostage of Caesar, they could do this without fear of breaking the law. In the event of not finding her in Ostrianum, they could but follow Ursus and the result would be the same. To act otherwise would be impractical. The Christians would quickly extinguish their lights and scatter in the darkness. Also, it would be a good idea to be well armed in case of strong opposition.

Vinitius saw the wisdom of this advice and recalling the counsel of Petronius, ordered his slaves to summon Croto to him. Chilo, who knew about everyone in Rome, felt much better at the mention of Croto. He had witnessed more than once the superhuman strength of this famous wrestler in the arena. Now he felt more at ease about going to Ostrianum. He was also more sure of getting that purse full of gold coins. He therefore sat down in good spirits at the table to which, after a time, he was called by the chief slave.

While eating, he told the servants that he had obtained for their master a miraculous ointment. Even the worst racehorse, if rubbed on the hooves with it, would leave every other horse behind in the race. A certain Christian had taught him how to prepare this ointment because some Christian elders were far more skilled in magic and miracles than the Thessalonians, even though Thessaly was much renowned for its witches. Christians confide in him most heartily. That is clear to everyone who knows the meaning of a fish. While speaking thus, he looked sharply at the slaves in the hope of detecting Christians among them and informing Vinitius about them. Not seeing anything unusual, he fell to eating heartily and drinking wine, while at the same time praising the cook and declaring that he would try to buy him from Vinitius. His joy was dimmed only by the fact that he had to go to Ostrianum. He consoled himself with the thought that he would go well disguised and in the company of two men, one of whom was so strong that he was the champion of the whole empire; the other, a favorite of Caesar...a noble patrician. Why should he be afraid? No one will dare harm him. Moreover, they will be lucky if they see the tip of his nose.

He began to recall his conversation with the laborer. He hadn't the slightest doubt that he was Ursus. He had heard from many sources about the great strength of this man. When he had need of a strong man, it was natural that Ursus with his great strength should be pointed out to him. The real proof, however, lay in the fact of the rage and anger shown on the face of the laborer when Chilo mentioned the names of Vinitius and Petronius and the missing girl. Furthermore, the laborer spoke of the penance due for killing a man recently, and had not Ursus killed Atacinus recently? His physical description also fitted the description given to him. The difference in the name was the only doubtful factor, but he knew that Christians took new names at baptism.

"If Ursus kills Glaucus," said Chilo to himself, "then all the better. If he does not, still not much harm done. That may even be a good sign, namely, that to commit murder comes extremely hard for Christians. After all, hadn't he painted the evil deeds attributed to Glaucus elaborately enough? He was so eloquent about it that even a stone would have been moved in sympathy, yet he had only barely talked him into it. If it weren't for the good fortune of mentioning some names, perhaps he would have refused. Evidently murder among Christians is a terrible thing. If Ursus will not murder Glaucus for such a great crime, then he will not harm him for such a small infraction. Moreover, when once I have pointed out to this ardent ringdove the nest of his turtledove, I will wash my hands of everything and transfer myself over to Naples. Christians speak about the washing of hands; that must be the way of ending things once you have finished with them. Yet how good these Christians are! How ill men speak of them! Gods...such is the justice of this world! I especially love this religion because it teaches not to kill. But if it forbids killing, then it must also forbid stealing, deceit and false testimony, hence I must say that it is not easy. It teaches that it is not enough to die bravely as the Stoics teach but one must live honestly and virtuously. If I ever possess enough property, then I also will become a Christian. A rich man can permit himself anything, even virtue. This must be a religion for the rich, and yet there are many poor people in its fold. What good does it do them? Why let virtue tie your hands? I must give this some thought in the future. Meanwhile, praise to you, O Hermes! Thank you for helping me find this girl, but if you did so for the yearling heifers with gilded horns, well...I don't want to know you. Shame on you, O Slayer of Argos! Such a wise god and did you not foresee that you will get nothing from me? However I will offer you my gratitude, but if you prefer two beasts instead, then you are a third one and you should be a shepherd and not a god. Have a care too, lest I, as a philosopher, prove to men that you do not exist. Then there will be no more offerings to you. Know also that it is much safer to be on good terms with philosophers."

Thus talking to himself and to Hermes, he stretched out on the sofa, put his mantle under his head and soon fell asleep. He awoke when Croto arrived. He went to greet him and began to examine with pleasure the magnificent physique of the wrestler who seemed to fill the room with his immense presence. Croto had already agreed upon the price with Vinitius and was just saying to him, "By Hercules! It is well that you have summoned me today because tomorrow I leave for Beneventum. The noble Vatinius asked me to compete with a certain Syphax, the most powerful black man in all Africa. Just imagine how his spinal column will crack in my arms and how I will break his jaw with my fist."

"By Pollux, Croto, I'm sure that it will be so!"

Chilo added, "That's the best way. Break his back and also his jaw. You are the man for it, Croto. But let me warn you, my Hercules, gird yourself well for tonight. You might meet up with a living terror. The man who guards the maiden has exceptional strength."

Chilo spoke thus only to egg him on but Vinitius added, "That is true. I did not see this myself but they tell me that he can take a bull by the horns and drag him wherever he pleases."

"Oh my!" exclaimed Chilo. He did not imagine Ursus to be that strong.

Croto laughed with contempt. "I undertake, worthy tribune, to carry away with one hand whomever you point out to me and with the other to defend myself against a dozen such as this Ligian. I will bring the girl to your house even if all the Christians in Rome were pursuing me like Calabrian wolves. If not, I will allow you to beat me with clubs."

"Don't let him do that, sir!" cried Chilo urgently. "They will hurl stones at us and how will his strength aid us then! Is it not better to take the girl from her own dwelling? Otherwise you will expose her and us all to danger."

"That is how it's going to be, Croto," said Vinitius.

"I take your money. I do your will. But remember that tomorrow I go to Beneventum."

"I have five hundred slaves in the city itself," said Vinitius. Then he withdrew to the library and wrote the following words to Petronius: "The Ligian has been found by Chilo. I go with him and Croto to Ostrianum and shall carry her off from her house tonight or tomorrow. May the gods pour down everything favorable on you. Be well. Joy does not permit me to write further."

Laying aside the pen he began to pace back and forth. With feverish thoughts he began to picture Ligia present here with him either tonight or tomorrow. His joy knew no bounds at the thought. Yes, he will be her slave; he will love her forever. Now he recalled once again what Acte told him of Ligia's love for him. It must then be merely a question of conquering a certain maidenish modesty and perhaps certain ceremonies which the Christian teaching evidently commanded. But once Ligia would be his, then all she could say is, "It is done," and then she would be compliant and loving.

Chilo's entrance interrupted his thoughts. "Sir, another thought occured to me. The Christians most likely have some kind of a sign or password without which we would not be able to enter among them. I know that in different houses of prayer it is so. It could also be tonight. Allow me then to go and find out about this because I think it is very important."

"Yes, I agree. You speak like a prudent man and I praise you for it. Go then to Euricius or anywhere else and find out what is required. But before you go leave your purse here."

Chilo frowned in displeasure. Any kind of parting with money was always unpleasant to him but he obeyed and left. It wasn't far to Euricius so that he returned soon with the necessary information.

"I have the password, sir. It is well that I did go because without the password we would not have been allowed to enter. Also I have inquired carefully about the road. I told Euricius that I need the password only for my friends because I myself cannot attend. I told him that I will visit with the apostle tomorrow and he will repeat to me the choicest parts of his sermon."

"What's that? You have to go tonight!" commanded Vinitius.

"I know that I have to but I will go hooded and I also advise you to do the same. We don't want to frighten off the birds."

They soon began to prepare to take leave because darkness was upon them. They put on Gallic cloaks with large hoods and took lanterns with them. Vinitius armed himself with the short Roman sword. Chilo put on a wig which he obtained on the way from an old man's shop and they went out hurrying so that they might reach the Nomentana gate before it closed.

CHAPTER XX

THEY walked by way of Vicus Patricius along the Viminal near the plain on which Diocletian later built his famous baths. They passed the remnants of the wall built by Servius Tullius and reached the Via Nomentana. Then turning to the left towards the Via Salaria, they found themselves among the sandpits and grave-yards.

It had already grown dark and due to the fact that the moon had not appeared as yet, the roads were dark. It would have been difficult for them to find the right roads had it not been for the Christians themselves who showed them because dark forms on all sides were hurrying on and they went along with them. Some of them carried lanterns covered somewhat by their mantles; others walked on in darkness evidently sure of the way. The trained military eyes of Vinitius easily distinguished the young from the old, women from men. Villagers leaving the city at night, as was their custom, took all these night wanderers for laborers going to sandpits or grave diggers who had their own night time celebra-tions. Now, there appeared more and more lanterns as they came closer to their destination. Some were chanting hymns in hushed tones, which to Vinitius seemed filled with sadness. Others talked among themselves. The name of Christ could be heard and the words, "Risen from the dead," were also distinguishable to him.

Vinitius, however, paid little attention to these words; he eagerly scrutinized the female forms passing by. Greetings of "Peace be with you" and "Glory to Christ!" were passed on to them but they did not answer. A certain uneasiness seized Vinitius and his heart began to pound; he thought he heard Ligia's voice and some female forms recalled her form, but it was only his imagination. On closer scrutiny he found that he was mistaken.

The way seemed extra long to him. Although he knew the neighborhood he could not place everything in the darkness. Many times they had to pass narrow passages, parts of wall or booths which he did not remember. Finally the edge of the moon appeared from behind a mass of clouds and lighted the place better than the dim lanterns. Something from afar began to glow like fire or the flame of a torch. Vinitius turned to Chilo.

"Is that Ostrianum?"

Chilo, on whom all this, the walk in darkness and all those ghostlike forms around him, made an unfavorable impression, replied in a somewhat subdued voice tinged with fear, "I know not, sir. I have never been in Ostrianum. They could have found a place closer to the city to praise their God." After a while, feeling the need for conversation in order to pick up his courage he added, "They convene like murderers...still they are not permitted to murder unless that giant Ligian has deceived me shamefully."

Vinitius who thought only of Ligia was also surprised now by the extreme caution and secrecy shown by the Christians for their assembly, hence he remarked, "Like all religions, this one also has its adherents among us, but the Christians are a Jewish sect. So why do they assemble here in secret when within the area of Trans-Tiber there are many temples to which the Jews take their offerings in daylight?"

"Sir, the Jews are their bitterest enemies. I have heard that before the present Caesar's time, it almost came to war between the Jews and the Christians. Those outbreaks compelled Claudius Caesar to expel all the Jews from Rome, but at present the edict is abolished. However the Christians hide from the Jews and from the populace who, as you know, accuse them of every crime."

They walked along in silence for a while, then Chilo, whose fear grew in proportion to the distance from the city gates, spoke up. "Returning from the shop of Euricius I borrowed a wig from a barber and I also have two beans in my nostrils. They shouldn't recognize me but if they do, they will not kill me. They are not bad people. On the contrary they are good and honest and I esteem their love."

"Do not be premature in your love for them."

They entered a narrow depression with ditches on each side and an aqueduct on one side of the ditches. The moon now shown fully and they saw a wall covered with ivy which looked silvery in the moonlight. Before them was Ostrianum.

Vinitius' heart began to beat faster. At the gate two men accepted the password and they entered within. They found themselves in a spacious place enclosed on all sides by a wall. Here and there were separate monuments and in the center was the entrance to the crypt. In the lower part of the crypt beneath the upper level of the ground were graves. The crowd was huge, so they all had to gather outside of the crypt itself. Here Vinitius saw many lanterns gleaming but there were also many without lanterns. With the exception of a few all were hooded and the young tribune thought with alarm that he may not recognize Ligia if she were hooded also.

However someone lighted some torches made of pitch around the crypt and suddenly it became much lighter and warmer. Songs were sung now at different locations. Vinitius had never heard such songs before. The same yearning which he noticed in the hymns murmured by separate persons on the way to the cemetery was heard now but more distinct and powerful. It soon filled the whole cemetery, penetrating and immense, as if together with the people, the pits, the hills around and the whole region itself was filled with yearning. There was also with it a humble prayer for rescue from wandering in the dark. Some hands were outstretched as if imploring from on high. When the singing ceased, there followed a moment of suspense so impressive that Vinitius and his two companions looked momentarily at the stars in fear that something unusual would descend on them all.

Vinitius had seen many different temples, in Asia Minor, Egypt as well as in Rome. He was acquainted with many religions. He heard many songs and hymns sung in their honor or praise but here for the first time he heard people, not fulfilling some kind of ritual, but calling from the heart with sincere yearning as children seek their father or mother. One had to be blind not to see that these people not only honored their God but also loved Him with their hearts and souls. Vinitius had never seen anything like it. In Rome, in Greece and elsewhere those who still paid homage to different gods did so to gain aid for themselves or through fear, but no one really loved these divinities. Even though his mind was occupied with Ligia and looking for her in the crowd, he could not avoid noticing what was happening round about him. Meanwhile, more torches were lit and it became lighter still. At the same time an old man who also wore a hooded mantle with bared head came from the crypt. He mounted a stone in order to be seen by all.

The crowd swayed before him. Voices near Vinitius whispered, "Peter...Peter." Some knelt, others extended their arms toward him. There followed a silence so deep that one heard every charred particle that dropped from the torches, the distant rattle of wheels on the Via Nomentana and the sound of the wind through the pines which grew close to the cemetery.

Chilo bent toward Vinitius and whispered, "This is he...the foremost disciple of Christ...a fisherman."

The old man raised his arm and with a sign of the cross blessed those present. The people fell on their knees. Vinitius and his companions, not wishing to betray themselves, followed the example of the others. The young man could not understand his first impression of the old fisherman. It seemed to him that Peter was a simple man and looked like it, yet in this seeming simplicity there was something of the extraordinary...something wonderful. He was not adorned with mitre on his head nor garlands of oak leaves about his temples...no victorious palm in his hand, nor golden tablet on his breast. He wore no white robe embroidered with stars. In short, he wore no insignia of the kind worn by priests, whether oriental, Greek, Egyptian or Roman...yet this simple fisherman had in himself a quality which Vinitius could not fully understand. He had in himself a truth which he was witness to. This truth and revelation he was willing to share with others. In fact, eager to do so since this was his mission. There was in his face a convincing power as pure as truth itself. And, Vinitius, who was a skeptic and who did not desire to yield to the charm and influence of this old man, could not wait to hear what words this man would utter and what was the teaching that Ligia and Pomponia believed in.

Meanwhile Peter began to speak. He spoke at first like a father instructing his children and teaching them how to live. He strongly urged them to renounce sinful excesses and luxury, to love poverty, purity of life and truth; to endure wrongs and persecutions patiently, to obey the government and those placed in authority, to guard against deceit and calumny and finally to give a good example to each other and even to pagans.

Vinitius, for whom good was only that which could bring Ligia back to him, and evil, everything which stood as a barrier between them, was angered by these counsels. It seemed to him that by urging purity, that old man dared not only to condemn his love for Ligia but to turn Ligia against him. He understood that if she were in this assembly, listening to these words and if she took them to heart, she must think of him as an enemy of that teaching and an outcast. Anger seized him at this thought. What's new about this? he thought to himself. Is that all that this religion is about? The cynics urge poverty and self sacrifice; Socrates urges the practice of virtue; the Stoics...even such a one as Seneca, who has five hundred tables of lemonwood and uses them for his feasts, praises moderation, truth, patience in adversity, endurance in misfortune...All this is old, stale like mouse-eaten grain; the people do not wish it because it smells of old age.

Vinitius was greatly disillusioned. He expected to discover some unknown, mysterious truth, a magical secret unknown to him until now. Besides, he thought that he would hear a splendid orator with high-sounding words. Instead he heard words which were simple and devoid of every ornament. He was astonished by the reverent attention with which the people listened.

The old man spoke on. He admonished the people to be kind, peaceful, just and pure, not that they might have peace during this life only but that they might live eternally with Christ after death in joy, in glory, in delight, as no one on earth can attain.

Vinitius, though predisposed unfavorably, noticed however that there was a difference between this teaching and the teaching of the Cynics, the Stoics and the other philosophers. The latter urged good deeds and virtue only as a reasonable and a practical way of living but this man taught something else. He promised something more than an earthly life which would be reasonable and practical; he promised immortality after death. Not just any kind of immortality, but one that was filled with happiness and joy for ever and ever. He spoke of this immortality as something sure to be obtained. In view of this kind reward, virtue took on a new sparkle, a new meaning. Suffering and tribulation on earth took on a different aspect. To suffer just because it is the only way of life and

nothing can be done about it and everything ends with this suffering...that is a belief which is much different from the one proclaimed by this old man. He promised eternal happiness after
death for the momentary bit of suffering on earth. A great reward
in eternity for the short life practicing virtue and good deeds for
the sake of Christ. That is altogether different. The greatest good
is this God of the Christians and whoever strives at goodness is the
child of this God and, as a child of God, he practices goodness
because of love for his God. Love then is the great difference.

Vinitius could not fully comprehend this. It never occurred to
the adherents of the different Roman gods to love them. They
merely tolerated them. Now he recalled the words of Pomponia,
spoken to Petronius, that the God of the Christians is One and
Almighty. At present he heard from the lips of this old man that
He is also all good and all truth. In comparison to such a God,
mere gods such as Jove, Saturn, Apollo, Vesta and Venus are but a
vain and noisy rabble. He was most astonished, however, when the
old man began to teach that this God is all love. He who loves his
neighbor and even his enemies obeys His command. And, it is not
enough to love people you know, people around you, but all people
of the world, the whole world, because Christ the Son of God died
for all. It is not enough to love those who love us but to love all in
Christ. Christ forgave those who crucified Him, the Jews who
incited the crucifixion and the Roman soldiers who actually did
the deed. He forgave all. To practice daily love, to forgive those
who persecute you and calumniate you, such is the mandate of
Christ-God.

At the words of the old man, Chilo was sure that his work had
gone for naught. No one hearing them, even Ursus, would dare kill
Glaucus now. But he consoled himself that if that is so then no
harm will befall him either if Glaucus ever found him.

Vinitius, reflecting upon all that he heard, began asking himself
What kind of God is this? What kind of teaching and what kind of
people is this? Everything that he had just heard was so strange to
him and he was dumbfounded by it all. The realization began to
sink in however that if he would wish to follow this religion, then
he would have to give up his former thinking...change his character
completely, overturn his present beliefs and turn them to ashes. He
would have to change his very soul. A faith that would enjoin him

to love the Parthians, the Syrians and Egyptians, Gauls and Britons...to forgive enemies...to return good for evil...to love them all...this seemed to him pure madness. But, at the same time, he felt that in this madness there was something mightier than the teaching of all the philosophers up to now. Because of its madness, it seemed impractical but because of its impracticability, it was divine. He rejected it from the bottom of his heart and soul but in the rejection he felt that something precious was eluding him. Once one has fully accepted and tasted it, then nothing on earth is so sweet. He was sure that in this religion nothing realistic can be found, yet reality in comparison with it is something so much lesser and so much more fanciful. He felt overwhelmed thinking of all this as if some great weight was pulling him down. "This cemetery is full of madmen," he thought. Yet, there was something new and wonderful in this mystery. All this which he now heard...of life, of truth, of love of God and man...all this blinded him as if a light shone before him. Now he came to the conclusion with alarm that if Ligia is here in this cemetery and she is listening to all that is spoken by this man and, at the same time taking it all to heart, then she can never be his mistress, his concubine.

Now for the first time came the realization that even if he found her, he could never possess her. With this thought a very sad feeling arose in him as if he had lost something very precious. With this came uneasiness and then great anger filled his being, an anger against all Christians but especially against this fisherman. This peasant, who looked so frail, now filled him also with awe...yes, and even with fear. It seemed to him that this old man, more than anyone else, stood in his way of happiness, tragically deciding his fate.

More torches were being lighted. The wind ceased to blow among the pines. The fisherman began to speak about Christ and His death. Silence abounded...all listened with bated breath. This man now spoke of something which he himself had witnessed and he spoke in a manner which gave proof of his witness to the final scene of Christ's last days as man. He saw...he knew.... The words came from a person who was really a witness. There was no doubt of that because every moment of those scenes were etched indelibly in the memory of this man. How on their return from witnessing the Crucifixion, he and John sat two days and two nights in the upper chamber of the Last Supper, neither eating nor sleeping...in suffering and in sorrow, in doubt and full of alarm, holding their heads in their hands, with the realization uppermost in their minds that their beloved Master had died. What sadness! On the third day, at sunrise, suddenly Mary Magdalen rushed in with the cry: "They have taken the Lord away!" Rising up they hurried to the sepulchre. John, being younger, arrived first but did not go in and awaited Peter; they entered together and saw that what Mary had said was true. They saw the winding sheet but the body was not there.

Fear fell upon them because they first thought that the Jews had taken the body away and both returned with even greater sorrow. Other disciples arrived and were told what had happened and they all lamented in their sorrow. They were sure that their Master would rule Israel. He was to be king, but now here it was the third day and nothing. It would appear that the Father Himself rejected His own Son. Now they were ready to die themselves without hope.

The remembrance of those terrible moments even now caused tears to fall from the eyes of the fisherman. This was clearly noticeable in the light of the torches. His head shook and he was unable to speak at times. Vinitius had to admit to himself that this man was telling the truth and he weeps over it. Weeping could also be heard among the listeners. They all heard the story of Christ's suffering, yet upon hearing of those cruel days from this witness, this Apostle of Christ, they could not prevent the tears from flowing with his. They soon ceased however because they were curious to hear the rest. The old fisherman resumed his talk: "When thus we were all sorrowing together, Mary Magdalen rushed in once again telling us that she had seen the Lord in the garden by the sepulchre. At first she did not recognize Him, thinking He might be the gardener, and begged Him to tell her where they had taken the Lord. But when He spoke the word, 'Mary,' she knew. She fell before Him in adoration crying the word, 'Rabboni-Master!' He then told her to spread the word, and so she ran, and she is here. They, the Apostles, sprang up with joy, tears turned into shouts of gladness. Later that evening Cleophas came to them with the news that he and his companion had seen the Lord on the way to Emmaus. They recognized Him by the breaking of bread at the inn. As soon as they recognized Him, He disappeared from view. They all shouted, "Christ has risen! Christ has risen!" Their joy knew no bounds. Then suddenly the Lord stood before them, although the door of the chamber was locked, and He spoke to them the most welcome words: 'Peace be with you!'"

"Yes, I saw Him!" continued the fisherman. "The others saw Him also. He was like a magnificent light and joy to our eyes and souls. And, we believed that He had risen from the dead just as He foretold and His glory will last forever. Were the oceans to dry up, were the mountains to turn to dust, His truth and His power will remain forever."

"After eight days, Thomas Didymus, who was absent at the first appearence, saw Him also and cried out, 'My Lord and my God!' The answer of the Lord to him was, 'Now that you have seen, Thomas, you believe, but I tell you that blessed are the ones who have not seen but believe in Me.'"

Vinitius listened with amazement. Something strange was happening within his soul. He forgot for a moment where he was and why he was there. He could not believe what he saw and what he heard. But he was convinced that one must be blind not to see the truth in the words of this old man who spoke the words, "I saw." There was something in his whole personality that denied any falsehood about him. Vinitius thought that he was dreaming...all this about him was due to his imagination only. But against this were the clear words: "I have seen!"

Peter further narrated what followed up to the time of the Ascension of the Lord. He paused at times for he was old and weary but he did not pause in uttering the words themselves which were engraved in his memory like fire. The people listened in rapture; most of them uncovered their heads in order to hear better, not to miss a single word. In spirit they were transported to Galilee, among the valleys and olive trees. They forgot where they were and joyfully walked with the Savior when He Himself walked the earth. When Peter spoke to them of the Resurrection, some uttered cries of joy and raised their arms to the heavens. They forgot Rome, they forgot the mad Caesar who ruled over them. Christ was present. Christ lived and lives now! Christ to them was everything. For them Caesar no longer mattered, nor Rome with its pagan gods.

Only Christ mattered, He it is Who fills them with complete happiness.

In the distance the crowing of the roosters could now be heard. It was after midnight. At this moment Chilo took Vinitius by the arm and whispered to him: "Sir, out there not far from the old fisherman, there is Ursus and a maiden with him. Look!"

Vinitius shook himself as from a dream and looked at the place indicated by the Greek and saw the face of Ligia.

CHAPTER XXI

AT the sight of Ligia, Vinitius shook from head to his toes. Immediately he forgot about the crowd, the old fisherman and all that he had heard and seen. His eyes were upon this girl whom he loved so much. After all his efforts in looking for her, she now stood not far away from him. The joy he now felt was almost enough to burst his chest. He, who thought that the goddess Fortune had to obey his every whim, now hardly believed that he was so fortunate. If it wasn't for the crowd, he would have rushed pell-mell toward her. He looked again. No, there was no doubt; it was she in person. There was enough light where she stood; he could recognize every contour of her body...every inch of her lovely face. The hood that she previously wore now fell to her shoulders and her dark, beautiful hair fell on her shoulders. Her face was upturned to hear every word spoken by Peter. She wore but a common mantle about her shoulders, but to Vinitius she was never lovelier. Again he noticed her whole bearing as one of a regal queen who had a touch of sadness about her. He felt his love for her and it knew no bounds. As a man dying of thirst, he now thirsted no more because the spring of living water was at hand. Standing by the giant Ursus, she appeared small, a mere child. He also noticed that she was thinner. In previous moments when he saw her, she inspired in him the impression of a beautiful flower with a beautiful soul. He now wanted to possess her all the more, to have her who was so different from the women he knew in Rome or elsewhere. For this flower he would give away all that he possessed. He would have stared at her longer had not Chilo begun to whisper to him and admonish him not to do anything rash which would spoil everything.

The Christians meanwhile began to pray out loud and sing hymns. One hymn called "Maranatha" which was usually sung last was now sung after which the old Apostle began to baptize the ones prepared by the presbyters and were ready for baptism. To Vinitius it now seemed that this night would never end but he realized that he had to be patient just as Chilo advised.

At last the crowd began to disperse and to return to their homes. Chilo whispered to Vinitius, "Let us leave now, sir, and wait for them at the gate. We are still wearing our hoods over our heads and some people are looking at us. This advice was prudent to Vinitius so they left and stood by the gate.

"We will follow them when they leave," said Chilo. "We will then see into what house they will enter and tomorrow you, good tribune, will give orders to surround that house and capture the maiden."

"No!" said Vinitius.

"What are you going to do, sir?"

"After they enter their home, we will go in and get Ligia. After all, Croto, you are ready for that are you not?"

"To be sure!" Croto replied, "and I promise to give myself to you as a slave if I won't be able to wring the neck of that bull who guards the maiden."

But Chilo began to urge them strongly not to undertake such a rash action. Croto was hired for protection only was he not? They will be taking too much of a chance. They are only two against perhaps many Christians who could be called to help them. If they lose her now, Vinitius will never see her again for they will hide her better next time. Why not act with certainty? Why act haphazardly?

Vinitius, in all his eagerness to get Ligia right away, momentarily felt the wisdom of Chilo's words and perhaps would have given heed to them had not Croto, who was only thinking of the reward money, cut in, "Sir, command this old goat to be quiet or permit me to hit him with my fist. Once, seven drunken gladiators attacked me at an inn and not one of them left that place on his own. I'm not saying to take the girl right now amid the throng because they could throw stones at our feet, but once she is home then I guarantee that she will be yours."

Vinitius was gladdened by these words and said, "That is how it is going to be. Tomorrow she may be elsewhere in a better hiding place."

"That giant of a man who guards the maiden looks to me like a very formidable man," said Chilo.

"I'm not asking you to hold his hands," answered Croto.

They had to wait quite a while yet before they saw Ursus and Ligia leaving. With them was a group of people among whom appeared the form of the Apostle Peter. Vinitius, Chilo and Croto followed at a distance.

"Yes sir," said Chilo, "your maiden is well protected by the elders. With her is the Apostle Peter. You see how the people kneel before him?"

Vinitius did not pay any attention to them however. His whole being was engrossed with Ligia and the thought that he would have her in his arms soon. He now thought of how to proceed in her capture. Being a soldier, he began to plan. He knew that it was a bold undertaking but he also knew that in military planning bold actions often meant success.

The road was long so at times he deliberated on the widening chasm that now loomed between Ligia and himself. This religion caused the difference; it put her on a pedestal above other women. He realized now that her religion made her different. Before, he only saw her beauty...he desired her for her physical attraction, but now he realized that this new religion ingrafted in her soul something new and unknown, especially to the world that he and Petronius belonged. He also realized that Ligia, even if she loved him, would not sacrifice any of her Christian truths for his sake. Every other woman whom he knew might become his mistress but she would only be his victim. When he thought thus, anger seized him but he felt that his anger was powerless. To carry off Ligia was indeed possible and most likely he would be successful in his attempt this night but he was equally sure that compared to her religion he was himself but a mere shadow. He, a Roman tribune who up to now was convinced of the invincible power of Rome, now for the first time felt that there was something more powerful than that, something that he could not fully understand. He asked himself what all this meant but could not give an adequate answer. The assembled crowd, Ligia listening with rapt attention to the words of the fisherman as he narrated the suffering, death and the Resurrection of Christ, the God-man Who had redeemed the world and promised happiness on the other shore of the Styx...all this he could not fathom. It was all a jumble in his brain.

Out of this chaos in his thinking, he was brought back to reality by the unhappy mutterings of Chilo who had begun to complain about his fate. He had agreed to find Ligia, sure. Well, he found her even at the peril of his life. He pointed her out to the noble tribune...so now what more do they want of him? He did not offer to carry the maiden away. They could not ask this of a poor and feeble man who was deprived of two fingers on his right hand and was devoted only to meditation, knowledge and virtue. What would happen to him if such a mighty tribune like Vinitius would meet with ill luck while bearing the maiden away? It is true that the gods have a duty to care for their chosen ones but did it not happen before that the gods looked the other way instead of watching what was going on in the world? The goddess Fortune is blindfolded as is well known and could not see even in the daylight much less at night. What would happen if that Ligian bear would throw a millstone at the noble Vinitius or a keg of wine or worse yet...a keg of water? Who will give assurance that instead of reward, the only son of his father will not receive punishment? He has attached himself to the noble Vinitius as Aristotle to Alexander of Macedon. If the noble sir would at least give him that purse which he had thrust into his waistband before leaving home, he would have means to hire help if the Christians capture him or if he needs to mollify the Christians. Oh...why don't they listen to reasonable advice of one who is prudent and experienced?

Vinitius, upon hearing the complaints of Chilo, took out the purse and threw it to Chilo who caught it neatly even though he lacked two fingers.

"There you have it, so be quiet!"

The Greek noticed that the purse was unusually heavy and he brightened up at once. "My only hope is that Hercules had a lesser chore to perform, but who is Croto if not another Hercules? You, sir, I will not call you demigod...you are a full god and I hope that in the future you will not forget your poor faithful servant whose needs will be necessary to provide for from time to time. Once a philosopher is sunk in books, he thinks of nothing else. Perhaps a little: a house with a small garden, even with the smallest portico for shade in the summer would befit such a generous donor as you, sir. Meanwhile I will admire your heroic deeds from afar and invoke Jove's aid for you and if need be I will raise such an outcry as to wake up half of Rome. What a wretched road this is! The olive oil burned out in my lantern and if Croto, who is as noble as he is strong, would carry me to the gate, he would be sure that he will be able to carry the maiden without effort and he would be doing a good deed and ensuring for himself complete success."

"I'd rather carry a sheep which died of mange a month ago," answered Croto, "but give me that purse which the noble tribune bestowed on you and I will carry you as far as the gate."

"May you break the big toe of your right foot!" replied the Greek. "What profit did you gain from the teaching of that worthy old man who described poverty and charity as the two foremost virtues? Did he not command you to love me? Never will I make of you even a poor imitation of a Christian, I can see that. It would be easier for the sun to pierce the walls of the Mamertine prison than for truth to penetrate your thick skull."

"Never fear." said Croto, "I shall not become a Christian. I know where I stand."

"If you but knew the first thing of philosophy, you would appreciate the fact that all gold is vanity."

"Attack me with your philosophy and I will in turn give you one blow to your belly with my head. Tell me, what will be the outcome?"

"That's the kind of answer Aristotle could have gotten from a bull."

It was beginning to dawn and they now could distinguish outlines of buildings and walls. The trees along the wayside and some gravestones began to take shape. They could also distinguish people with their mules laden with vegetables hurrying towards the city. The coming day seemed to be clear with a promise of good weather. Vinitius had his eyes constantly on the slender form of Ligia up ahead.

"Sir," said Chilo, "I should offend you if I were to presume that your generosity will ever end, but now that you paid me, I do not speak in order to gain something further from you. I advise you once again, go home and get your slaves and a litter after you find out to which house Ligia enters. Do not heed this big elephant Croto who only wishes to take advantage of your generosity and squeeze your purse for more money.

"Here's my fist between your shoulders...that means that you will perish," said Croto.

"Take a swig of my Cephalonian wine...that means that nothing will happen to me!"

Vinitius did not say anything because he was amazed at the scene ahead of him. Two guards at the gate knelt down before the Apostle for his blessing. Peter placed his hand upon the iron helmets of the soldiers and then made a sign of the cross over them. It had never occurred to Vinitius that Christians could have adherents in the army also. Evidently, he thought, this new doctrine was spreading like wildfire all over the city. This astonished him greatly.

After they had passed some vacant places beyond the wall, the Christians began to disperse. Now they had to be more cautious in pursuit of Ligia and Ursus. Chilo fell to complaining more about his ailments, especially the pain in his legs and began to drop behind. Vinitius did not oppose this, knowing that the cowardly and feeble Greek would be of little use to him at the time of seizure. He would have permitted him even to depart altogether but the latter was drawn to the scene by curiosity. So, he remained several feet behind them to see what would happen.

The people surrounding Ligia dispersed. The Apostle and his group went one way and Ursus and Ligia turned toward a narrow road. About a hundred yards from this intersection, they entered a house with a shop up front which sold olives and poultry.

Chilo, who was about fifty feet from Vinitius, hurried over to him in order to take counsel. Vinitius commanded, "Chilo, go and see if there is a back entrance to this house." Chilo left and soon returned and said, "No, sir, this is the only entrance." Then, once again he tried to dissuade Vinitius but to no avail. He looked at his face and realized that the tribune would not be held back for any reason now. That look showed Chilo a face pale from emotion... the eyes burning with resolve.

Croto began to breathe harder with his massive chest heaving and moved his head from side to side. Not one flicker of worry could be detected on his face.

"I'll go in first," he said.

But Vinitius commanded, "You will follow me!"

Chilo sprang to the edge of the nearest building and watched from behind it, waiting for what would happen.

CHAPTER XXII

ONLY inside the entrance did Vinitius comprehend the difficulty of his undertaking. The house, being large and several stories high, was one of the numerous kind built in Rome, especially in the poorer side of the Tiber called the Trans-Tiber section. They were built so poorly that scarcely a year passed when one did not collapse. Bee hives they were called, with numerous chambers and little dens. Overcrowding in these houses was a constant problem. In a city where many streets had no names, houses like these had no numbers; the owners committed the collection of rent to slaves, who many times were not aware themselves how many tenants they had to collect from. To find someone in one of these houses was very difficult, especially when there was no gatekeeper.

Vinitius and Croto came upon a narrow, corridorlike passage walled in on four sides, forming a kind of entrance to the whole house. There was a fountain in the middle whose stream fell into a stone basin fixed in the ground. There were stair entrances in all directions beyond, entrances to all the different apartments above. Due to the hour, most were asleep and there was a stillness everywhere.

"What shall we do, sir?" asked Croto.

"Let's wait here. Someone may appear. We should not be seen from above." But, Vinitius momentarily reflected that Chilo's advice was prudent. With slaves guarding the only exit, the search would be easy enough. Now, if they began asking questions at the different apartments, there was a strong possibility that the Christians, who most likely were not a few in this house, may easily hide

Ligia. Vinitius was about to decide that it was better to go back for the slaves when someone entered. It was a man approaching the fountain while holding a sort of strainer in his hand. Evidently he had some vegetables which he wished to rinse. Vinitius looked at him and recognized Ursus.

"That's the Ligian," he whispered.

"Shall I break his bones now?"

"Wait!"

Ursus was not aware of their presence. They happened to be in the shadow of the entrance and he began to wash the vegetables at the fountain. It was evident that after a whole night spent in the cemetery, he was now preparing something to eat. After he finished the chore, he disappeared in one of the entrances. Croto and Vinitius followed him through the same opening. They were surprised to find that this entrance led into a sort of garden with a few cypresses and myrtle bushes and then to a small house attached to a windowless stone wall of another building.

Both understood that this was for them a favorable circumstance. In the courtyard where the fountain was, unusual sounds would doubtless bring other tenants out. This little house with its private garden made the capture quieter and easier. First they would take care of Ursus or others if they were there, then getting the girl, make their exit quickly without disturbing the neighbors. On the streets, no one would dare accost them. Vinitius would only reveal his identity to the guards and summon their help in the event of pursuit.

Ursus was about to enter the little house when he heard footsteps behind him and turned to look. Seeing two men approaching, he asked, "What do you want here?"

"You!" cried Vinitius. Then turning to Croto, ordered: "Kill him!"

Croto leaped at Ursus like a tiger and before the Ligian knew what was happening, he was in a vicelike grip.

Vinitius was so confident of the mighty strength of Croto that he didn't even wait the outcome of the struggle. He sprang to the door of the little house, pushed it open and found himself in a room which was lighted only by a fire glowing in the fireplace. This light fell on the face of Ligia. There was another person in the room, an old man who was with them at the cemetery.

Vinitius ran in so suddenly that before Ligia could recognize him, he seized her by the waist and lifting her rushed toward the door. The old man tried to bar the way, but Vinitius, holding the girl with one hand, with the other pushed him aside. The hood fell from his face and Ligia recognized him. She became white as a sheet and the voice of alarm died in her throat. She struggled but to no avail. Vinitius, holding her firmly, rushed out into the garden. As he did so, a terrible sight struck his eyes.

In his arms Ursus was holding Croto who was doubled up with a broken back. His head hung in death with blood flowing from his mouth. On seeing Vinitius carrying Ligia, Ursus struck Croto with his fist, threw him aside and sprang at Vinitius like a raging wild beast.

"Death!" was the sudden thought of the tribune. Then, as if in a dream, he heard the far-off voice of Ligia crying, "Ursus, don't kill him!" Then darkness descended on him and he knew no more.

Chilo, hidden behind the corner of the alley, awaited the outcome. His curiosity was stronger than his fear. He pondered the whole situation. If Vinitius would manage to capture the girl, he himself would fare well. Vinitius was an important person in Rome and he would doubtless help him in the future. As to Ursus, he was more at ease now knowing the great strength of Croto whom he had seen more than once victorious in the arena. If the Christians would dare to pursue the tribune, then he might come to the assistance of the tribune and say to the crowd of Christians that he, Chilo, has authority from Caesar himself and then call the guards. He still thought that the action of Vinitius was rash but considering the strength of Croto, the venture might succeed. He waited a long time and began to be alarmed at the delay.

If they don't find her hiding place right away, then there is a possibility of an uproar and alarm made by the Christians. However, he did not hear a sound up till now. The thought that Ligia might evade Vinitius once again did not disturb Chilo too much. If she was gone again, then he, Chilo, would start searching for her once more, but not without further remuneration. "Whatever happens will be to my advantage," he mused.

He suddenly held his breath; it seemed that someone was peering out of the entrance of the building. Chilo clung closer to the wall and looked again. Yes, a head peeped out and disappeared.

Then, looking more intently, he was struck dumb in amazement for what he saw turned him to stone.

In the doorway appeared Ursus with the body of Croto hanging over his shoulder. Looking around, Ursus began to run along the empty street toward the river.

Chilo made himself as flat as possible against the wall. "If he sees me, I'm lost," he thought. But Ursus ran past the corner quickly and disappeared.

Chilo, without waiting any longer and with his teeth chattering from fear, ran the other way with a speed of a much younger man, the remnants of his hair standing on end. With extreme alarm he thought: "If he turns around and sees me and catches up to me then I'm lost. Save me, O Zeus...Apollo.... Save me Hermes.... Save me God of the Christians.... I will leave Rome. I will return to Naples, but save me from the hands of that demon!"

The Ligian seemed to him at that moment a superhuman being. He might be some god who had taken on a human form. He was ready to believe in all the gods of the world and all the myths against which he usually jeered. Maybe the God of the Christians killed Croto...then what would happen to him who rose against this God?

Only when he had run past a few more alley ways and begun seeing some workers on the roads did he pause for breath. With the corner of his mantle he wiped the sweat from his forehead and murmured, "I am old and need peace."

There was more and more movement about the city. Slaves were evidently awakening and beginning to make their morning preparations. Chilo sat at the side of the road and rested; he felt a biting cold. He soon rose again and began walking home but he first made sure that the purse was still in his possession.

As he approached the river he wondered if he would see the body of Croto floating by...muttering to himself, "By the gods, if that Ligian is human he can make millions. If he polished off Croto so easily who can resist him? For every appearance in the arena he would get as much gold as he weighs. He protects this girl better than Cerberus protects Hades. May Hades swallow him up! What a man! I don't want anything to do with him. He's too strong. What shall I do? A dreadful thing happened. If he broke the back of such a strong man like Croto, then what must have happened to

Vinitius? His soul must now be hovering about that dreadful house awaiting burial. By Castor! He is a noble patrician, a friend of Caesar, and a nephew of the famous Petronius, a man well known and cherished in all Rome. Moreover, he is or was a military tribune. His death will be avenged. Should I go and notify the Praetorian guards?"

He began to ponder the question seriously. "Woe is me! Who guided Vinitius to this awful house if not I? All his slaves know about me. What will happen if they accuse me of causing his death? Even if it did come out that I did not want his death, it still will be put forth that I was the cause of it. Either way it bodes no good for me. And if I leave Rome suddenly, that too will be no good since I will be under suspicion."

One way was just as bad as another...it only remained for him to choose the lesser evil. Rome was a large city but Chilo felt that it would be too small for him. Another person could go to the Praetorian guards and tell them the whole story; then wait for developments peacefully. The authorities would then do the rest and find out everything. But, with his past and the suspicion in which he was generally held by everyone he came in contact with, he had no chance to come out of this mess blameless.

On the other hand, to flee would only confirm the opinion of Petronius that Vinitius had been betrayed and murdered through a conspiracy in which Chilo took part. Against such an influential person as Petronius, a man like Chilo had no chance no matter where he would flee. He would be found and punished severely. Would it not be better then to go to Petronius and relate the whole episode? Yes, that would be best. Petronius is a peaceful man and Chilo was sure that he, at least, would listen to him to the end. Furthermore, Petronius was aware of all that had transpired up to now with Vinitius, so he should believe him and be sure of his innocence.

First, however, it was necessary to know definitely what did happen to Vinitius. Chilo did not know. He saw Croto dead on the shoulders of Ursus and he was most likely thrown into the river but that's all he knew. Vinitius could be dead but he also could be alive...perhaps wounded. It occurred to him now that even Christians would not dare to kill such an important man as Vinitius because if they did, they would draw upon themselves severe persecution. It was then more likely that they only detained him forcibly and that he was still alive. They will hold him until Ligia could find for herself a better hiding place. That must be it.

Chilo felt much better. Now, if that Ligian beast did not tear him apart first then he, Vinitius, must be alive. And, if he is alive then he himself will testify that I did not betray him. In such a case, not only does nothing threaten me (O Hermes, count on two heifers again!), but there will be need of my talents in finding her new hiding place. I sought Ligia, now I will seek Vinitius and then I will seek Ligia again, but I have to know whether he is dead or alive.

It occurred to him that he could go to the baker Demas in the evening and ask about Ursus. But he rejected this idea at once. He had no desire to have anything to do with Ursus. If Ursus did not kill Glaucus, then evidently he had been dissuaded by some of the elders to whom he must have spoken of his intention regarding Glaucus. The mere thought of Ursus brought a shiver to his entire body. He might go to Euricius and from him try to find out what had transpired in the house where Ligia and Ursus lived. Meanwhile, he would return home, take a warm bath and rest. The events of the night had wearied him tremendously.

One thing gave him comfort, however, and that was the possession of the two purses which he received from Vinitius...one at his house...and the other just recently. Due to this sudden windfall, he decided to eat more sumptuously and drink a better wine than usual.

When the wine shops opened up, he indulged in his good fortune to the extent that he forgot food and a good warm bath. So that finally with weary and uncertain steps he managed to get home and immediately fell asleep.

He awoke in the evening, or rather he was awakened by the slave which he bought recently announcing to him that someone waited for him on the outside regarding some important business.

Chilo became wary immediately. He dressed and peered out to see who it could be. He almost had heart failure when his eyes rested on the huge form of Ursus waiting for him outside. He was unable at first to say a word. Finally he blurted out, "Syra, I am not in. Tell him that you did not find me home!"

"But, sir, I have already told him that you were sleeping. He wanted me to wake you up right away."

"Oh gods, I'll have you..."

But Ursus, entering inside, interrupted him and asked him, "Are you Chilo Chilonides?"

"Peace be with you! Peace be with you! Peace...Peace...I don't seem to know you. Who are you?"

"Chilo Chilonides," answered Ursus, "your master Vinitius summons you to him right away. I will take you to him."

CHAPTER XXIII

AS Vinitius regained consciousness, he felt an excrutiating pain. At first he could not figure out where he was and what was happening to him. He sensed a roaring noise in his head and his eyes were covered as if with mist. Gradually however full consciousness returned and when his eyes cleared, he noticed three people bent down over him. He recognized two of them. One was Ursus, the other was the old man whom he hurled aside when he picked up Ligia and was fleeing with her. The third person was unknown to him. This man held his broken left arm and was attending to it. Vinitius first thought that he was being tortured. Through clenched teeth he moaned, "Kill me outright. Don't torture me!"

The three men paid no attention to his words. The old man spoke to the one holding the arm of Vinitius, "Glaucus, are you certain that his head wound is not serious?"

"That's right, Crispus. I attended to many a wound in my time in Naples and elsewhere and I'm sure it is not serious. When Ursus hurled him against the wall of the house he was lucky to have put his hand in front of him and thereby saved himself."

Crispus spoke again, "I know that you have taken care of many a brother and you are well known as a good doctor. That is why I sent for you now."

"Ursus, who summoned me, revealed that only yesterday he was willing to kill me.

"Yes, I was aware of that because he first told me about it and I put his mind at ease and assured him that we Christians have no cause to fear you. You certainly are no traitor to us Christians here

in Rome. You are even an elder in our Roman Christian community."

Ursus spoke up sadly, "It must have been an evil man who
incited me against you, Glaucus."

"Well, thank God that it is past. Now we must consider this
young wounded man here. Saying this, he began to manipulate the
arm in order to set it right. The pain was so great that Vinitius
fainted. After bringing him to, Glaucus finished the job on the arm
with the necessary splints. When the work was completed, Ligia
appeared and Vinitius raised his eyes toward her.

She stood at his cot holding a basin of water in her hands.
Glaucus took a sponge and moistened the head of the patient.

Vinitius kept looking at Ligia and could not believe his eyes. All
this seemed a dream to him. Only after a while he whispered,
"Ligia."

The basin trembled in her hands; she turned her eyes toward
him full of sadness. "Peace be with you," she said in a low voice.

She stood there, her face full of pity and sorrow. He kept looking
at her beautiful dark hair and her figure which was covered with
the dress of a peasant girl. His gaze was so intent that she began to
color under his close scrutiny. He now saw that it was on account
of him that she was forced to hide and to dress thus and live in
poverty. He wanted to adorn her with riches and now he felt so
sorry that he was the one who forced this condition on her. If he
were only able to stand up, he would eagerly have fallen at her feet
to beg her forgiveness.

"Ligia, you did not allow me to be killed!"

She answered with her usual sweetness, "May God make you
well soon."

Her words were as balm to him. Knowing how much harm he
caused her, she was still willing to wish him well. A great feeling of
tenderness for this girl engulfed him, so much so that he felt
weaker still. Yes, he felt weak but at the same time happy that he
could once again gaze upon this lovely girl whom he loved so
much. She was now more than ever a goddess to him.

Meanwhile Glaucus finished his work on the arm and began
attending the wound on the head. This did not take long and he
soon finished. He told Ursus to give the patient some water.

Vinitius drank greedily, a fever having made him very thirsty. The pain in his arm and in his head was gradually diminishing.

"Give me another drink." he asked Ursus.

Ligia left the room with the empty basin. Crispus, after whispering something with Glaucus, approached the cot and spoke up, "God did not allow you to commit an evil deed. He permitted you to live in order that you may change your designs toward this poor girl and stop persecuting her. You are now defenseless and in our power but Christ teaches us to forgive and to love our enemies. We have dressed your wounds and as Ligia said we will ask God to return you to health. Remember the kindness we have shown you. May it prevent you from persecuting her. It is necessary for us all to leave this place; our safety demands this."

"Do you wish to leave me like this?"

"We wish to leave this house. Persecution from the prefect of police will no doubt reach us here if we stay. It is not our fault but the anger of the law will fall upon us."

"You will not be persecuted...I will protect you."

Crispus did not want to tell him to his face that it was not only a matter of persecution from the police but also the fear that Vinitius would continue to pursue Ligia and that they did not have any confidence in him even if he promised not to do so.

"Sir, your right arm is well. Take this tablet and stylus; write to your servants to bring a litter in the evening and take you to your home where you will receive greater care and you will be more comfortable. We dwell here in poverty as you see. The old widow who lives here with her son will soon return. Her son can take your message. Now we must get ready to leave you and find another place for the girl."

Vinitius grew pale. He understood by these words that they wanted to separate him from Ligia again. He felt that if he lost her now, he may never find her again. He was aware that many things had come between him and her due mainly to what he knew about her now and about her religion. He needed time to think. He needed time to talk over different things with her. He understood that if he promised these people that he would no longer harm her, and that they should take her back to Pomponia, they would not believe him. He supposed that they were right in believing so. No...no promises of his would be believed. He, being a believer of the Roman gods, could swear by these gods but that kind of swearing would do him no good in their eyes, he knew.

He desperately wanted to converse with Ligia, to convince her somehow that he would change toward her...that he would no longer persecute her. This he meant from his heart but he needed time for all this. For him it was of utmost importance that he see her every day to talk to her. This was, he felt, the only way for him to retain his sanity. Just as a drowning man is saved by a plank or an oar, so too he must have her near him or else he did not know what would happen to him. Hence, collecting these thoughts, he spoke to Crispus, Glaucus and Ursus.

"Hear me out, Christians. Last night I was present at Ostrianum and heard the teaching of your religion from the lips of your Apostle Peter. Although I do not understand it, I am sure of one thing: You Christians are good and honest people. Your good deeds have convinced me of this. Tell the widow who lives here with her son to remain...you also remain. No harm will come to any of you. You who are a doctor know very well in what condition I am. You know that I cannot be moved this day nor for some days to come. You know this. I am sick...I have a fever and my arm is broken and cannot be moved. Therefore I declare to you all that I will not leave. I will not leave this house unless you yourselves will throw me out by force."

Here he stopped and paused for a while because he was still very weak. Crispus however answered him, "No one is going to use force against you. We only wish to save our necks."

"Let me get my breath," said Vinitius irritably, not being used to any contradiction of his will. After a short pause he spoke again, "There will be no inquiry from the police as to Croto's where-abouts. He was to leave for Beneventum today. People will believe that he has left for that city. When we entered this house, no one saw us except a certain Greek who was with us at Ostrianum. I'll tell you where he lives and you can summon him here. I will then order him to keep silence for he is in my employ. I will write a note that I have gone to Beneventum and this note you can take over to my house so that they will believe that I am not here. If that Greek has already notified the authorities, I'll tell them that I myself killed Croto who caused my arm to be broken. This all I will do and I will swear it on the shade of my father and mother. You may all remain here and no harm will come to you, I promise you."

"Well then," said Crispus, "in that case Glaucus can remain; he and the widow can take care of you."

Vinitius frowned at these words. "Listen to me old man. I owe you gratitude for what you have done, and you seem to me an honorable man but you're not saying what is in your heart. You are afraid that I will summon my slaves to this house and take Ligia by force, is that not true?"

"Yes, that is so."

"Then consider this: I will speak to Chilo the Greek in front of you and also you will see me writing the note telling my people of my departure to Beneventum. I will not be able to send anyone else from here or give word in any way. That should be clear to you all. Think about it, old man, and don't irritate me." Here, he frowned. Obviously he suffered not only physically but with inner turmoil. He resumed speaking. "Do you think that I will deny the fact that I want her near me? But, as I said before, I will no longer attempt to take her by force and this you will have to believe. And I promise you something else. If she leaves me now, then I will tear off these bandages. I will not eat nor drink. My death will fall on you and on your brethren. It would have been better if you had killed me!"

He paused, his face pale from anger and weakness. Ligia, who had heard all this from the other room and was certain that he would act thus, now entered fearfully. She did not want to be the cause of his death for anything. She only felt pity for him now that he was hurt and bedridden. From the time of her escape she mingled with religious people. She was absorbed with the life of sacrifice and charity towards others. She led a very severe life for that reason and she was convinced that Christ Himself wanted her to make all kinds of sacrifices for His sake. It was the life of many such maidens which caused the change in the soul of humanity for years to come. However, she often thought of Vinitius. He was too much in her life to be oblivious to him. Many a time she prayed for him; she prayed that a time would come when she would repay him good for the evil that he caused her. Now the time had come. Her prayers were answered.

She approached Crispus and with a face uplifted in charitable resolve, she spoke to him as if inspired, "Crispus, let him remain with us until the time when Christ will heal him."

The old presbyter, always looking for religious direction and seeing her exalted countenance, thought that it must be Christ speaking through her. Fearful of going contrary to Christ's wishes, he nodded his head.

"Let it be then as you wish." he said.

This sudden obedience to the words of Ligia by the old man made such an impression on Vinitius that he could only stare at her in bewilderment. It seemed to him that these Christians looked upon Ligia as a kind of priestess to be revered and obeyed. He too felt a certain reverence for her. He was sure that henceforth he would not be able to treat her as before. Now, he was the one dependent on her, not vice-versa. He felt like a defenseless child in her care. But, he was entirely happy that it was so, and was eager for it to continue in such a way forever.

He wanted to thank her, but to thank her in a way unusual for him and strange too because he wanted to show her his humility. That was why he could not utter a word right away; his eyes only followed her every move. His eyes lit up because she consented to stay near him. His one fear was that he might lose these precious moments. He was so touched by her goodness and his own happiness that when, after a while, she undertook to give him some water to drink, he wanted at first to kiss her hand in thanks but he was afraid to do so because he might spoil everything. Yes, he Vinitius, who not long ago at Caesar's feast forcibly kissed her lips, was now afraid to do or say anything that would cause her discomfort of any kind. He, who promised himself that if he found her he would pull her hair and flog her at will, now did not know what to say for fear that an imprudent or thoughtless word would take her away from him.

CHAPTER XXIV

VINITIUS did not wish to mar the joy that he now felt. Therefore he was a bit apprehensive about well meant but unwanted help from outside. Momentarily he reflected that if in truth such help would be forthcoming, could he not then take Ligia by force? However he immediately rejected this kind of thinking. He was always a willful man and he had done many things in his life for which he was later sorry. However, this act, if he were to commit it, would be so low and base that he could not lower himself to that level. He was capable in the past of acting harshly, especially in anger, but now being sick and perplexed by inner turmoil, he definitely was not willing to repay Ligia in a way befitting a Nero or a Tigellinus. His military upbringing made him sense that justice would be muddied if he were to stoop that low.

He was also amazed to know that once Ligia stood by him in his desire to remain in the house, the others did not demand further proof of security for themselves against persecution by him. After the unusual happening in Ostrianum everything seemed so strange to him. This mixed up his whole thinking. However, sobering up a little in his thinking, he felt it necessary to get in touch with Chilo and so once again he persisted in asking them to summon Chilo to him. He reassured them once more that everything that he would say and do would be done and said in their presence so that they need not fear any treachery.

Crispus and the others finally agreed to this and decided to send Ursus to summon Chilo. Vinitius informed Ursus where the Greek lived and writing a few words on the tablet turned to Crispus and

183

said, "I'm writing this because this man has a very suspicious nature and is crafty in the bargain. Many times when I called for him by my slaves, they were told by his servant that he wasn't home. He did this whenever he had no news for me and did not wish to contend with my possible anger against him."

Ursus replied, "Once I find him, he will come with me whether he likes it or not." After saying this he left hurriedly.

It wasn't easy to locate someone in Rome even having the best of directions. Ursus however possessed that certain sense which comes naturally to some people, a certain hunting instinct by which they come upon their prey without too much difficulty. Thus it was with Ursus. It did not take him long to find out the residence of Chilo.

He did not recognize him though. Previously he had seen Chilo only once and that was at night by the mill. Furthermore, looking at this haggard and fearful man before him, he did not in the least associate him with the forceful and important looking personage who talked with him at the mill and who convinced him to kill Glaucus.

After the first moment of mortal fear, Chilo realized that he was not recognized by this giant and began breathing again. The note written to him by Vinitius calmed him still further. In it he could not find any indication of his guilt against Ligia and the Christians. He was now convinced that the only reason that the Christians spared Vinitius was because of his importance and influence as a high Roman official and dignitary.

"So now Vinitius will protect me too," he mumbled to himself, "for surely I am not being summoned just to be killed."

Breathing a huge sigh of relief, he spoke to Ursus, "My friend, did not my good and worthy friend Vinitius send a litter for me? My legs hurt me and it is such a long way to go."

"No, we will go on foot."

"And if I refuse to go?"

"Don't do that! You must go!"

"I'll go...I'll go. I assure you and most willingly. But I want you to know that I am a good friend of the prefect of the police and no one can force me to go against my will. I'm also a philosopher and a sage which give me other means at my disposal, so think of that too. However I will go willingly as I have said. Only permit me to put on a warm mantle with a hood. It is a cool day and I have a slight cold. He proceeded to put on the heavy mantle which he wore the night before. He hid his face as much as possible with the hood so that on the way, perhaps with better light, Ursus would not be able to recognize him.

"Where are you taking me?" he asked when they were on the way.

"To the Trans-Tiber section."

"I have come to Rome rather recently, therefore I am not acquainted with that part of the city. I'm sure however that many good and honest people live there."

To the simple soul of Ursus, these words were indeed strange. He himself heard Vinitius say that Chilo accompanied him to the cemetery and then saw him entering the house of the widow. He paused a moment and faced Chilo.

"Do not lie, old man. This past night you have been there."

"Oh," Chilo put in hurriedly. "Did you say Trans-Tiber? I was unaware what that section was called. Yes, my good man, I was indeed there, but do you know why? Only because I wished to dissuade Vinitius from such a mad venture. I was also present at Ostrianum because for some time I have been instructing Vinitius in order to convert him to Christianity. I therefore wanted him to hear the holy words of the Apostle himself. May the true light begin to shine in his soul and in yours too. You are a Christian are you not?"

"Yes," answered Ursus in a humble tone.

Chilo was more sure of himself now. "My good friend is a powerful man in Rome and a close companion of Nero himself. If but a hair of his head is disturbed, Caesar will seek revenge."

"A greater power than Caesar's protects us."

"Sure, but what do you intend to do with Vinitius?"

"I do not know," answered Ursus. "Christ has commanded mercy and forgiveness!"

"That's exactly right! Remember that always...mercy and forgiveness! Otherwise you will burn in hell like a blood sausage on a skillet."

Ursus began to sigh sadly. Chilo was now sure that with this simple giant he could do whatever he wished. Wanting to know more about what had happened the previous night he asked, "What did you do with Croto? Tell me the truth now!"

"Vinitius will tell you all about it."

"That means that you have knifed him to death."

"No. I was totally unarmed."

The Greek could hardly believe this. Such strength was indeed phenomenal.

"May Pluto, that is to say, may Christ forgive you!"

They walked silently for a while; then Chilo resumed speaking. "I won't give you away to the Praetorian guards."

"I fear Christ, not the guards!" answered Ursus firmly.

"And rightly so...rightly so...but I will have to pray for you very hard and I'm not sure whether my prayers will be heard. There is nothing more serious than murder! Unless you give me your solemn promise that you will never, never kill again in the future."

"I did not want to kill him. It had to be done and I did it unwillingly."

Chilo wanted to protect himself against the future anger of the giant and kept on insisting that he make a vow not to kill in the future. He also wanted to know more about Vinitius but Ursus was reluctant to discuss the matter with him and answered only in monosyllables.

They finally arrived at their destination. Chilo, upon seeing the house and remembering the awful things which happened there the night before, blanched with fear. He imagined all sorts of things. He was sure that Ursus was looking at him in a strange way.

"It is a small consolation to me," he mumbled to himself, "if this giant kills me unwillingly or not. May paralysis take hold of him and all the Ligians to boot. Grant this, O great Zeus, if you can."

Wrapping himself closer in his spacious mantle and making sure the hood was up, he kept complaining to Ursus that he was cold. The worst moment for him came when they had to pass the murky entrance. He breathed a sigh of relief when finally they stood at the door of the little house inside.

He still was apprehensive, not knowing what would happen to him. He suddenly heard voices singing from within. He turned to Ursus and asked, "What is that?"

"You say you are a Christian and don't recognize that? We

Christians sing to honor Christ. Miriam is back evidently and perhaps brought back the Apostle with her."

"Take me immediately to Vinitius."

"He is in the same room with the others. It is a large room where all of us usually congregate."

They entered. It was quite dark inside; only the flame of a few candles lit up the interior. Chilo approached the cot upon which Vinitius lay and spoke to him in mournful tones, "Oh, sir, why did you not heed my advice?"

"Be quiet and listen," Vinitius ordered as he looked upon Chilo to make sure that the Greek paid attention to what he was about to tell him.

"Croto hurled himself upon me in order to kill me and rob me. Understand? I managed to kill him with my *sica* (dagger). He wounded me though and these people are taking care of me and my wounds."

Chilo immediately understood the words of Vinitius. If he wanted to speak thus with him then it was obvious that he made some agreement with the Christians. Being crafty himself, he did not pause to inquire further but agreed with Vinitius in his own thoughts.

"Sir, that Croto was a complete rascal! Did I not warn you against him? All my teaching bounced from him as from a wall. Now that he made an attempt on your life, death is a welcome kindness to him. How could he do such a thing to his benefactor? This shows clearly what a scoundrel he was. Oh gods!"

Vinitius spoke again. "Were it not for my knife which I had with me, he would have killed me."

"Blessed be the moment, sir, when I advised you to take even your knife."

Vinitius now looked upon him inquiringly, "What did you do today?"

"Now sir, did I not assure you that I would pray for your health?"

"And nothing else?"

"I was getting ready to come to see you when this good man came for me."

"Here is a tablet," said Vinitius. "You will go with it to my house and tell my freedman that I have left for Beneventum, giving this tablet to him. Tell him that I was suddenly summoned by Petronius so that I had no time to make preparations for the trip." Now he spoke with greater emphasis. "I have left for Beneventum, do you understand?"

"Yes, sir, I understand perfectly. Did I not bid you goodbye at the Capenan gate? From the moment of your parting my heart was so sad that if your generosity does not console me, I shall fall apart in sad tears and wailing just as the wife of Zethos did at their parting."

Vinitius, although sick and used to the Greek's craftiness, had to smile at the quickness of the latter's grasping the situation correctly. He added, "I will then give you something to allay your tears. Give me the tablet."

Chilo, completely sure of himself now, undid his hood and approached unafraid. As he did so the light fell on his face. Glaucus immediately rushed toward him and took his arms in a firm grip and cried, "Don't you recognize me, Cephas?" and there was something terrifying in his voice.

Chilo looked up at him and in one moment was stricken with fear. "I'm not he...not he...have pity...have pity." And he fell on his knees in mortal fear.

Glaucus turned to the others and said mournfully, "This is the man who after wounding me severely sold my family into slavery and left me to die in the inn on the way from Naples to Rome."

His story was well known by all the brethren in Rome. All were aghast at this scene. The man who caused this tragedy to befall Glaucus was now before them in this house. Ursus, who now took a better look at Chilo, suddenly recognized him as the man who came to him by the mill.

"He is the same man who wanted me to kill Glaucus!"

"Mercy...Mercy..." moaned Chilo. Turning to Vinitius he cried, "I put all my faith in you, sir. Tell them to have mercy on me. Sir, please."

Vinitius, now knowing what tragedy Chilo caused, had not a shred of pity for him. His heart knew no pity and as a soldier he himself would ask vengeance against such a crime as Chilo committed. He now spoke up, "Kill him and bury his carcass in your gardens. Someone else will take my message to my house."

To Chilo these words were as a seal of doom. He began to shake with mortal fear. He imagined his bones being crushed in the arms of Ursus.

"On your God, mercy! I am a Christian.... have pity on me! I was christened and if you don't believe me christen me once more. Glaucus, that was all a great mistake. Do not kill me. Have pity!"

His voice tapered off in agony of fear and alarm. Then at the table stood up Peter the Apostle. Silence reigned for a brief moment. Then Peter spoke, "The Master Himself has said, 'If your brother has sinned against you, warn him and forgive him. If he sinned against you even seven times seven, which means innumerable times, forgive him also. Never stop forgiving. Our mercy then must be endless, must be everlasting just as His love and mercy for us all is endless and everlasting.'"

A great silence followed. Glaucus stood for a long time, his hands covering his eyes, tears falling from his face. Finally, with a face completely resigned to the will of God, sad countenanced beyond compare, he turned to Chilo and said, "Cephas, may God forgive you as I forgive you."

Ursus, after embracing Glaucus, spoke up, turning to Chilo, "May God forgive you as I also forgive you."

Chilo, crouching on the floor and turning his head from side to side could not comprehend fully what was happening and expected to be killed at any moment. He definitely did not expect to be forgiven by Glaucus. The meaning of his words and the words of Ursus finally penetrated his brain and he looked about wildly.

"Go in peace," the Apostle told him.

Chilo stood up. He was still unable to utter a sound. He slowly sidled up to the cot where Vinitius lay as if still seeking protection from him. He did not then fully realize the meaning of the tribune's rejection of him. That thought came to him later. He was now beginning to realize that he was forgiven by Glaucus and Ursus and he wanted to flee this house immediately. Reaching the cot he entreated Vinitius eagerly and fearfully, "Give me the tablet, sir, give me the tablet." And, grasping the tablet, he made a hurried bow, first to Vinitius then more hurriedly to the rest of the people in the room, and left the house as quickly as he was able.

In the garden he paused, partly because it was dark there but mostly with a fearful thought that surely Ursus would follow him here and kill him. He would have run like mad from that spot but suddenly his legs turned to stone because Ursus indeed appeared at his side. Chilo could only moan the words, "For the love of your God, have mercy on me!"

Ursus spoke quietly, "Do not be afraid. The Apostle told me to lead you out of here. Also, if you wish, I will even go with you to your home."

"What are you saying? What? You are not going to kill me?"

"No, I will not kill you...and if I grabbed you extra hard, please forgive me."

"Help me to get up, please. You won't kill me? Then help me only to the street. I will manage on my own from there."

Ursus helped him up as if he were merely a feather and placed him on his feet. Then he went with him through the narrow corridor until they got to the door which led outside.

"I will go on by myself," said Chilo trembling.

"May peace be with you."

"And with you too...and with you."

After Ursus left him, he breathed a great sigh and began walking slowly, turning his head from one side to the other, still not understanding everything that had transpired. After a few paces, he paused and asked himself, "Why didn't they kill me?"

He still did not understand even though he was with the Christians on many occasions, and even after hearing the Apostle's sermon on love and forgiveness. He kept repeating the question, "Why didn't they kill me?"

CHAPTER XXV

VINITIUS too could not fully understand what had transpired and was just as mystified by the events as was Chilo. He ascribed the reason for their treatment of him in such a manner partly to Ligia, partly to the beliefs of their religion and also partly to the fact that he was well known and honored as a dignitary in Rome. But their treatment of Chilo was to him completely baffling. Their readiness to forgive Chilo and his crimes was unheard of to his way of thinking. Why did they not kill him? This question had no answer for him. They could have done so without fear of incrimination from anybody. All they had to do was to bury him in the garden or throw him into the river. There were so many bodies recovered from the Tiber every morning that no one would even try to identify him. For all that Chilo had done, they had a perfect right to kill him. Even in the arena, mercy was granted to certain gladiators or even to enemy hostages such as Caractacus, king of the Britons, who was taken by the late Claudius and who still lived in the city and fared quite well too. Vengeance for personal wrongs however was proper and justified to his way of thinking. True, he had heard in Ostrianum that mercy should be shown even to enemies but he thought that this was merely a theory which is impossible to put in practice. Perhaps it was some kind of holy day of their religion at which time they did not dare to kill anyone. He heard that there were certain customs among different nations which prohibited them even from going to war at certain times of the year. If that were so, then why did they not give Chilo up to the authorities for punishment later? The Apostle indeed spoke of forgiveness; he said to forgive one another not only seven times but seventy times seven times, which means always. Glaucus forgave Chilo and this was hard for him to understand.

Chilo had done the most terrible wrong that one man can do to another. At the very thought of how he would act against a man who would kill Ligia, for instance, he knew that there would not be enough punishment for such a man at his hands. But Glaucus had forgiven...and Ursus also.... Ursus could kill any one in Rome with impunity, being as strong as he was. All he had to do was to kill the reigning wrestling champion and thus take his place to reign as king himself without fear of anyone. Who on earth can best the man who was able to kill Croto with bare hands.

To all these questions there could be perhaps one answer. They acted thus because they possessed a certain goodness...a goodness so great that no other was equal to it. This love of neighbor was something new. An unbounded love of man which commands one to forget one's own self, one's wrongs, one's happiness and misfortune and live for others. As to a reward for this kind of life, Vinitius heard of it at Ostrianum, an eternal reward in some kind of heaven. To him this was something unheard of: to renounce material goods, to give up delight and choose poverty, all this was to him utter madness, a life filled with wretchedness.

"This kind of life is for the weaklings, not for the strong of earth," he thought. "They are like sheep ready to be eaten by wolves." To his Roman nature all this was abhorrent. Weakness had no part in his nature.

However there was something that struck him as very strange. It was the look of peace and joy upon the faces of these Christians after the departure of Chilo. The Apostle placed his hands on the head of Glaucus and said, "In you Christ has triumphed."

Hearing these words, Glaucus raised his eyes which shone as if in joyous light, as if a certain kind of happiness had been poured into him. Vinitius, who could understand the joy and delight born of vengeance, looked at him with astonishment thinking him mad. To his surprise he watched as Ligia approached the grizzled old man and kissed his hand. A queen kissing the hand of a peasant! The earth indeed had turned upside down! Next Ursus related how he conducted Chilo to the street and had asked forgiveness for any harm done him and was even willing to accompany him to his home. The Apostle blessed him also. Crispus then declared that this day was indeed a day of victory. What kind of victory? For the life of him, Vinitius could not understand.

When Ligia came up to him with a drinking vessel, he held her hand for a moment and asked, "Then you have also forgiven me?"

"We are Christians; we cannot keep anger in our hearts."

"Ligia, whoever your God is, I honor Him only because He is yours."

"You will also honor Him in your heart when you come to love Him."

"Only because He is yours," repeated Vinitius in a fainter voice. He closed his eyes from emotion and weakness.

Ligia left but soon returned and bent over him to see if he were sleeping. Vinitius, sensing that she was near, opened his eyes and smiled. She placed a hand over them lightly as if to incline him to slumber. A great sweetness seized him then. He was ill with fever and complete weakness engulfed him. Night came and his fever increased. He could not sleep. He followed Ligia with his eyes wherever she went.

At times, he fell into a kind of doze in which he saw and heard everything around him mingled with feverish dreams. It seemed to him that in some old deserted cemetery stood a temple in the form of a tower in which Ligia was priestess. He saw her on the top of this tower with a lute in her hands...all in light like those priestesses who come out at night to honor the moon with hymns and whom he had seen in the East. He began to climb this tower but with great effort. He wanted to reach Ligia and take her away from there. Behind him, Chilo followed with his teeth chattering from fear and repeating the words, "Do not do this, sir; she is a priestess for whom He will take vengeance." Vinitius did not know who this He was, but he felt that he was about to commit a great sacrilege and he became greatly alarmed. When he reached the top, the Apostle Peter stood suddenly in front of Ligia and said. "Do not dare! She belongs to me!" Then the Apostle took her away with him by a path filled with rays of light caused by the moon and disappeared. Vinitius stretched out his hands toward them to take him along also but there was no answer.

He woke up suddenly and looked about the room. The lamp still shone with light but a little dimmer. All were seated by the fire warming themselves for the night was cold and the room rather chilly. In the midst of them Vinitius recognized the Apostle Peter, Ligia, Glaucus, Crispus, Miriam the widow and her son Nazarius; Ursus too was there. All were listening intently to the words of the Apostle. Vinitius looked at Peter with superstitious awe, something akin to the fear and awe that he experienced in his dream. Perhaps this man had some kind of magic with which he drew people to him. He tried to hear what was being said by him, thinking surely that he was speaking of him and warning Ligia against him. But he was mistaken altogether. The Apostle was talking about Christ again.

"They only live with the name of Christ on their tongues," he thought.

Peter was relating to them the events of that night of suffering which Christ endured. "A company of soldiers came to seize Him that night. When the Savior asked whom they were seeking, they answered, 'Jesus of Nazareth.' But when He told them, 'I am He,' they all fell to the ground and dared not to raise a hand against Him. Only after the second inquiry did the Master allow Himself to be seized."

"The night was cold," Peter continued, "but my heart was aflame with anger. I drew the sword and cut the ear of the servant of the high priest. I would have defended Him more than my own life but He forbade further use of the sword, telling me, 'Put up your sword. Shall I not drink the cup which the Father has prepared for Me?' Then they seized and bound Him."

When he had spoken thus far, Peter placed his palm on his forehead and was silent. Ursus, unable to restrain himself, sprang to his feet, trimmed the light so it shone brighter, sat down nervously and muttered out loud: "No matter what they would do to me...if only I were there." He stopped suddenly because Ligia put her finger to her lips for silence. But his face spoke louder than words. Had he been there how eagerly would he have given up his life in defense of the Savior. He would have been a match for all those soldiers and the officials too. Tears came to his eyes at the thought of this and because of his sorrow and mental grief. He should have summoned others to help him defend his divine Master...the mighty Ligians would heed his call. He paused in a flurry of emotion asking himself if the Redeemer would want that…and tears came to his eyes.

After a while Peter resumed the narrative. Vinitius however did not hear him; he had another dream. This time he saw an immense body of water and on the water a boat. In the boat were Peter and Ligia. He began to swim toward this boat but the pain in his broken arm thwarted his efforts to swim. The wind hurled waves all around him and he began to sink. He called out for help. He saw Ligia kneeling before the Apostle begging him to rescue Vinitius. The Apostle then turned the boat toward him, stretched out an oar toward him and helped him to get inside the boat.

His dream continued. It seemed to him that he now saw a multitude of people rowing after them. But the waves soon engulfed many of them; others were in the water yelling for help. Peter, with a huge fisherman's net began to reach out and save them one by one and pulled them into the boat which mysteriously grew larger and larger. Vinitius wondered how they all could fit in the boat but more and more were pulled in and still there was room. Ligia took him by the arm and showed him a magnificent light on the distant shore towards which they were sailing. This dream blended in with what he had heard in Ostrianum from the lips of Peter about Christ appearing miraculously to the Apostles on the lake. As they approached the lighted shore, the weather grew calmer by degrees. The huge crowd in the boat began singing joyfully; there appeared a rainbow overhead. At last the boat reached the shore. Ligia then took his arm and said, "Come, I will lead you." And she led him onward into the beautiful light.

Vinitius woke again fitfully and soon dozed off once more. The feverish dream persisted. This time it seemed to him that he was still on the lake in the boat surrounded by crowds. He began eagerly to look for Petronius and was astonished that Petronius was nowhere to be found. He woke up again. Now he was able to distinguish Ligia sitting by his bedside. This stirred him profoundly and brought him to full consciousness. Everyone else had departed; she alone was at his side. She was sitting with her eyes closed, evidently very weary after the past events of the night at Ostrianum and the whole day, and now the coming evening. Through all this she had no opportunity for sleep. Vinitius looked at her profile, at her long lashes, at her hands lying peacefully on her knees. Now, he realized that there was another beauty which he did not know of which is pure and clean and which is much more beautiful than all the Greek and Roman beauties made by hand.

Watching her now at his bedside, he was certain that she was taking care of him due to her faith; had he not persecuted her, caused her worry and anguish? Yet he wished that the reason for her vigil here was because she truly loved him, his face, his eyes and everything about him. There were other women who loved him for those reasons. He felt however that if she were like the other women, something would be lacking. This was a strange feeling and yet it was true, he felt. He was awakening more and more to feelings which astonished him. As he gazed upon her, she opened her eyes and seeing him awake and looking at her, said quietly, "I am with you."

"I saw your soul in my dream," he replied.

CHAPTER XXVI

NEXT morning when he awakened, he was still very weak but the fever was gone. Ligia was not present. Ursus, bending by the fireplace, was raking up ashes and seeking live coals beneath them. Soon he began to blow at the live coals with a sound like the bellows of a blacksmith. Vinitius, recalling that this man crushed Croto the day before, looked with amazement upon his huge back which resembled the back of a Cyclops and his limbs, strong as columns.

"Mercury be thanked that he did not break my neck," he thought. "By Pollux! If all the Ligian men are like this one, the Danubian legions will have hard work with them."

Aloud he said, "Hey, slave!"

Ursus drew his head from the fireplace and smiled at him in a manner which was almost friendly and answered, "God give you a good day and good health but I am not a slave. I am a free man."

This information came as a pleasant surprise to Vinitius who wanted to converse with him about Ligia and it was much more convenient to do so with a free man rather than with a slave. His patrician pride still considered slaves as merely base creatures. Therefore, he was glad to know that Ursus was free.

"Did you not belong to Aulus Plautius?"

"No, sir. I serve Callina just as I served her mother but I do so of my own free will." Here, he turned again to the coals in the fireplace. Soon he had a good fire going. He rose and said, "With us there are no slaves."

"Where is Ligia?"

"She just departed a moment ago. She watched over you the whole night."

"Why didn't you relieve her?"

"Because she wished to do so and it is for me to obey her wishes." Here, his eyes darkened, and he added, "You would not be alive right now if it had not been for her."

"Are you sorry that you did not kill me?"

"No, sir, Christ commands us not to kill."

"What about Atacinus and Croto?"

"I could not do otherwise," muttered Ursus. He looked at his hands somewhat ruefully as if to say that while he was a Christian, his hands are still pagan.

"All this is your fault, sir. Why did you raise your hand against her, a king's daughter?"

Anger momentarily flushed the face of Vinitius. A peasant and a barbarian dared to speak to him thusly and even blame him for all that happened. Being weak however and alone and sick on his cot, he felt helpless, so he restrained his anger. He did so for another reason too. He wanted to learn more details about Ligia from him so he forced himself to be calm.

He then proceeded to ask Ursus about his people, the Ligians. Ursus told him what he knew. It was for the most part what Vinitius himself had heard previously from Aulus Plautius. After the wars of the Ligians, some hostages were brought over to Rome among which was the queen herself, Ligia's mother. It wasn't long after when she died in captivity and Ligia was given to Pomponius who in turn placed her in the care of his daughter Pomponia Graecina. Vinitius who knew most of the story was always happy to hear about the royal ancestry of Ligia. As a king's daughter she could very well occupy a position at Caesar's court equal to the daughters of Rome's first families.

Ursus ended with the following: "We used to live in the forests where the trees were plentiful and large. Our enemies did not dare to make war on us; only sometimes when the wind blew toward us, they used to burn our forests, but they were afraid to attack us openly. No, sir! we did not fear any of them, not even the Roman Caesar."

"The gods gave Rome dominion over the earth," said Vinitius severely.

"The gods are evil spirits," replied Ursus without guile, "and where there are no Romans, there is no supremacy." Here he fixed the fire again and spoke as if to himself, "When Callina was taken to Caesar's palace, I was afraid that harm would befall her. Immediately I wanted to go to the Ligians, gather them together and come to her rescue. The Ligians would have come. They are a good people although still pagan. Even now, if ever Callina returns to Pomponia, I will seek her permission to go to them. Christ was born far away and they are till now ignorant of Christ and His teaching. He knew best where to be born but if He had come into the world among us in the forests, we would not have tortured him, put Him to death. That is certain. We would have taken care of the Child and guarded Him well. Never would He have lacked for game, mushrooms, beaver skins or amber. He would have lived in comfort among us."

Thus speaking, he placed a bowl of food prepared for Vinitius close to the fire in order to warm it. His thoughts evidently still wandered among the wild forests of his home. The food was soon warm enough for eating and taking it over to Vinitius, he said to him, "Glaucus advises you to move even your good arm as little as possible so Callina commanded me to give you food."

Ligia commanded! There was no denying her wishes. To Vinitius, to go contrary to her wishes would be like performing some sacrilegious act. Therefore, he uttered no word and permitted Ursus to spoonfeed him. However his hands were so large that this chore was done rather clumsily. He tried so hard though that Vinitius had to smile at his efforts. This brought on a comment by Ursus, "It's easier for me to pull a bull by the horns than do this."

Interested in this remark, Vinitius asked, "Did you really pull a bull by the horns?"

"I was afraid to do so until my twentieth year, but after that I did many times." He tried once more to feed Vinitius but gave up in disgust. "I'll have to ask Miriam or Nazarius to feed you."

Ligia's pale face appeared from behind a curtain. "I'll help you," she said. She came out after a moment. Obviously, she was preparing to take her rest. Vinitius, knowing that she had not slept for practically two days, began to urge her to go to sleep, but she answered, "I will do so after I feed you."

She then proceeded to feed him. Vinitius was overcome by this

unexpected pleasure. Yes, he desired her very much and her nearness to him brought him great joy, yet he felt that this indeed was
a person most cherished by him, a lovely and dear one who was
more important to him than any other person or thing in the whole
world. Seeing her so pale and tired, he took pity on her even
though he wanted her by him so much. He tried to prevail upon
her to go and get her rest because she needed it. "Enough," he said.
"Go, rest, my divine one."

"Please don't call me divine. I'm merely human like everyone
else." She smiled at him however saying that somehow she did not
feel sleepy then and she would stay by his side until Glaucus came.

Her words were as music to his ears. His heart was filled with
joy and gratitude. He wanted to express this feeling of gratitude.
"Ligia, I did not understand you fully until now. I'm convinced
now that I tried to possess you by a wrong road. I beg you to return
to Pomponia. My hand will not be raised against you in the future.
You can believe me now."

Her face took on a sad expression. "I would be happy to see her;
to see her even from a distance, but I cannot return to her at this
time."

"Why?"

"Through Acte, we Christians are aware of what is going on in
Caesar's palace. Did you not know that Caesar, at the insistence of
Poppaea, sought vengeance on me? He even summoned Aulus and
Pomponia to him and demanded to know where I was hiding.
Fortunately Aulus could reply firmly, 'Sire, you know that I have
never lied; I swear to you now that I did not help her escape and I
do not know where she is now.' Caesar believed him and afterward
forgot about the matter. I have not even written to them so that
they would be able to testify, if the need arose, that they had no
word from me at all. The elders advised me in this matter. Perhaps,
you do not understand but for us Christians lying is forbidden
even if it were at the cost of our lives. Such is our religion which
we wish to put in practice. All this is the reason why I did not try
to reach Pomponia. Every now and then, she is told that I am alive
and well and am in safe hands. That is sufficient for her to know."

She broke off, engrossed in sad thoughts, but soon continued.
"I too know that Pomponia misses me. But we have our consolation."

"Yes, your consolation is Christ, but I don't understand."

"For us there is no true parting and if sorrow and suffering come upon us, we believe that we can suffer for the sake of Christ...even with joy in our hearts knowing how much He suffered for us. Even death, which for you is the end of everything, for us it is but the beginning, the beginning of a life that will be everlasting in eternal peace and joy. There must be something of value in a religion which teaches us to be merciful to one another, forbids falsehood, purifies our souls from hatred and ensures a happiness which is eternal after death."

"Yes," said Vinitius. "I was in Ostrianum and heard these things which sound so strange to me. And now I can see firsthand your practical works due to your religion, how you have treated Chilo and also me. As I say, all this is strange to me, but you, O Ligia, are you really happy in your religion?"

"Yes," she answered. "Christ is our happiness; with Him we cannot but be happy."

Vinitius looked at her and could not comprehend. "Then, you do not wish to return to Pomponia?"

"I do. With all my heart if that be the will of God."

"Well then, let me say once again, please return. There will be no danger to you on my part."

"No, I cannot at this time. I dare not expose Aulus, Pomponia and their son to danger. Caesar does not like Aulus and Pomponia. If I were to return...well, you know how quickly news is spread all over Rome by slaves. The news of my return would soon come to the ears of Poppaea who hates me, and you know what the result would be."

"Yes, you are right! Caesar would persecute you just to show that his will must be done. But then, suppose that he could be persuaded by Petronius that you be taken to the Palatine and then from there once again be given to me.... I will then return you to Pomponia. What do you think?"

Ligia replied sadly, "Vinitius, do you really want to see me in his palace once again?"

He gritted his teeth and shook his head, "No! You are right. I spoke like a fool!" He saw a precipice before him without a bottom, a future without hope. He was a patrician, a military tribune, a powerful man, but now he saw another power threatening him, a power which belonged to a madman whose evil actions were numerous in the past, in the present, and no doubt would be in the future. Only such people as the Christians disdain this power and do not fear it, knowing that this power is merely temporary and ephemeral. Sure, he could put them to death now but eventually they would overcome this evil which threatens them. Everyone else was in mortal fear of Caesar's power but not the Christians. They feared a much greater power than Nero's or any other on earth.

Vinitius now fully understood the extent of the evil which ruled the Roman world. He could not return Ligia to Aulus and Pomponia because the monster would remember her and turn his anger upon her and other innocent victims such as Aulus and Pomponia. Even if he, Vinitius, would take Ligia as his wife to his home he still would not be sure of her safety. One moment of ill humor and Nero could cause ruin to befall Vinitius and all whom he loved. For the first time, he felt that either the world must change and be transformed or life would be impossible with such a tyrant as ruler. He now understood that in times like these only Christians could be happy.

He was filled with great sorrow when he realized that it was he who complicated the life of Ligia in the present tragedy. He spoke, "Do you know that you are much happier than I am? You live in poverty yet you have your faith, your Christ. Me...I have only you and when I lost you I was like a beggar without bread and without shelter. You are more dear to me than the whole world. I never stopped looking for you because I could not live without you. Had it not been for the hope of finding you, I would have thrown myself on my sword. Now, I fear doing this too because if dead, I would not see you again. Do you remember that talk in the garden at the house of Aulus? There, you drew the sign of the fish on the sand. I did not know then what it meant. Do you remember how we played ball? I loved you then. Aulus came and interrupted our talk. Pomponia told Petronius that God is One, Almighty and All-merciful. We did not understand that your God is Christ. May He give you to me and I will love Him even though right now He seems to me a God of slaves, foreigners and beggars. You sit by me, yet you only think of Him. Think a little of me too, otherwise I will despise Him. To me you are divine. Blessed be your father and mother; blessed be the land that gave you birth. If I could, I would

fall at your feet right now and pay homage to you, O divine one!
You don't know how much I love you." Speaking thus, he placed
his hand on his forehead and closed his eyes. His natural inclinations knew no bounds whether in anger or in love. However, he
spoke from the bottom of his heart and with sincerity. All his
feelings came to his lips in an upsurge of emotion.

To Ligia, some of his words sounded like blasphemy, yet her
heart beat faster. She could not resist the feeling of pity for him and
for his suffering. She was moved by his sincere devotion to her.
This proved that he belonged to her body and soul...like a slave.
This feeling brought her temporary happiness. She recalled the
first words which he spoke to her at the house of Aulus. He spoke
of love to her even then and managed to rouse her as if from sleep.
Now, with joy showing in his face mingled with pain...wounded,
broken, loving, full of homage and submission, he was to her as she
desired him to be from the first moment when she laid eyes on
him, one whom she could love with all her heart and soul.

Suddenly, she realized that a moment might come in which his
love would seize her and bear her away like a whirlwind. She felt
that she was now on the edge of a precipice. Was it for this that she
escaped before? Was it for this that she had hidden herself from
him? Who was this proud Vinitius? An Augustian, a soldier, a
friend of Nero. Moreover, he took part in Caesar's madness as was
proven to her at that feast which she could not forget. He attended
temples and paid homage to the pagan gods. He perhaps did not
believe in them, yet the fact remained that he gave them official
honor. Furthermore, he pursued her to make her his slave and
mistress and at the same time to thrust her into a world of excesses,
luxury, crime and dishonor. Right now he had changed seemingly,
but had he not said just now that if she thought more of Christ
than of him, then he was ready to hate Christ? This thought was to
her unbearable. All this made her realize that if she gave way to her
feelings for him, she would endanger her very soul. This alarmed
her greatly.

At this moment of her internal struggle, Glaucus came in to take
care of his patient. Vinitius was not glad to see him; his appearance
interrupted his conversation with Ligia and when questioned, he
gave gruff answers. If Ligia had any illusions, this unkind treatment of the doctor by Vinitius dispelled them. Yes, he could

change but only for her benefit; his heart still remained proud and selfish, not capable of accepting the sweet teaching of Christ, even incapable of the feeling of mere gratitude.

She left filled with internal turmoil and worry shown on her face. Formerly, she offered Christ a heart which was pure as the driven snow. Now, that calmness was disturbed profoundly. A poisonous insect penetrated the interior flower of her soul. In spite of the fact that she had no sleep for two nights, she slept fitfully. She dreamed that at Ostrianum Nero, at the head of a group of Augustians, gladiators and others, was trampling crowds of Christians with his chariot wreathed in roses. In this dream she saw Vinitius come to her and take her in his arms to his chariot, whispering to her, "Come with us."

CHAPTER XXVII

FROM that time on Ligia did not permit herself to be alone with Vinitius. She approached his couch less frequently even with the others present. Vinitius followed her with imploring glances, wordlessly telling her that he waited patiently for her; that he suffered but dared not complain lest he might turn her away from him; that she alone was his health and delight. Seeing this mute outpouring of his love for her, she was filled with compassion. The more she tried to avoid him, the more pity she had for him and by this itself, the more tender the feelings which rose in her. Peace left her. At times she told herself that it was her duty to care for him. Had not her religion commanded to return good for evil? Then again, by talking to him might not she try to convert him to Christianity? But, deep in her heart she knew that he attracted her very much; she was eager to listen to his words—flaming words of love—to see his face and see the look of devotion upon it. Thus she lived in constant struggle. At times it seemed that a kind of a net entangled her and she was becoming more and more enmeshed in it. She had to confess to herself also that she felt a great need to see his face and hear his words. So, she struggled with all her might not to go and sit by his side. When she approached him and his face lit up, there was also joy within her. One day she noticed tears in his eyes and for the first time the thought came to her that she could wipe them with her own kisses. Terrified by this feeling she spent the following night in prayer and self-contempt, weeping all the while.

As for Vinitius, it seemed that he had made a vow to be patient.

Only at brief moments his eyes flashed with self-will, anger and petulance, but he forced himself to restrain these feelings, at the same time looking at her as if seeking her pardon. Never had she a greater feeling of being loved by him than at these moments of his stuggle for patience. She knew what he was going through and she loved him the more for his efforts. At the same time she herself felt guilty knowing that his efforts were for her sake alone...but feeling guilty did not erase the feeling of happiness in her.

Gradually, in his conversations with the others, even with Glaucus, there was less and less pride. It even occurred to him that this man and all the other Christians around him were human beings too. He was astonished at such thoughts. He found that he liked Ursus and liked to talk to him. The giant had much to tell him of his past life in the wilds of his native land, also about Ligia and her family and about life of the Christians in general. While always regarding Ligia as a person on a higher plane, he still found many fine traits about all of them.

However, he could not stand Nazarius because it seemed to him that he was in love with Ligia. It was pure jealousy on his part. When Nazarius offered Ligia a present of some quail one day, buying them in the market with his own money, Vinitius did not like this at all. After Nazarius departed he turned to Ligia and said bitterly, "Why do you accept gifts from him? Don't you know that Jewish people are considered even by Greeks as inferior?"

"I do not know what the Greeks call them but I know that he is a Christian and my brother." She was surprised at his outburst because she expected him to be over and done with such petty feelings. She looked at him sadly. He in turn bit his lips and resolved to restrain himself in the future regarding Nazarius.

"Forgive me, Ligia. You are a daughter of a king, but I am sorry."

His determination to control himself bore fruit to the extent that when Nazarius entered the room later on, he promised him a gift of peacocks and flamingos upon his return to his own house.

Ligia understood what such victories over himself must have cost him and the more he gained these victories the more her heart turned toward him.

It was very difficult for him to understand the Christian religion. He would love it only because it was Ligia's but to understand it and love it for its own sake, that was something else again. What he witnessed at Ostrianum and what he saw of the daily living in practice of Christianity, convinced him that this was not an easy religion to live by. It was not a religion which one could put on and take off at will. This religion gave some kind of power, a superhuman power, to cause a fundamental change in the souls and hearts of people. This change was so fundamental that it could turn the inhabitants of the earth upside down in their beliefs. It could embrace the whole world in its fold; ingraft love and justice in human beings...justice and good will and equality for all. No more slaves...everyone equal in the eyes of God. This world would then be different from the one ruled by Jupiter and Saturn up till now. He could not doubt either the supernatural origin of Christ or His Resurrection or the miracles which He performed. The eyewitnesses who spoke of them were trustworthy and despised falsehood too much to have one suppose that they were telling things which had not happened. Roman skepticism, moreover, permitted disbelief in gods but belief in miracles. Vinitius, therefore, stood before a kind of marvelous puzzle which he could not solve. On the one hand, this religion seemed to him alright in theory, but on the other hand, impossible in practice. It seemed mad in some of its tenets.

According to him, people of Rome and of the world might be bad but the order of things was good. Had Caesar been an honest man such as Thrasea for instance, what more could one ask? No, Roman peace and supremacy were good; distinction among people right and just. But this religion would destroy all order, all distinction. What would happen then to the dominion and ruling power of Rome? Could the Roman consider the whole herd of barbarians equal? To him this was impossible. As to him as a person, this religion stood opposite to all his previous ideas and habits, his whole character and understanding of life. It seemed impossible for him to accept it and all that it stood for. He both feared and admired it but his whole being shuddered at accepting it. When he thought that it was this religion which separated him from Ligia, then he began to hate it.

Still he had to admit that it was this religion which adorned Ligia with that exceptional, unexplained beauty of which he was aware. This beauty augmented rather than diminished her physical beauty. He was sure of this. Then he wished anew to love Christ

Who could give such beauty to human beings. He now felt that he either must love Christ or hate Him. Nothing in between. He could not remain indifferent, not with his nature, his temperament. These two opposing currents were pulling him from one side to the other. He wasn't sure of his feelings and thoughts. In silence he bowed his head to that God and paid homage to Him for the sole reason that He was Ligia's God.

Ligia was aware of his inner turmoil. She saw how he struggled against the tenets of the Christian religion and how his nature was rejecting them. She felt great pity, compassion and gratitude for the silent respect which he showed Christ. This inclined her to him with irresistible force. She thought of Pomponia who grieved daily because Aulus still remained a pagan and that she might lose him forever. She too found a being close to her heart, this Vinitius whom she loved, and the fear that she too might lose him forever. This caused her great pain.

At times she deluded herself in thinking that he might become a Christian, but she knew that this was merely an illusion on her part, just wishful thinking. She knew him too well. Vinitius a Christian? Hardly! If the considerate, discreet and stable Aulus did not up till now become a Christian in spite of the efforts of Pomponia, how then could she expect this proud Roman, this haughty tribune, to become one? No, there was no hope of that.

However, this conclusion filled her with great sadness. This sentence of condemnation, instead of making him repulsive to her, made her pity him even more. She wanted to sit by him and explain to him the sweet teaching of Christ, so she tried it, but he said, "You are my only religion and life. I want no other," and, saying this, he placed his head on her knees. In that moment she could not breathe; a quiver of ecstasy rushed over her from head to foot. Seizing him by his temples she tried to raise his head, and when her lips touched his hair for a moment both of them were overcome with delight.

Ligia rose at last and rushed away with a fire in her veins and giddiness in her head. However, this moment was the drop that overflowed the cup. Vinitius did not realize how dearly he would have to pay for that moment of happiness. Ligia now realized what she herself needed. She spent a sleepless night in tears and in prayer. She felt unworthy and defiled. Next morning, seeking out

Crispus in the garden, she opened her soul to him, imploring him to allow her to leave this house of Miriam since she could not trust herself any longer.

Crispus was an old man. He was also harsh and unforgiving where moral actions were concerned. He had no words of consolation for the poor girl who was as pure as the driven snow. His heart swelled with indignation at the very thought that Ligia whom he had guarded from the time of her flight, whom he loved as a daughter, could have found a love other than pure in her heart. Up to now, he believed that nowhere in the world did there beat a heart more pure and devoted to the service of Christ. He wanted to offer to Christ this pearl, this jewel, this precious work of his own hands. Disappointment caused him grief and amazement.

"Go and beg God to forgive your sin," he said gloomily. "Flee before the evil spirit! God died on the cross to redeem your soul with His blood but you have expressed love for one who wants to make you his concubine. God saved you by a miracle but now you opened your heart to impure desire and love for the son of darkness. Who is he? The friend and servant of Anti-Christ, his co-partner in crime and debauchery. Where can he lead but to perdition, to the Sodom which he himself belongs but which God will destroy with the flame of his anger. But, I tell you that it would have been better had you died rather than have this satan creep into your bosom and fill it with the poison of iniquity!"

He was carried away by his sense of righteousness to the extent that he did not realize how adamant and unforgiving were his words. He was not aware that this girl still remained pure, that she only wished to flee from that love that she confessed to him with compunction and sorrow. Crispus wanted to transform her into an angel and she had fallen in love with an Augustian of Nero. The very thought of this filled his unforgiving heart with horror. No, how could he forgive her? He shook his emaciated hands over the stricken girl.

Ligia felt guilty but not to that degree. She was sure that her decision to withdraw from this house was a victory in itself for her, victory over temptation, and would lessen her fault, but this man rubbed her into the dust. She expected some semblance of mercy from him whom she had considered up to now as a father, but not this. She wanted to find courage, consolation and strength, but not downright condemnation.

Suddenly they saw two men approaching them, one the Apostle Peter and the other a short man whose name was Saul, but he was better known to all as Paul. He was renowned for his teaching and preaching and especially for his numerous epistles.

Ligia in despair ran up and clung to the feet of Peter, weeping all the while.

"Peace be with you," said Peter and seeing the girl weeping at his feet, asked what happened. Crispus informed them of the girl's plight, her sinful love and her desire to flee. Bitterly, he spoke of his own sorrow that a soul which he wished to offer to Christ, pure and unstained, had defiled itself with earthly love, a love for a man who shared in all the crimes to which the pagan world had sunk and which called for God's vengeance.

Ligia, all the while he was talking, remained at the feet of the Apostle as if she were certain that she would find refuge there and mercy too.

The Apostle listened to the end, bent his head toward the poor girl and then raised his eyes toward Crispus and said to him, "Crispus, don't you know that our Divine Master attended a wedding feast in the town of Cana and blessed the love of man and woman?" Crispus looked with astonishment at Peter, who continued. "Don't you know that Christ permitted Mary Magdalen to wash his feet and forgave her sins even though she was a prostitute? Would Christ then turn away from this pure maiden here? She is as pure as the lily of the field and you want to cast her aside as a sinner?"

Ligia, hearing this, nestled more closely to Peter now confident of her true refuge. The Apostle spoke to her, "While the eyes of him whom you love are not open to the light of truth, avoid him lest he bring you to sin, but pray for him and know that there is no sin in your love. And, since you wished to avoid temptation by leaving, this will be accounted to your merit with the Lord. Do not weep and be of good cheer for I tell you that the grace of the Redeemer has not deserted you and your prayers will be heard. After sorrow, there will come days of gladness."

When he said this, he placed both hands on her head and blessed her. His face glowed with unearthly light and goodness.

The penitent Crispus tried to justify himself by saying, "I have sinned against mercy but I thought that by admitting within her heart an earthly love she had denied Christ."

"I denied Him three times," Peter answered, "and still He forgave me and commanded me to feed His sheep."

"And, because Vinitius is an Augustian, a friend of Nero the Anti-Christ."

"Christ has softened harder hearts than his," replied Peter.

Then, Paul of Tarsus, who up till now remained silent, spoke up, "I am the one who persecuted the servants of Christ and brought them even to death, I am he who, during the stoning of Steven, looked after the garments of them who did the stoning; I am the one who wished to root out the truth, yet the Lord chose me to proclaim this truth over all the earth. I have proclaimed it in Judea, in Greece, on the Islands and also in this godless city. The seed of Christ will be sown here also as elsewhere and a bountiful harvest will come one day."

To Crispus, this short bent man now seemed what he really was: a giant who would shake the world to its foundations and gather in lands and nations under the banner of Christ.

CHAPTER XXVIII

PETRONIUS TO VINITIUS:

Have pity on me carissime! Do not imitate the Lacedonians or Julius Caesar. He, at least, wrote, *"Veni...Vidi...Vici"* (I came...I saw...I conquered), but in your letter I read, "I came..I saw..I fled!" The last part is so contrary to your nature that some explanation is necessary. You say that you were wounded; that the Ligian killed Croto as easily as a Caledonian dog would kill a wolf, and that so many strange things occurred to you. As for the giant who killed Croto, all I can say is that this man is worth his weight in gold. It depends on him alone to become the favorite of Nero. When I return to the city I must make closer acquaintance with him. I will make a bronze statue of him. Our bronze-bearded Emperor will burst with curiosity when I tell him that the model of the statue is alive. Formidable bodies are really becoming scarce these days. You can hardly find one in Italy or in Greece, much less can one be found in the East. As to the Germans, they are more bulky than strong. Try to find out from this Ligian whether there are more like him where he comes from. This knowledge will come in handy when one of us is attempting to prepare for a feast or a test of strength in the arena.

Praise to all the gods that you have come out from all this without much harm. Most likely they spared you because you are a noteworthy person in Rome and a high tribune in the army. Everything that happened to you astonishes me greatly, from Ostrianum to the house where you were wounded and also the treatment you received from the Christians. There are many points which I cannot understand and if you want to know the truth, I understand the Christians even less. I feel somewhat guilty because I have contributed to the events which happened to you, so please write me soon and try to elucidate. I say write soon because we here do not know from day to day where we are going to be. With Bronze-beard plans change like the winds in autumn. At present he wants to go to Greece but Tigellinus wants him to return to Rome. He claims that the Romans yearn for him. You may rightly surmise that they yearn, not for him but for the gifts of bread and circuses. So, right now I do not foresee where we will go. If we go to Greece, we may also journey to Egypt. In your present state of mind such a trip will be beneficial to you. Perhaps you may want to go to your estates in Sicily. Even that would be preferable to your remaining in Rome. Write soon and Farewell!

I add no particular wish for you at this time because, by Pollux, I really do not know what to wish you.

After receiving the letter from Petronius, Vinitius did not feel like replying. He felt that it would do no good, that he did not know how to express himself about his deep feelings. If he wrote now, he was sure that it would make no sense to Petronius. Something had changed in him, changed to the very core. All that he had held dear up to now was to him of no use or of little worth. He was tired and listless. The thought of going to Beneventum and from there to other places only brought the question to him: What for? What good will it do me? Even the banter and wit of Petronius would not appeal to him. That would only annoy him, he was sure.

Being alone in Rome also displeased him. All his acquaintances, his friends, were away. This feeling of loneliness finally caused him to take up his pen and write to Petronius as follows:

You want me to write to you and explain more fully. I will try but I'm not sure whether I will write more clearly than before. There are still many knots which I am unable to loosen. I described to you my stay with the Christians and their kind treatment of me. No, my dear uncle, they did not treat me in such a kind way only because I am important in the world. Look how they treated Chilo! I even urged them to bury him in their garden. No, I was not spared because I happened to be a son of a consul. Such considerations mean little to them. They are like no one we know; you cannot judge them by the same measure we judge other people. I tell you, if I were sick and lying in my own home, I would not have received more consideration. I would perhaps have more comfort but less kindness.

Know this also. Ligia is like the other Christians. Had she been my sister or my wife, she could not have nursed me more tenderly. I was very happy thinking that only love for me made her so tender but I soon found out that I was mistaken. Not mistaken about her love...because I still cling to the thought that she does love me...but to the fact that she would be as tender to any other human being, for such is the teaching of their religion.

No, Ligia was not indifferent to me. I could see that, but she left the house of Miriam, she left me. Why? Did I mention to you that I told her I would return her to Pomponia? Aulus and his family are at present in Sicily but I would have been willing for her to return to them. She knows however that her return may cause them harm so that is why she refused. She left me although nothing of me really threatens her.... I keep trying to find an answer to that and I cannot. She might have rejected me freely if she had not loved me. But supposing that she does? She still decided to run away. Why? Is it because she really loves me that she ran away?

The day before her flight I met an unusual man, a certain Paul of Tarsus. He spoke to me of Christ and His teaching. His every word was so powerful that it seemed to me, were it heeded, it would turn the whole foundation of our society and of our life upside down. Regarding Ligia he said, "If God opens your eyes to the light perhaps then you will find her." I ponder these words and try to find a hidden meaning in them. I have found out that the Christians are not enemies of humanity. They are enemies only of our way of life, our gods and our crimes. Knowing this, I feel that Ligia perhaps fled from me as from a person who belongs to this way of life. I think that she really loves me and that is why she has fled. Realizing this, I desire to send out all my slaves everywhere shouting, "Come back, Ligia!" I would not have stopped her loving her God and practicing her religion. To me, what harm can one more god be? I haven't much belief in all the others. One more, one less, what harm in that?

I know definitely that the Christians do not lie and that they say their Christ rose from the dead. A mere man cannot rise from the dead. Paul of Tarsus, who is a Roman citizen although a Jew, told me that this was foretold about Christ in old Hebrew writings: His birth, His teaching and His death. All this is very unusual. Paul's statement that there is but one God, not many, seems sound to me. Seneca is also of this opinion and there have been others, as you know. Christ lived, gave Himself up to be crucified for the salvation of the whole world and rose from the dead. All this is perfectly certain and understandable. So why can't I offer Him an altar as to other gods? It would not even be difficult for me to renounce all the other gods. You know yourself how little I esteem them all. But there is one thing I have found out about the Christians and that is that it is not enough for Christians to honor Christ, they have to live according to His teaching and this is something which I cannot do right now...it is beyond me at the present time. That is why I cannot promise the Christians that I will live according to their teachings. Were I to promise that, I would be a liar. Even Paul told me this openly. You know how much I love Ligia and what I wouldn't do for her and yet I cannot do something that is impossible for me to do...like for instance, I cannot change my eyes from black to blue, which is the color of her eyes. It is not in my power to do so. Perhaps in the past I seemed to you rather dull but I assure you I am not. Let me tell you my thinking on this subject. I know not how Christians lead their lives but I know this: where their religion begins, Roman rule ends—our mode of life for example. To them there is no difference between the conquered and the victors, between rich and poor, between master and slave. In the place of the pagan law of Caesar, there is the heavenly law of Christ. His mercy, His goodness...this is opposed to our Roman way of life, our instincts, our cruelty and our crimes.

Ligia means more to me than all the riches in the world, but that is something else again. Just to agree with words means little if you do not mean what you say and do not live according to your words. A Christian feels in his soul that his religion is true and he is willing to die for it. Do you understand all this? My nature shudders at this religion and were my lips to glorify it, were I to say that I will conform to its precepts then I will only deceive myself knowing that I do so just for the sake of Ligia. Putting my regard for her aside, there is nothing more repulsive to me than this religion. Paul of Tarsus understands this and so does their first Apostle Peter who in spite of all his simplicity and low origin is the highest among them. Do you know what they are doing in my behalf? They are all praying for me, for something which they call grace that is like a special favor given by God Himself to hu-

man beings. But nothing seems to come to me except a greater uneasiness and a greater yearning for Ligia.

Yes, Ligia left me again but before she left she made a cross out
of two twigs of boxweed. When I woke up I found it near my
bed. I have it with me here in my library and I always approach it
with awe and reverence as if it were some divine object. I love it
because her hand fashioned it but I also hate it because it divides
us. Peter, although a poor fisherman, is in reality a high personage
of some kind and it is he who has cast a spell on all of us.

You write that my letter is full of sadness and uneasiness. Sadness there must be because I have lost her again; uneasiness, because something is being changed radically in me. I sincerely
admit that things in this religion are repugnant to me, yet, since I
have come in contact with it, nothing is the same any more. Is
this magic or is it caused by my love for Ligia...I don't know.
Circe changed the bodies of men just by touching them but with
me, I feel that my very soul is being changed. No one but Ligia
could have done this...rather, Ligia through this strange religion
of hers.

When I returned home from the house of Miriam, no one expected me. My household, all the slaves, thought that I was still
in Beneventum. I found the house in a mess, feast in progress and
the slaves treating themselves to my stores of food and wine. Most
of them were drunk. They expected death rather than to see me in
person. You yourself know how strict I am with my household. At
seeing me enter they all fell on their knees, some even fainted in
fear. Well, do you know what I did? On first impulse I wanted to
call for rods and whips, but a feeling of pity came over me, a pity
for all those wretched souls lamenting loudly in front of me.
Among them were slaves who served under my grandfather, Marcus Vinitius, who brought them from the Rhine in the time of
Augustus. I left them there without a word and went and shut myself in the library.

Strange thoughts and feelings came over me, especially the feeling that I should not treat these miserable creatures in the tyrranical way I previously treated them. Involuntarily, the thought
occurred to me that they too were human beings. For two days
they moved about in fear thinking that the only reason I delayed
punishment was because I was pondering the cruelest way to do
it. However, dear Petronius, I did not punish them in any way
and I do not intend to. Summoning them on the third day, I said
to them, "I forgive you. In the future strive to make up for what

you have done with diligent service." They all fell on their knees shouting thanks and calling me their father, their lord and master. And, I am ashamed to admit it, I was really moved by this, seeing their tearful faces and the gratitude evident on them. Strangely enough, at that moment I felt that the sweet face of Ligia was smiling at me and nodding her approval.

As to the slaves, I noticed one thing: In their daily duties afterwards they showed more zeal and effort due to my act of forgiveness. They now seem to outdo one another in their eager efforts to please me. Seeing this, I am reminded of the words of Paul of Tarsus: "Love is a stronger motive than fear." I now see that in certain cases his opinion is correct. I saw it to be true in my dealing with my clients who come for a handout every day when I am home. You know that I have never been stingy with them. My father acted rather haughtily with them as a matter of principle and taught me to do the same. But, when I saw their torn mantles and hungry faces I felt sorry for them. I handed out food and clothing, at the same time conversing with them, which I had not done previously. I called some by name and asked about their families. In their eyes I noticed tears of gladness because I decided to consider them as human beings, not merely as cattle to be fed as a strict rite. Once again I seemed to sense that Ligia was looking at me with approval.

Is my reason failing me? Is love for Ligia confusing everything in me? I don't know. But this I know: She is looking at me from afar and I am afraid to do anything that might displease her.

So it is, Caius; my very soul is being changed, transformed. Sometimes I feel that this is going to affect my manhood, my energy, and in the future I will be useless not only for high counsel and feasts but also for war. This must be magic of some kind. I am now changed to such a degree that I will tell you what I thought while lying sick at the house of Miriam. I came to the conclusion that if Ligia were like Poppaea, Nigidia, Crispinilla and the other divorcees of Rome, I would not love her as I do now. But because I love her for that which divides us, then you can guess what turmoil abounds in me.

If life can be compared to a spring, then in my spring you will find chaos instead of water. I live only in the hope of seeing Ligia again. I shall not leave Rome. I could not endure the society of the Augustians. Here in Rome, I from time to time hear about Ligia through Glaucus who visits me now and then. Also from the lips of Paul whom I invited to visit me, I may hear news of her too. No, I would not leave Rome even if they offered me the rule of Egypt.

I also want you to know that I had a statue made of Gulo. Too late did I recall that he carried me in his arms when I was a mere child and he was the one who taught me for the first time to set an arrow to a bow. I can't understand why I feel so sorry for him now but I do.

If all this that I write makes you wonder, then know also that it makes me wonder no less. But, I wanted to tell you the truth about everything as I see it. FAREWELL!

CHAPTER XXIX

VINITIUS did not receive a reply to his letter. The reason for this was that Petronius expected Nero and his whole entourage to return to Rome soon. As a matter of fact news of his returning soon spread over the city and caused joy in the hearts of the rabble eager for gifts of grain and oil, great supplies of which were amassed in Ostia. At last his definite return was announced in the Senate. Nero, however, took his time, sailing by sea and visiting the coast cities at leisure. He even took time to sing and play the lute on stage in the city of Minturna after which he was tempted to return to Naples once more.

During all this time Vinitius remained mostly at home, thinking of Ligia and all those new things which occupied his soul. From time to time Glaucus paid him a visit and brought him news of Ligia, as little as it was. He did not know her present hiding place, however he told the tribune that she was well. Once, on seeing the sad face of Vinitius, he tried to comfort him by telling him that Peter chastized Crispus for being so harsh with Ligia when she confessed her love for him. He was sure now she was not indifferent to him. At first he wanted to rush over to Peter and implore him to persuade Ligia to return. However Glaucus informed him that Peter was temporarily away from the city. Furthermore, at Vinitius' appeal that he would even become a Christian himself so that he could be near Ligia, Glaucus presented the argument to him that in order to become a Christian one must want it for its own sake. It was necessary to desire Christianity through love of Christ alone. The mere motions of accepting the faith will do him no good. He must be convinced of its truth. Glaucus told him, though, that he would pass the word on to Paul of Tarsus when he returned to the city and he might then give instructions to Vinitius on the tenets of Christianity. Anything that would delay seeing Ligia was not pleasing to Vinitius and it irked him now listening to Glaucus and his explanations, but he now began to realize that other reasonings rather than his own immediate desires might have merit of their own and this was different from the way he would have reacted in the past...in an angry, selfish way. He did not realize himself now the extent of that difference in his feelings.

After Glaucus left, Vinitius was more lonely than ever. He took up his dreary searching about the city as he used to do in the past. When that proved fruitless, he gave himself up to weariness and impatience.

The moment came when his former nature rose up in him in full force like an onrush of a wave toward shore. He kept telling himself that he had been a fool all along, that he should demand from life all the pleasures that it can give. But this, he felt inwardly, was for him a last trial of whether he could forget Ligia or not. He would throw himself into the old life of pleasure with blind energy and impulse. Life demanded this he told himself.

After the dreariness of the winter months, the city was coming alive with the nearness of spring and the imminent arrival of Nero. Immense receptions were being prepared for his coming. The warmer weather was filling the people with a better outlook on life. The Forum and the Campus Martius were filled with humanity.

Along the Via Appia, the usual place for drives outside the city, an exodus of richly ornamented chariots had begun. Excursions were made to the not-too-distant Alban Hills. Youthful women, under the pretext of honoring Juno or Diana, left home to seek adventures and pleasures outside the city. Here one day Vinitius came across the splendid chariot of Chrysothemis. Her chariot was surrounded by a group of young men and even old senators whose position in the Senate forced them to remain in the city. Four beautiful Corsican steeds were harnessed to her chariot. She scattered smiles and light banter around her, playfully brandishing her golden whip. Whe she spied Vinitius, she called him over, invited him into her chariot and then asked him to her villa for a banquet. This lasted all night. Vinitius drank so much wine that he did not know when they brought him home drunk. He remembered one thing though. When Chrysothemis mentioned Ligia in an off-handed way, he got very angry and emptied a goblet of wine on her head.

The following day, Chrysothemis evidently overlooked the offense for she decided to visit him at his own house. They took a ride up the Via Appia together, had something to eat and spent the evening together at her villa. Here, she confessed to him that Petronius and her new-found lute player were no longer her lovers; she had tired of both of them and now her heart was free.

They appeared together in different places for about a week but the relationship did not last. Even though Ligia's name was never mentioned, Vinitius could not free himself from thoughts of her. Her eyes seemed to follow him everywhere. He felt that what he was doing now would surely bring sadness to her and he was miserable on that account.

After the first scene of jealousy when Chrysothemis remonstrated with him on his treatment of two Syrian damsels whom he purchased, he let her go in a manner which was rude but he did not care any more how he treated her. He wanted to be rid of her. Although he did not cease altogether his search for bodily pleasure, he soon found that it was no use, even if he blamed her for his present immoral actions. He tried to justify them by telling himself that she was the cause of his evil as well as good actions. Finally came the moment of disgust and weariness for this kind of life which he was now leading. It was becoming loathsome to him too; he began reproaching himself more and more and thereby felt more wretched than ever before. Then he fell into a state of listlessness of such magnitude that even the news of Nero's arrival in Rome did not dispel it. He did not even go to see Petronius; the latter had to send his own litter for him with an invitation to come and visit him.

At first, Vinitius responded to the joyous greeting of Petronius mechanically and unwillingly. After a while, however, his pent-up emotions burst forth in a torrent of words. He began to relate the events which happened to him and everything which he felt and thought. Then he began to complain. Due to all this he now could not make the right kind of judgments and decisions.... he could not make correct distinctions about things which were happening to him any more. Nothing seemed real to him...all was a fantasy or such...he did not know. Regarding the Christian religion, he did feel a certain attraction to it, yet at the same time a real aversion also. At times he felt sure that he could honor Christ but the aversion followed when he thought of Christ's teaching and then came serious doubts that he could follow it in good conscience and truthfully. Even if he did possess Ligia, he was now convinced that he would not possess her completely because he would have to share her with Christ. As far as daily living was concerned, he went merely through the motions from day to day, without hope, without the promise of happiness. There was darkness around him and he was constantly groping to be led into the light.

Listening to all this, Petronius gazed upon him with pity. He looked at his haggard face, at the hands which seemed to grope for something as he spoke. He approached the young man and touching his temple lightly said, "Do you know that you have some gray hairs?"

"I will not be surprised if all my hair turns gray soon."

Both were silent for a moment. Petronius, who considered himself a man of the world and quite sensible in matters pertaining to life in general, did not know what to say to all this. This was indeed a mystery to him. Yet, life could be happy or unhappy depending how one acted on these matters. He himself could be serene in time of unfortunate events which might occur. So, to him it only was one's attitude to life. Just as an earthquake can topple a temple, so could misfortune crush a person if that person permitted it. Life itself could be beautiful if it were not for the diverse entanglements which mar its beauty.

What Vinitius was talking about was something else. He was engulfed in a spiritual dilemma for which he, Petronius, had no ready answer. Even with all his knowledge, tact and wisdom, he could not bring forth ready answers. All he did in answer is to finally mutter, "All this must be due to some kind of spell."

"I thought so too," answered Vinitius. "Even now it seems to me that I'm under some kind of strange influence which I cannot understand."

"Perhaps you could go to the priests of the temple of Serapis. They may give you some advise in this matter." This was merely a half-hearted expression on the part of Petronius. There was no conviction in it. As a cynic, which he claimed to be, this sounded strange even to himself as he said it.

Vinitius rubbed his forehead in frustration. "I've seen sorcerers who I am sure used questionable methods in order to gain profits for themselves. These Christians live in poverty; they forgive their enemies, preach submission to authority, urge the practice of virtue and mercy. What profit could they gain from sorcery and why should they use it?"

Petronius had no answer for this and he muttered somewhat angrily, "This is a new sect. By the divine dweller of the Paphian groves! Their beliefs go contrary to good living. You admire the goodness and virtue of these people but I tell you that they are enemies of life just as disease and death itself. As it is, we have enough of disease around us. Who needs Christians? Just think: disease, Caesar, Tigellinus, Caesar's poetry, cobblers who rule in place of noble Quirites, freedmen who sit in the Senate. By Castor! I have had my full of them all! Take my word for it, this sect is destructive. Have you tried to dispel your sadness and use a little of good life instead?"

"Yes, I tried."

"Ah, traitor," said Petronius laughingly, "news spreads quickly; you have seduced Chrysothemis."

Vinitius merely waved his hand in disgust.

"Anyway, I want to thank you for that. I will send her a pair of slippers embroidered with pearls. In my language of love this means: Depart! I owe you a two-fold kind of gratitude. First, that you refused to accept Eunice, and second, that you have freed me of Chrysothemis. Hear me now. You have before you one who was used to rising in the morning, bathing, writing satires, possessing Chrysothemis, but one who was bored to death and often had gloomy thoughts. And, do you know why? Because I failed to notice something wonderful which was close to me. A beautiful woman is worth her weight in gold, but a loving one too is indeed a pearl. You cannot purchase such a one no matter how rich you are. Now, I say to myself that I will fill my life with happiness and I will drink of it till my hand becomes powerless and my lips grow pale. What will happen in the future, I care not! And, this is my latest philosophy."

"You always believed thus...nothing new in it."

"Yes, but in the past something was lacking: substance." When he said this he summoned for Eunice. She came in, a very beautiful girl dressed in white and joy was evident in her face. A slave no longer, but a goddess of love and happiness. Petronius opened his arms to her and said, "Come."

She ran to him, sat on his knees with her hands around his neck and her head cradled on his breast. Joy and happiness caused her cheeks to glow with a beautiful pink color and her eyes became misty. To Vinitius' eyes, these two formed a magnificent couple. Petronius stretched out his hand and from a nearby vase took some violets and sprinkled them over Eunice. He pushed the tunic from her arms and exposing her breast said, "Happy is the man who has found love in such a beautiful being. Are we not a pair of gods? Look at her. Has Myron or Scopas, Praxiteles or Lysippos ever created more wonderful lines of body than this one possesses? Have you seen anything more beautiful made from marble? Warm, rosy and full of life? There are people who love their rich vases so much that they kiss them constantly but I prefer to look for pleasure where it may really be found."

He then proceeded to place kisses on the arm and breast of Eunice. She quivered with delight. Petronius then turned to Vinitius. "Look at us and then compare us to your gloomy Christians and if this sight doesn't cure you of them, then you may just as well go to them."

Vinitius, with his nostrils flaring at the smell of violets and at the scene before him, grew pale. He thought that if he had done the same to Ligia it would have been sacrilegious. "Even at this moment," he mused, "I'm thinking of her."

"Eunice," said Petronius, "have the slaves bring us garlands and have them prepare a meal for us."

When she departed, he turned to Vinitius and said, "I wanted to give her her freedom but do you know what she told me? 'I would rather be your slave than Caesar's wife.' I freed her without her knowledge anyway. The praetor did this for me without requiring her presence. She is also unaware that this house, as well as all my possessions, will belong to her after my death. Love changes people; it has changed me. I used to love the smell of verbana; now I prefer violets."

"Please, let's not talk about perfumes!"

"I wanted you to see Eunice and talk about her only because you yourself may have someone close to you, even among your slaves, who loves you. A true and simple heart, a heart which could be like salve for your ills. You say that Ligia loves you? But what kind of love is the kind that flees from you. No, Ligia is not Eunice."

"Yes, I realize that," answered Vinitius. "When I saw you kissing Eunice in that way, I thought that if I were to kiss Ligia the same way, it would be some kind of sacrilege for which I would be immediately punished as if I defiled some goddess. Ligia is not Eunice, that is true, but I understand the difference in another way than you do. For you, love changed your nostrils and you prefer violets to verbana; for me, it has changed my soul. That is why even in my misery and desire I prefer Ligia to be like she is rather than like the others."

"In that case no harm is being done to you. But I don't understand you."

"Yes, it seems that we don't understand one another any more."

After a while of silence, Petronius spoke up in a voice which for him was unusually angry. "May Hades swallow up these Christians. They have filled you with uneasiness and destroyed your former vigor. May Hades devour them, I say! You must be mistaken thinking that their religion is good. Being good brings happiness, beauty, love and power, but your Christians call all this vanity and without much importance. You are mistaken when you say that they are right because if we return good for evil, then why should people be good?"

"No," answered Vinitius. "You are mistaken about them. The reward is not the same. According to their teaching this reward begins in a future life, a life without end."

"When we see this future life with our own eyes, then we shall know what it is like. I'm not disputing that. All I'm saying is that these Christians are simpletons and useless people. Ursus killed Croto because he was the stronger and had limbs of steel but the rest are impotent and the future of the world does not belong to simpletons."

"For them true life begins with death."

"Which is to say that day begins with night. Do you still intend to go after Ligia?"

"No, I cannot repay her in such a way. I promised her that I will not."

"Do you intend to accept the religion of the Christians?"

"I want to but my nature cannot endure it at present."

"Are you able to forget Ligia?"

"No."

"Then struggle along as best as you can."

Word was given that the meal was ready. On the way to the dining room Petronius suddenly came upon an idea which he thought might help Vinitius. He said, "You have seen much of the world but only as a soldier. Come with us to Greece. Caesar has not given up the idea of going there. Believe me, that will be some journey! A journey of Bacchus and Appolinus in one package. Singing, dancing, thousands of lyres and lutes! By Castor! That will be a sight to behold. Nothing like that has ever been experienced before."

He seated himself at the table beside Eunice and when the slaves placed a wreath on his head, continued. "What have you seen in all that time of your military service? Nothing. Have you seen the Grecian temples and visited them at leisure? Have you been in Rhodes and seen the Great Colossus? Have you been in Sparta and Athens and seen the wonders there? Have you been to Alexandria? Have you seen the pyramids? The world is wide; everything does not end with our Trans-Tiber. I intend to accompany Caesar on this journey and when he returns to Rome, I shall make my own trip to Cypress. This is the wish of my golden-haired goddess and we will both offer doves to the divinity in Paphos; and I want you to know that whatever she desires, will be done."

"I am only your slave," said Eunice.

"Then I am a slave of a slave. You know how much I adore you."

He turned to Vinitius and said, "Come with us to Cypress but first remember that you must go and visit with Caesar. It is not safe to stay away from him for long. Tigellinus may even use this as an excuse to cause you harm. He has no personal hatred for you but he does not like you even for the reason that you are my relative. I'll pass the word that you have been sick. We'll have to think of an answer if he happens to ask about Ligia. It may be best if you wave your hand and say that she was with you until you got tired of her. He will understand that. Tell him also that sickness kept you at home; that your fever was increased by not being able to attend his singing performance in Naples; that only the hope of hearing him in the future pulled you through. Don't be afraid to exaggerate. Tigellinus plans on something extraordinary as a spectacle for Caesar here in Rome. I hope that he doesn't try to undermine my influence in bringing these things up. I am also not sure how you will react to all this when you come face to face with such an eventuality."

"Do you know that there are people who are not afraid of Caesar and live as if he cannot do anything to them?"

"Yes, I know. You are referring to your Christians."

"Yes, they alone. All the others are filled with constant fear. We too do not know what will happen to us at the whim of Caesar."

"Stop telling me about your Christians. They do not fear Caesar because, no doubt, he hasn't heard of them yet and even if he did, he considers them as nothing, as withered leaves. But, I will tell you once again that your Christians are useless and incapable of anything worthwhile. You yourself mentioned that your nature is repugnant to their teaching and you know why? Because you know deep down that they are all useless and incompetent and their teaching is worthless to such as you. Don't bother yourself or me with them. We are made from a different mold. We are able to live and die but what can they do?"

These last words of Petronius impressed Vinitius and when he returned home, he began to think about them. Indeed, perhaps the goodness and charity of the Christians was proof only of their weakness and incompetence. Those who are strong and formidable and worthy of note cannot forgive so easily. This must be the answer of the Roman soul: "We shall be able to live and to die." The Christians can only forgive, that's all. They cannot understand true love or true hatred.

CHAPTER XXX

NOT long after his return to Rome Nero was sorry that he had returned and soon was planning to leave again. As a matter of fact he issued an edict about his coming departure but he assured the Roman populace that he wouldn't stay away for long and the public affairs would not suffer during his absence.

In view of his coming journey, he went to different temples in order to give offerings to the gods for a successful trip. The Augustians, among whom was Vinitius, accompanied him. On the second day when Nero was visiting the temple of Vesta, an event occurred which changed all his plans.

Nero feared the gods although he did not believe in them. Of all the gods, he feared Vesta most. At the sight of the goddess and the sacred fire in front of it, a sudden terror seized him; his teeth began to chatter. A shiver ran down his body and he fell backwards. He would have fallen to the ground had not Vinitius, who happened to be just behind him, held him up and prevented his fall.

Nero was carried out of the temple and taken to the Palatine. After he recovered somewhat, he announced to the Augustians that his plan of leaving Rome must be put off. The goddess spoke to him and warned him against leaving so soon.

To the public it was announced that Nero, seeing the sad faces of the Romans and moved by pity for them, as a father for his children, would remain with them and share their lot in the city, whether good or bad.

The people rejoiced at this decision for it meant games in the circus and free distribution of wheat and olive oil. So, they raised shouts of joy in honor of the divine Caesar.

Nero, upon hearing their shouts, paused in his dice game, turned to the Augustians and remarked, "Yes, there was need to defer the journey but I still intend to go to Greece and Egypt. I will give command to cut through the Isthmus of Corinth. I will have a sphinx put up, one which is seven times larger than the one which gazes out into the desert. This sphinx will have my face and the future ages will speak of this monument and praise me."

"With your verses you have already built a monument to yourself, not seven but thrice seven times greater than the pyramid of Cheops," said Petronius.

"And my songs?" Nero wanted to know.

"Alas, if only a monument could be built which would sing out with your voice a daily call to sunrise. Ships would come from everywhere in the future ages to hear your divine voice and be enthralled by it."

"Alas, how can this be done?" asked Nero.

"But, you can command to be built a chariot of basalt in which you are driving four magnificent horses."

"True, I can do that."

"You will bestow a gift to humanity."

"In Egypt I will marry the goddess Luna and then I will really be a god."

"And you will give us stars for wives. We will form a new constellation; we will call it the Constellation of Nero. However, command Vitelius to marry the river Nile so that he may beget baby hippos. Give the desert to Tigellinus who then can become the king of the jackals."

"And what will you assign to me?" asked Vatinius.

"May Apis bless you! You have arranged such splendid games in Beneventum that I cannot wish you anything but good. However make a pair of boots for the sphinx whose paws must grow cold at night. After that you can make sandals for the two colossi. Every one of you will have some chore to perform. Domitius Afer, for example, will be treasurer since he is renowned for his honesty. I am glad Caesar when you dream of Egypt and I'm sad that you deferred the journey."

Nero replied, "Your mortal eyes did not see what I saw. The gods reveal themselves only to whomever they wish. The goddess appeared to me and distinctly said, 'Postpone the journey!' It happened so suddenly that I was terrified."

"We were all terrified," said Tigellinus, "especially the Vestal Virgin Rubria."

"Rubria?" asked Nero. "What a beautiful neck she has!"

"But she blushes at the sight of the divine Caesar."

"True. I noticed that too. There is something divine in every Vestal Virgin and Rubria has great beauty also."

After a pause Nero asked, "Why do people fear the goddess Vesta more than the other gods? Why is this so? Though I am the chief priest, even I was seized with fear. I now remember that I fell backward and had it not been for someone behind me, I would have fallen. Who was it that supported me?"

"I," answered Vinitius.

"Oh, it was you, O Son of Mars! Why weren't you with us in Beneventum? I was told that you were ill. Indeed your face shows that you were sick. I heard that Croto wished to kill you. Is that true?"

"It is. I defended myself and he broke my arm."

"You defended yourself with a broken arm?"

"A certain barbarian helped me. He was stronger than Croto."

Nero looked at him with astonishment. "Stronger than Croto? Are you jesting? Croto was the strongest man alive."

"I tell you Caesar what I saw with my eyes."

"Where is this pearl? Has he already made himself king of the gladiators?"

"I cannot tell, Caesar; I lost sight of him."

"You did not inquire even where he came from?"

"I had a broken arm and was not able to make inquiries."

"Seek him out and find him for me!" ordered Nero.

"I will occupy myself with that little chore, Caesar," said Tigellinus. "I will find him for you."

Nero turned to Vinitius again and said, "I thank you for supporting me. I could have fallen and injured myself. Once you were a good companion but now I hardly ever see you. By the way, how is that girl...too narrow in the hips...with whom you were in love...the one I took from Aulus Plautius to give to you?"

Vinitius became momentarily confused. Petronius however

came to his aid. "I will lay a wager, sire" said he, "that he has already forgotten her. Do you notice his confusion? Ask him rather how many others there were since and perhaps he will be able to answer you. The Vinitii are good soldiers but better gamecocks. Punish him, sire, by not inviting him to the games which Tigellinus is preparing in your honor on the pond of Agrippa."

"I will not do that. I trust, Tigellinus, that beautiful maidens will not be lacking there."

"Could the Graces deny their presence when Amor himself is going to be there?" answered Tigellinus.

Nero began to say wearily, "I am bored here in Rome. I cannot endure this city. Were it not for Vesta herself, we would have been away from here by now. These narrow streets stifle me. I smell their foul air even here in my gardens. I wish an earthquake would level it down to the ground or some angry god destroy it. Then I would show you all how a city should be built, a city worthy of a ruler of the world."

"Caesar," Tigellinus spoke up, "you say if some angry god would destroy the city?"

"Yes, so what?"

"Are you not a god?"

Nero waved his hand in an expression of boredom and said, "We shall witness your endeavors on the pond of Agrippa. You all underestimate me. Your minds are small and you do not see that I need to perform great things."

Then he sat down and closed his eyes giving others to understand that he needed rest. The Augustians began to wander off. Petronius took Vinitius by the arm and walked off with him.

"You are invited then to share our amusement. Bronze-beard postponed the journey but you may be sure he will outdo himself in madness. He considers Rome as his footstool. We all will become somewhat mad with him. In these mad ventures try to find some amusement and forgetfulness yourself. By Jove! We have conquered the world and have a right to amuse ourselves. You, Marcus, are a very handsome young man. If you could only observe your countenance; you truly resemble those ancient Quirites. Others look like freedmen by comparison. Prove to yourself that Christians are enemies of life and mankind. You may be grateful to them for treating you with kindness but you should detest their religion which denies you pleasure and love. Take pleasure where you can find it. I repeat: You are handsome and Rome is full of divorced women."

"I'm still amazed that all this does not weary you."

"Who told you that? Oh, it wearies me all right...but I'm not as young as you are. Moreover, I have other hobbies which you do not have. I love books, I love poetry, I love precious gems and many other things which you do not care about. Finally, I have my Eunice. I know that I cannot make an esthete out of you. I am satisfied with what I have; you are still seeking. If death were to come to you right now, you would die sadly, even with your courage, because death would come to you too soon. As for me, I would accept it philosophically knowing that I have tasted all the sweetness that life could offer me and there is nothing more to hope for. I shall endeavor to remain joyful to the end. There are cheerful skeptics in the world. For me, Stoics are fools, but Stoicism at least tempers men while your Christians are full of sadness and they contribute only sadness to this world of yours. During the festivities which Tigellinus will arrange for us at the pond of Agrippa, there will be women from the first houses of Rome. Will there not be even one beautiful enough for you? There will be young girls dressed as nymphs appearing in public for the first time. Such is our Roman world! The weather now is getting warmer and will not cause naked bodies to get goose pimples. You, handsome Narcissus, should know that no one will be able to resist you even though she be a Vestal Virgin."

"I will need much luck to find the one I really want."

"Whose fault is that? The Christians! But I'm not surprised. You can't expect much from a religion whose symbol is the cross. Hear me, Marcus, Greece created wisdom; we Romans created power. What can this religion create? If you know the answer to that please let me know."

"You seem unduly worried that I will become a Christian."

"Not so. But I'm concerned that you will spoil your life. If you cannot be a Grecian, at least be a Roman. Possess and enjoy! There is a kind of method in our madness. I despise Bronze-beard because he is a Greek clown. If he acted as a Roman tyrant only, I would recognize and evaluate his madness because of his position as tyrant. Promise me, Marcus, that if you happen to meet up with a

Christian on your way home, stick out your tongue at him. If he happens to be Glaucus, the doctor, he may not even be surprised. Farewell, till we meet on the pond of Agrippa."

CHAPTER XXXI

Praetorian guards surrounded the groves on the banks of the pond of Agrippa lest the numerous crowds of spectators might annoy Caesar and his guests. Everything that Rome possessed of wealth and beauty was present at this feast which had no equal in the history of the city. Tigellinus wished to surpass others in lavishness: first, to thank Caesar for remaining in Rome and, second, to prove to Nero that no one else could entertain him as well as he. Therefore, he made lavish preparations, even beginning during the time when Caesar was still in Beneventum and in Naples. Orders were sent out everywhere throughout the whole empire for rare birds, rare fish, plants, vessels and rugs which were to enhance the splendor of the feast. Total revenue of several of the provinces went to defray the huge expense, but the powerful favorite of Nero had no need to hesitate. His influence grew daily. He was becoming more and more indispensable to Nero.

Petronius surpassed him greatly in polish, intellect, wit, for he knew better than anyone else how to amuse Caesar in conversations of various kinds. However, in his misfortune, he surpassed Caesar too, thereby rousing his jealousy. Caesar always consulted him whenever there was a discussion of taste, poetry and song. However, Nero did not have to show restraint of any kind in front of Tigellinus. Moreover, the title of Arbiter of Elegance, which was attributed to Petronius, rankled his self love because he wanted that title for himself as emperor of the world. That title should be his too.

Tigellinus had sense enough to recognize his own deficiencies

234

and he was well aware that he could not compete with Petronius, with Lucan and some of the others in matters of poetry and song and talented speech. He resolved therefore to overcome his handicap by the eagerness of his services and above all by such magnificence and exposure that even the imagination of Nero would be impressed.

He therefore arranged the preparation of a great feast on a gigantic raft framed with golden timbers. The borders of this raft were decked with magnificent shells found in the Red Sea and the Indian Ocean, shells brilliant with colors of pearls and of the rainbow. The banks of the pond were planted with palm trees; there were groves of lotus flowers and roses. In the midst of these, fountains were hidden, fountains of perfumed water. There were statues of gods and goddesses; gold and silver cages of all sorts of birds of various colors.

In the center of the raft appeared an immense tent or rather just the roof of a tent with the sides exposed. This roof rested on silver columns. Under this roof, tables were prepared for guests, tables loaded with Alexandrian glass, crystal and other precious vessels, the plunder from Italy, Greece and Asia Minor. The raft had the appearance of an island because of the greenery abounding on it. It was pulled with gold and silver ropes tied to numerous boats shaped in the form of swans, fish and flamingos. In these boats sat naked rowers of both sexes, their hair beautifully adorned in oriental fashion.

When Nero arrived at the main raft with Poppaea and the Augustians and sat down beneath the purple-colored roof, the rowers in the boats began to row slowly and the raft with the feasting dignitaries aboard began to be pulled slowly in a circle around the pond. There were numerous other small boats surrounding them and also smaller rafts filled with naked women playing on lyres and harps. This all resembled a huge, colorful floating circus with music and song.

The groves on the banks also sounded with music, horns and trumpets everywhere.

Nero, with Poppaea on one side of him and Pythagoras on the other, was very pleased at this gala performance and did not spare praises on Tigellinus. But as from habit, he looked at Petronius in order to find out what the Arbiter of Elegance thought of all this.

Petronius however kept silent. Only when he was asked directly by Nero did he deign to give his opinion: "I think, Caesar, that ten thousand naked maidens make less impression than does only one."

However, despite what Petronius thought, Nero was pleased. It pleased him especially to have this floating feast which was something new. Such exquisite dishes were served that even the imagination of Apicius would have been sated by the sight of them; there were wines of so many kinds that even Otho, who used to serve eighty varieties at a time, would have hidden in shame under water.

Among all the Augustians, Vinitius stood out as the most handsome. A strong face of a soldier, touched a bit with sorrow, gave clear indication of that. Above the body of a soldier rested the proud head of a Grecian god. In a word, he was a true patrician, subtle, refined and handsome. Petronius, in saying that none of the ladies of Caesar's court would be able or willing to resist him, spoke like a man of experience. All gazed at him, not excepting Poppaea and even the Vestal Virgin Rubria whom Nero wished to be present at the feast.

Wines, cooled by snow brought from the mountains, soon warmed the hearts and heads of the guests. The water of the pond shimmered in the sunshine. Above birds of all kinds flew about. The May weather was just right, neither too hot nor too cold. The whole pond heaved from the strokes of the oars which beat the water in time with the music. The raft continued to circle the pond and the guests continued to get drunker and drunker.

The feast was not half over when the order in which all sat at the table was no longer observed. Caesar himself gave the example. Rising and approaching Vinitius, who sat next to Rubria, he commanded him to move and he sat in his place and began whispering something in Rubria's ear. Vinitius found himself next to Poppaea who extended her arm and asked him to adjust her arm band. When he attempted to do so with hands which trembled a bit, she turned to him and cast a glance at him as if in modesty and shook her golden curls as if in resistance.

Meanwhile the sun sank slowly beneath the tops of the grove. Most of the guests were drunk by now. The raft circled near the shore on which, among trees and flowers, were seen groups of people disguised as fauns and satyrs, playing on flutes and bagpipes and drums with groups of maidens representing nymphs. Darkness fell at last amid drunken shouts raised in honor of the goddess Luna. Meanwhile the groves were lighted with thousands of lamps. From various places on the shore appeared new groups formed of the naked wives and daughters of noted Roman families. These with voice and manner began to lure partners.

The main raft touched shore and Caesar and his Augustians vanished amid the groves, grottos artificially arranged amid fountains and springs. Madness seized all. No one knew where Caesar was; no one could distinguish a senator from a dancer or a musician. Satyrs and fauns fell to chasing the nymphs with loud shouts. Soon the lamps were extinguished; darkness covered some parts of the grove. Shouts, laughter and loud whispering could be heard everywhere. Rome had not seen anything like this before.

Vinitius was not totally drunk but he was aroused nonetheless. The fever of pleasure swept him along also. Entering the grove, he rushed out with the others attempting to catch one of the more beautiful nymphs. Groups of these maidens led by one dressed as Diana tried to entice him. He rushed forward wanting to see her at closer range. Managing to see her closer, he was thunderstruck because it seemed to him that she was Ligia.

The group encircled him and he noticed now that the girl dressed up as Diana was not Ligia. He stood on the spot with beating heart, breathless. His illusion of seeing Ligia was so great that it deprived him of strength. Suddenly, he was seized with a yearning for her as never before. Love for Ligia engulfed him like a wave. Never had she seemed to him more pure, more dear and beloved as in that forest of madness and frenzied excess. A moment ago he himself wanted to drink of this cup and share in the debauchery. Now, disgust and repugnance possessed him. He wanted fresh air. He determined to flee but barely had he moved when before him stood a veiled figure of a woman who placed her hands on his shoulders and whispered, "I love you. Come with me...no one will see."

Vinitius stood still, unable to move.

"Who are you?" he asked finally.

She leaned her head toward him and insisted, "Hurry! See how empty it is here. I love you!"

"Who are you?"

"Guess." As she said this she pressed her lips to his through the veil, drawing his head to her and kissing him long.

"Night of love. Night of madness." she said breathlessly. "You may have me today...it is possible."

The kiss filled Vinitius with disgust and uneasiness; his soul and heart were elsewhere with Ligia, so, pushing back the veiled figure, he said, "Whoever you are, I do not want you. I love another."

"Remove the veil," she said lowering her head.

At that precise moment the leaves of the nearest myrtle rustled and parted and a man appeared. The woman vanished but from a distance her laugh was heard, a laugh strange and ominous. The man who stood before Vinitius was Petronius. "I heard and saw," he said.

"Let's leave this place," said Vinitius. And they left. They passed through the grove now partly lit and found their litters on the outside.

"I will go with you," said Petronius. He then entered the litter of his nephew and both were carried to the house of Vinitius. They were both silent on the way. When they reached the house Petronius spoke, "Do you know who that veiled woman was?"

"No. Was it Rubria?"

"No."

"Who then?"

Petronius lowered his voice. "The fire of Vesta was defiled for Rubria was with Nero. It was the Augusta Poppaea herself who was with you."

A moment of silence followed.

"Caesar was unable to hide his desire for Rubria," continued Petronius. "Perhaps Poppaea wanted to avenge herself against Nero by being with you. I am glad that I was able to prevent her wish. Had you refused her, knowing who she was, then you would have been lost, and perhaps I too along with you."

Vinitius burst out, "I have had enough of Rome, Caesar, feasts, the Augusta, Tigellinus and all the rest of the scoundrels! I cannot live this way. Do you understand me?"

"Marcus, you are losing all sense of judgment!"

"I love only her!"

"So what?"

"This...that I don't want any other love. I do not want your way of life, your feasts, your shamelessness, your crimes!"

"What is the matter with you? Are you becoming a Christian?"

The young man seized his head with his hands and repeated in despair, "Not yet...not yet."

CHAPTER XXXII

PETRONIUS returned home shrugging his shoulders and greatly dissatisfied. It was clear that he and his nephew had ceased to understand one another. Previously, he had much influence over him; a few words spoken ironically usually swayed him to his way of thinking. This was all ended. He had lost the key to reach the soul of the young man. This filled him with dissatisfaction and even with uneasiness which was heightened by the events of the night.

"If this is just a passing fancy of Poppaea and not something deeper," he thought, "then there will not be any great danger. However, if otherwise, then Vinitius will surely be ruined when he attempts to resist her as he surely would. Being his only close relative, she will use her influence with Caesar against me too. This is bad."

Petronius was a man of courage and did not fear death but since he believed that he gained nothing from death, he refrained from inviting it unnecessarily. He wondered if it might be safer to send Vinitius away from Rome on some journey. If only he could send Ligia along with him, he would do so with pleasure. However, he thought that he might not have too much difficulty in persuading Vinitius to leave even without Ligia. He would then spread the word on the Palatine that he had to leave Rome due to illness. This way he would remove danger from Vinitius as well as from himself. Moreover, he wasn't sure that the divine Augusta knew that she was recognized. In all probability, she thought that she had not been. Still it was prudent to prepare for the eventuality in the future when and if it did arise. Above all, Petronius wanted to gain time. Once Caesar left Rome for Greece and Egypt, then all danger would cease. In Greece and in Egypt, Petronius was sure of victory over his arch rival Tigellinus.

Meanwhile he determined to keep in close touch with Vinitius and urge him to leave Rome. He even thought that perhaps it might be a good idea to talk Caesar into expelling all the Christians from Rome. This way, Ligia and all the Christians would leave and Vinitius would also follow her wherever she would be.

It was not too long ago when the Jews in Rome, out of hatred for the Christians, began to cause disturbances and fights between the Jews and the Christians. Caesar Claudius, being unable to distinguish one from the other, issued an edict which expelled all Jews from Rome. Could not Nero do the same but this time expel all the Christians?

To suggest such an idea to Nero was not difficult; Caesar almost always agreed to the requests of his Augustians, especially when they meant to do harm to decent people. To make his plan succeed, Petronius decided to prepare a feast and invite Nero. The latter would then be more prone to accede to his request. Once the edict was issued, then he would see to it that Vinitius and Ligia would meet somewhere, even in Greece, and then they could live in happiness forever and practice Christianity to their heart's content.

In the meantime he visited Vinitius more often, first because he had a sincere affection for him, secondly because he wanted to talk him into taking the journey.

At one of his visits to Caesar, Petronius found out that Nero definitely was preparing to go to Antium. The day he found this out, he went to Vinitius to tell him about it. Vinitius had, however, just found out about it himself and he showed Caesar's invitation and the list of the invited.

"As you see, my name is there as well as yours," he told his uncle.

"If I wasn't among the invited, that would mean the end for me. I don't expect anything like that happening before the journey to Greece. I shall be useful to him there I suppose. Barely have we returned to Rome, then we must leave again and drag ourselves over the weary road to Antium, but we have to go. There is no way out of it. Caesar's invitations are just as forceful as commands."

"What would happen if anyone who is invited decided to disobey and remain in Rome?"

"He would quietly be invited to go on another journey, a much longer one, a journey from which there is no return. What a pity that you have not left Rome as I suggested. Now, you have to go to Antium!"

"I have to go to Antium. Don't you see in what times we live? What cringing slaves we have become?"

"You only notice this now?"

"No. But you have tried to explain to me that Christians are enemies of life, that what they teach places rigid shackles on good living. But tell me, what greater shackles are there than the ones we ourselves carry, you, I and the others? You yourself told me that Greece created beauty and wisdom but Rome created power and strength. Where is our power? Where is our strength?"

"If you wish to philosophize, call Chilo. I have no desire to do so right now. By Hercules! I did not create these times we live in. Why should I answer for them? Instead let us talk of Antium. I wish to remind you that great danger lies in wait for you there. Yet you cannot refuse to go."

Vinitius motioned carelessly with his hand. "Danger? We are all wandering in the shadow of death; more and more often a head rolls by order of Caesar."

"Yes, you are right but I can recall a few who have outlived the times of Tiberius, Caligula, Claudius and now perhaps will outlive Nero. An old and miserly man, as Domitius Afer even, has done so and he lived as a scoundrel all his life."

"Perhaps that is exactly why he lived so long," put in Vinitius. He began to go over the list of invited guests: "Tigellinus, Vestinus, Sextus Africanus, Aquillius Regulus, Sullius, Marcellus and on and on, all a bunch of ruffians and scoundrels. And they are the ones who govern the world. They would do better to go into the provinces, jingle their *sistra* and earn their bread by telling fortunes."

"Or by exhibiting trained monkeys, dogs, or flute-playing asses." added Petronius. "Yes, all that is true. But let's talk of something more important. Listen to me. Despite the fact that I spread the word on the Palatine that you were ill, your name was placed among those invited. I see the obvious hand of Poppaea in this. Nero knows you as a soldier and does not need you where poetry and song are concerned. It must be the work of Poppaea, which to me means that her desire for you was not a mere fancy."

"For an empress, she takes too many chances."

"Certainly, but she can ruin you and with you me also. May Venus inspire her with an infatuation for someone else soon. You must observe the greatest caution in her presence. Our Bronze-beard seems to be getting tired of her. Now he prefers Rubria or even Pythagoras. Even so, he would wreak vengeance on both of us through his wounded pride."

"I did not know that I was speaking with Augusta in the grove. Anyway, I told her that I loved another. You know that."

"I implore you by the infernal gods, don't lose the remnant of good sense which the Christians have left you. How can you hesitate between possible danger and sure danger? Have I not told you that if you have wounded the vanity of Poppaea, there will not be any help for you? By Hades, if life is so bitter to you that you want to end it now, then cast yourself upon your sword or open your veins. This way you may have an easier death than the one prepared for you by Poppaea herself. At one time I could talk some sense into you, but now I don't know. Furthermore, your presence in Antium and your tactful behavior where Poppaea is concerned would not lessen your love for Ligia. Remember too, Poppaea saw her in the gardens of Caesar and would immediately surmise whom you mean when you say that you love someone else. Then she would take revenge on her too. Can't you understand that?"

Vinitius listened to all this in a sort of distracted way. Suddenly, he said, "I've got to see her!"

"Who? Ligia?"

"Yes."

"Do you know where she is?"

"No."

"Then you will search for her again throughout the city?"

"I really don't know. All I know is that I have to see her."

"That's fine. I'm sure when you see her she will advise you to act the same way as I'm advising you, even though she is a Christian. She certainly doesn't wish you ruin."

Vinitius shrugged his shoulders. "She saved me from the hands of Ursus."

"Then hurry up and find her. Bronze-beard won't postpone his departure for long. Sentences of death can be issued from Antium too, remember."

But Vinitius did not listen. He began thinking of the best method of seeing Ligia again.

Luckily something happened which gave him hope of seeing her. Chilo appeared unexpectedly at his house the next day.

His appearance when he entered was wretched and worn. Signs of hunger showed on his face, his clothing was torn. The slaves who had orders to let him in allowed him to enter as usual. Presenting himself before Vinitius he said sadly, "May the gods shower you with immortality and dominion over the earth."

Vinitius at first wanted to throw him out, but on second thought he wondered if Chilo perhaps had news of Ligia. So, his curiosity overcame his disgust and he asked, "Is that you? What have you been doing?"

"Everything has gone bad with me, O Son of Jove! Real virtue is rare these days. A philosopher and sage must be satisfied to buy some meat for his table only once in five days and wash it down with his own tears. Ah, sir, the money that you have given me is gone. The slave whom I bought to write down my memoirs robbed me and fled. I am ruined. To whom can I go but you, O Serapis, whom I love and deify. For you I have exposed my life to danger."

"Why have you come? Have you any news for me?"

"I come because I need your help and I also have good news for you. You remember Eunice, sir, she who is of the house of Petronius. I had helped her in the past by giving her a miraculous thread from the girdle of the goddess Venus. I have another such thread for you." Here he stopped because he saw anger gathering on the forehead of Vinitius. To anticipate the outburst, he quickly added, "I know where divine Ligia is living. I will show you the street and the house."

Vinitius had some difficulty in repressing the emotion which enveloped him at this news.

"Where is she?" he asked with a strained voice.

"With Linus, who is an elder of the Christians. Ursus is still with her and guards her but he still works for Demas the miller on the night shift. If you surround the house at night, you will not meet Ursus. Linus is old and besides him there are only two older women."

"How do you know this?"

"You remember, sir, the Christians had me in their hands and spared me. Of course Glaucus was mistaken as to my identity. He is an old man and feeble too; his mind is clouded also. That is why he blames me for his troubles although I am innocent. But I forgive him. As a sign of forgiveness, I wanted to get better acquainted again with the Christians and to find out what was happening to my former friends. I love them all, sir. Should I not have learned about them? To wish them well? This way I found out about Ursus and Ligia and the house she dwells in now. Hear me, sir. The house stands apart and you will have no difficulty surrounding it at night with your slaves and the divine Ligia will be yours without trouble whatsoever. It now depends on you whether that beautiful king's daughter will reside in your house. If you do accomplish this, noble sir, remember that it was the son of my father who brought you this joy."

Vinitius felt strongly tempted. Yes, it should be easy just as Chilo suggested to surround that house with his slaves and then Ligia would be his forever. And why shouldn't he take her? She was his by Caesar's command. It is true, he had promised not to take her by force but he vowed by the gods, and he does not believe in the gods, nor the God of the Christians Whom he hasn't accepted. So what is there to prevent him? Once he makes Ligia his mistress, then all the gods and all the religions of the world won't take her away from him.

He began to pace the floor of the library with feverish steps. Suddenly his eyes rested on the cross which Ligia formed for him with her own hands. He stopped and stood transfixed. Thoughts rushed to his head. Will he repay all the kindness she had shown him with such a base and cowardly act? For all her goodness and love repay her by dragging her by her hair so that she will have to submit to him? Treat her like a slave, she...a king's daughter? How could he do this when he is sure that he loves her with all his heart and soul? Yes, he wants her but not against her will. He wants her as a loving maiden who wishes to be with the one she loves of her own free will. He knew now that his love for her needs more, needs her consent, her love and her soul. Blessed be the roof where she will come willingly. Then his happiness will be inexhaustible as the ocean, as glowing as the sun. Seizing her by violence would destroy this kind of happiness forever and defile that which is most precious to him. Terror seized him at this thought. He glanced at Chilo who, watching him closely and uneasily, was scratching himself under the rags which he wore.

The sight of Chilo brought disgust to Vinitius. He now wished to trample this worm of a man into the dust. He would punish him as he deserved. With this determination he spoke aloud, "I will not do as you suggest and, as a reward for your sliminess and treachery against the Christians, you shall receive three hundred lashes."

Chilo grew pale. There was so much cold resolution in the face of the tribune that he could not delude himself that Vinitius was joking. He threw himself on his knees before Vinitius and with a broken voice pleaded, "How, O King of Persia? Why? Why, O Noble Tribune? O Pyramid of Kindness, O Colossus of Mercy! For what? I am old and hungry. I have served you well. Why do you punish me? Why do you repay me thus for the good that I have done you?"

"As you have done to the Christians," said Vinitius. Thereupon he called his slave and issued orders for the punishment.

Chilo sprang forward and embracing the feet of Vinitius pleaded once more, his face covered with deathly pallor. "Sir, I am old! Fifty lashes not three hundred! One hundred only. Please...please...mercy."

But there was no mercy in Vinitius. He gave orders and the slaves dragged Chilo away.

"In the name of Jesus Christ!" called out Chilo in desperation.

Vinitius paid no attention to that cry either. He felt better now; he thought that he was acting correctly. This thought enlivened him. He felt relieved that he had overcome the temptation of seizing Ligia by force. This he considered a great victory. He was convinced that he made a great approach toward Ligia and that she would be pleased, that she would be pleased too about the punishment which he inflicted upon Chilo who was a traitor to the Christians.

It did not even occur to him that he had done a grievous wrong to Chilo. He had him flogged for the same thing which he rewarded him just recently. He was too much of a Roman yet to be pained by another man's suffering and to occupy his mind with the fate of a miserable Greek. His mind turned to Ligia and he spoke to her in his soul, "I will not repay you with evil for the good which you have done me and I have punished the worm who wanted me to raise my hands once more against you." Suddenly he paused. Would Ligia be pleased with this act of punishment? Her religion commands forgiveness. Perhaps she would want me to forgive Chilo. With this thought in mind he was about to summon the slaves to bring Chilo back to him when a slave appeared before him and announced, "Sir, the old man fainted, perhaps he is dead. Am I to command further flogging?"

"Revive him and bring him back to me."

After some time Chilo stood before him, pale as a sheet with wobbly legs. He began to utter disjointed words. "Thank you, thank you, merciful sir. I owe you my life."

"Dog! Remember that I forgave you because of the Christ which you mentioned to me and by Whom I too was forgiven by the Christians."

"O sir, I will serve Him and you."

"Be silent and listen! You will go with me and show me the house wherein Ligia now resides."

Chilo wanted to walk but was really not able to, he was so weak. He pleaded, "Sir, I am really weak and hungry. I will gladly go but first please allow your slave to give me a bit of food, even the food which you serve to your dogs."

Vinitius ordered him fed and also gave him some money. Chilo, although very weak, made a great effort to go willingly. "Let the wine warm me a little first, sir, then I will be all right. I could then walk with you even to Greece."

They left. The way was long because, like most of the Christians, Linus lived in the Trans-Tiber section too and not too far from the house of Miriam. At last, reaching their destination, Chilo pointed out the house to Vinitius. It was a small house standing apart, surrounded by a wall covered entirely with ivy. Chilo said, "Here it is, sir."

Vinitius turned to him and spoke firmly, "Now listen to me! Forget that you have served me. Forget where Peter, Miriam and Glaucus dwell. Forget this house. You will come each month to my house where my freedman will give you two pieces of gold. But, if you again spy on the Christians, then I will have you flogged and give you up to the prefect of the city."

Chilo bowed down, "I will forget, sir, I will forget everything."

However when Vinitius vanished beyond the corner of the street, he stretched his hands after him and threatening with his fists exclaimed, "By the gods and by the furies, I will never forget!"

Then he grew weak again.

CHAPTER XXXIII

VINITIUS directed his steps to the house where Miriam lived. Before the gate he met Nazarius who was at first confused at seeing him. However he greeted the lad cordially and asked to be conducted into the house.

Besides Miriam, Vinitius found Peter, Glaucus and Paul of Tarsus inside. At the sight of the young tribune, astonishment reflected upon their faces but he greeted them all pleasantly. "I greet you in the Name of the Christ Whom you honor."

"May His Name be glorified!" they answered.

"I have seen your virtue and experienced your kindness, hence I come as a friend."

"We greet you as a friend," answered Peter. "Sit down, sir, and partake of our food and drink as a welcome guest."

"I will sit down and share your repast but first listen to me, all of you, so that you may know my sincerity. I know where Ligia is dwelling. I have just come from observing the house wherein she dwells. It is as you know the house of Linus. Caesar gave her to me so I can say that I have a right to her. I have at my disposal here in the city about five hundred slaves. I could surround the house of Linus with my slaves and take Ligia by force. However, I have not done so, and I will not do so."

"For that reason the blessing of the Lord will be upon you and your heart will be purified," said Peter.

"I thank you. But listen to me further. I have not done so although I am living in sadness. Before I began to know you, I would have taken her by force but your virtue and your religion,

249

though I do not profess it, have changed something in my soul so that I now abhor violence. I can't understand it but I assure you that it is so. I come to you who are as parents to Ligia and say to you: Give her to me as a wife and I swear that not only will I not forbid her to confess Christ but I myself will begin to learn this religion."

He spoke with head erect and decisively, still he was filled with emotion and his legs trembled from the weight of his words. When silence followed these words, he continued as if to anticipate an unfavorable answer. "I know what obstacles lie in my path but I want you to know that I love Ligia more than myself. Though I am not a Christian I want to assure you that I am neither your enemy nor the enemy of Christ. I want to be sincere so that you will trust me. Another would say, 'Baptize me,' but I say, 'Enlighten me,' for I may not be ready for baptism as yet. I believe that Christ rose from the dead because people who love truth say so; people also saw Him after He had risen. I have seen for myself that your religion encourages virtue and mercy, not the crimes of which you are accused. I do not know much about your religion, a little from your deeds, a little from Ligia, a little from my talks with you. Still, I repeat: It was sufficient to make a profound change in me. Formerly, I held my slaves with an iron hand; I cannot do so now. I knew no pity in the past; I know it now. I was fond of pleasure, but the other night I fled from the pond of Agrippa, my whole being filled with disgust. Formerly, I believed in superior force, that might was right. Now I have abandoned that belief. I want you to know that I do not recognize myself. I am disgusted with Caesar's feasts, the wine, lyres, garlands, the songs and the whole court of Caesar and their crimes and debauchery. When I think that Ligia is as pure as the snow on the mountains, I love her more. When I think that she is what she is because of her religion, I love and desire that religion. But, since I do not understand it fully, since I do not know whether I will be able to live this religion in practice or if my nature can endure it, I am in a turmoil of indecision and uncertainty and I suffer much."

Here, his brows constricted as if in pain and his cheeks flushed with emotion. After a short pause he continued, "As you see I'm tortured within myself. I have been told that in your religion there is no room for life or human joy or happiness or law or order or authority or Roman rule. Is this true? I have been told that you are all madmen. Tell me, please tell me what you bring. Is it a sin to love? Is it a sin to feel joy? A sin to want happiness? What is the truth? Your deeds and words are clear as water but what is underneath? You see that I am sincere. Scatter the darkness for me. Men say this also: 'Greece created beauty and wisdom; Rome created power; but they? What do they bring?' Tell me then what do you bring? If there is brightness beyond your doors, open them for me."

"We bring love," said Peter.

Paul of Tarsus added, "If I speak the tongues of angels but have no love within me, I am merely as a sounding brass."

The heart of Peter was stirred seeing this poor suffering soul before him which was struggling to attain freedom like a caged bird trying to reach the open air and to fly to freedom. He stretched his hand toward Vinitius and said, "To him who knocks the door will be opened. The favor and grace of God is upon you; for this reason I bless you, your soul and your love in the name of the Redeemer of mankind."

At this Vinitius sprang forward to Peter and astonishing to all present, took the hand of this poor fisherman and pressed it to his own lips in gratitude.

Peter was pleased for he understood that his sowing had borne fruit, that his fishing net had gathered in one more soul.

Those present were pleased also at the show of humility and gratitude of Vinitius toward the Apostle and shouted, "Praise to the Lord in the highest!"

Vinitius was radiant with joy and said, "I see that joy can dwell among you because I feel happy. I feel that you can convince me of other things in the same way. However, I must say that this cannot be done here in Rome. Caesar is going to Antium and I must go with him. It's like a command that I should be there. You yourselves know that not to obey means death. If I have favor in your eyes please hear my request. Come with me to Antium. It will be safe there for you and you can safely spread your teaching to those who will listen. In Caesar's court Acte may be a Christian, at least I heard that it may be so. There are Christians among the Praetorian guards. I myself have seen them kneeling before you, Peter. In Antium I have a villa in which we can assemble to hear your teaching. Glaucus told me that you are willing to go to the ends of the earth for one soul. Please come there with me."

Hearing this, they began to make plans thinking that the conversion of such a personage as Vinitius to Christianity would mean a great deal in the pagan world. They were ready indeed to wander to the end of the earth for one soul and since the death of their Master they had in fact done so, hence a negative answer did not even come to their minds. However, due to important commitments, Peter was unable to leave right then but Paul of Tarsus was happy to accompany Vinitius to Antium. He had some free time before he again would return East in order to visit churches and freshen them with new zeal for the faith. Too, Paul could leave by boat from Antium so it would work out fine.

Although sad that Peter could not accompany him, Vinitius was glad to have Paul go with him to Antium and to learn from him about the new faith. He now turned to the Apostle with a request: "Knowing Ligia's dwelling I could go to her and ask her to be my wife but I prefer to ask you, Peter, to permit me to see her. I don't know how long I will be in Antium and with Caesar, no one is sure of his tomorrow. Petronius told me that I should not be altogether safe there. Please let me see her before I leave. Let me ask her to forget the evil that I have caused her and if she would be willing to share the future with me."

Peter smiled and answered, "Of course. Why should this joy be denied you? I tell you also, have no fear of Caesar for nothing will happen to you." He then sent Miriam to fetch Ligia telling Miriam not to divulge the name of the person awaiting her, so that her delight would be the greater for that reason. It was not far to go and after a short time they could see Miriam leading the girl by the hand.

Vinitius wished to rush forth to meet her but the sight of that loved one caused so much joy in his heart that at first he became weak and unable to move a step; his heart beat wildly within him.

Ligia ran in not suspecting anything. At the sight of him she stood transfixed. Her face flushed suddenly and then grew pale. She looked all around but met only smiling faces. These faces reflected joy and gladness. Peter approached her, took her by the hand and said, "Ligia, do you love Vinitius here present?" A moment of silence followed. Her lips began to quiver like that of a child preparing to cry. Then, with humility, obedience and fear in her voice, she whispered, kneeling at his feet, "I do."

At that moment Vinitius knelt down beside her in front of Peter who placed his hands on both of them and said, "Love each other in the Lord and for His glory for there is no sin in your love."

CHAPTER XXXIV

THEY walked in the garden hand in hand. Vinitius related what had transpired, how he found out where she lived, about his visit to Miriam's house where he met Peter and Paul and the others, and his words to them. He confessed to her that he tried to forget her but was unable to do so. He told her how much he yearned for her during all this time, how much he dreamed of her. The cross which she left for him, the one she formed herself out of boxwood twigs had reminded him of her and he looked upon it constantly. His love for her seized his entire soul and he was miserable without her. True, his acts in the past toward her had been bad and misguided but she must know that they had their origin in his love for her. Even from the first time when he saw her in the house of Aulus, he was madly in love with her. His search for her, his being at Ostrianum, and finally his attack upon her at the house of Miriam, all that stemmed from his great love. Will she then forgive him now? He acted wildly, he knew, but it was all from love. When he was hurt and she watched at his bedside, he felt great joy for she was near; how he wasted away when she left. He also blessed the moments when he became acquainted with her religion. It was this which brought him to Miriam's house and to ask the apostle Peter for her hand in marriage. Blessed be that moment for now she is at his side and will no longer flee from him.

"I did not flee from you," she said.

"Then why did you go away?"

She raised her beautiful eyes to him and then inclining her head she said with modesty, "You know why I fled."

Vinitius was silent for a moment, his heart filled with great joy. Then he resumed talking. He told her that she was different from other women whom he knew in Rome...the divorcees...the wicked glorified prostitutes of Nero's court. He now recognized her beauty for what it was, the beauty of a soul as well as body; this beauty which he was sure the new Christian religion would cause to flourish in future generations. Yes, he was glad that she fled from him and he assured her that she would be sacred to him always. Taking her hand with a great outpouring of love, he could only whisper, "Ligia."

He wanted to know from her what she herself thought and felt about him from the first moment she saw him. She confessed to him that she loved him even in the house of Aulus. If only he promised her that he would take her from the Palatine to Aulus and Pomponia, then she would have told them of her love for him and would have begged them to forgive him.

"I swear to you that it was not my intention to have you taken away from the house of Aulus. Petronius can vouch for that because he was the one who talked me into it. I told him that I wanted to marry you. I said to him, 'Let her anoint my door with wolf fat and let her sit at my hearth,' but he ridiculed me and gave Caesar the idea of demanding you as a hostage and then giving you to me. How often in my sorrow have I cursed that moment, but perhaps fate ordained thus for otherwise I should not have understood you and Christ."

"Believe me, Marcus, it was Christ Who led you to Himself in this way."

Vinitius raised his eyes in wonder. "True, everything that happened seemed to have some kind of design, for in seeking you I met the Christians. In Ostrianum I listened to the Apostle in amazement; I had never heard the like before. You have prayed for me too."

"I did."

They passed near the summer house covered with ivy and approached the place where Ursus, after killing Croto, turned his wrath upon Vinitius.

"Here I should have perished were it not for you."

"Please don't remind me of that awful moment and please don't hold it against Ursus. His only thought was to protect me."

"Could I blame him for trying to defend you? Had he been my slave I would have freed him immediately."

"Had he been a slave Aulus would have freed him a long time ago."

"Do you remember my telling you to return to Pomponia but your fear was for their safety. Do you remember that?"

"Yes, Marcus."

"Well, now you may return to them safely."

"How, Marcus?"

"I mean when you are my wife. Should Caesar question me regarding you, I will be able to answer, 'I married her and she visits Aulus and Pomponia with my permission.' Caesar will not remain long in Antium because he still wants to make that trip to Greece, but even should he stay longer than anticipated, I myself don't have to be with him always. When Paul of Tarsus teaches me your faith, I will receive baptism. I will then try to regain friendship with Aulus and Pomponia and I will seat you at my hearth, O my beloved!"

She raised her eyes to him and said, "And then I shall say, 'Wherever you are, Calus...there I, Caia, am also!' "

"I swear to you, my love, that never will there be a woman more honored as I will honor you in my house as my wife."

For a time they walked in silence, their whole beings filled with great feelings of love which both felt so strongly for each other. The beauty of spring and of the flowers matched the beauty of these two happy souls. They halted finally under a fine cypress growing near the entrance of the house. Ligia leaned against his breast and he began to entreat her: "Please tell Ursus to go to the house of Pomponia for your childhood toys and different playthings and your possessions which have remained in their house. Let him take them all to my house."

She blushed a bit at this and responded, "Custom decrees otherwise."

"I know. The *pronuba* (bridesmaid) usually brings them over to the house of the future husband. But please, this time have them brought to me." He pleaded like a child. "It will be soon when they return from Sicily. Do this for me, my loved one."

"Let Pomponia do as she wishes in this matter," answered Ligia, blushing still more.

They stood by the cypress, their faces aglow with their love. In the silence of the afternoon they only heard the pounding of their hearts and in their mutual ecstasy, that cypress, the myrtle bushes about and the ivy of the summer house became for them a paradise of love.

Miriam appeared at the door and invited them to the afternoon meal. They sat down with the apostles who gazed upon them with pleasure as on the young generation which, after their death, would preserve the faith and continue to sow the seed of Christianity. Peter blessed and broke bread. There was calmness and immense happiness among them.

"See," said Paul, turning to Vinitius, "are we enemies of life and happiness?"

"I now know," answered Vinitius, "because never have I been so happy as right now with you."

CHAPTER XXXV

LATE that same evening, while returning home by way of the Forum, Vinitius noticed the litter of Petronius which was carried by eight strong Bithynian slaves. With a sign of his hand he stopped the litter and peered inside the curtain. He saw that Petronius was dozing.

"Pleasant dreams," he remarked as Petronius woke up.

"Oh, it's you! I was dozing a bit. I spent last night at the Palatine and came home late. I have just bought some books which I want to take with me to Antium. Well, what's new with you?"

"Are you visiting the bookshops?"

"Yes, I don't want to bring disorder into my library so I'm collecting a special supply for the journey. I was looking for some works of Musonius and Seneca and certain editions of Perseus and Virgil which I do not have. Oh! How tired I am! How my hands ache from taking the scrolls off the racks. You know how it is in bookshops. One becomes curious and starts looking here and there. I've already been to several and now I'm tired and sleepy."

"You were at the Palatine last night? What is new there? Say, how about sending your litter home and coming with me to my house if you are not too tired. We will talk of Antium and I also have something to tell you."

"All right. You, of course know that we leave for Antium the day after tomorrow."

"How could I know about that?"

"You don't know? You must be living in another world! Then I am the first to tell you this? Yes, be ready; we will definitely leave the day after tomorrow. Peas dipped in oil have not helped; a cloth around his thick neck has not helped; Bronze-beard is still hoarse. Due to this there is no thinking of delaying any longer. He curses Rome and its dampness. He would like to level it to the ground or destroy it by fire. He wants to breathe the sea air. He claims that the smells which are wafted from the narrow streets onto the Palatine are driving him slowly into the grave. Today, sacrifices were offered in all the temples to restore his divine voice, and woe to Rome and especially to the Senate if his throat doesn't get better soon."

"If his voice is gone then there will be no reason for him to go to Greece."

"Do you think it is the only talent that our divine Caesar possesses? He wants to appear at the Olympic games as a poet reciting the masterpiece *Burning of Troy*, and as a charioteer, as a musician and esthete, even as a dancer! He wants to receive all the crowns intended for victors. Do you know why that monkey grew hoarse? Yesterday he wanted to equal our Paris in dancing! He danced for us the adventures of Leda during which he sweated and caught cold. He was as wet and slippery as an eel freshly taken out of the water. He changed masks one after another, whirled around like a top and waived his hands like a drunken sailor. I tell you, pure disgust seized me when I looked at that huge belly and skinny legs. Paris was teaching him for two weeks but you can imagine him trying to imitate Leda and the Swan. What a swan he was! And he wants to appear in this pantomine before the public, first in Antium and then in Rome."

"People are already offended because he sang in public; but to think that a Roman Caesar will appear publicly as a mimic. No! Even present-day Rome will not endure that!"

"My dear, Marcus, Rome will endure anything; the Senate will pass a vote of thanks to the Father of his Country and the rabble will be elated to see Caesar as its clown."

"How much more can he debase himself and debase Rome?"

Petronius shrugged his shoulders. "You live by yourself and think only of Ligia and of the Christians so you do not know what happened a couple of days ago. Nero actually took part in a marriage ceremony with Pythagoras. He was dressed as a maiden. Imagine that! Well, you would think that the measure of his madness was complete but no. The *flamens* (priests) came to perform the ceremony with pomp and solemnity. I was there! Believe me, I can endure quite a bit but I thought that the gods, if there be any, should have given some kind of sign. But, Caesar does not believe in gods and he is right."

"In that case he is a high priest, a god, and an atheist all in one person!"

"True," agreed Petronius with a laugh, "that had not occurred to me but it is some mixture, is it not? I might add too that this high priest who does not believe in the gods and this god who reviles other gods fears them like an atheist."

"The proof of that is what happened in the temple of Vesta."

"What a world we live in!"

"Our world is like our Caesar and that must end soon; it cannot go on like this."

Conversing in this way they entered the house of Vinitius who ordered supper to be served. He then turned upon Petronius a happy face and exclaimed, "No, my dear uncle, such a world will not last for long; it must be renewed."

"We shall not renew it," answered Petronius. "Even for the simple reason that in Nero's time a man is like a butterfly. He lives in the sunshine of favor and at the first cold wind he perishes, even against his will. By Jove! More than once I asked myself how could someone like Lucius Saturninus for instance reach the ripe old age of ninety-three? He survived Tiberius, Caligula and Claudius. That's some feat. But never mind. Will you permit me to send for Eunice? I am no longer sleepy and I wish her to be joyous with me. We will have our talk about Antium later; how you should behave there will be very important in regards to Poppaea."

Vinitius gave orders to send for Eunice. However, he wasn't worried about Antium: "Let those worry who cannot live otherwise than in the rays of Caesar's favor. For me the world does not end on the Palatine, especially if one has something much more important in his heart and soul." He spoke in such a carefree manner and with such animated joy that this struck Petronius, who looking at him more closely observed, "What is it with you? You appear as happy as I remember you when I saw you wearing the golden *bulla* on your neck."

"I am happy. I invited you purposely in order to tell you so."

"What happened?"

"Something for which I would not exchange the whole Roman empire." Then he sat down, rested his head on his hand and asked, "Do you remember the time we were together in the house of Aulus and you called a girl Dawn and Spring? Do you remember that beautiful girl?"

"What are you talking about? Of course I remember Ligia."

"I am engaged to marry her."

"What?"

Vinitius sprang up and called the chief slave. "Let all the slaves stand before me. All of them quickly."

"You are engaged to marry Ligia?" Petronius asked. Before he recovered from his astonishment, the whole room was filled with slaves. Panting old men, men in the prime of life, women, boys and girls. All stood apprehensive against the walls. Vinitius turned to his freedman and said, "Those who have served twenty years in my house are to appear tomorrow before the magistrate and receive their freedom; those who have not served out their time will receive three pieces of gold and double rations for a week. Send an order to the village prisons to remit the punishment of all those there; strike the fetters from their feet and feed them sufficiently. I want all of you to know that a happy moment has come to me and I want all to share in my happiness."

For a moment they all stood in silence not understanding; finally when they did comprehend, they all uttered cries of joy and thanks. Vinitius dismissed them with a wave of his hand and sat down by Petronius.

"Tomorrow," he said, "I will command them to meet again in the garden and to make such signs on the ground as they choose. Ligia will free those who make a sign of a fish."

"A fish you say? Oh yes. I remember. According to Chilo, that is the sign of the Christians." Then he extended his hand toward Vinitius and said, "Happiness is where you find it. May the goddess Flora strew pretty flowers under your feet and Ligia's for a long time. I wish you everything that you yourself wish."

"I thank you. I was afraid that you would try to dissuade me, but that would be a loss of time and effort on your part."

"Me? Dissuade you? By no means! On the contrary I tell you that you are doing well."

"Ha! You have forgotten that you advised me otherwise before."

"I have not forgotten," answered Petronius without blinking, "but I can change my opinion, can't I? My dear Marcus, here in Rome everything changes. Husbands change their wives, wives change their husbands, so why shouldn't I be able to change my mind whenever I so desire? Remember that Nero was only a whisper away from marrying Acte. If he did that we would have now for ourselves a worthy Augusta. By Proteus and his empty spaces in the sea! I shall change my opinion as often as I find it convenient and worthwhile. I'm sure that Ligia's royal descent is more certain than Acte's. Now, let me admonish you about Antium. Be on your guard against Poppaea. You know how vengeful she is."

"I worry not one bit about her. Even one strand of my hair will not be disturbed by anyone in Antium."

"If you think that you can astonish me again, you are mistaken, but tell me why are you so certain of that?"

"Because the Apostle Peter told me so."

"Ah, the Apostle Peter told you so. Against that there is no argument. However permit me to advise you to take precautions even for the very reason that your mighty apostle may turn out to be a false prophet. For, should the Apostle Peter be mistaken, then he might lose your faith in him which, I am sure your Apostle Peter may need in the future."

"You can say what you want, but I believe him. And, if you think that you will be able to turn me against him by repeating his name as in a circle, then you are totally mistaken."

"One more question then: Have you already become a Christian?"

"Not yet, but Paul of Tarsus will accompany me to Antium and he will explain to me the teaching of Christ after which I will receive baptism. What you thought about Christians that they are the enemies of life is wholly false."

"Well, that's fine and I am glad for you and Ligia." After a while he shrugged his shoulders and said, "Yet, it is mystifying how rapidly this religion has spread."

"Yes. You are right. There are thousands and tens of thousands in Italy alone. There are many also in Greece and in Asia. They are numbered even among the Praetorian guards. There are even some in Caesar's palace, I believe. Some of the members of the house of Cornelius are Christians. Presumably Acte is one as well as others. This faith is renewing the earth and it alone can do it. Don't shrug your shoulders because you yourself don't know whether you may become one in the future."

"Me, a Christian? Not by the son of Leto! No, I will never become one! I will not accept Christianity even if it contains all the truth and wisdom in the world. To become a Christian would mean to renounce many things and I have no desire to renounce any of my possessions. It requires effort and as you know I'm quite lazy and do not intend to exert myself unnecessarily. It means self-denial and I don't intend to deny any pleasure in my life. With your nature, like fire and boiling water, it was possible but not for me. I have my precious gems, my beautiful vases and above all, my lovely Eunice. I do not believe in the gods but I arrange them to my own liking here on earth and they serve me, not I them. I shall go along this way till the arrows of the divine archer pierce me or, which is more likely, until Caesar commands me to open my veins. I love the smell of violets and the precise order of my house. I even love our gods but only as rhetorical figures. I'm also looking forward to the trip to Greece with our fat, thin-legged, incomparable genius, the one and only Nero."

The thought of him becoming a Christian evidently put him in a humorous mood because he began to sing in an undertone the song of one of the poets: "I will entwine bright swords in myrtle...after the example of Harmodios and Aristogeiton."

He did not finish because the arrival of Eunice was announced and supper was soon served during which they were entertained by music and song. Vinitius recounted the visit of Chilo and the result of the lashes, during which the happy thought occurred to him to visit the apostle Peter.

Petronius murmured drowsily, "Your thought was good because the result was good but as for flogging Chilo, I don't know. In your place I would have rewarded him with gold but since you decided to flog him, then perhaps it might have been better to flog him to death. Who knows, maybe some time in the future, senators themselves will bow to him like they now bow to Vatinius our noble cobbler. Well, I bid you good night for I am very sleepy."

Removing his wreath, he and Eunice took their departure. Vinitius entered his library and wrote to Ligia as follows: "When you open your beautiful eyes I want this letter to bid you good day. I'm writing now though I shall see you tomorrow. I have learned today that Caesar is leaving for Antium the day after tomorrow and as you know I have to go with him. To refuse now would mean my death and I have not the courage to die at present. However if you don't want me to go, say the word and then it would be up to Petronius to make the necessary excuses. As a result of my happiness, I gave rewards to all my slaves; those who served in my house for twenty years and over will receive their freedom; others will receive appropriate rewards for serving me well. I'm sure this will meet with your approval because it seems to me to be in accord with your religion which, I hope, will soon be mine. My slaves will have you to thank for their freedom and I will tell them so. I myself want to be your slave; you have made me so happy. I curse the necessity of my going to Antium but I am glad that I am not as wise as Petronius, otherwise I would be forced to accompany Caesar to Greece. I will think of you constantly while I am in Antium and this will compensate for my stay there. Otherwise it would be unbearable for me. Whenever I can, I shall try to break away and visit you in Rome. If I cannot come personally, I shall write you letters and send them by a trusted slave. I salute you, O divine one, and embrace your feet. Please forgive me if I offend you by calling you divine; if you forbid it I shall obey, but now I know no other salutation which befits you better than that. I love you with my whole soul!"

CHAPTER XXXVI

IT was well known in Rome that Caesar wanted to visit Ostia and see the largest ship in the world which recently docked there with a huge supply of wheat from Alexandria. His plan was to travel by way of the Via Littoralis and on to Antium.

From early morning crowds lined the route of departure; people of all nations and all tongues gathered to feast their eyes on Caesar and his retinue. The trip to Antium was not long and the palaces and villas in that city were well equipped with all kinds of comfort and luxury. However, Caesar's custom was to take with him everywhere he went, even to Antium, all the exquisite and luxurious objects in which he found delight, beginning with all sorts of musical instruments and domestic furniture and ending with statues and mosaics. He was accompanied therefore by whole legions of servants and slaves, not mentioning numerous Praetorian guards. As to his guests, each Augustian had his own private retinue.

In the early morning, herdsmen from the Campania, wearing goatskins on their legs, drove forth five hundred she-asses through the gates so that Poppaea, upon her arrival might have her usual bath in their milk. The crowds, even that early, gathered to see the animals and listen to the whistling of whips and the wild shouts of the herdsmen. After the animals passed by, crowds of young men and girls rushed about sweeping the road carefully and covering it with flowers and pine needles. The entire road to Antium was strewn this way.

As the morning hours passed, the crowds grew bigger; some

brought their whole families to witness the sight and they brought provisions with them for the day. They ate their noon meal under the open skies, amid the noise and shouts all around them. People were conversing at leisure about the retinue and wonders to be seen by those who had not yet witnessed the travels of Nero or the other Caesars. Those who had traveled abroad began to confront others with tales of the splendors of faraway places and things, tales of India and the archipelagos surrounding Britain, where the spirit of Briareus imprisoned the sleeping Saturn, and of the hisses and roars of the faraway oceans. Some had read of these places as narrated by Tacitus and Pliny, so they knew what was being discussed. They spoke of the great ships which brought so much wheat to the people of Rome and Italy. They attributed that to Nero and praised him for it. Their general mood in regards to Nero was good; he it was who nourished many of them and amused them. Hence a greeting full of enthusiasm was awaiting Nero and his retinue.

First came a detachment of Numidian horses which was part of the Praetorian guard. They wore yellow uniforms, red sashes and had earrings pierced through the lobes of their ears. Their black faces gleamed in the sun. The points of their bamboo spears glittered like flames. After they passed by, the crowd saw the Praetorian guard on foot take their places on both sides of the road. There were wagons carrying tents of all colors but especially purple and red. There were wagons laden with oriental rugs of all shades and hues; kitchen utensils and citrus tables; pieces of mosaics; cages with exotic birds from the East, North and West; birds whose tongues and brains were to be assigned for Caesar's table; vessels with wine and baskets with fruit. The more delicate objects were carried separately by slaves, such as vessels and statues of Corinthian bronze, Etruscan and Grecian vases of gold and silver; vessels of Alexandrian glass. Each division of slaves carried certain matching objects. This all looked like a huge religious procession and this resemblance became more striking when the musical instruments of Caesar were carried: harps, Grecian lutes, Hebrew lutes, Egyptian lyres, formingas, cithras, flutes, horns and cymbals. All these instruments gave rise to the thought that Apollo and Bacchus themselves had set out on a journey through the world.

After the instruments came the rich chariots filled with acrobats, male and female dancers grouped artistically with rods in their hands. There were boys and girls taken along for pleasure, not to serve in any capacity. They were a select group chosen from all Greece and Asia Minor, beautiful children resembling cupids with faces heavily made up with cosmetics lest the wind and the sun darken their delicate complexions.

A cohort of tall Sicambrians followed. They were noted for their blond and red hair and blue eyes. They bore standards, Roman eagles, tablets with inscriptions on them, statues of the gods and finally statues and busts of Nero. They were all a muscular lot, their limbs sunburnt and powerful looking. They bore heavy weapons and looked formidable indeed. The earth itself seemed to bend beneath their measured and weighty tread. They looked with contempt on the rabble as if assured of their own strength and power which they sometimes used against the reigning Caesars. Their looks were haughty when turned on the crowds; many of them forgot that they themselves rose to their present position from the ranks of manacled slaves. Their number on this march was not numerous because the greater part of them remained to guard the city and keep it in order.

Nero's lions followed the Praetorian guards. These together with tigers and other animals were led by slaves, so if the wish of imitating Dionysius should occur to Nero, he would have them handy to attach to his chariots. They were led chained by Arabs and Hindus but the chains were so camouflaged by twining flowers that they resembled flowery leashes. The lions and tigers, tamed and trained by skilled handlers, looked at the crowds with green and seemingly sleepy eyes. At times though, they raised their massive heads and breathed in the human smell all around them while licking their jaws with spiny tongues.

Now came Caesar's vehicles and litters, large and small, gold and purple, inlaid with ivory and pearls or glittering with diamonds. After them came another cohort of Praetorians in armor. These were composed of Italian mercenaries, called the Cohors Italica. At last Nero appeared greeted with shouts.

The Apostle Peter, who wanted to see Nero once in his life, was in the crowd. He was among a group of elders accompanied by Ligia and Ursus. Ligia's face was hidden by a thick veil. Ursus protected her from the sometimes wild and boisterous crowd. He picked up a huge stone which was nearby and which was meant for the future building of a temple. He brought it for the apostle to stand on. The crowd muttered at first when Ursus forced himself forward but when they saw him pick up that stone which four of the strongest among them could not even budge, then their mutterings turned into amazement and cries of *"macte"* (well done) were heard around him.

Meanwhile Caesar appeared. He was sitting in a chariot drawn by six white Idumean stallions whose hoofs were shod with gold. The sides of the chariot were exposed so that the crowds could see Caesar go by. Although it was a spacious chariot and had room for several people, Nero preferred to ride alone with only two dwarfs at his feet. He was dressed in a white tunic and a purple toga which cast a bluish tinge on his face. On his head was a laurel wreath. He had grown quite fat recently, the double chin was very noticeable. This made his mouth appear closer to his nose, almost touching his nostrils. His bulky neck was protected as usual by a silk scarf which he kept arranging now and then with his fat hand which was very white with red hair growing on it. He did not permit the red hair to be plucked because he was told that to do so would bring on trembling of the fingers and cause his lute playing to suffer.

On his face one could see total boredom and vanity—it was a horrible face. He turned his head from side to side, blinking at times and listening carefully to the manner in which the multitude greeted him. On all sides he was met with shouts of applause: "Hail divine Caesar! Hail Emperor! Son of Apollo! Apollo in person!"

When these shouts reached his ears he managed a weak smile. At moments however clouds of annoyance for the rabble would pass over his face; for Rome was always cynical and skeptical as well as derisive. It criticized even men of state whom it loved and admired. It was a fact that even during the triumphal march of Julius Caesar into Rome, Romans began to shout: "Romans, hide your wives, the old lecher is coming!" Nero's monstrous vanity however would not endure the least bit of criticism or blame. Even so, from time to time he heard shouts of "Bronze-beard, Bronze-beard. Where are you taking your flaming beard? Are you afraid to leave it in Rome because it would ignite the city?" Those who uttered such cries did not know that their jest concealed a dreadful prophecy.

Nero had shaved off his beard some time ago. He had offered it shorn in a golden cylinder to Jupiter. These cries about his beard did not offend him much but soon he heard other shouts of "Mother killer! Where is your wife? Where is Octavia? Abdicate! Murderer!" When Poppaea appeared immediately after him, they shouted at her with names such as *"flava coma"* (yellow hair, meaning prostitute), Nero's ear would catch these names and then he would turn to the crowd with his polished magnifying glass pressed to his eye and pierce them with a look which wanted to remember the perpetrators of such a crime. Once, as he looked thus, his eyes met a man with a white beard who was standing on a huge stone. They looked upon each other for a brief moment. It occurred to no one in that brilliant retinue nor to anyone in the crowd that at that moment two powers were looking at each other, one of which would pass as quickly as a bloody dream and the other, dressed in simple garments, would take over in eternal possession the world and the city.

Caesar passed and after him eight Africans bore a magnificent litter in which sat Poppaea who was so detested by the people. She was also dressed in purple. Immovable and indifferent to the shouts around her, she looked like some beautiful but wicked divinity carried in procession. In her wake followed a whole court of servants, male and female; after these came a whole line of wagons carrying materials of clothing of all kinds.

The sun was sinking noticeably now. The passage of Augustians was taking place. The indolent Petronius was greeted warmly by the crowds. He was being carried in a litter with Eunice at his side. Tigellinus traveled in a chariot drawn by ponies ornamented with white and purple feathers. He was clearly noticed because he kept rising and turning his neck towards Nero's chariot. Among others, the crowd greeted Licianus with applause, Vitellius with laughter, Vatinius with hissing. Toward Licinius and Laecanius, the consuls, the crowd seemed indifferent but Tullius Senecio, for some unknown reason, received applause as did Vestinus.

The whole retinue seemed interminable. It appeared to the watching crowds that everyone of note, and everything of value, was leaving Rome and migrating to Antium. It was Nero's custom to travel with at least a thousand vehicles and about six thousand people.

The crowd pointed fingers at different personalities passing by:

dignitaries like Domitius Afer and Lucius Saturninus received little applause; Vespasian was applauded warmly. He had not gone yet on his famous expedition to Judea from which he would return to Rome to be crowned Caesar. Young Nerva, Lucan, Annius Gallo came next. There were also many chariots of famous women of Rome who were renowned for their beauty, wealth or vice.

The eyes of the onlookers took in the chariots, the horses, the strange livery of the servants from all over the world. In all that procession of glamour, one hardly knew what to look at and not only the eyes but the imagination was dazzled by the gleam of gold, the flashing of precious stones, the glitter of brocade, pearls and ivory. It seemed that the very rays of the sun were dissolving in that abyss of brilliancy.

There were many poor people watching; people with sunken bellies and hunger in their eyes. Yet, the spectacle inflamed even them because they felt a certain kind of pride within them and because being Romans, they felt the might and invincibility of Rome. Contributions of the entire world were sent here and before this might the whole world knelt in homage. Indeed there were few among that multitude who doubted that this power would not endure for generations and outlive all nations. Nowhere in existence was there anything strong enough to oppose it.

Vinitius, riding at the end of the retinue, sprang out of his chariot at the sight of the Apostle and Ligia. He expected to see them but his joy was not diminished by this fact. He greeted them with radiant face and spoke hurriedly to Ligia, "You have come. I thank you for coming. It is a good omen for me. I bid you farewell but not for long. On the road I shall place relays of horses and every free day I shall come to you. Farewell!"

"Farewell, Marcus!" Then she added in a lower voice, "May Christ go with you and open your soul to Paul's words."

"Dearest, let it be as you say. Paul prefers to travel with my people but he is with me and will be my companion as well as teacher. Please, raise your veil so that I can at least get a brief glimpse of you. Please!"

She raised the veil and showed him her beautiful and smiling face. "Is this all right?" Vinitius looked at her full of love and turning to Ursus said, "Ursus, guard her as you would your own eyes; she is my lady as well as yours." Seizing her hand he pressed it to his lips to the astonishment of the crowd around them who wondered about this show of honor by an Augustian to a girl dressed plainly.

Vinitius departed quickly because Caesar's retinue had already pushed ahead quite a ways. The Apostle blessed him with a sign of the cross. Ursus began to praise him knowing that this pleased his lady.

The whole retinue moved on and finally disappeared in a cloud of golden dust. Th group around the Apostle watched for some time after the departing retinue until Demas, the miller, approached Peter, kissed his hand and asked him to join his group.

They partook of supper and left for home as evening was approaching and it was growing dark. They crossed the Tiber by the Aemilian bridge going along the Aventine Hill between the temples-of Diana and Mercury. From that height the Apostle looked at the dwellings below him. Sunk in silence, he meditated on the immensity and might of the city to which he had come in order to announce the word of God. Till now he knew the power of Rome through its legions in various lands which he visited. Today he saw that power personified by the evil emperor. Now, looking at Rome from the heights, he considered this city which was immense, predatory, ravenous, unrestrained, rotten to the core, but powerful. This Caesar whom he saw with his own eyes had committed fratricide, matricide, he was a wife-slayer. His followers the Augustians were a cut from the same cloth. Their profligacy was well known in Rome and elsewhere. Nero was a clown but he was also lord of thirty legions of soldiers and through them he ruled the world. These courtiers of Nero, these Augustians covered with gold and scarlet, uncertain of tomorrow, were mightier than kings.

Peter, thinking of all that, marveled that God could give such might to Satan; that God could yield this earth to him to knead, to overturn and trample upon; to squeeze blood and tears from it; to twist it like a whirlwind; to encompass it like a tempest; to consume it like a flame. In spirit he spoke to his master, "Lord, how shall I begin in this city to which You have sent me? All seas and lands belong to it; all beasts of the forests and the creatures of the seas also; it owns other kingdoms and cities and thirty legions guard them. But I, O Lord, am a poor fisherman. How shall I conquer its malice, how shall I begin? Thus thinking he raised his gray trembling head toward heaven, praying from the depths of his soul.

His prayer was interrupted by Ligia who said, "The whole city looks like it is on fire."

At that moment the sun began to disappear below the horizon. As it was disappearing the whole expanse of heaven was filled with a red gleam. From the place where they were standing, Peter's glance embraced the whole area below the Janiculum Hill. Somewhat to the right they saw the long extending walls of the Circus Maximus; above it the towering palaces of the Palatine. Directly in front of them beyond the Forum Boarium and the Velabrum, the summit of the Capitol with the temple of Jupiter was visible. A section of the Tiber was visible from afar and it seemed to be flowing with bloody waters. As the sun disappeared behind the horizon the gleam became redder and redder, like a fire which embraced the seven hills and extended to the whole region about. "The whole city seems on fire," repeated Ligia.

"The wrath of God is upon it," Peter replied.

CHAPTER XXXVII

VINITIUS TO LIGIA:

I am sending this letter by my slave Phlegon who is a Christian, hence he will be one of those who will receive his freedom at your hands, my dearest. He is an old servant of the house so I can write to you with full confidence and without fear that this letter will fall in hands other than yours. I write from Laurentum where we have halted because of the heat. Otho once owned a beautiful villa here which he donated to Poppaea. She, although divorced from him, chose to retain it for herself. When I see the women who surround me now and I think of you, I cannot but wonder how different you are from them, and I admire and love you and wish only to speak of you. But, I have to tell you of our journey. At Laurentum Poppaea prepared for Nero a magnificent reception at the villa I spoke of. She invited only a few of us; Petronius and I were included among them. After dinner we sailed in golden boats over the sea which was as calm and blue as your eyes, O loved one! We rowed the boat ourselves for it flattered the Augusta that men of consular rank or their sons were doing the rowing. Caesar, sitting at the rudder in a purple toga, sang a hymn in honor of the sea; this he composed the night before with Diodor who had arranged music for it. Other boats and musicians from India who played on large shells accompanied us. Dolphins swam about as if enjoying the music. Do you know what I was doing? I was thinking of you and yearning for you. I wanted to gather up all the sea and the music and give it to you for a present.

Would you like to live by the sea? I have some land in Sicily on which there is an almond forest which has rose-colored blossoms in spring and whose branches almost touch the water in places.

273

There we will go. I will love you and we will both praise Christ together. I know that this religion does not oppose love and happiness. Do you want that? Let me continue what happened here.

When we rowed some distance from the shore, someone spied a sail in the distance. A dispute arose as to whether it was a common fishing boat or a big ship from Ostia. I was the first to recognize it; Poppaea then turned to me and said that from my eyes evidently nothing is hidden and dropping her veil over her face she inquired if I could recognize her thus veiled. Petronius answered immediately that it was not possible to see the sun behind a cloud. She replied that love alone could blind such a keen eyesight as mine and naming various women of the court, tried to find out whom among them I loved. I answered calmly but at last she mentioned your name and as she did so she withdrew her veil and looked upon me with evil and inquiring eyes.

I was grateful to Petronius who at that precise moment tipped the boat with his oar and attention was turned from me. I don't know what I would have done or said if she had reviled you or spoken ill of you in any manner. I'm sure that I wouldn't have been able to hide my true feelings. Who knows I might have broken her head with my oar but luckily it did not come to that. You remember that incident on the pond of Agrippa about which I told you? Petronius is alarmed on my account and he again implored me not to offend Poppaea's vanity. Petronius however does not understand me any more and does not realize that apart from you I know no pleasure or love. For Poppaea, I only feel disgust and contempt. You have changed my soul so profoundly that I have no wish to return to my former self. But, do not be afraid. Poppaea does not love me for she is incapable of true love and her desire arises only from anger against Nero. He is still under her influence and perhaps still loves her; even so he does not hide from her his open transgressions and shamelessness.

I'll tell you something else. Peter told me in parting that I shouldn't fear Caesar, that nothing threatens my life here and I believe him. Some inner voice tells me that he is to be believed and since he blessed our love, neither Caesar nor all the powers of hell could take you away from me. Oh Ligia, when I think of this I am as happy as if I were in heaven. If anything I write may offend you, please forgive me. I am not as yet baptized but my heart is like an empty chalice which Paul is to fill with the sweet doctrine professed by you, the sweeter to me because it is yours. I wish to drink from this chalice as eagerly as a thirsty man standing at a pure spring. I want to find favor in your eyes in everything I do.

In Antium my days and nights will pass listening to Paul who is popular among my people so much so that they surround him whenever they can in order to listen to him. They see in him a wonder-worker and an unusual man. Yesterday I saw joy reflected on his face when I asked him what he was doing and he said to me: "I am sowing." Petronius knows that he is among my people and wishes to speak to him as does Seneca who heard about him from Gallo.

But the stars are growing pale, O Ligia, and the dawn will soon be upon us. Everyone else is sleeping except me. I'm thinking of you and loving you, my future wife!

CHAPTER XXXVIII

VINITIUS TO LIGIA :

Have you ever been in Antium, my dearest? Perhaps with Aulus and Pomponia? I will be happy to visit this city with you in the future sometime if you so desire. All the way from Laurentum there are villas along the seashore. Antium itself is an endless succession of palaces and porticos whose columns are reflected in the water in fair weather. I have a residence here also; it overlooks the sea. It has an olive garden and cypress trees behind the villa. When I think that this place will be also yours in the future, its marble seems whiter to me, its groves more shady and the sea bluer. How good it is, my dear Ligia, to live and love. Old Menikles who is the caretaker has planted irises around the villa. At the sight of them I was reminded of the irises in the house of Aulus, the flowers which you love so much. These irises will remind you of your childhood home so I'm sure that you will like it here.

Immediately after our arrival I had a long talk with Paul at dinner. We spoke of you and then I listened while he explained the teaching of Christianity. Even if I could write like Petronius, I could not explain everything which passed through my soul and mind; I didn't know that there could ever be such such happiness in this world, such beauty and peace which up to now people were not aware. I'll tell you all about this when I see you in Rome.

Sometimes I cannot understand how our world can put up with a person like Nero, the madman. Late one evening we were gathered with Nero who began reading his poem on the destruction of Troy by fire. He stopped suddenly and complained to us that as yet he had not seen a burning city. He envied Priam and called him fortunate because he was able to see his own birthplace up in flames. Whereupon Tigellinus spoke up: "O divinity, say the word and I will put the torch to Antium." But Caesar called him a fool. "Where," he said, "can I get away from the foul smells of Rome but here in Antium? Is it not the smells of Subura and the Esquiline which cause me to get hoarse? Would not a burning Rome present a spectacle a hundred times greater than a burning Antium?" All of us broke in to tell him what a great tragedy that would be to burn the city which had conquered the world and to turn it into ashes. Caesar argued that seeing Rome burning, his poem would surpass the poem of Homer. He then began to describe how he would rebuild Rome and how the coming ages would admire his achievement, greater than any other. Some of the drunken revelers began shouting "Do this! Do this!" He answered them by saying, "Before I do that, I must have with me more faithful and devoted followers." I was alarmed listening to all this because you are in Rome. I laugh at this fear and alarm; even a mad Caesar would not dare to permit such madness. Still, see how I fear for the one I love. Would it not be better, considering everything, to leave the house of Linus, which as you know, is situated in the narrow confines of the Trans-Tiber section?

Go to the house of Aulus and Pomponia, my dearest. I worry about this. If Nero were in Rome, news of your return would reach him quickly through the slaves and perhaps turn his attention to you and bring about the possible persecution against you. However he will remain here for some time yet and everyone will forget about you and cease to speak of you. Linus and Ursus could accompany you there. Besides, I live in the hope that before the Palatine sees Caesar, you, my goddess, shall be dwelling in my house. Blessed be the day, the hour, the moment when you shall cross my threshold. If Christ permits this to be, then I shall serve Him and give my life for Him. But perhaps I speak incorrectly. We shall both serve Him as long as life lasts for both of us.

I love you with all my heart and soul!

CHAPTER XXXIX

URSUS drawing water from a cistern was humming to himself. It was an old Ligian song and Ursus was happy because his lady was especially radiant this evening. Vinitius paid her a sudden visit from Antium and they were both conversing joyfully in the calm of the evening. Among the cypresses in the garden of Linus, they seemed as white as two statues; their clothing was not moved by the least breeze. A golden and lily-colored twilight was sinking on the world about them.

"Will any harm come to you, Marcus, for leaving Caesar and coming here?"

"No, my dearest, Caesar announced that he would shut himself up for two days with Terpnos and compose a new song. He sometimes does this and at that time doesn't care for anything else or to see anyone else. Anyway, what is Caesar to me now that I am near you and looking at your sweet face? I missed you so much. Sometimes I would fall off to sleep and suddenly wake up with fear that you are in some kind of danger. Also, I would think that the relays of horses which I have left at different points have been stolen. But, everything went off smoothly. No courier of Caesar's made as fast a trip from Antium to Rome as I have. Besides, I could not stay away any longer. I love you, my dearest."

"I had a feeling you were coming! Twice, I had Ursus run to your house inquiring about you. They all laughed at my fears here."

Indeed, she seemed to expect him because instead of the usual dark dress, she wore a soft white stola, from the beautiful folds of which her arms emerged like primroses out of snow. A few rosy anemones adorned her beautiful black hair.

Vinitius pressed his lips to her hands, then they both sat on a stone bench amidst the grape vines, holding hands and inclining their heads toward each other, looking at the twilight whose last gleams were reflected in their eyes.

The wonderful evening of peace and quiet immersed them both in rapture and delight. Vinitius spoke, "How calm it is here and how beautiful the world is. I feel happier now than I have ever been. I used to think that love was just a flame coursing through the veins and sensual desire. Now, for the first time, I know that it is possible to love with every drop of one's blood and every breath, and at the same time feel such sweet and immeasurable calm as if Sleep and Death had put the soul to rest. For me this is something new. Now I begin to understand this happiness of which people are not aware. Now I understand why you and Pomponia have such peace. Yes, it must come from Christ! He alone can give this kind of happiness."

Ligia placed her head on his shoulder and replied, "My dear Marcus." She was unable to continue because joy, gratitude and happiness filled her soul and the knowledge that now, at last, she was free to love. This deprived her of speech for the moment and her eyes filled with tears of joy.

Vinitius, drawing her slender form closer to him said, "Ligia, may the moment be blessed when I heard His Name for the first time."

"I love you, Marcus," she responded in a low but firm voice.

Both became silent unable to speak because they were overcome with a tremendous feeling of love. After a while, when the garden about them changed to a silver-like reflection from the moon above, Vinitius spoke, "I know. Barely had I kissed your hands when I read the question in your eyes. No, I have not been baptized as yet but you know why? Paul said to me, 'I convinced you that God came into this world and gave Himself to be crucified for its salvation but Peter will baptize you.' And I, my dearest, want you to witness my baptism. I also want Pomponia to be my godmother. This is the only reason that I am not baptized yet though I believe in the Savior and His teaching. Paul convinced me; he converted me, and could it be otherwise? How could I not believe that He was God since He rose from the dead? Others saw Him in the city of Jerusalem and on the lake of Genesareth and also on the mountain top; people whose lips have never known a lie claimed to see Him so why shouldn't I believe it? In Ostrianum I said to myself regarding Peter: 'That man speaks the truth!' At first I was of the opinion that there was neither wisdom nor beauty in it but now I am convinced of the truth of it, its wisdom and beauty. I would be less a man if I did not want this truth to rule the world instead of falsehood, love instead of hatred, virtue instead of crime, faithfulness instead of promiscuity, mercy instead of vengeance. Who of right mind would not wish the same? Christianity teaches this and more. Others desire justice but Christianity is the only religion which makes one's heart just, makes it pure like your heart and Pomponia's, makes it faithful too. One would be blind not to see this. If in addition Christ promises eternal happiness in eternal life after death, what more could one wish for? If I were to ask Seneca why he urges the practice of virtue if vice brings more sensual pleasure, he would not be able to give me a satisfactory answer. But now I know that I should be virtuous because virtue and love flow from Christ, and because when death closes my eyes, I shall find unending happiness in heaven and you enjoying it with me. Why should not all embrace this religion which speaks the truth and destroys the power of death? Who can prefer evil to good? At first I thought that this religion was the enemy of happiness but now I am convinced that it not only does not take away happiness but it enriches it. All this must be true because I have never been so happy before. If I had taken you by force and possessed you, I would never have heard the words which you just said: I love you. And I could not have forced you even with the might of Rome to utter them, but you said them now and you meant them with all your heart as I mean them also. Oh Ligia, reason alone tells me that this religion is divine and my heart feels it fully. Who can resist two such forces?"

Ligia listened to him focusing her pretty eyes on him which in the light of the moon shone like beautiful stars.

"Yes, Marcus, that is true," she said, nestling her head more closely to his shoulder.

They were both extremely happy because they understood that they were united not only by their love for one another but also united by another power, irresistible yet sweet, by which this love of theirs became endless. Treason, deceit and even death had no dominion over it. Their hearts were certain that no matter what happened, they would not cease to love one another and to belong to each other. For that reason peace and joy filled their souls. This kind of love was not only deep and pure but also new, such a love the world cannot give. For him in this love all was united: Ligia, the teaching of Christ, the light of the moon and the still night, so that to him the whole universe seemed filled with it.

After a while he spoke, "You will be the soul of my soul and the dearest possession in the world to me. Our hearts will beat as one and we shall pray in gratitude to Christ. What a thought! Love together, praise Christ together and after this life to live together in eternal joy. What more can I ask for? You know what I think? It is this: In time no one will be able to resist this religion. In two hundred...three hundred years the whole world will accept it for how can it be otherwise? People will forget Jupiter and there will be no gods but Christ and temples in His honor. I heard Paul's conversation with Petronius about all this and you know what Petronius replied: 'That's not for me.' He could find no other answer."

"Please repeat Paul's words to me," requested Ligia.

"It was at my house one evening. Petronius began to speak lightly and to banter about as is his custom, whereupon Paul asked him, 'How can you deny, O wise Petronius, that Christ existed and rose from the dead since you were not there but Peter and John saw Him and I saw Him and heard His words on the road to Damascus? Let your wisdom then first of all show us up as liars and then only deny our testimony.' Petronius replied that he had no intention of contradicting Paul's words; he knew that many incomprehensible things were done which trustworthy people affirmed, but he added, 'The discovery of some new foreign god is one thing and the acceptance of his teaching is another. I refuse to believe anything that destroys life and mars its beauty. It doesn't matter whether our gods are true or not, they are beautiful, they are pleasing to us and allow us to live without a care in the world.' Paul replied, 'You are willing to reject the religion of love, justice and mercy because you fear that it will bring all kinds of anxieties and cares, but think, Petronius, is your life really free from anxieties and fear? Not one of you, even though you are all rich and powerful among your own, no one among you, I repeat, knows that when he falls asleep at night, he may not wake to a death sentence in the morning. But, tell me, if Caesar professed this religion which urges love and justice, would not your own happiness be more assured and would you not be more free than before? You are alarmed that this religion would mar your pleasure, but would not, on the contrary, life be more pleasing to all? As to life's beauties and ornaments, if you have built so many temples to gods who are evil, revengeful, adulterous and faithless divinities, what could You not do in honor of One God of Truth and Mercy? You are pleased with your lot in life but you could have been born poor or deformed or deserted...would it not then have been better for you if people confessed Christ? In Rome even wealthy parents, unwilling to rear children, cast them out of their houses; these children as you know are called alumni. Chance might have made you also an alumnus like one of them. But if parents live according to our religion, this could not happen. If you had married a woman you love, you would want her to be faithful to you. But, look around you! What is happening? What vileness, what shamelessness among the women of Rome! You yourselves are astonished when you come across a woman you call *univira* (a one-man woman). But, I tell you that women who believe in Christ and live by His teaching will be true to their husbands just as Christian husbands will be true to their wives if they heed Christ's teaching. You are not sure of your rulers; you are not sure of your wives; you are not sure of your servants and slaves. The whole world trembles before you but you tremble before your own slaves because at any moment they might rise against you as they have done in the past. You are now rich and influential but you do not know how you will fare tomorrow. Your riches may be taken away from you and you may be cast aside from Caesar's favor. You are still young but you may have to die tomorrow. Today you are rich, tomorrow you may be exiled to poverty. Now, you have a thousand slaves; tomorrow these same slaves may take your own life and if all this is so, how can you and others like you live in peace and calm and be truly happy?'"

"'I proclaim however a love and a religion which commands rulers to love their subjects; masters, their slaves, slaves to respect authority and serve with obedience and love. Through this religion, I proclaim justice and mercy, and finally, I proclaim and promise through Christ Himself a happiness and joy that will be eternal. How then, wise Petronius, can you say that this teaching spoils life and its beauty? How can you say that it is the enemy of life when, on the contrary, it greatly improves living at all levels and for all people. You and everybody else would be a hundred times happier and a hundred times more secure of tomorrow if you would live under its dominion rather than under the dominion of ruthless and evil Roman emperors?'"

"Thus spoke Paul but all Petronius could answer at the end was, 'That's not for me, Judean. I prefer my Eunice to your religion but I'll tell you one thing: I would not want to debate with you on any platform!'"

"I listened to Paul and when he spoke of the women of Rome, my heart surged with joy that you, my dearest, are different from them. I thought of Poppaea who cast aside two husbands for Nero; Calvia Crispinilla, Nigidia and the numerous others who have no honor nor shame and I compared them all to you. You are like the pure lily among them, from a rich field in springtime, and I thanked Christ for keeping you thus. I know that you will never desert me, never be unfaithful and I am grateful to Christ and to you. I will try to show Him my gratitude and I will never cease to love and honor you for what you are and what you will be to me always. I'm glad that you fled from Caesar's house. Neither do I care for Caesar's house any longer. I do not want its luxury and music; I want only you. Say the word and we will leave Rome at the first opportunity and settle somewhere else."

Without raising her head Ligia raised her eyes to the silver tops of the cypress trees and answered, "Very well, Marcus. You wrote to me of Sicily where Aulus wants to settle down in his old age. We could go there if you wish!"

"All right, my dearest, we will go there. My property is not far from the land that belongs to Aulus. It's wonderful there. The climate is better and the nights brighter than here in Rome. I'm sure that you will like it there."

They began to talk and make plans for the future. Vinitius said, "There, we will forget our anxieties. We will walk among the groves in the shade among olive trees. O Ligia, what a life it will be for both of us. To love and cherish one another, to gaze upon the sea together, to look at the sky and honor our God together and to live in peace and justice for the rest of our lives."

Both were silent looking toward the future. He drew her closer to him; every part of that garden was so peaceful as if in unison with the peace and happiness in their souls.

"Will you permit me to visit Pomponia?" asked Ligia.

"Yes, dear. We will invite them to our house or visit them together or you may go there by yourself as you wish. We can take Peter with us and Paul also if they wish to come. Paul will be able to convert Aulus I'm sure. We will be as soldiers in virgin territory and we will be able to found colonies of Christians."

Ligia, taking his hand in hers wanted to press it to her lips but he whispered, "No, Ligia. It is I who honor you and exalt you. Please give me your hand."

"I love you!" said Ligia.

For a while all they heard was the beating of their hearts. There was not the slightest movement in the air; the cypress trees stood motionless as if they too were holding still for this couple of loving souls.

Suddenly the silence was broken by an unexpected roar, deep as if coming from under the earth. A shiver ran through Ligia's body. Vinitius stood up and said, "The lions are roaring in their dens."

Both began to listen. Now the first roar was answered by others and seemed to come from all sides and from all parts of Rome. There were several thousand lions quartered in various arenas of Rome and frequently in the night time they approached their gratings and let out roars which loudly spoke of their yearning for freedom and the forests. Thus, on this night they began their roaring, answering one another all over Rome and they filled the city with their fearful and mournful raging. There was something terrifying about these sounds, and Ligia whose bright and calm visions of the future were dissipated by these cries, felt a sudden and dreadful fear and sadness.

But Vinitius, encircling his arm around her, with a protecting voice, said to her, "Fear not, my dearest. The great games are at hand and all the dens are full.'"

Then both entered the house of Linus accompanied by the fury of lions which was growing louder and louder.

CHAPTER XL

IN Antium meanwhile, Petronius gained new victories daily over other Augustians who were vying for the favor of Caesar. The influence of Tigellinus reached a record low. In Rome, where there was always an occasion to do away with people who seemed dangerous to Nero, and to plunder their holdings to settle political cases, and to produce spectacles in the arena which astounded everyone by their luxury—not to mention bad taste—or even to satisfy the monstrous whims of the mad Caesar, Tigellinus was ready for anything and in this way he became indispensable to Nero. But in Antium, among the palaces and close to the shining sea, Nero led a Hellenic existence.

From morning till night Nero and his attendants read verses and discoursed on their structure and completion, studied drama, listened to music and took part in the theater. In other words Nero led a life of poetry and music which the genius of Greece had invented. Under these conditions, Petronius, who was incomparably more refined than Tigellinus and the other courtiers, was certainly in his proper element. He was witty, eloquent, always ready with the right word and right suggestion for procuring activities of good taste and elegance.

Caesar sought his company, listened to his opinions, asked for his advice when he composed rhymes and showed toward him a livelier friendship than ever before. It now seemed to all that the influence of Petronius would culminate in his final victory over all, especially Tigellinus, his arch rival. This victory, they were sure, would last for a long time.

Even those who in the past had shown dislike toward this exquisite Epicurean began now to crowd around him, vying for his favor. More than one was even sincerely glad in his heart that this kind of victory came to a man who knew what to think of a person and who received with his usual cynical smile all the flattery which now poured over him. They knew that he was not vengeful nor did he use his influence toward the destruction of others. There were even moments when he could have destroyed Tigellinus himself but he preferred to ridicule him and expose his vulgarity and lack of refinement.

In Rome the Senate drew a sigh of relief for no death sentences had been issued for a month and a half. They all spoke of the heights which this favorite of Nero had finally reached and they preferred a favorite of Caesar who was refined to one who was brutal and ruthless as Tigellinus was. The latter was becoming more and more frustrated as days wore on. Nero daily repeated to all that in the entire world there were only two geniuses who were capable of understanding the Hellenic life of poetry and music to the utmost: he and Petronius.

The amazing flexibility of the latter confirmed to the others that his influence would now be secure. Who else could converse with Caesar in such a way regarding poetry and music? Nero had only eyes and ears for criticism from the lips of Petronius, the Arbiter of Elegance, when he began his compositions.

Petronius with his habitual indifference seemed to attach no importance to his position. As usual he was seemingly indolent, skeptical and cynical. People whom he talked to had the impression that he was having fun with them, with himself and with Caesar. At moments he even criticized Nero to his face and when the others thought that he really went too far each time, he was able to turn the criticism in such a way that it came out as praise. By this, they were convinced that there was no situation from which he could not extricate himself to his own benefit.

About a week after the return of Vinitius from his visit to Rome, Nero was reading an excerpt he composed in honor of Troy. When he had finished everyone shouted his praise, that is everyone except Petronius. Interrogated by a glance from Nero, he replied, "Merely common verses, fit only for the fire!"

Those present looked at him with surprise. Nero was astonished to hear such words. No one dared to criticize him in this way since his childhood. The face of Tigellinus lit up suddenly with vengeful satisfaction. Vinitius grew pale thinking that Petronius, for the first time, had too much to drink.

Nero however inquired in a honeyed tone in which he could not disguise his wounded pride, "What fault do you find in them?"

Petronius turned toward him an animated face. "Don't listen to them. They understand nothing. You ask me what fault do I find in these verses? Well, I'll tell you. Although these verses are equal to those of Virgil, Ovid and even Homer, they are not worthy of you. The fire that you describe does not burn sufficiently; it is not hot enough. Don't listen to the praise of Lucan here. Had he written them then I would concede greatness to him but in your case it is different. And do you know why? You are greater than they. From him who is gifted of the gods, more is required. But you are getting a little lazy. You would rather sleep after the noonday meal than sit down to compose. I am sure that if you really try you will be able to compose a work of art unknown to the world up to now. So Caesar, to your face I say: 'Write something better.'"

Saying this, Petronius seemed as if he were merely chiding and carelessly giving his honest opinion. However, Nero's eyes filled with misty delight.

"Gods gave me some talent but they have given me something more...they have given me a true companion, friend and honest judge, the only man who can speak the truth to my eyes."

Then he stretched out his fat hand, overgrown with reddish hair, to a golden candelabrum plundered from Delphi in order to burn the verses. But Petronius seized them before the flame touched the paper.

"No! No! Even these are worthy to be preserved for the good of mankind. Leave them Caesar to me!"

"In that case," replied Nero standing up and embracing Petronius, "allow me to find a proper cylinder in which I shall send them to you."

"True, you are right," he continued after a while. "My fire of Troy does not burn enough; it is not hot enough. I thought that it would be sufficient to equal Homer. I do not think highly enough of my talents. Now, you have opened my eyes. But, do you know why it is so? I have never had a proper model to look at; I have never seen a burning city. That is why I cannot produce it correctly in verse."

Petronius answered, "Only a great artist realizes this fact."

Nero grew thoughtful. Then he spoke, "Answer me one question, Petronius. Do you regret the burning of Troy?"

"Do I regret it? By the lame consort of Venus, I do not! Not in the least. And I'll tell you why: Troy would not have been consumed had not the god Prometheus given fire to man and if Greece had not made war on Priam. Aeschylus would not have written his Prometheus had there been no fire, just as Homer would not have written his *Iliad* had there been no Trojan war. I think it is better to have Prometheus and the *Iliad* than some small shabby city which I'm sure was wretched and dirty to boot and which if it now existed would only annoy you with its complaints and quarrels."

"This is what we call speaking with sound reason," said Nero. "For the sake of art and beauty it is permitted to sacrifice everything. Happy were the Greeks who produced Homer and supplied him with substance for his *Iliad* and happy Priam who beheld the ruin of his birthplace. As for me I have never seen a burning city."

Silence followed, broken finally by the heated words of Tigellinus: "I told you, Caesar, to command me and I will burn down Antium to the ground for you or, if you wish to preserve these villas and palaces; give but an order and I will burn all the ships in Ostia or I will build a wooden city on the Alban Hills into which you can throw a burning torch. Do you wish it, O Caesar?"

"Am I to gaze at the burning of wooden sheds?" asked Nero casting a look of contempt on him. "Your mind is indeed empty, Tigellinus, and I see clearly that you set little value on my talents or my Troyad. You do not understand that no sacrifice is big enough for me."

Tigellinus was confused at this answer. Nero however kept speaking in another vein. "The summer will soon be over. What a stench there must be in Rome now. And we have to return there for the summer games. O gods!"

"When you dismiss the Augustians, Caesar, permit me to remain with you for a moment," said Tigellinus.

An hour later Vinitius, returning with Petronius from Caesar's villa observed, "I was very much alarmed about you today. I thought that you were drunk and ruined yourself beyond redemption. You are playing with death."

"That is my arena," answered Petronius carelessly, "and it amuses me that I am the best gladiator in it. See how it ended? My influence increased as of this evening. Nero will send his verses in a capsule which I will wager will be immensely expensive and also of poor taste. I shall give it to my doctor for him to preserve my toilet articles in. I acted like this for another reason. Tigellinus will try so much harder now to imitate me and I can imagine what will happen. The moment he tries to make a witty remark will be as if a bear were trying to walk a tight rope. I shall have myself a good laugh when I see that. Perhaps, if I wished I could destroy Tigellinus and become the Praetorian prefect in his place and have Bronze-beard in my power. But, I am lazy and I prefer my present life such as it is and even prefer Caesar's verses to becoming prefect of the Praetorians."

"What dexterity! To be able to turn rebuke into flattery. But tell me, are those verses really so bad? I'm no judge in these matters."

"Those verses aren't any worse than the others. Lucan has more talent in his little finger than our Bronze-beard in his whole body, but even in him there is something. Above all there is an immense love of poetry and music. In two days we are to be with him to hear his music in honor of Aphrodite. There will be only you, me, Tullius, Senecio and young Nerva. But, as regards Nero's verses and what I said about them, that I use them after feasting as Vitelius uses flamingo feathers to throw up, is not altogether true. At times his verses are not bad at all. Hecuba's words are touching. She complains of the pangs of birth and Nero was able to come up with some good expressions, perhaps because he gives birth to every verse in torment. At times I'm even sorry for him. By Pollux! What a strange mixture of a man! Caligula was crazy, but even he did not attempt to do things which Nero perpetrates."

"Who can foresee to what lengths he will go?"

"No one indeed! He may even try some things which not only will shock the present generation but also future generations as well. However, there are some things which please me and keep me from being bored to death and those are poetry, music and the arts in general. Under another Caesar I would perhaps be bored even more. Your friend Paul is eloquent, that I grant him, and if people like him start preaching Christianity, our gods will have a difficult time defending themselves. I agree with him that if Nero were a Christian, all of us would feel much safer. But, your prophet from Tarsus does not understand me nor my way of thinking. To me all this is a game, although I admit a serious and deadly one at times, but a gamble like playing dice for instance. There is a kind of pleasure in the danger of the moment and the chances one takes even towards the safety of life itself. This uncertainty is enticing to me and I play because it pleases me for the danger involved. Christian virtues would only bore me just like the discourses of Seneca. Paul's eloquence has gone for naught as far as I am concerned only because of this. People like me are reluctant to accept this religion. With a disposition such as yours, you could either hate it or accept it wholeheartedly. With me it is this way: I recognize the truth in what they say but I do so while yawning. Yes it is true, we are mad; we are on the edge of a precipice; something is breaking up underneath; something is dying around us.... Yes, all this is true. But I say to you that we will succeed in going down manfully. In the meantime we do not wish to put burdens on life or wish for death before it takes us. Life exists for itself alone, not for death."

"I feel sorry for you, Petronius."

"Don't feel more sorry for me than I feel for myself. Once you were a good companion among us and during your campaign in Armenia you longed to see Rome."

"I long to see Rome now."

"Sure, because you love that beautiful Vestal Virgin, Ligia, who lives across the Tiber. I don't blame you for it nor am I surprised. I'm more surprised at the fact that despite your religion which you say gives you happiness, there is sadness on your face. Despite the fact that you will possess the one you love soon, there is sadness. Pomponia is always sad also. Don't try to persuade me that this religion is cheerful. You have returned from Rome sadder than ever. If Christians love this way, well, by the bright curls of Bacchus, I shall not imitate them."

"That is something else. I swear to you, Petronius, not by the curls of Bacchus but by the soul of my father, that never in times past have I experienced even a foretaste of such happiness as I enjoy today. But, I yearn greatly for Ligia and when I am away from her

I have a feeling that some danger is threatening her. I don't know what danger or whence it may come but I feel it as one feels a coming tempest."

"I will take it upon myself to try to get permission for you to leave Antium. Just give me two days and I think that I will be able to accomplish it. Poppaea is somewhat more quiet now and as far as I know, no danger threatens from that side."

"This very day she asked me what I was doing in Rome although I kept my departure secret."

"Perhaps she hired people to spy on you. However even she must count with me these days."

"Paul told me that God sometimes forewarns us but does not permit us to believe in omens, hence I guard myself against forebodings of danger but I cannot ward it off completely. I will tell you what happened. It will help me to get it off my chest. Ligia and I were sitting side by side one night as calm as now and planning our future. I cannot tell you how happy and peaceful we were. All at once lions began to roar. That is common in Rome nowadays but I tell you that since that moment I have no peace of mind regarding the safety of Ligia. It seems to me that this raging of lions is a warning sound of threatening misfortune in the future. You know that I do not frighten easily; that night however something happened which filled all the darkness with terror. It came so unexpectadly and strangely that I still hear those sounds in my ears. I have this fear in my heart as if Ligia calls to me to save her from some forthcoming danger to her. Please obtain permission for me to leave. Otherwise I just might leave without it. I cannot remain here much longer."

Petronius began to laugh. "Sons of consuls and their wives are not given up to lions as yet, I assure you. Any other death may meet you but not that. I ridicule omens and fates. Last night was warm and stars were falling like rain. Some people have evil forebodings at this sight but I thought to myself that if among these stars is my own star then I shall not lack for company." Then, after a while he added, "If your Christ rose from the dead, then He will be able to protect you and Ligia."

"Yes, He could," asserted Vinitius.

CHAPTER XLI

NERO, playing his lute, sang a hymn in honor of Venus, the Lady of Cypress. He composed these verses himself. That day he was in voice and he really felt that his music and verse had captivated his audience. This feeling gave him confidence and stimulated him so much that he appeared inspired.

For the first time in his life, he refused to listen to the praises round about him. He merely sat with his head bowed and was silent. Suddenly, raising his head he said, "I am tired and need a little fresh air. Tune the instruments while I am gone." So saying he wrapped a silk scarf around his throat and turning to Petronius and Vinitius who were sitting apart by themselves, commanded them, "You two come with me. You, Vinitius, will give me support for I am still weak. Petronius will speak to me about music and poetry."

They left to walk on the terrace which was paved with alabaster and sprinkled with saffron.

"Here one can breathe more freely," said Nero. "My soul is moved with emotion because I now know that I can appear publicly to sing that song which I had just sung to you. No Roman has ever achieved such a triumph as I will get from the people of Rome."

Petronius answered, "Yes, Caesar, you should appear in Rome and also in Greece. I admire you with all my heart and soul, divinity!"

"I know that you are rather lazy in your praises but you are sincere, just as sincere as Tullius Senecio, but you know more about music and poetry than he does. Tell me truthfully, what is your opinion of music?"

"When I listen to poetry, when I see you in a chariot driven by four beautiful horses, when I look at a beautiful statue, temple or picture, I feel that I comprehend what I see and my enthusiasm is the result of what I see; but when I listen to music, especially if it is your music, new delights and beauties open up a fresh vista for me. As I try to embrace them, ever more delights flow in like waves of the sea. Hence I say that music is like the sea. We stand on one shore and look afar but cannot see the other distant shore. So too, it is true with music: we hear it, evaluate it, are pleased with it, yet we are never satisfied but always yearn for more."

"Ah. What deep feelings you have about music!" said Nero.

They walked a while in silence which was broken only by the rustle of their feet upon the saffron on the terrace walk.

"You spoke my mind exactly," said Nero. "I say that in all Rome you alone are able to understand me. I feel the same about music as you do. When I play and sing I visualize things which I thought never existed. I know that I am Caesar and that the world is mine, yet music opens up to me new kingdoms, new seas, new delights unknown before. I feel them close. I see Olympus. I feel the presence of the gods. New and unearthly breezes blow over me. I behold an immeasurable greatness within my bosom and all around me as if it were a calm but bright sunshine. At these moments, I, Nero, Caesar and god, feel as small as a flicker of dust. Can you believe all this?"

"I can. Only great artists feel small in the presence of art."

"This is the night of sincerity," went on Nero excitedly. "I open my soul to you as a friend and I will say more. Do you think that I am blind to what is going on? Do you think that I am ignorant of what people are saying and writing on the walls about me? The different insults? That I am a mother-killer, a wife-murderer? They think me a monster and a tyrant because Tigellinus obtained a few sentences of death against my enemies. Yes, I know what they think. They talk about me so much that even I ask myself, 'Am I so cruel?'"

"However," continued Nero, "they do not understand that a man's deeds sometimes must be cruel but the man himself is not cruel. You perhaps may not believe me when I say that at moments when music caresses my soul, I am like a child in a cradle. I swear by the stars above that I speak the truth. People are not aware how much goodness and kindness lie within my heart and what treasures I see in it when music opens the door to them."

Petronius did not doubt for a minute that Nero spoke sincerely at this time, and that music indeed brought out the more noble inclinations in his soul which was overwhelmed by mountains of egotism, profligacy and crime. He said, "People should know you as I do. Rome had never been able to appreciate you."

Caesar leaned more heavily on the arm of Vinitius as if he were bending under the weight of injustice and said, "Tigellinus told me that even in the Senate they whisper that Diodor and Terpnos play better on the lyres than I do. They refuse me even that. But tell me, you are always truthful, do they play better than I do?"

"Not in the least! Your touch is more refined and you are stronger. In you, one can see the artist; in them, merely good lyricists. When one listens to them, one can appreciate you better."

"If that is true, then let them live. They will never guess what a service you have done them right now. Anyway, if I condemned these two, I would only have to get two others in their place."

"And people would say that out of love for music, you destroy musicians. Never kill art for art's sake, divinity."

"How different you are from Tigellinus. You can see that I am an artist and, for an artist such as I am, there are places to reach such as haven't been reached up to now; delights and joys which I have not possessed as yet. I cannot live merely a common life. Music tells me that there are extraordinary aims to strive for. At times it seems to me that I must do something which no man has ever done. I must surpass acts of man in good as well as in evil. I know that people say that I am mad. But I am merely seeking. And, if I am going mad it is because of the impatience that I feel in wanting to accomplish things which I seek. Do you understand me? I want to be greater than any other man who ever lived and the greatest artist who ever existed."

Here he lowered his voice so that Vinitius would not be able to hear and, turning closer to Petronius whispered in his ear. "Do you know that the reason why I condemned my mother and my wife to death was because I wished to lie at the gates of the unknown world, the greatest sacrifice that one could put there. I thought that after that, something very unusual would happen to me, that here doors would open beyond which I would see something very extraordinary and unknown. No matter whether it was wonderful or terrible. It mattered only that it be great and unusual. It seems however, that it wasn't sufficient. Something greater is now needed and this I will do!"

"What do you intend to do?"

"You will see sooner than you think. Meanwhile be assured that there are two Neros, and if this artist causes pain and death even, and even if he strives to live a frenzied life like Bacchus, it is only because the boredom and staleness of ordinary life stifles him.

"I will free myself from this boredom, from this staleness even if I have to use fire and sword. How this world will miss me when I am gone. No man really knows what a superior artist I am, perhaps not even you, Petronius. But precisely because of this I suffer and I tell you sincerely that my soul is sad and as gloomy as these cypresses which are there in front of us. The weight of supreme power and highest talents is indeed hard to bear."

"I sympathize with you, O Caesar, and with me the earth and the sea, not to mention Vinitius here who idolizes you."

"He too has always been dear to me," said Nero, "though he serves Mars not the Muses."

"First of all he serves Aphrodite." Suddenly, Petronius decided to try to settle the affair of his nephew with one stroke and at the same time eliminate any danger that might threaten him. So, he said, "He is in love as was Troilus with Cressida. Permit him, O Caesar, to visit Rome for he is pining away. Do you know that the Ligian hostage whom you have given him has been found and Vinitius, when leaving Rome, left her in care of a certain Linus? I did not mention this to you because you were composing your hymn and that was far more important. Vinitius wanted her as a mistress but when he found out that she was as virtuous as Lucretia, he fell in love with her and now desires to marry her. She is a king's daughter, hence she will cause him no shame, but he is a soldier, so he sighs, withers and groans. He does nothing without his emperor's permission."

"The emperor does not choose wives for his soldiers. What good is my permission?"

"I have mentioned Caesar that he idolizes you."

"All the more may he be certain of my permission. That is a beautiful girl but too narrow in the hips. The Augusta complained to me that she bewitched our child in the Palatine gardens."

"But I told Tigellinus that the gods are not subject to evil charms. You remember his confusion to that, divinity, and how you yourself exclaimed, '*Habet!*'"

"I remember."

Here he turned to Vinitius. "Do you love this girl as Petronius claims?"

"I love her, sire," replied Vinitius.

"Then I command you to set out to Rome tomorrow and marry her and don't appear before me without the marriage ring."

"Thank you, Caesar, from the bottom of my heart."

"Oh, how good it is to make people happy! Would that I do nothing other than that the rest of my life."

"Grant us one more favor, divinity. Please declare your will in this matter before the Augusta. Vinitius would never venture to wed a woman who is displeasing to our Augusta. You will then dissipate her prejudice with a word by declaring that you have commanded this marriage."

"I am willing. I cannot refuse anything to you or Vinitius."

He turned back toward the villa and they followed. Their hearts were filled with joy over the victory and Vinitius had to use self-restraint to avoid throwing himself on the neck of Petronius in gratitude, for it seemed now that all danger and obstacles were removed.

Inside, young Nerva and Tullius Senecio were entertaining the Augusta with conversation. Terpnos and Diodor were tuning the lyres.

Nero entered, sat down in an armchair which was inlaid with tortoise shell, whispered something in the ear of a slave and waited.

The slave returned shortly holding in his hands a golden jewel-box which he presented to Nero who opened it and took out a necklace of opals.

"These are jewels worthy of the evening," said he.

"The light of the goddess of dawn, Aurora, shines through them," answered Poppaea, thinking that the necklace was for her.

Caesar, now raising, now lowering the necklace, said at last,

"Vinitius, you will present this necklace from me to the young daughter of the Ligian king whom I command you to marry."

Poppaea's look of surprise and anger passed from Caesar to Vinitius and finally rested on Petronius, but he, leaning casually on the arm of a chair passed his hand along the back of the harp as if to fix its form firmly in his mind.

Vinitius, meanwhile, after giving due thanks to Caesar for the gift approached Petronius and said softly to him, "How shall I ever thank you for what you have done for me today?"

"Sacrifice a pair of swans to the goddess Euterpe," replied Petronius. "Praise Caesar's songs and laugh at omens. Henceforth the roar of lions will not disturb your sleep, I trust, nor that of your Ligian beauty."

"No, I am entirely at rest."

"May fortune favor you but be careful for Caesar is taking up his lyre again."

Caesar, in fact, did take up the instrument and raised his eyes. All conversation ceased and all stood still as if petrified. Terpnos and Diodor accompanied Nero, looking now at Caesar, now at each other, waiting for the tones of the song.

At that moment there was a commotion at the door entrance. Caesar's freedman Phaon appeared suddenly from behind the curtain. Close behind him was the consul Laecanius.

Nero frowned.

"Pardon, divine Emperor!" exclaimed Phaon. "Rome is burning! The greater part of the city is in flames!

At this news all sprang forward.

"O gods! I shall see a burning city and finish my *Troyad*," cried Nero. Then he turned to the consul. "If I go at once, shall I see the fire?"

"Sire," said Laecanius as pale as a ghost, "the whole city is one sea of flames! Smoke is suffocating the inhabitants and people are fainting everywhere or casting themselves into the flames. Rome is perishing!"

A moment of silence followed broken by the cry of Vinitius, *"Vae misero mihi!"* And, casting his toga aside, he rushed forth in his tunic. Nero raised his hands and exclaimed, "Woe to you, O sacred city of Priam!"

CHAPTER XLII

VINITIUS had barely time to command a few slaves to follow him, then springing onto his horse he rushed forth into the deep night along the empty streets of Antium toward the town of Laurentum. The terrible news still held him in shock. He wasn't altogether sure that all this was not a nightmare; he only had a feeling that misfortune rode along with him, sitting behind him on his horse and shouting in his ear: "Rome is burning!" This specter was lashing his horse onward. Laying his head on the horse's mane, he rushed on, unaware of the obstacles in the way and relying on the horse to avoid them.

In that calm night the horse and rider seemed like an unearthly vision of the night. The Idumean horse, folding back his ears and stretching his neck forward, shot on like an arrow past the motionless cypresses and the white villas hidden among them. The sound of hooves on the flagstones roused some dogs here and there which followed the strange vision with their barking, then howling mournfully, raised their heads to the moon. The slaves who followed Vinitius soon fell far behind, their horses being much inferior to the one Vinitius was riding.

He soon reached Laurentum, passed it like a tempest and turned toward Ardea in which, as in Aricia, Bovillae and Ustrianum, he kept relays of horses. Remembering these relays, he coaxed more speed from his mount.

Beyond Ardea it seemed to him that the sky on the northeast perimeter was covered with a rosy hue. That could be dawn, he thought, but it could also be the reflection of the fire, and despair seized him. He remembered the consul's words: "The whole city is one sea of flames!" At this thought fear for that dear creature whom he loved so much seized him again. He wondered whether he would be able to reach her before the whole city turned to ashes. He did not know in what part of the city the fire began but he supposed the Trans-Tiber section, with all its packed wooden houses, timber yards and store houses, along with the wooden sheds which served as slave marts, might be the first food for the flames.

In Rome small fires were frequent. During these fires, deeds of violence and robbery were committed, especially in the poorer sections of the city. What then could happen in the Trans-Tiber section which was filled with poor people and rabble of all nations? Here the thought of Ursus, his superhuman strength brought a little hope to Vinitius, but then who, even the strongest of men, can do anything against such a fire which was raging now in Rome?

Too, the fear of rebellion of the slaves was a factor. For many years past Rome seriously considered this problem. Many remembered the times of Spartacus and were only awaiting the right opportunity to rebel against their masters. Now, the moment was here, an opportune time if there ever was one. Perhaps murder was raging in Rome now together with the fire. Another thought: Perhaps the Praetorian soldiers by the order of Caesar were slaughtering the Roman populace.

This last thought made the hair on his head stand on end with fear. He recalled all the conversations that Nero had about burning cities; his complaint being that he never witnessed a burning city; his contemptuous answer to Tigellinus who offered to burn Antium or an artificial wooden city; finally his complaints against Rome and the pestilential alleys of the Subura. Yes, Vinitius was convinced: Caesar himself ordered the burning of Rome and all the people there would be slaughtered by his command. Yes, the monster was capable of such a horrendous deed. Fire, chaos and slaughter. And among all this...is Ligia.

The groans of Vinitius were mingled with the laboring pants and snorts of the speeding horse. Who can save Ligia from the burning city, from murder and chaos? A horse rider, rushing also like the wind but in the opposite direction, flew past Vinitius. In passing, he shouted: "Rome is burning! Gods!"

Vinitius raised his eyes to the skies and began to pray. "Not to the gods whose temples are burning do I pray but to You alone Who can give mercy. You know pain and sorrow and suffering; have pity on us. If You are what Peter and Paul claim You are, then save Ligia for me; take her in Your arms and bear her away from the flames. You have power to do this. Save her and I will give You my blood. She loves and trusts You. You promise life and happiness after death but death will be with us always and she does not wish to die right now. Let her live. Take her in Your arms and carry her away. You can do this, unless You don't want to."

He stopped suddenly because he felt that further prayer of this kind would turn into a threat and he did not want to offend this Divinity at a time when he needed His help so much. He was terrified at the mere thought of this. The white walls of Aricia which was mid-way to Rome now gleamed in the distance.

He rushed pell-mell into the city, past the temple of Mercury. Evidently the people there already knew of the catastrophe for there was much feverish movement round about. People stood around the temple holding torches and trying to gain protection from their god Mercury. There also were people on the road now. They were hurrying hither and yon. Vinitius, riding in, was met with shouts of, "Rome is burning! May the gods rescue Rome!"

The horse he was riding was at the end of his strength and stumbled forward toward the inn where the relay station was. Slaves stood before the inn as if expecting him. At his command they rushed to get him a fresh horse. Vinitius, seeing a detachment of Praetorians nearby, asked the centurion, "What part of the city is on fire?"

"Who are you?" asked the centurion.

"Vinitius, a tribune of the army, an Augustian. Answer on your head!"

"The fire broke out in the shops near the Circus Maximus. When we were dispatched, the center of the city was on fire."

"And the Trans-Tiber?"

"The fire had not yet reached that section I think, but it is engulfing new parts of the city with each moment and with a force that nothing can stop! People are perishing from heat and smoke; all rescue is impossible."

The slaves brought a fresh horse. The young tribune sprang

upon it and rushed on. He was heading for Albanum, leaving Alba Lunga and its beautiful lake on the right. The road from Aricia lay at the foot of the mountain which hid the horizon completely, but Vinitius sensed that reaching the heights leading to Albanum he would be able to see a great distance, even Rome itself. The lowlands of the Campania stretched on both sides of the Via Appia, along which only the arches of the aqueducts ran toward the city and nothing was there to obstruct the view of Rome.

"From the top I will be able to see the flames," he said to himself. Before he reached the top, however, the smell of smoke came to his nostrils. At the same time the summit shown crimson as if gilded. "The fire!" he thought.

The night had paled long since; with the dawn visibility increased. On all the nearer hills, golden and scarlet beams were shining which could be attributed to the coming daylight or the city burning. Vinitius reached the top at last and a terrible sight met his eyes. The whole lower reach was covered with one gigantic cloud of smoke hanging close to the earth. In this gloom, aquaducts, villas, towns, trees and roads disappeared. Beyond this cloudy plain he could discern the burning city itself on the hills far away.

The conflagration did not have the appearance of one pillar of fire as happens when a single building burns; it was rather a long belt of smoke above which a wave swelled completely black in some places and in others with a rosy tinge. Still elsewhere it resembled the redness of blood. The fire flickered and quivered in places like a serpent, winding and unwinding itself. This monstrous wave seemed at times to cover even the river of fire itself which then became as narrow as a ribbon but later this ribbon illuminated the smoke from beneath, changing its lower rolls into waves of flame. The two sides of the fire extended upwards and outwards, hiding the horizon completely. The Sabine Hills were not visible at all.

It seemed to Vinitius that not only Rome but the whole world was on fire and that no living being could save himself from the onslaught of fire and smoke. The wind blew with growing strength from the region of the fire bringing the smell of burnt objects. Now daylight appeared and the sun lit up some of the tops surrounding the Alban lake. The bright, golden rays of the morning sun appeared reddish and sickly through the haze of smoke. The closer he got to Albanum, the denser became the smoke. It was pretty bad where he was; what must be going on in Rome itself? This thought struck Vinitius with terror.

Despite his despair, he tried to reassure himself somewhat with the thought that it was impossible that all parts of the city were in flames. Perhaps some areas remained untouched by the fire. In any case, Ursus could guide Ligia out through the Janiculum gate. And, it is unlikely that the whole population of Rome would perish. Many should be able to escape, so why not Ursus and Ligia? Surely God is watching over her and will protect her. He Who Himself conquered death will save her from death.

Thus reasoning, he began to pray once more, making promises and vows to Christ. He remembered that the Apostle Peter was still there and grew a bit calmer. Peter, for him, was almost a superhuman person. From the time he heard him in Ostrianum, this impression clung to him, giving him now the assurance that every word of that fisherman would come true. Since Peter blessed his love and promised him Ligia, she could not perish in the flames. The city may burn but no harm will befall her, no spark of the flames will fall on her garments.

Now, he felt much better. All things seemed possible. Peter speaks to the flames, they part, and Ursus and Ligia pass safely on with fire raging on both sides of them. Moreover, Peter sees future events; no doubt then he foresaw this fire and warned Ligia about it, and the Christians also so that they too could flee to safety. Who knows, Ligia may even be on this road coming towards him any minute now.

That seemed to him most likely as he saw numerous escaping on the road, heading for the heights of the Alban Hills. Now, he had to slacken his pace on account of the congestion of people on the road. Besides pedestrians with bundles on their backs, he met horses with packs, mules and vehicles laden with personal property; there were also many litters of the wealthier citizens being borne by slaves.

At Ustrianum he changed horses again. It was much more difficult for him to wade through the crowds. They were everywhere. The streets were swarming with fugitives. He could see them erecting tents at different locations for the protection of their families. Some people lay by the wayside wailing to the gods or cursing their fates. He found it difficult to get information because of this chaos around him. Those whom he questioned did not answer or answered with terrified faces that the city was perishing and the world was coming to an end. There was much disorder caused by greater and greater crowds fleeing from the fire. Some searched in vain for their loved ones; half-wild shepherds from the Campania crowded to the town to hear news or to find plunder made easy by the general uproar. Here and there crowds of slaves of every nationality and gladiators fell to robbing and pillaging and even fighting with the soldiers who tried to prevent their atrocities and to defend the citizens.

Junius, a senator whom Vinitius spied at the inn surrounded by a detachment of Batavian slaves, was the first to give him more detailed information on the fire. "It had begun at the Circus Maximus in the section which is nearest to the Palatine and the Caelian Hills. Soon the fire raged and expanded with unusual rapidity toward the center of the city. Never since the time of Brennus had such a catastrophe come upon Rome. The entire circus was soon demolished by the fire as well as all the shops surrounding it." cried Junius. "The Aventine and the Caelian area are also on fire. The flames surrounding the Palatine have already reached the Carinae." Here, Junius, who possessed on the Carinae a beautiful villa, filled with works of art which he loved, seized a handful of earth and scattered it on his head, all the while moaning despairingly.

Vinitius shook him by the shoulder and cried, "My house is also on the Carinae, but if everything is perishing, let it also perish." Then remembering that Ligia may have gone to the house of Aulus, he asked, "What about the Vicus Patricius?"

"On fire!"

"What about the Trans-Tiber?"

Junius looked at him in surprise. "Never mind the Trans-Tiber," he wailed.

Vinitius retorted, "I'm more concerned about that section than any others!"

"Perhaps you could get there by the Via Portuensis but the heat there must be terrible; the smoke alone would choke you. I doubt if the fire reached that whole section as yet. Anyway, the gods alone know what is going on out there." Then lowering his voice he said,

"I know that you won't betray me if I tell you what I saw. There is something very strange about this fire. People were forbidden to save the circus. Those who tried to save the burning homes were actually murdered. Another thing: I saw men running through the city and throwing burning torches into the buildings. It is clear to me that the city was put to the torch by someone's command. Many are convinced of this and they are crying out in anger against Caesar. I can say nothing more. This is the end of Rome." Again he began to moan, "Woe to you Rome and woe to us!" Vinitius did not wait to hear any more. He leaped onto his fresh horse and galloped on. However he found it almost impossible to buck the tide, and the heat of the fire was more and more intense. Even the uproar of the fleeing and terrified populace could not drown out the terrible hissing of the flames.

CHAPTER XLIII

VINITIUS realized how difficult it would be for him to enter the city. The crowds on the Via Appia were getting thicker. The homes and temples on either side were commandeered by the fleeing populace. The temple of Mars was broken into for shelter during the night. Even the cemeteries were occupied. The crypts were being fought over and taken with bloodshed.

Ustrianum was merely a mild prelude to what was going on closer to Rome. All respect for authority ceased; members of families became separated; all distinction of rank and privilege was disregarded. Slaves were seen hitting citizens with sticks; drunken gladiators with wild shouts ran about pillaging, robbing and trampling over people. Many barbarians who were brought to Rome in order to be sold as slaves and who were locked up in booths at the slave market now managed to free themselves and began running amuck. For them this was the time of freedom to murder, to take revenge. Yelling insanely, they ran about with howls of joy scattering the people, robbing and bearing away the younger women. They were joined by all the riffraff, the penniless and the wretched poor of the city, emerging as they were from the woodwork of the slums, from the alleys and the foul streets.

People of all nationalities: Asiatics, Greeks, Thracians, Germans and Britons were howling in their own tongues, now sure that their time of freedom had come as a reward for their misery and suffering.

In the midst of the surging throng, there were seen shining helmets of the Praetorians under whose protection the more peaceable population had taken refuge and who, in hand to hand combat, had to put off the onslaught of the rampaging hordes of frenzied attackers. Vinitius had seen captured cities in his time but he had never witnessed such a sight in which despair, tears, pain, wails of lament, wild delight, madness, rage and license were mingled together in such immeasurable chaos. Above this horrible scene roared the fire surging up the hilltops of the greatest city on earth sending into the whirling throng its fiery breath and covering it with smoke through which it was impossible to see the blue sky.

The young tribune with much effort and exposing his life to danger at every moment, finally reached the Appian gate, but there he saw that he could not reach the heart of the city from that direction because of the terrible heat and smoke. He understood now that he had to return to Ustrianum, cross the river below the city and approach Rome by the Via Portuensis which led directly to the Trans-Tiber section. This was not an easy task on account of the crowd. He would have to open passage by force. He had no arms with him so when he got to the temple of Mars and saw a detachment of soldiers there standing guard, he approached the centurion and commanded that he and his soldiers follow him. Vinitius himself took command of the soldiers and forgetting for the moment the teaching of Paul regarding love of neighbor, he pressed on forcibly and unmercifully. He and his men were followed by curses and showers of stones but he gave no heed to all this. He heard voices all around him shouting, "Nero burned the city! The clown! Mother Killer!" They cried that they had had enough of Nero and his madness. It was clear to Vinitius that if a leader were found to head this angry populace, these threats could be changed into open rebellion. Now, they turned on him and his Praetorians and he had to wage pitched battles in some places in order to proceed. He finally did so, passing across the Via Latina, Numitia, Lavinia and Ostiensis, and passed around villas and gardens, cemeteries and temples and at last managed to cross the Tiber. There was now more room and less smoke since the wind was blowing the other way. From the fugitives, Vinitius found out that only some alley-ways and streets were on fire but they were sure that nothing could stop the fire from reaching all parts of that section, especially when people themselves were spreading the fire purposely and permitted no one to put it out, shouting that they were commanded to do so. Now, Vinitius had not the slightest doubt that Nero himself ordered the fire. Vengeance against him would be just and proper. No outside enemy of Rome could have done worse. Nero's madness exceeded itself in this monstrous act. Vinitius felt that Nero's hour had struck. The heinous buffoon had to be toppled over with his crimes. A man of stature could stand up against him and lead the crowd in open rebellion. Here, vengeful thoughts began to fly in his brain. What of himself? The house of Vinitius was important enough to have many consuls and was known throughout Rome. The crowds need only a name.

Once when four hundred slaves of the prefect Pedanius Secundus were sentenced to death, Rome almost verged on civil war. What could happen today in view of this dreadful calamity surpassing almost everything which Rome had undergone in the course of eight centuries of its existence? Why should not he, Vinitius, be the one to stand at the head of rebellion against this madman? He was stronger than the other Augustians, more youthful and active than the others. True, Nero commanded thirty legions stationed on the borders of the empire, but would not these legions and their leaders rise up at the news of the burning of Rome and its temples? And in that case Vinitius himself would become Caesar. Perhaps Christ would assist him in this. Perhaps this was His inspiration. "Oh, would that come true!" he exclaimed. He would take vengeance on Nero for this danger to Ligia and his own fear. He would then begin the reign of truth and justice; he would extend Christ's religion from the Euphrates to the misty shores of Britain; he would array Ligia in purple and make her mistress of the world.

But these thoughts which burst forth in his head like a bunch of sparks from a blazing house now died away as quickly as sparks. First of all, the need was to find Ligia. He looked now at the catastrophe close up and fear seized him again, and in the face of reality, of the sea of flame and smoke, the confidence with which he believed that Peter would rescue Ligia died in his heart. Despair entered into his heart again. He found it more difficult now to go ahead. People living in that section of Rome, having had more time to save themselves and their goods, were storming out laden with their earthly possessions. The streets became clogged. Narrow alley-ways were completely impassable. Sometimes Vinitius saw streams of humanity flowing at each end of the street toward one another. Families became separated, mothers calling woefully for their children. There were shouts and curses on all sides. The young tribune's hair stood on end at the sight and at the thought of what was happening nearer the fire. Amid shouts and howls it was difficult to ask about anything or understand what was said.

New billows of smoke, black and heavy, rolled toward them. The wind blew them away and Vinitius managed to pass forward slowly toward the alley in which stood the house of Linus. The heat of the July day plus the heat of the fire became almost unbearable. People who remained in their houses thinking that the fire would not reach this section, now had to flee. The throng increased by the minute. The detachment of soldiers were now remaining behind. In the crush someone wounded his horse. The animal reared up his head and refused to go on. The crowd recognized an Augustian and shouted, "Death to Nero and his Incendiaries!" Vinitius now felt peril for his own life, but luckily the wounded horse bore him away just in time. Soon, however, the horse stopped altogether and Vinitius was forced to go on foot. Slipping along the walls and sometimes waiting for the fleeing crowds to pass him, he was more and more convinced that his efforts were in vain and that Ligia was safe somewhere. But, he had to go on. He had to find out for himself. He was unable to see and the smoke was stifling him. Tearing off a piece of his tunic he covered his face and eyes.

At the turn of the Vicus Judeorum on which stood the house of Linus, Vinitius saw flames amid the clouds of smoke. He remembered that the house was surrounded by a garden; between the garden and the Tiber was a small field. Hopefully, he thought, the fire might have stopped at this vacant space. In that hope he ran forward amid the flying sparks.

At last he came to the cypresses in the garden. The house as yet was not burning. He ran in thankful for this. The door was closed but he pushed it open and rushed in. There was no living soul inside. He cried out. "Ligia." There was no answer. Silence, except the roaring fire. He cried again for Ligia but no answer.

Suddenly he heard again the gloomy roars of lions. Evidently the dens had caught on fire and the lions, crazed by the fear of the fire, began raging mightily. A shiver ran through him. Another foreboding of evil hit him again. This feeling lasted but a moment. He ran to search the complete house. Coming to Ligia's private room he thought at first that she might have fainted and had not heard his shouts but she was not there. Seeing one of her garments hanging on a hook, he clutched it running out of the house. "I must seek them among the crowds beyond the gates of the city," he thought. He now saw that he had to flee for his own life. He ran out of the house at full speed toward the Via Portuensis from where he had come. The fire seemed to pursue him now with its burning breath and surrounded him with smoke and covered him with sparks from head to feet. In his mouth there was a taste of soot and burnt objects; his lungs were aching from his efforts. He said to himself, "Perhaps it would be best for me to cast myself into the fire and perish." His head, neck and shoulders were streaming with sweat. He was losing consciousness and at this moment he was half-convinced in a feverish sort of way that all he had to do was to find Ligia and then die.

When he was about to fall from exhaustion, he saw the end of the street. This sight gave him fresh strength. Passing the corner he found himself in the street which led to the Via Portuensis. The sparks were no longer around him. If he could reach the Via Portuensis, he would be safe. He ran forward with his remaining strength. He threw off his tunic which began smoldering and, having only Ligia's clothing around his face and mouth, he kept running. Suddenly he heard human cries up ahead, "The rabble is plundering the houses," he thought, but he ran on toward the voices. No matter, someone might assist him. In this hope he shouted for aid with all his might. But this was his last effort. His eyes were blinded by a red glow, his breath failed his lungs, strength failed his bones...he fell!

They heard him, however, or rather saw him. Two men ran toward him with gourds of water. Vinitius, who had fallen but had not lost consciousness, seized one of the gourds with both hands and drank greedily. "Thanks," he said. "Place me on my feet. I will try to walk." The other man poured some water on his head and after a moment the two of them carried Vinitius to the others who surrounded him and asked if he had suffered seriously. This tenderness astonished him. "People," he cried out. "Who are you?"

"We are breaking down houses so the fire won't reach the Via Portuensis," they answered.

"You came to aid me when I had fallen. Thanks!"

"We do not refuse aid to anyone."

Vinitius, who from the beginning of his ride saw only brutal crowds, slaying and robbing, looked at them more closely and said, "May Christ reward you!"

"Praise His Name!" they all cried.

"Linus? Where is Linus...does anyone know?"

A voice among them replied, "He left by the Nomentanum gate to Ostrianum two days ago. Peace be with you, O king of Persia." It was Chilo.

Vinitius rose to a sitting posture and saw Chilo before him.

"Your house is gone, sir," said the Greek. "The whole section of Carinae is in flames. But you will always be as rich as Midas himself. O, what a tragedy! The Christians, O Son of Serapis, had predicted this a long time ago. Fire would destroy this city, and this is it!"

Knowing that Ligia was most likely safe, since she left with Linus, Vinitius became suddenly weak. It was certainly good news. But, he asked again, "Have you seen them?"

"I saw them, sir. May Christ and all the gods be thanked that I am able to repay you for all the good that you have done me by telling you this good news. But, O Cyrus, I shall repay you more. I swear this by this burning city."

Although it was evening, it was still very light because the fire had increased. It seemed that not even one part of the city would be spared. The sky above was red as far as the eye could see and the night became fiery scarlet instead of black.

CHAPTER XLIV

THE fiery light reflected from the burning city and filled the sky as far as the eye could see. The moon rose large and full from behind the mountains. It seemed to look with amazement upon the city which ruled the world until now and which was perishing. In the rose-colored abysses of the heavens crimson stars were glittering, but unlike usual nights, the earth was lighter than the skies. The burning city illuminated the surrounding areas. In this light the faraway mountains were barely visible as well as towns, villas, temples and aqueducts upon which were swarms of people looking at the fiery scene of the burning city.

Meanwhile the fire was reaching all parts of Rome. There was no doubt now that criminal hands were spreading the fire since new fires were being started away from the main conflagration. From the heights upon which Rome was founded, the flames flowed like waves of the sea into the valleys occupied by houses of five and six stories high, shops, booths, movable wooden amphitheaters built to accommodate various spectacles and finally storehouses containing wood, olives, grain, nuts, pine cones and clothing of all kinds, which was distributed to the rabble from time to time as a favor from Caesar. In these places, the fire, finding much that was flammable, became almost a series of explosions, spreading quickly. People standing on the heights outside the city or on aqueducts knew from the color of the flames what was burning. The furious power of the wind threw out thousands and millions of burning shells of walnuts and almonds which shot out into the sky like countless flecks of bright butterflies. These, driven by the

311

wind, fell on other parts of the city, on aqueducts and fields of Rome. All hope of rescuing the city seemed remote. There was more and more confusion everywhere. From one side people were fleeing and, from the other, many tried to get closer in order to see better. All were shouting, "Rome is perishing!"

Violence and robbery were spreading. It seemed that only the sight of the perishing city could restrain an outburst of slaughter which would begin when the whole city would turn into ruins. Slaves were only awaiting a leader, like Spartacus. The citizens began arming themselves as best as possible under the circumstances. The most frightening reports were rampant at all the gates. Some declared that Vulcan, commanded by Jupiter, was destroying the city with fire. Others that Vesta was taking revenge for the Vestal Virgin Rubria whom Nero defiled. People with these convictions did not bother to save anything, but beseeching the temples, implored mercy from the gods.

More prevalent than any other rumor spreading about was the one that Nero himself ordered this fire to free himself from the odors which rose from the Subura; that he wanted to rebuild the city from scratch and call it Neronia. Rage seized them at this and as Vinitius believed, if a leader had taken advantage of the outburst of hatred, Nero's hour would have struck years sooner. Another report, more gruesome, spread the notion that Nero had gone mad, that he ordered the Praetorians to fall upon the whole populace and slaughter them all. Others swore that wild beasts were let out of their dens at Nero's command. People had seen lions with burning manes running wildly about; elephants and bisons were trampling others. There was some truth to this because elephants in their fright had broken open their enclosures and gained freedom, destroying everything in their flight. Many thousands of people lost their lives, according to the belief of some. There were even those who, losing their families, threw themselves into the flames in despair. Many were suffocated by smoke. Fires which were started in many locations at the same time did the most damage because the people fleeing from one ran into another and lost their lives. In terror and bewilderment, people did not know where to flee. Streets became obstructed and many small streets were completely blocked. Many perished from the heat of the fire after hiding in places where they thought they had found shelter.

In places not reached by the flames were found afterwards hundreds of bodies burned to a crisp, though here and there some unfortunates tore up flat stones and half-buried themselves in defense against the heat. Hardly a family inhabiting the center of the city survived totally, hence along the walls, at the gates, on all roads were heard howls of despairing women, calling for their dear ones who had perished in the throng or the fire.

And so, while some were imploring the gods, others blasphemed them because of this awful catastrophe. Old men were seen coming from the temple of Jupiter Liberator, stretching forth their hands and crying, "If you are the Liberator, save us, save our altars, save the city!" Their despair finally turned against the old Roman gods who, in the minds of the populace, were bound to watch over the city. But, they had proved themselves powerless so they insulted them now. It happened on the Via Asinaria that when a company of Egyptian priests appeared conducting a statue of Isis, which they carried out from the temple near the Caelemontan gate, a crowd of people rushed among the priests, attached themselves to the chariot and pulled it to the Appian gate and seizing the statue placed it in the temple of Mars while they beat to death the priests of that deity who dared to resist them. In other places people invoked Serapis, Baal or Jehovah, whose adherents, swarming out of the alleys in the neighborhood of the Subura and the Trans-Tiber, filled the field near the walls with shouts and uproar. In their cries were heard tones as if in triumph. When therefore some of the other citizens joined in the chorus and glorified the Lord of the World, others indignant at this glad shouting, strived to repress it with violence. Here and there, hymns were heard such as "Behold the Judge has come this day of wrath and disaster." All this deluge of people encircled the burning city like a tempest-driven sea.

Neither despair nor blasphemy nor hymn singing helped however. The destruction seemed inevitable and pitiless like predestination. Around Pompey's amphitheater stores of hemp caught fire, likewise ropes used in circuses, arenas and every kind of machine at the games, and with them the adjoining buildings containing barrels of pitch with which the ropes were smeared. In a few hours all that part of the city beyond which lay the Campus Martius was so lighted up by bright yellow flames that for a time it seemed to the spectators, half-conscious from terror, that in the general ruin the order of night and day had been lost and that they were seeing sunshine. But later, a monstrous gleam extinguished all other colors of flame. From the sea of fire, gigantic fountains shot up to the heated sky and pillars of flame spread into fiery branches and feathers which the wind bore away, turning them into golden threads and sparks, and swept them on toward the Campania and toward the Alban Hills. The night became brighter; the air itself seemed penetrated not only with light but also with flame. The Tiber flowed on as a living fire. The hapless city turned into a raging hell. It seized more and more space, took hills by storm, flooded the lower places, drowned valleys. It raged on, roared and thundered.

CHAPTER XLV

MACRINUS, a weaver, to whose house Vinitius was carried, washed him and gave him clothing and food. When the young tribune recovered his strength sufficiently, he declared that he would search further for Linus that very night. Macrinus, who was a Christian, confirmed Chilo's report that Linus with Clement, the elder priest, had gone to Ostrianum where Peter was to baptize many new confessors to the faith. It was known also that before leaving for Ostrianum two days ago, Linus entrusted the care of his house to a certain Gaius who would remain there while Linus and Peter and others living there went with him. For Vinitius, this was proof that neither Ligia nor Ursus had remained behind in Linus' house with the caretaker.

This thought gave him great comfort. Linus was an old man for whom it would be difficult to walk daily to the distant Nomentanum gate and back to the Trans-Tiber, hence it was very likely that he lodged these few days with some co-religionists beyond the walls and with him Ligia and Ursus. Thus, they escaped the fire. Vinitius saw in this the kind providence of Christ and his heart was filled with gratitude and love. In his heart he vowed that he would repay Christ for this act of mercy and love even with his life if it came to that.

Now he would hurry to Ostrianum with Chilo; he would find Ligia and Peter and the others and take them all away to safety, perhaps even to Sicily. Let Rome burn; in a few days it will be a heap of ashes. Why remain in the face of disaster, madness and cruelty of the rabble? In Sicily, he had lands, many slaves and many comforts. Ligia would be surrounded with calm and peace under Christ's protection with Peter's blessing. If he could only locate them soon.

But to do so was not easy. Vinitius recalled the difficulty he had previously when passing from the Via Appia to the Trans-Tiber. He resolved to go in the opposite direction this time. Going by the Via Triumphalis, it was possible to reach the Aemilian bridge; then he would pass the Campus Martius outside the gardens of Pompey, the Pincian Hill and proceed on toward the Via Nomentana. That was the shortest route. Macrinus and Chilo, however, advised him not to take it. The fire had not reached these areas yet, it was true, but all the market squares and streets would be densely packed with people and their possessions. Chilo advised him to go by way of the Vatican fields to the Flaminian gate, then cross the river at that point and push on outside the walls beyond the garden of Acilius to the Salarian gate. After a moment's hesitation, Vinitius decided to take their advice.

Macrinus had to remain behind in care of his house but he provided two mules which would also serve Ligia in a further journey. He also offered a servant to go along but Vinitius refused, judging that the first detachment of soldiers he would meet would pass under his orders.

Going through the Pagus Janiculensis (Janiculum District), he and Chilo soon reached the Via Triumphalis. There were many vehicles there too but they managed to push on without too much difficulty, as the inhabitants had fled for the greater part by the Via Portuensis toward the sea. Beyond the Septimian gate they rode between the river and the gardens of Domitius. The road became freer; only at times did they have to struggle against the current of incoming people. They urged their mules forward as best as they could. Chilo riding closely behind Vinitius kept muttering to himself almost all the way. "Well, at least we have left the fire behind and now it is burning our backs. Never yet has there been so much light on this road in the night time. O Zeus! If you don't pour down torrents of rain on this fire, you don't love Rome and I don't blame you. The power of man will not quench these flames. Such a great city! A city to which Greece and the whole world paid homage but now the first Greek who comes along will be able to roast beans in its ashes. Who could have foreseen this? Now, there will no longer be Rome and Roman rule. Whoever wants to walk in the ashes of Rome when they grow cold and whistle disdainfully while he's walking may do so with impunity. O gods! To whistle disdainfully over such a world-ruling city! What Greek or even barbarian ever hoped for this? And still...one may whistle because a heap of ashes, whether left after a shepherd's fire or a burnt city, is mere dust which the wind will blow away sooner or later."

Thus muttering to himself, he turned now and then toward the fire with a face that was both joyful and malicious.

"It will perish. It will perish!" he continued to mutter. "Where will the world send its wheat, its olives and money? Who will squeeze out gold and tears from the world in the future? Marble does not burn but it crumbles in the fire. The Capitol and the Palatine will both crumble into dust. O Zeus! Rome was like a shepherd and other nations like sheep. When the shepherd was hungry he slaughtered the sheep, ate the meat and offered the skin to you, O mighty father of the gods! Who, O Master of the Clouds, will do the slaughtering now? Into whose hands will you place the master's whip? For Rome is burning as truly as if you yourself burnt it with your lightning and fire."

"Hurry up!" urged Vinitius. "What are you doing back there?"

"I'm weeping over the fate of Rome, sir, the city of Jove."

They rode on accompanied by the noise of the burning city and the sound of birds on the wing. Many doves had their nests about the villas and surrounding towns. Birds of the field and birds from the seashore flew around them. Many mistook the gleam of the fire for sunlight and began to fly blindly into the fire. Vinitius spoke. "Where were you when the fire broke out?"

"I was going to my friend Euricius who as you know has or had a shop near the Circus Maximus and I was just meditating on the teaching of Christ when people began to shout, 'Fire!' They gathered around the circus at first for safety but when the flames seized the whole circus and began to appear in other places as well, each had to think of his own safety."

"Did you see soldiers throwing torches into the houses?"

"What have I not seen, O grandson of Aeneas! I saw people making a way for themselves with swords; I have seen battles waged in the streets and the entrails of those who were trampled on the pavements. Ah, sir, if you had seen all that, you would have thought that barbarians had entered the city and were slaughtering the populace. There were cries that the end of the world has come. Some lost their heads to the extent that they refused to flee and allowed the flames to envelop them. Some were in shock; others howled in despair. I also saw some who howled in delight. O sir, there are many wicked people who do not recognize and appreciate your good and mild rule. Those just laws which you enact by which you take from everybody and keep for yourselves. Yes, sir. There are people who will not be reconciled to the will of the gods."

Vinitius was too much occupied with his own thoughts to note the irony of Chilo's words. A shudder of terror overtook him at the thought that Ligia might have been in the midst of such chaos on the streets of Rome. Hence, he asked once more, "But you have seen them in Ostrianum with your own eyes, have you not?

"I saw them, O son of Venus. I saw the girl, the good Ligian, holy Linus and the Apostle Peter."

"Before the fire?"

"Yes, before the fire, O Mithra."

Vinitius was still doubtful whether Chilo was not lying, so reining in his mule, he looked at the Greek fiercely and inquired, "What were you doing there?"

Chilo became confused. Although it seemed to him now, as to many others, that with the destruction of Rome the domination of Rome would also come to an end, nevertheless he was face to face with Vinitius and the young tribune forbade him to spy on the Christians, so he answered warily, "Sir, don't you believe me when I say that I love them? I was in Ostrianum because I am half a Christian. Pyrrho taught me to esteem virtue more than philosophy, hence I cling more and more to virtuous people. Besides, I am poor. When you were in Antium, I suffered hunger frequently while bending over my books. Therefore I sat by the wall in Ostrianum, for the Christians, though poor themselves, distribute alms more frequently than the other inhabitants of Rome altogether."

This reason seemed sufficient enough to Vinitius and he inquired less severely, "And, do you know the present temporary location where Linus is staying?"

"You punished me severely for curiosity, sir."

Vinitius ceased talking and rode on.

After a while Chilo spoke up. "In the past you would not have found the maiden but for me, sir. If we find her again, I hope that you will not forget the poor sage who rides with you."

"You will receive a house with a vineyard at Ameriola."

"Thank you, O Hercules! A house with a vineyard. Thank you. Thank you! With a vineyard?"

They were passing the Vatican Hill now and turning to the right; after passing the Vatican field, they would reach the river and then the Flaminian gate. Suddenly Chilo reined in his mule.

"Sir, a lucky thought just came to me."

"Speak!"

"Between the Janiculum and the Vatican Hills, beyond the gardens of Agrippina, are excavations from which stones and sand were taken for the building of the Circus of Nero. Hear me, sir. Recently, the Jews who are numerous in the Trans-Tiber section have begun to persecute the Christians. You recall the disturbances during the time of Claudius who was forced to expel them from Rome. Well, now they are back in full force thanks to the protection of the Augusta. They feel safe so they began to persecute the Christians once again. I know this; I have seen it. No edict against the Christians has been issued but the Jews complain to the prefect of the city that Christians murder infants, worship an ass head and preach a religion which is not recognized and approved by the Senate. They attack the houses of worship so fiercely that Christians are forced to flee and hide."

"What do you wish to say?"

"This, sir, that the synagogues exist openly but the Christians are forced to worship in secret and assemble in ruined sheds outside the city and also in the pits. Those who live in the Trans-Tiber section often choose that place which was excavated for the building of the circus and various houses along the Tiber. Now, when the city is perishing, the adherents of Christ are praying. Without doubt we shall find a number of them in those excavations. So, my advice is to go there first since it is on our way."

"But, you said that Linus had gone to Ostrianum," cried Vinitius impatiently.

"But, you promised me a house with a vineyard. For that reason I wish to seek the maiden wherever hope is to find her. They might have returned to the Trans-Tiber after the outbreak of the fire.

They might have gone around the city as we are doing right now. Linus has a house; perhaps he wished to be nearer his house. If they did return, I swear to you by Persephone that we shall find them at prayer at the sandpits. At least we will be able to get some word of them there."

"You are right. Lead on." Chilo then turned to the left toward the hill. For a while the slope of the hill concealed them; then they passed the circus and turned left again. Thereupon they entered a dark passageway and in the darkness Vinitius was able to see many gleaming lanterns.

"They are there," said Chilo. "There will be more of them today than usual because the regular houses of prayer are burnt or filled with smoke."

"True," said Vinitius. "I hear singing."

Voices in song indeed reached them from the dark opening. Soon Vinitius and Chilo found themselves amid a whole assemblage of people singing and praying. Chilo slipped down from his mule and beckoning toward a youth who sat nearby said to him, "I am a priest of Christ and a bishop. Hold the mules for us. You will receive my blessing and forgiveness of your sins." Then without waiting for the boy to answer, he thrust the reins to him and with Vinitius joined the crowd.

They pushed through a dark passage until they reached a spacious cave from which stones had been taken recently for the walls bore signs of fresh fragments.

It was brighter there than in the corridor. In addition to the tapers and lanterns there were torches also. By the light of these Vinitius saw a crowd of kneeling people with their arms upraised in prayer and supplication. He did not see Ligia anywhere about. Neither did he see Linus nor Peter. The faces around him were solemn and full of emotion. Some showed alarm, some hope. Light was reflected in the whites of their upraised eyes. Some were singing hymns, others with faces pale as chalk were praying fervently.

Meanwhile the hymn stopped and above the assembly appeared Crispus who was known to Vinitius. His face was stern, pale and fanatical and he hurled his words at the assembly, words that were scathing and full of accusation.

"Bewail your sins for the hour has come. Behold the Lord has sent down flames to destroy Babylon, the city of crime and shame. The hour of judgment has struck; the hour of wrath and disaster is here. The Lord promised to come and He will soon be here. He will not come as a meek Lamb Who offered His blood for our sins but He will come as a Judge Who in justice will hurl sinners and unbelievers into the pit. Woe to the world! Woe to sinners! There will be no mercy for them. I see You, Lord Christ! Stars are falling upon the earth, the sun is darkened, the earth opens its gaping maw, the dead rise from the graves but You are triumphant amid sounds of trumpet and legions of angels, amidst thunder and lightning. I see You, O Lord, O Christ!"

Then he was silent, only raising his eyes as if perceiving something. A dull roar was heard from without. Houses were crashing down into ruin with loud sounds. Most of those present thought that indeed the last hour had come. Terror seized them at this visible sign of Christ's second coming at the end of the world. Many cried, "The day of judgment is upon us!" Some covered their faces with their hands believing that the earth would be soon shaken to its foundations, that beasts would rush forth, beasts of hell, and hurl themselves on them. Others cried, "Christ have mercy on us!" Some confessed their sins in loud voices, others cast themselves into the arms of loved ones fearing to be soon separated.

There were also faces filled with rapture, with smiles. They showed no fear; these were the people who in religious ecstasy and exultation began to cry out words unknown, in a strange language. Above all this clamor rose the voice of Crispus, "Watch and pray! Renounce earthly loves! Christ will condemn those who love others more than Him. Woe to the rich! Woe to the depraved! Woe to husband, wife and child!"

Suddenly a roar shook the quarry. It was louder than the others. All fell to the earth stretching out their arms in the form of a cross as if to ward off any evil by this religious sign. There was much weeping, especially from the children. After a while silence followed, broken only by whispers of the blessed name of Jesus. At that moment a calm and reassuring voice was heard. "Peace be with you!"

It was the voice of Peter the Apostle who had entered the cave a moment earlier. At the sound of his voice terror dissipated as if by a miracle. People rose from the crowd. Those who were near the Apostle fell on their knees before him as if seeking protection. He stretched out his hands over them and cried, "Why are you troubled? Who can say when the final hour will strike? The Lord punished Babylon with fire but His mercy will be on those whom baptism has purified and you, whose sins are redeemed by the blood of the Lamb, will die with His name on your lips and peace in your hearts. Peace be with you!"

After the merciless words of Crispus, the words of Peter fell like a balm on all present. Not the fear of God but the love of God was more important to them now. These people loved Christ about Whom they had learned from the Apostles' narratives. Not a merciless judge but a mild and patient Lamb was their God. A God Whose mercy surpasses all understanding, surpasses all wickedness that man can perpetrate. This was great comfort to them all. A great solace and thankfulness filled their hearts. Voices from all sides were heard now crying to Peter: "We are your sheep, feed us, take care of us." Others cried: "Do not forsake us in this hour of peril."

Seeing all this Vinitius approached Peter with trepidation, took hold of Peter's mantle and said, "Help me, sir. I have sought her in the smoke of the burning city and among the people, but nowhere can I find her. I believe though that you can restore her to me."

Peter placed his hand upon the fevered brow of the tribune and spoke to him, "Have trust and come with me."

CHAPTER XLVI

THE fire raged on. The Circus Maximus was entirely in ruins. Entire streets and alleys were filled with rubble. The wind had changed and was now blowing from the sea causing the fire to spread to the Caelian, Esquiline and Viminal hills. Finally, some efforts at rescue were being organized. Tigellinus, who came to the city only on the third day, now ordered some houses to be demolished so that the fire reaching empty spaces would die of itself. A remnant of the city was thus to be saved. It was no use at all to fight the raging fire itself. It had to die of its own accord. There was need also to guard against looting and other atrocities. Incalculable wealth perished in the fire; people's entire possessions were destroyed. As many as a hundred thousand people were wandering around the walls—hungry, dissolute and wretched. No one thought of sending for new supplies to alleviate the needs of the populace. This was mostly due to the general disorder and disregard for authority which existed throughout the catastrophe. Only after the arrival of Tigellinus, were orders sent to Ostia for fresh supplies.

Meanwhile the crowds grew more and more threatening. The house where Tigellinus lodged was surrounded by people who throughout the day and night cried out for help, for bread and a roof over their heads. Vainly did the Praetorians try to maintain order; they were met with resistance and even armed clashes occurred here and there. The crowds abused Caesar, the Augustians, the Praetorians and others. Yells of, "Kill us too. We don't care!" were hurled at the soldiers. Tigellinus, looking at night on the thousands of camp fires around the city, said to himself that those were fires in hostile camps.

Flour was finally brought in and as much baked bread as was possible to get from Ostia and from the neighboring towns and villages. When the first batch of supplies came in, the maddened crowd seized the supplies and fought over bread and flour and other provisions in such frenzied ways that they trampled under-foot much of the supplies. Flour from torn bags was strewn about and looked like snow on the ground. The uproar continued until the soldiers dispersed the crowds unmercifully with arrows and missiles.

Never since the invasion of the Gauls under Brennus had Rome beheld such disaster. People began to compare these two events saying that even when Rome was destroyed by the Gauls, the Capitol remained intact. Now, the Capitol was encircled by a dreadful wreath of flame. The marbles, it was true, were not blazing, but at night, when the winds swept the flames aside for a moment, rows of columns in the lofty sanctuary of Jove were visible, red as glowing coals. In the days of Brennus, moreover, Rome had a disciplined, integral people, attached to the city and its altars, but now crowds of many-tongued people roamed nomad-like around the walls of burning Rome, a populace composed for the greater part of slaves and freedmen, excited, disorderly and ready under the pressure of want to turn against authority and the city.

But the very immensity of the fire, which terrified every heart, disarmed even the crowds to a certain measure. Every one thought famine and disease would surely follow. To complete the tragedy, the heat of July mixed with the heat of the fire to make things unbearable. Night brought little relief for even then it was stifling hot.

Round about the raging volcano which was the city itself was an endless camp formed of sheds, tents, huts, vehicles, bales, stands, all engulfed in smoke, a sea of terrified people around the island of fire.

Various reports began to spread among these crowds, some favorable, many ominous. People told of immense supplies of wheat and clothing which were to be brought to the Emporium and distributed free to the populace. It was said too that provinces in Asia and Africa would be stripped of their wealth by Caesar's command and the treasures thus gained would be given to the inhabitants of Rome so that each man might be able to build for himself his own dwelling.

On the other hand, word spread that the water in the aqueducts was poisoned, that Nero intended to annihilate the city and destroy the inhabitants to the last man, woman and child, that he was planning to move to Greece and from there to rule the empire. Each report spread very quickly and found belief among the rabble, causing outbursts of hope, anger, terror or rage. Finally, a kind of fever mastered these nomadic thousands. The belief of Christians that the end of the world by fire was at hand spread even among the adherents of the pagan gods and increased daily. People fell into shock and even madness. In clouds of smoke the various gods were seen gazing down on the ruin. The hands of many stretched toward these gods to implore pity, but also to shout curses at them.

Meanwhile soldiers, aided by some inhabitants, continued to tear down houses on the Esquiline and the Caelian hills and also in the Trans-Tiber. By doing this some areas were saved from total ruin. But in the city itself numerous treasures, accumulated through centuries of conquest, were destroyed; priceless works of art, splendid temples, precious monuments of Rome's past and recent glory, and more, were lost.

Some spread reports that the soldiers were tearing down houses not to stop the fire but to prevent any part of the city from being saved. Tigellinus sent messenger after messenger to Antium each time imploring Caesar to come and placate the despairing people with his presence. But Nero moved only when the fire reached the Domus Transitoria, and then he hurried so as not to miss the moment in which the conflagration should be at its highest. Tigellinus assured him that he would lose nothing of the immensity of the burning city.

Meanwhile the fire reached the Via Nomentana but turned from it, with the change of the wind, toward the Via Lata and the Tiber. It surrounded the Capitol, spread along the Forum Boarium and destroyed everything which it had spared before and then approached the Palatine again.

Nero, on his way back to Rome, decided to approach the burning city at night so as to sate himself all the better with a view of the perishing Capitol. Therefore he halted in the neighborhood of Aqua Albana and, summoning to his tent the tragedian Aliturus, wanted to learn from him the various poses of a tragedian and also learn the necessary words to be used. He wished to know above all that in stating the words, "O sacred city, you seemed more enduring than the goddess Ida..." whether to raise both his hands or, holding the lute in one hand, lower his arms to his side in a tragic pose. This question was to him of utmost importance. Starting at last at nightfall, he took counsel of Petronius whether, to the lines describing the catastrophe, he might add a few magnificent blasphemies against the gods, or whether, considered from the standpoint of art, they would not have rushed spontaneously from the mouth of a man in such a position, a man who was losing his birthplace.

At last, at about midnight, Nero and his court composed of whole detachments of nobles, knights, freedmen, slaves, women and children approached the walls of Rome. Sixteen thousand Praetorians, arranged in battleline formations along the road, guarded his safety and held back the enraged crowds. The people cursed, shouted and hissed on seeing the retinue but dared not attack it. However, in some places applause was heard from the rabble which, owning nothing, lost nothing in the fire and which hoped for a more bountiful distribution than usual of wheat, olives, clothing and money. Finally, all these noises were drowned out in the blare of trumpets and horns which Tigellinus ordered to be sounded.

Arriving at the Ostian gate, Nero declaimed, "Houseless ruler of a houseless people, where shall I lay my poor head for the night?" Then passing the Clivus Dalphini, he ascended the Appian aqueduct on steps prepared especially for him. The Augustians followed, and then the choir of singers bearing cithras, lutes and other musical instruments.

All held their breaths waiting to hear what he would say, words which for their own safety they ought to keep in memory. But, he stood in solemn silence. In his purple mantle and wreath of golden laurels on his head, he gazed on the burning flames. When Terpnos gave him the golden lute, he raised his eyes to the sky as if waiting for an inspiration.

The people pointed at him from afar as he stood in the bloody gleam. In the distance fiery serpents were hissing. The ancient and the most sacred edifices were crumbling, the temple of Hercules built by Evander; the temples of Jupiter, Luna and others were burning as also was the house of Numa Pomphilius; the sanctuary of Vesta and many others were all perishing from the fire. Yet, Caesar Nero, with a lute in his hand and a theatrical expression on his face, did not think of the perishing city but he thought only of his posture and prophetic words with which he might best describe the greatness of the catastrophe, rouse most admiration and receive the warmest plaudits. He detested this city, its inhabitants. He loved only his own songs and verses. Hence, he rejoiced in his heart that at last he saw a tragedy like this one. The verse-maker was happy; the declaimer felt inspired; the seeker of emotions was sated. The destruction of Troy was nothing compared to the destruction of this mighty city. What more could he desire? Here and now this mighty Rome lay in flames at his feet. Yet, down below and among the crowds afar and near, in the darkness, he began to hear the mutterings, the rumblings, the sounds of uneasiness, the ominous sounds of rage and hatred. No matter! Let them mutter! Let them rage! They are senseless rabble. They do not understand that ages will pass, thousands of years go by, but this very moment will be remembered and glorified by future generations of the present poet and singer. He, Nero, much greater than Homer and his flimsy *Burning of Troy*. Really, can Homer be compared to him and even Apollo himself with his hollowed-out lute?

Here, he raised his hands, and striking the strings of his lute, pronounced the words of Priam: "O nest of my fathers! O precious cradle!" His words in the open air mingled with the sounds of the fire and the murmur of the throng seemed strangely weak, uncertain and barely discernible; the sounds of the accompanists, a mere buzzing of insects. The senators, dignitaries and all assembled on the aqueduct, bowed their heads and listened in silent rapture. He sang long, gradually showing sadness on his face. At moments when he stopped to catch his breath, the chorus of singers repeated the last verse. Then Nero, casting off from his shoulders the tragic robe called the *syrma* with a gesture learned from Aliturus, struck the lute and sang on. When at last he had finished the lines composed, he improvised, seeking grandiose comparisons in the spectacle unfolding before him. His face began to change. He was not moved by the destruction of Rome but he was inspired now by the pathos of his own words to such a degree that his eyes filled with tears. Finally, he dropped the lute at his feet and stood as if petrified like one of the statues of Niobe which ornamented the courtyard of the Palatine.

Soon a storm of applause broke the silence but in the distance this was answered by the howling of multitudes. No one doubted then that Caesar had given orders to burn the city to afford himself a spectacle and sing a song at it. Nero, when he heard that cry from the hundreds of thousands people, turned to the Augustians with a sad, resigned smile of a man who suffered from injustice.

"See," said he, "how these Quirites value my poetry and song!"

"Scoundrels!" cried Vatinius. "Command the Praetorians to attack them!"

Nero turned to Tigellinus. "Can I count on the loyalty of the Praetorians?"

"Yes, divinity," said the prefect.

However, Petronius shrugged his shoulders and remarked, "On their loyalty, yes, but not on their numbers. I advise you, Caesar, to remain here where it is safe, but someone has to pacify the crowds."

Seneca was of the same opinion and the consul Licinius also. Meanwhile the feverish excitement of the crowds was increasing. They began to arm themselves with stones, tent poles, sticks, staves from the wagons and whatever objects they could find. The Praetorian captains now sent word that they were able to hold back the crowd only with great difficulty. Since they had no orders to attack, they did not know what to do.

"O gods! What a night!!" cried Nero. The raging fire on one side and the raging crowd on the other called forth for some beautiful and memorable phrases on his part. He was trying to come up with some words, when turning to the Augustians and the people around him, he saw only pale and fearful faces. He finally realized the danger himself and began to show fear.

"Give me a dark mantle with a hood." he cried out. "Must it really come to a fight with the crowd?"

"Sire," said Tigellinus with an uncertain voice, "I've done what

I could but there is danger threatening. Speak to the people, O Caesar, and make them promises."

"Shall Caesar speak to the rabble? Let one of you do so in my name. Who will undertake it?"

"I," answered Petronius calmly.

"Go my friend. You are always faithful to me even in my direst need. Go and promise them anything."

Petronius turned to the retinue and with a careless motion spoke out, "Senators here present, also Piso, Nerva and Senecio, follow me." Those whom he named followed him, not entirely without hesitation but with a certain confidence which his calmness had given them. Petronius, halting at the foot of the arches, gave command to bring him a white horse and mounting rode on at the head of those whom he named toward the howling mob. He was unarmed, having only a thin ivory cane which he usually carried with him.

When he had ridden up, he pushed on with his horse into the crowd, not caring about the upraised hands holding various weapons, inflamed eyes, sweating faces, bellowing and foaming lips. A mad sea of people surrounded him on all sides. A sea of armor rose all around him; angry hands stretched out for the reins of his horse. Through it all he rode on, contemptuous and indifferent. The crowd seeing him so cool and unafraid, subsided somewhat. Finally some recognized him and cries of, "Petronius, Petronius, Arbiter of Elegance," were heard all around.

Even though he had never striven for the favor of the populace, he was their favorite patrician. He was known throughout Rome as a humane and magnanimous person. His popularity had increased especially since the affair of Pedanius Secundus when he spoke in favor of mitigating the cruel sentence which condemned all slaves of the prefect to death. All slaves of Rome especially loved him since that time. Evidently he would speak for Nero himself.

Petronius waved his white toga for silence.

"Silence. Silence." cried the people on all sides.

When there was some semblance of quiet Petronius spoke out, "Citizens, let those who hear my voice repeat what I say to the others. Behave yourselves like human beings, not like animals in the arena."

"We will. We will. Quiet everybody. Let us hear Petronius."

"Then listen! The city will be rebuilt. The gardens of Lucullus, Maecenas, Caesar and Agrippina will be opened to you. Tomorrow will begin the distribution of flour, wine and olives so that every one of you will be full. Then Caesar will prepare games for you in the circus, such as the world has not seen yet. During these games, gifts will be given out to all of you. You will be richer than you have been before."

A murmur answered his words and it grew louder and spread as word was passed along. From time to time shouts of anger were still heard but then they turned to joyous shouts of *"panem et circenses"* (bread and circuses).

Petronius wrapped himself up in his toga, and listened for a while without emotion. The uproar increased but soon the people were yelling that Petronius had something else to say. Finally, when they had quieted down he cried, "I promise you bread and circuses. Now give a shout in honor of Caesar who feeds you. Then go to sleep and cease to be an unruly mob, for the dawn will soon be upon you."

He turned his horse and pushing through the mob calmly once again rode slowly to the ranks of the Praetorian soldiers. When he returned to Nero, he saw the fear depicted on his face and those around him because they did not know what the shouts were all about. They thought that the crowd was going to attack Petronius and those with him. Now they were relieved to see Petronius calmly approaching them. Nero ran up to him and asked, "Well, what are they doing? Is there going to be a fight?"

Petronius began to breathe deeply. He finally answered, "By Pollux! Their sweat almost overcame me. Will someone please pass some perfume spray to me; I'm almost fainting." Then he turned to Caesar. "I promised them flour, wine and olive oil and also the opening of the gardens and also games in the circus. They worship you once again and are howling in your honor. Gods! What a foul odor the plebians have."

"I had the Praetorians ready," cried Tigellinus, "and if you had not quieted them, they would have been silenced forever by my soldiers. It is a pity, Caesar, that you did not allow me to use force."

Petronius looked at him and shrugged his shoulders. "That still may come. You may have to use force tomorrow."

"No," cried Caesar, "I will give command to open the gardens and to distribute food and wine and other goods. Thank you, Petronius. I will prepare games for them and on that occasion I will sing the same song which I sang tonight." Then, he placed his hands on the shoulders of Petronius and asked, "Tell me truly, how was my performance tonight?"

"You were worthy of the spectacle as the spectacle was worthy of you," he answered. Then turning toward the fire he spoke, "But, let us take a last look and bid farewell to the old Rome."

CHAPTER XLVII

PETER'S words brought great comfort to the souls of the Christians. Although they were sure that the end of the world and the last judgment would come, now that end seemed less imminent. Perhaps the Lord would allow them to live through the reign of Nero, this reign of Anti-Christ as he was called. Thus comforted, they began to disperse. Some left for their temporary shelters, others returned to their homes in the Trans-Tiber which were preserved from the fire. There were not many of those however.

The apostle Peter, in the company of Vinitius and Chilo, was finally able to break himself away from the surging crowd of Christians, some of whom wished merely to touch his cloak. At last they found themselves on the outside.

Peter, turning to Vinitius, blessed him and said, "Fear not. The hut of the quarryman is not far from here. There you will find Ligia. Linus and Ursus are there also. Christ saved her for you."

Vinitius almost fell on hearing this great news. The sleepless night, the past events, his fear and alarm had exhausted him completely. Now, the news that Ligia was near and that he would see her soon, almost took the last remnant of strength away from him. He fell on his knees before the Apostle and began thanking him heartily.

"Don't thank me, son. Thank Christ. He protected her for you."

Chilo looked in wonder. Finally he remarked, "What a mighty God! But, sir, what shall I do with the mules yonder?"

"Rise and come with me," said Peter to Vinitius.

Vinitius rose with shining face. Tears of joy and gratitude were visible in his eyes. His lips moved as if in prayer.

Chilo repeated his words, "Sir, what shall I do with the mules? Perhaps this good prophet would prefer to ride instead of walk."

Vinitius himself was not sure but when Peter told him that the hut was close by, he told Chilo to return the mules to Macrinus.

"Forgive me, sir, if I remind you of the house in Ameriola."

"You will get it."

"O grandson of Numa Pompilius, I was always sure of it but now that this good prophet is a witness to your generosity, I need not remind you that you promised also a vineyard. Peace be with you. I shall find you, sir. Peace."

Peter and Vinitius turned right toward the hills. Along the way Vinitius said to Peter, "Wash me with water of baptism so that I may call myself a real confessor of Christ for I love Him with all my heart and soul. Wash me for I am ready. Whatever you will command me to do, I will do. Tell me what should I do, how should I act."

"Love men as your brothers for only with love you may serve Him."

"Yes, I understand. I did believe in the Roman gods although I never loved them, but I love Him Who is one, just and merciful. I'm ready to confess Him and Him alone. Even if Rome and all the world perish, I will still believe in Him."

"For that He will bless you and yours."

Meanwhile they turned into a narrow ravine at the end of which a faint light was visible. Peter pointed at a hut nearby. "There is the hut of the quarryman of whom I spoke. He gave refuge to Ligia, Linus and Ursus when they could not return to the Trans-Tiber due to the fire."

The hut was more of a cave than a dwelling place. It was rounded out from the extended face of the hill and enclosed by a wall of reeds. The door was closed but through the opening which served as a window, the interior was visible, illumined from inside by a lamp. A giant of a man rose from guarding the door to see who was approaching. "Who are you?" he demanded.

"Servants of Christ," answered Peter. "Peace be with you, Ursus."

Ursus bent down to greet the Apostle and then recognizing

Vinitius, he greeted him warmly saying, "It is you, sir? Blessed be the name of the Lord. You will bring joy to Callina." He then opened the door and they all entered. Linus was lying on a bundle of straw, his face showing the suffering that he was undergoing on account of sickness and old age. Near the fire sat Ligia with a string of fish by her side, evidently cleaning them for a meal. She did not raise her eyes thinking that it was only Ursus entering. Vinitius uttered her name and stretched his hand toward her. At the sound of his voice Ligia looked up suddenly and her face showed joy and astonishment at seeing him. Without a word she sprang up quickly and rushed to embrace him.

Vinitius took her in his arms with a feeling of happiness and joy that knew no bounds. He kissed her forehead, her eyes, her hair, repeating her name and embracing her with delight. As was his love for her, so too his delight at seeing her was great indeed.

At last he began telling her what had transpired, how he searched for her, how he even reached the house of Linus to look for her there, how terrified he was at not finding her there, how much he had endured before the Apostle assured him that she was all right.

"But now that I found you, I won't leave you to the danger of the fire and the raging crowds. People are killing one another, slaves are revolting and plundering. God alone knows what miseries may yet come to Rome and its inhabitants. O, my dearest, let us all go to Sicily. My land is your land; my home, your shelter. Listen to me. In Sicily we will find Aulus and Pomponia. I will give you back to them and then take you from them as my wife. O my love, Christ has not washed me through baptism yet but ask Peter if I have not just asked him to baptize me? Even here in this hut. Believe me, Ligia, and all of you, please believe me for I speak sincerely."

Ligia listened to these words with radiant face. All Christians in Rome lived in fear and had to hide from persecution. A journey to Sicily would put an end to all danger and open up a new phase of happiness in their lives. Perhaps, if Vinitius had wished to take only her, then she may have demured, but when he also wanted the others to go there, then she would obey. As a sign of obedience she bent down to kiss his hand uttering the historical Roman wife's willingness to go with her husband, "Where you go, Caius, there I, Caia, also go."

Confused somewhat at uttering words which were only said at times of marriage she blushed deeply. But Vinitius' face glowed with pleasure. He turned to the others and said, "Rome is burning at the command of Caesar. Even in Antium he complained that he had never seen a great fire of a burning city. Since he did not hesitate at such a terrible catastrophe, what then would prevent him from perpetrating other crimes in the future? Who knows whether this madman will not order troops of soldiers to begin murdering the populace with their swords? Who knows what danger there is here? Perhaps civil war, famine, murder, will be the future lot of Romans. Please flee with me and Ligia to Sicily. There you can wait until the storm passes and when it is over you may return to continue sowing the seed of the teaching of Christ."

As if in confirmation to his fears for them, they heard cries of rage and terror coming from outside. The quarryman went out to look and soon reappeared inside saying with quaking voice, "People are killing one another near the circus of Nero. Slaves and gladiators have attacked the citizens."

"Do you hear that?" cried Vinitius.

"The cup is full to overflowing and disasters will abound," said the Apostle. Then he turned to Vinitius and said, "Take the maiden whom God has chosen for you, take Linus and Ursus with you also, and flee to Sicily."

Vinitius who had come to love the Apostle very much exclaimed, "I swear, teacher, that I will not leave you to the mercy of this danger and destruction in Rome."

"The Lord will bless you for your kind heart and noble feeling, but you do not realize that the Master Himself thrice repeated to me the words, 'Feed my sheep.'"

Vinitius became silent not knowing what to respond.

Peter continued, "I cannot leave my flock in the day of disaster. When there was a storm on the lake and we were all terrified in the boat, the Lord did not desert us. Why should I, His servant, desert my flock, those whom He has given me?"

Then Linus raised up his emaciated head and said weakly, "O Peter, Christ's appointed shepherd, why should I not follow your example?"

Vinitius rubbed his forehead as if struggling with his thoughts, then taking Ligia by the hand he spoke to all present: "Hear me, Peter, Linus and you, Ligia. I only spoke as my own human intellect dictated. However all of you reason according to Christ and His teaching. I don't fully understand that yet and my inclination and my thinking is still different from yours. But since I love Christ and want to be His servant, I here kneel before you and swear to you that I too will not leave my brethren in the days of trouble." Then he raised his eyes and with religious fervor exclaimed, "Do I understand You at last, O Christ? Am I now worthy of You?"

His hands trembled, his eyes glistened with tears, his whole body shook with faith and love. Peter took an earthen vessel filled with water and, pouring the water over the head of Vinitius said solemnly, "I baptize you in the name of the Father, the Son and the Holy Spirit. Amen."

Religious fervor seized all present. A divine light seemed to fill the whole room and they felt Christ's blessing upon them.

Meanwhile the shouts of fighting and the roar of the flames were still heard on the outside.

CHAPTER XLVIII

THE homeless people of Rome made camps at different locations which were preserved from the fire. Some of the famous gardens were available to them, such as the gardens of Domitius and Agrippina and also the gardens of Pompey, Sallust and Maecenas. All kinds of animals preserved in various zoos and enclosures throughout the city were rounded up (that is those which were still living) and were killed and roasted. Peacocks, flamingos, swans, ostriches and gazelles, African antelopes and deer, all these went under the knives. Provisions began to appear also from Ostia in such abundance that the Tiber was filled with all kinds of boats and barges. Flour was sold at an unheard of price of three cents for a large bag; mostly though, it was distributed free of charge. Immense supplies of wine, olives and chestnuts were handed out free. Sheep and cattle were driven in daily from outlying areas. Some people were better off now than they were before the fire, especially those who had nothing previously; they had at least plenty to eat now. The danger of famine was averted but the looting and robbery went on unabated. A nomadic life ensured safety for thieves, especially when they proclaimed themselves as admirers of Caesar and welcomed him enthusiastically wherever he appeared.

Atrocities of all kinds were perpetrated daily and nightly. Kidnappings of young boys, women and girls went on every day. Every morning the banks of the Tiber were strewn with bodies which no one bothered about. They soon decayed and filled the air with foul odors. Sicknesses broke out at different places and there was fear of great pestilence.

337

The city burned on. Only on the sixth day did the fire weaken when it reached the empty spaces on the Esquiline where many houses were demolished purposely. But the piles of burning cinders still smoldered on. As a matter of fact, a new fire broke out on the seventh night amid the buildings belonging to Tigellinus but did not last long and did not spread. Burnt houses were falling from time to time and threw up showers of flames and pillars of sparks. But the glowing ruins began to appear black on the surface. After sunset the sky ceased to gleam with a bloody light; only from the piles of cinders tongues of flames still arose here and there.

Of the fourteen districts of Rome there remained only four including the Trans-Tiber. Flames consumed all the others. When, at last, the piles of cinders turned into ashes, an immense empty space was visible from the Tiber to the Esquiline, gray, gloomy and dead. In this space stood rows of chimneys like columns of graves in a cemetery. Among these columns moved gloomy crowds of people in the daytime; some seeking objects of worth, others looking for bones of their dead relatives and friends. At night above the ashes and ruins of former dwellings, dogs howled mournfully.

All the aid and provisions which the crowd received by order of Nero did not assuage their anger nor restrain the ugly talk of the people against him. Only the homeless criminals and ruffians, who could now eat, drink and rob, were contented. People who lost their property, lost their families or friends were not won over by the opening of the gardens and the distribution of bread and the promise of gifts at the games. The catastrophe had been too great and unparalleled. Some were brought to despair at the news that the name "Rome" would be forever abolished and a new name for a new city would replace it, the name "Neropolis." The feeling of hatred for Nero and his courtiers rose every day. Despite the flatteries of the Augustians, Nero was fearful that his influence would wane among the senators and among the populace. Tigellinus proposed summoning the legions of soldiers from Asia Minor. Vatinius, who laughed even when being slapped on his face, lost his humor; Vitellius lost his appetite.

Counsel was taken on how to avert the danger which was threatening. The Augustians were sure that with the fall of Nero their own cause would be nil because the people blamed them as well as Nero. In some places they were blamed even more than Nero himself, so to save themselves, they must save Caesar and free him from all suspicion. Poppaea, who understood that Nero's ruin would mean her own also, took counsel with the Hebrew priests. It was known throughout Rome that she practiced the faith of the Hebrew Jehovah. Nero, one moment fearful, another moment filled with childish delight, began composing new verses about the fire.

A long and fruitless consultation was being held in the house of Tiberius which had survived the fire. Petronius was of the opinion that it would be best to leave all this and go to Greece, thence to Egypt and Asia Minor. After all, the journey had been planned before, so why defer it? Especially now, when in Rome there was sadness and danger.

Caesar accepted this proposal with eagerness but Seneca spoke up after a few moments of thought, "Yes, it is easy to go but it will be more difficult to return!"

"By Heracles!" replied Petronius, "We will return at the head of the Asiatic legions!"

"This I will do!" exclaimed Nero.

Tigellinus however opposed the idea. He was unable to come up with anything himself and if he thought of the suggestion by Petronius, he would have gladly presented it to Nero. But now, being jealous of Petronius, he spoke out, "Hear me, O Caesar. This advice is dangerous. Before we reach Ostia, civil war will break out. Perhaps one of your surviving relatives will proclaim himself Caesar in your absence and what shall we do when the legions themselves take his side?"

"Then we'll try not to have any more relatives around; that is easy! We will get rid of the rest of them."

"Yes, that is possible but it is not just a matter of your relatives. Only yesterday my people heard in the crowd that a man like Thrasea should become Caesar."

Nero bit his lip. He raised his eyes and said, "Insatiable and thankless rabble! They have enough flour and have coal in which to bake their bread; what more do they want?"

"Vengeance," said Tigellinus.

Suddenly Nero rose and began to declaim, "The people want vengeance and vengeance calls for a victim." Then forgetting everything else he cried out with glee, "Quick, give me a tablet so that I can write that verse down. Lucan himself could never compose such a line so quickly. Have you all noticed how quickly it came to me?"

"O Incomparable One!" exclaimed the others.

Nero wrote down the line and said, "Yes, vengeance demands a victim." Then he cast his glance around the room. "Supposing we tell the people that Vatinius gave command to burn Rome and offer him up to the anger of the people?"

"O divinity. Who am I?" exclaimed Vatinius.

"True, one more important than you, perhaps you, Vitellius?"

Vitellius grew pale and began to laugh, "My fat will start another fire."

But Nero had someone else in mind, one who really would satisfy the anger of the people, and turning to Tigellinus said, "Tigellinus, it was you who burned Rome."

A shiver ran through those present. They all realized that this time Nero did not jest, that he was deadly serious.

The face of Tigellinus took on a nasty expression like that of a dog ready to bite. "Yes, I burned Rome but at your command!" he exclaimed. Then he glared at Nero who glared back at him with hate in his eyes. Finally Nero spoke quietly, "Tigellinus, don't you love me?"

"You know that I do, sir."

"Then sacrifice for me."

"Divine Caesar, why present me with the sweet cup when my lips are unable to drink from it? The people are now muttering and rising in anger. Do you want the Praetorian soldiers to do the same?"

A feeling of terror held those present in silence. Tigellinus was the prefect of the Praetorian Guard and his words held the clear meaning of a threat. Nero himself understood this and his face became suddenly pale with fright.

At that moment however Epaphrodites, Caesar's freedman, entered announcing that the divine Augusta wished to see Tigellinus as there were people in her apartments whom the prefect should hear.

Tigellinus, bowing to Caesar with a face both calm and contemptuous, went out. Now, he showed them all. When they wished to strike at him, he bared his teeth and made them all understand his importance. Knowing the cowardice of Nero, he was sure that he would never raise a hand against him now.

Nero sat a moment in silence, then remarked sadly, "I have reared a serpent in my bosom."

Petronius shrugged his shoulders as if to say that it wasn't difficult to destroy this kind of snake. Nero noticed this and asked, "Speak out. Tell me what to do. You have more sense than any of the others and I know that you love me."

Petronius was almost ready to say, "Appoint me prefect in place of Tigellinus and I'll give him to the people and pacify the city in a day." But his innate laziness got the better of him. To be prefect meant to bear Caesar on his shoulders and to take care of the thousand daily affairs which were demanded of a prefect of a city. Why should he want that? Was it not better to read poetry in his library or hold close to his breast the divine body of Eunice and kiss her lovely lips? Hence he merely replied, "I advise the journey to Greece."

"Ah!" exclaimed Nero. "I expected something more from you. I know that the Senate hates me. If I depart now, who can guarantee that they will not acclaim someone as my successor as emperor? The people so far have been faithful but they may follow the dictates of the Senate. By Hades, if the Senate and all the people had but one head!"

"Permit me to say, divinity, that if you save Rome, you will have to preserve some Romans too," said Petronius with a smile.

"What do I care for Rome and the Romans! I know that I would be obeyed in Greece. Here, only treason surrounds me. All of you are ready to desert me, I know. You know not what a great artist you will get rid of. Future ages will weep because such a great artist as I had been deserted by you and the people. Not one of you realizes yet what a great artist I am."

Then he turned to Petronius with a hopeful face, "Petronius, the people murmur, but if I take my lute and sing that song which I sang at the fire, don't you think that I will be able to move their hearts as Orpheus moved wild beats?"

To this, Tullius Senecio, who for some time impatiently fidgeted to return to his slave women remarked, "Beyond doubt, Caesar, if they permit you to begin!"

"Let's all go to Greece." Nero shouted.

At that moment Poppaea appeared and with her Tigellinus strode in triumphantly. He began to speak slowly and with emphasis, his tone hard as iron, "Hear me, O Caesar, for I have found the solution. The people want vengeance; they want not one victim but hundreds and thousands. Have you heard the story of a certain Chrestos who was crucified by Pontius Pilate? And do you know who the Christians are? Have I not told you about the foul crimes and ceremonies and their predictions that fire would come and cause the end of the world? People hate and suspect them. No one sees them at temples offering gifts and in the stadia nor at the horse races. Never has any one of them proclaimed you as god. They are enemies of the human race, of the city and of you. The people murmur against you but you did not give orders to burn the city nor did I burn it. The people want vengeance. Well, let them have it. The people want blood and games...well, let them have them. The people suspect you...well, let that suspicion turn toward the Christians."

Nero listened with amazement at first but as Tigellinus continued speaking, his face began to take on an actor's role. His face successively assumed expressions of anger, sorrow, sympathy and indignation. Suddenly he rose and casting his toga aside, he raised both hands and stood silent for a minute, then he spoke in a tone of a tragedian actor: "O Zeus! O Apollo! All the gods! Why did you not come to our aid? What had this magnificent city done to these wretches that they burned it so unmercifully and inhumanely?"

"They are your enemies and the enemies of mankind," put in Poppaea.

"Punish them!" cried some of those present. "Punish the firesetters, O Caesar, for the gods themselves cry out for vengeance."

Nero sat down, dropped his head on his breast and was silent as if he were stunned that such an atrocity was perpetrated. After a while, wringing his hands as if in despair, he cried, "What punishments, what tortures befit such a crime? But the gods will inspire me to punish them appropriately. I will give the people such a spectacle that they will remember me for all time, and they will be grateful to me."

The face of Petronius clouded up with disgust and acute distaste. He thought of the danger that would hang over the heads of

Ligia and Vinitius as well as all those people whose religion he rejected, but of whose innocence he was absolutely sure. He visualized future bloody orgies and these he fervently despised. Above all, he was determined to save Vinitius whom he loved, and who would certainly go mad if Ligia perished at Nero's bloody hands. He understood the extreme danger of this endeavor but he did not hesitate; his whole life was a succession of these turns of fate and events of his own wisdom and perspective. Thus he began to speak, and as always quietly, freely and almost carelessly criticizing and ridiculing this latest madness of Tigellinus and Caesar.

"Yes, so you seem to have found victims. You may send them to the arena. You may dress them in animals' skins. That is all true, but hear me. You have authority; you have the Praetorians; you have power, then be sincere and honest to yourselves. Deceive others but don't deceive yourselves! Condemn the Christians; put them to the torture and to death but at least have the courage to say that it was not they who burned the city.

"You call me the Arbiter of Elegance, hence I tell you that I care not for your wretched comedies. All this reminds me of events when actors play parts of gods and kings to amuse the rabble at the Asinarian gate, and when the play is over, they wash down onions with sour wine or get beaten up with clubs. But you, be real gods, be real kings. You are powerful enough to permit it. As for you, O Caesar, you have reminded us of future generations. How do you want them to judge you? By the divine Clio! Nero, ruler of the world! Nero, a god! Nero burnt Rome because he was as powerful on earth as Zeus himself. Nero loved his city so much that he sacrificed it to poetry. None did the like in history. I therefore beseech you in the name of the double-crowned Libethrides, do not renounce such glory. Songs of praise will sound in your honor for all ages. What will Priam be in comparison to you? We do not say that the burning of Rome was good but it was colossal and uncommon. I tell you also that the people will not dare to raise a hand against you. Have courage. Guard yourself against acts unworthy of you because if you do, then future ages may say, 'Nero burned Rome but as a timid Caesar and a timid poet he denied the great deed out of fear, and cast the blame on innocent people.'"

The Arbiter's words produced the usual deep impression on Nero but Petronius did not delude himself; he knew that this was the fatal roll of dice and the words but a desperate means of saving Vinitius and the Christians from slaughter. What's more, it would probably destroy him too. Yet he did not hesitate one instant. This was his arena and he had thrown the challenge. What the outcome would be, he knew not. He thought, the die are cast, now we will see how much fear for his own life outweighs in the monkey his love for glory.

Deep down however, he felt sure that the fear for his own life would be the stronger.

Meanwhile, silence followed his lengthy speech. Poppaea and all present turned their eyes on Nero who began to open his mouth and raise his lower lip almost to his nostrils as he usually did when he was not sure of himself. Disgust and trouble began to be evident on his features.

Noting this, Tigellinus cried out. "Permit me to leave when people here wish to expose your person to danger and, besides, call you a cowardly Caesar and a cowardly poet, an incendiary and a comedian. My ears cannot stand to hear this."

At this Petronius thought to himself, "I have lost!" But, turning toward Tigellinus, he measured him with a glance in which there was contempt, such a look of contempt that only a refined person could throw at a ruffian.

"Tigellinus," said he. "It was you whom I called a comedian for you are one at this very minute."

"Is it because I do not wish to listen to your insults?"

"No! It is because of your masquerading as a comedian with your boundless love for Caesar. You, who only a short time ago were threatening him with the Praetorian soldiers. This we all understood clearly as did Caesar himself."

Tigellinus was flabbergasted. He did not think that Petronius would dare cast such dice on the table. He paled and was speechless. This was however the last victory of the Arbiter of Elegance over his arch rival because at that moment Poppaea spoke up in defense of Tigellinus. "Sire, how can you permit that such a thought had even come to the mind of anyone here? Furthermore, how can anyone even say this in your presence?"

"Punish the insolence!" roared the fat pig Vitellius.

Nero raised his lip to his nostrils once again and turning his nearsighted eyes toward Petronius said, "Is this the way you repay me for all the friendship which I have accorded you?"

"If I'm mistaken then show me the error but know that only love for you dictates these words which I have spoken."

"Punish the insolent one!" again roared Vitellius.

"Punish him," some others cried out.

There were murmurings and movements because the Augustians began to withdraw from Petronius. Even Tullius Senecio, his constant companion at the court, walked away from him as did young Nerva who had shown him the greatest friendship up to now. Petronius remained standing alone on one side with a smile on his lips. Gathering the folds of his toga closer to himself he awaited the verdict of Caesar.

"You all wish me to punish him, but he is my friend and companion. Though he has wounded my heart, let him know that for the sake of friends this heart has nothing but forgiveness."

"I have lost" thought Petronius with finality. Caesar rose and the conference was at an end.

CHAPTER XLIX

PETRONIUS went home. Nero and Tigellinus went with Poppaea to her apartments where some people who had previously spoken to Tigellinus awaited them. These included two rabbis from the Trans-Tiber dressed in solemn robes with mitres on their heads, a young secretary who assisted them and Chilo.

At the sight of Nero they all rose, extended their arms and bent their heads in greeting. The older rabbi spoke, "Greetings, O ruler of rulers and king of kings! Greetings, O Caesar, Guardian of the Chosen People, lion among men. Your reign is like sunlight, like cedars of Lebanon, like the beautiful spring, like the balsam of Jericho!"

"But you don't call me god?" demanded Nero.

The rabbis blanched in fear; the older one spoke again. "Your words, sir, are as sweet as a cluster of grapes, as a ripe fig. Jehovah filled your heart with goodness. Your predecessor, Caesar Caius Caligula, persecuted our people because we did not call him god, preferring death to violation of the law."

"And, did he not order them thrown to the lions?" asked Nero.

"No, sire. Caesar Caligula feared the anger of Jehovah." Saying this they raised their heads for the mention of Jehovah gave them courage, and confident in His might, they looked upon Nero more boldly.

"Do you accuse the Christians of burning Rome?"

"We, sire, accuse them only of being enemies of our Law, enemies of the human race, enemies of Rome and also our enemies. We know that they threatened the world and the city with fire. Any way, this man in whose veins flows the blood of the chosen people and through whose lips no lie has passed will tell you about them."

Nero turned to Chilo. "Who are you?"

"Your obedient servant and admirer, O Cyrus, also a poor Stoic."

"I hate Stoics!" exclaimed Nero. "I hate Thrasea, Musonius and Cornutus. Their kind of talk only irritates me. I despise them because they have contempt for art and because they prefer to live in squalor and filth."

"Sire, Seneca, who taught you in your childhood days, has a thousand tables made of citrus wood. Say the word and I shall have twice as many. I am a Stoic only from necessity. Dress my Stoicism, O Radiant One, in a garland of roses: put a pitcher of wine before it and it will sing the song of Anacreon the Epicure in such a way that will deafen him and all the Epicureans."

Nero smiled. It pleased him to be called Radiant One. "You please me," he said aloud.

"The man is worth his weight in gold," added Tigellinus.

"Add your generosity to my weight, sire, otherwise the wind will disperse any reward," said Chilo.

"In any case you will never outweigh Vitellius, " said Nero.

"O Silver-tongued One! My wit is never that heavy."

"I see that your belief, whatever it is, does not prevent you from calling me god."

"O Immortal One! My belief is only you. All Christians despise me for this. That is why I hate them."

"What do you know of the Christians?"

"Will you permit me to weep, O divinity?"

"No! That will only annoy me."

"And you are thrice right. Eyes which beheld your countenance should forever be free from tears. But, sire, protect me from my enemies."

"Speak of the Christians," said Poppaea irritably.

"As you wish, O Isis! From my youth I devoted myself to philosophy and the pursuit of knowledge. I sought wisdom among the ancient sages in the Academy of Athens and also Alexandria. Hearing of the Christians, I supposed that they were merely a new school of thought so I made their acquaintance. To my misfortune! The first Christian to whom evil fate brought me was one Glaucus, a physician of Naples. From him I soon learned that the Christians worship a certain Chrestos who promised to exterminate all people except the Christians and destroy every city in the world by fire, including the city which they hate most, Rome. They hate everybody; they poison fountains. They hate all the temples and all our gods. Chrestos was crucified but he promised that when Rome was destroyed by fire, he would come again and give Christians domain over the world."

"People will understand now why Rome was burned," interrupted Tigellinus.

"Many understand even now, sire, for I go about and tell them the truth. Allow me to tell you my reasons for vengeance. Glaucus the physician did not at first reveal to me that their religion taught hatred. On the contrary, he told me that Chrestos taught love. My sensitive heart could not resist loving Glaucus. I trusted him. I shared every morsel of bread with him, every piece of coin, and do you know how he repaid me? On the road from Naples to Rome he thrust a knife into me. Then he sold my wife, my beautiful Bernice to a slave merchant. If only Sophocles knew my history, but what am I saying? One better than Sophocles is now listening to me."

"Poor man," said Poppaea.

"Who sees the face of Aphrodite, my lady, is not poor. I gaze at it this moment. Coming back to my story: I sought at first consolation in philosophy. When I came to Rome, I tried to approach the Christian elders and bring justice on Glaucus. I wanted my wife returned to me. I became acquainted with their chief priests, one they call Peter the Apostle and another named Paul of Tarsus who was a prisoner in this city but was liberated later. I got to know Linus, Cletus and others. I know where they lived before the fire. I know where they used to meet. I can point out a sandpit on the Vatican Hill and a cemetery beyond the Nomentanum gate where they perform their shameless rituals. I saw the Apostle Peter there. I saw Glaucus kill children so that Peter could sprinkle the heads of those present with their blood. I also saw Ligia, the fosterchild of Pomponia Graecina. She boasted to others that she brought with her the death of an infant for she bewitched the little Augusta, your daughter, O Cyrus, and yours too, O Isis."

"Do you hear that, Caesar?" asked Poppaea.

"Can that be?" exclaimed Nero.

"I could forgive them the wrongs they did to me but when I heard what she had done to you, I wanted to kill her with my knife. Unfortunately, I was prevented from doing so by Vinitius who loves her."

"Vinitius? But did she not flee from him?"

"She fled at first but Vinitius searched and found her in the Trans-Tiber section. We went there with the wrestler Croto whom the noble Vinitius hired to protect him. But the slave of the girl named Ursus crushed Croto. He is a man of unusual strength, sire, who can twist the neck of the strongest bull as easily as one may twist the neck of a poppy stalk. Aulus and Pomponia love him for his strength."

"By Hercules! Anyone who could overpower Croto deserves a statue of himself to be placed in the Forum. But, old man, you are mistaken. Vinitius killed Croto with a knife."

"That is how people fool the gods, sire. I myself saw Croto's ribs being crushed in the arms of Ursus. He then wanted to kill Vinitius also and would have killed him had not it been for Ligia who saved him. Vinitius was ill for a long time after that incident but they nursed him in the hope that he might become a Christian, and as a matter of fact he did become one of them."

"Who, Vinitius?"

"Yes, sire."

"Perhaps Petronius also?" asked Tigellinus hopefully.

Chilo squirmed, rubbed his hands together and said, "I admire your sagacity, sir; yes, Petronius too might be one of them. He might indeed."

"Now, I understand, sire, why he defended the Christians so strongly."

Nero laughed. "Petronius, a Christian? An enemy of life and luxury? Don't be foolish and don't tell me to believe that, for, if you do, then I won't believe anything you told me."

"But the noble Vinitius became a Christian, sire," said Chilo hurriedly. "I speak the truth. Lies disgust me and I hate them. Pomponia Graecina is a Christian, little Aulus is one. Ligia is a Christian. I served Vinitius faithfully but he flogged me unmercifully. I was old and sick then but he flogged me and I swore vengeance. O sire, avenge my wrongs. Punish them all. I will deliver them all to you. Peter the Apostle, Linus, Cletus, Crispus,

Ligia and Ursus. I will also point out others to you. I will indicate houses of prayer they use. Without me you won't be able to find them. In misfortune, I have sought consolation up till now in philosophy; now I will find it in the favors that will descend upon me from your bounty. I am old. I have not tasted life; let me begin now."

Nero asked, "Is it your wish to be a Stoic in front of a full dish?"

"Rendering service to you, sire, is fulfillment in itself," said Chilo.

"You are not mistaken in that, philosopher."

Poppaea wanted vengeance on Vinitius and Petronius. Her fancy for Vinitius was only temporary but her pride was wounded at his rejection of her. Therefore, she was both angry and jealous. The fact that he preferred another over her was to her a monstrous thing which must be avenged. As for Ligia, she hated her from the moment she laid eyes on her in the garden of Caesar. Ligia's beauty made her jealous and fearful that Nero might recognize her true beauty some day and that she herself might be replaced by Ligia. Therefore as a possible rival she hated her and vowed her death.

"Sire, " she cried. "Avenge your child."

"Make haste, make haste. Otherwise Vinitius may hide her somewhere. I will point out the house where she is now residing after the fire." Chilo squirmed.

"I will give you ten men and you can go right now." said Tigellinus.

"Ten men? Sire, you did not see Croto in the arms of this giant. If you give me fifty men, even then I will only show the house from a distance. If you also do not imprison Vinitius, then I am lost."

Tigellinus glanced at Nero. "Would it not be well to take care of the uncle and nephew at the same time?"

Nero thought for a moment and answered, "No. Not now. People won't believe us if we spread the word that Petronius, Vinitius and Pomponia had burned Rome. Their houses were too beautiful. Their turn will come later. Today other victims are needed."

"Then, sire, give me soldiers as a guard against Vinitius," asked Chilo.

"Tigellinus will see to that."

"You will lodge with me," said Tigellinus.

Chilo was delighted at this and cried feverishly, "I will betray them all but let us hurry, let us hurry."

CHAPTER L

AFTER leaving the conference with Nero, Petronius ordered his litter bearers to carry him home. His palace and villa on the Carinae were saved from the fire due to the fact that it was surrounded by gardens on three sides. The small Cecilian forum fronted his property so that on all sides there were empty spaces. This luckily prevented the fire from igniting his house and thus it was saved.

The Augustians and others who lost all of their possessions in the fire considered him very fortunate. He was always referred to as one whom the goddess Fortune favored. His recent popularity and favor with Caesar seemed to confirm that belief.

Now, however, this so-called "Lucky son of the goddess Fortune" had time to reflect on the fickleness of that lady. He could now compare her to the goddess Chronos who was known to gorge herself on the flesh of her own children.

He reflected to himself, "If my house had indeed been destroyed in the fire and all my possessions had been consumed by it—also my gems, my Etruscan vases, my Alexandrian glass and my Corinthian bronze—then perhaps Nero might have forgotten the offense. By Pollux! To think that it was within my power to become the prefect of the Praetorians. I would then have denounced Tigellinus as the real perpetrator of the tragedy, which indeed he was. I would have dressed him in the painful tunic and given him over to the populace for punishment. That way the Christians would have been spared and Rome then could well be rebuilt peacefully through my efforts. Who knows, perhaps better times would then

have come for honest people. I should have done so out of regard
for Vinitius. In case of too much work as prefect, I could have
relayed some work to him and Nero himself would not have
minded. Vinitius would then proceed to baptize the whole Praetorian guard and perhaps Caesar too. By Jove! I'd love to have seen
that! Nero pious...Nero virtuous...Nero merciful. What a sight that
would be!"

At this he began to laugh as if he had not a care in the world.
After a while his thoughts turned to another direction. For a
moment he imagined that he was back in Antium and Paul was
saying to him, "You call us enemies of life but tell me, Petronius,
if Nero were a Christian and lived according to our religion, would
not your tomorrow be more secure?"

Thinking of these words he said to himself: "By Castor! No
matter how many Christians will be murdered, others will take
their place. He is right. Our world cannot last this way much
longer. Scoundrels have to be erased sooner or later. I myself have
learned much in life, yet I have not learned to be a big enough
scoundrel. Therefore it will be necessary for me to open my veins.
Anyway, it had to end this way. If not exactly this way, it had to
end some way. I'm only sorry that I will have to leave my Eunice
and my Myrrhene vase but Eunice is free and the vase will go with
me. Bronze-beard will not get it. I'm sorry also for Vinitius.
Though I was bored less of late than ever before, I am ready. There
are many beautiful things on this earth but there are so many vile
people and for that reason I do not regret parting. He who knew
how to live should know how to die. Although I was part of that
ignoble gang around Caesar, yet I was much freer than any one of
them."

Here he shrugged his shoulders. "They may all think that my
knees are trembling at this moment and that terror has raised the
hairs on my head. What I will do when I get home is take a good
bath in water smelling of violets. My golden-haired one will herself
anoint me, then after some refreshment we shall recline and listen
to the song in honor of Apollo. I have always said that it is not
worthwhile to think of death; it thinks of us without any help from
us. It would be something if indeed there were beautiful Elysian
fields and beautiful meadows in which one can roam around after
death. Well, I'll find out. Without doubt Eunice will come to me

sometime and we will be happy together there. I will be certainly better off than I am now. Just to think of Nero's herd of clowns! What buffoonery, trickery and all sorts of vileness. By Persephone! I have had enough of all of them!"

He was aware that something had indeed separated him from them already. He had known that well before but he noticed now more than ever how much contempt he had for Caesar and his clowns at court. Yes, he had enough of them indeed.

He began to think a little about his position. Thanks to his acute intellect and reasoning, he was sure that death by Nero's command did not threaten him right away. Nero had chosen the occasion to utter a few lofty phrases about friendship and forgiveness, thus binding himself for the moment. He mused, "Nero will have to seek pretexts and before he finds them much time may pass. First of all he will have games during which Christians will undergo suffering and death. My time will come later. The immediate danger threatens Vinitius."

He resolved to rescue Vinitius with all the skill that he possessed. Vinitius now lived with him since his own house was destroyed. Petronius told the litter bearers to hurry.

On seeing Vinitius he asked him, "Have you seen Ligia lately?"

"I have just come from her," answered Vinitius.

"Listen to me and don't lose time on questions. It has been decided this morning to put the blame for the fire on the Christians. Persecution, torture and death threaten them. Pursuit may begin any moment. Take Ligia and flee at once even beyond the Alps if necessary. Hasten because the Palatine is closer to the Trans-Tiber than my house."

Vinitius was too much of a soldier to hesitate and lose time in useless questions. He listened with frowning brows, his face intent and purposeful. His nature was such that when danger threatened, he was ready for battle.

"I go." said he.

"One word more. Take a purse of gold, take weapons and some people in case you need to rescue her promptly!"

Vinitius was already at the door.

"Send me word by a slave." cried Petronius.

When left alone Petronius began pacing back and forth, thinking of the events which transpired. He was aware of the fact that

Linus together with Ligia and Ursus returned to his home in the Trans-Tiber. Some of his property was burned but the main house was intact. He supposed that Caesar and Tigellinus did not know as yet where Ligia was and that Vinitius would get to her in time. He now began to reflect on what actions Tigellinus would pursue against the Christians. No doubt he would send his soldiers in a giant round-up in the city and outside. A small number of soldiers would not be able to take Ligia with Ursus guarding her, and sending Vinitius to help was wise.

Of course it was dangerous to act against Nero's orders but he had to take that chance. In case of a successful rescue and flight of Ligia and Vinitius, Nero's vengeance would definitely descend on him and that, sooner than he wished, but he did not worry about it. On the contrary he felt elated that he would put a crimp in their plans. He determined to do his utmost in this venture and spare no money and effort to thwart them.

The entrance of Eunice interrupted his thoughts. At the sight of her he immediately forgot about everything else. He gazed on her beautiful figure and lovely face with the eyes of an esthete.

She was dressed in a gorgeous violet robe called the *Coa vestis* which emphasized her beautiful womanly lines to perfection. Knowing in her heart that she was admired by the man she loved filled her with delight and she blushed with pleasure.

"What do you wish to tell me, my dearest?" asked Petronius.

"Sir, Antemios arrived with his singers and asks if you wish to listen to them?"

"Let him wait a while. They will sing during a meal. Amid these ashes of Rome we will listen to the song of Apollo. By the groves of Paphos how beautiful you look in that dress. Aphrodite herself could not look any better."

"Oh sir," exclaimed Eunice.

"Come here, Eunice, and embrace me. Do you love me?"

"More than anyone else, even Zeus himself." She then kissed him most tenderly and snuggled up to him. After a while Petronius spoke, "Perhaps not too long hence I may have to leave on a long journey."

"Take me with you, sir," she replied fearfully.

Petronius changed the subject.

"Tell me, are there any asphodels in the garden plot?"

"The cypresses and the flowers are yellow on account of the fire; the leaves have fallen from the myrtles and the whole garden seems dead."

"All Rome seems dead and soon it will be a real graveyard. An edict against the Christians will soon be issued and persecution against them will begin. Thousands will perish."

"Why punish the Christians, sir? They are good and peaceful."

"Perhaps for that very reason."

"Let us go to the sea. Your eyes cannot bear the sight of blood."

"Yes, but meanwhile I must bathe. Come and annoint me. By the girdle of Venus never before have you looked lovelier. I will order a bathtub made in the form of a shell and you will be a beautiful pearl in it. Let us go, golden-haired goddess."

They left and after his bath they both reclined at table. They ate, drank and listened to the beautiful songs sung by the choir accompanied by the musicians on harps and lyres. They cared not for Rome and its ashes; they were happy together thinking only of their mutual love which was to them like a divine dream. However, before they were finished, the main slave entered and announced, "Sir, a centurion with a detachment of soldiers is outside and wishes to see you."

The song and the music ceased. All present were alarmed at the news for it was well known that Caesar did not communicate thus with his friends. Soldiers were sent only when there was bad news.

Petronius was not alarmed but he was a bit irritated at the intrusion.

"They might have let me dine in peace," he muttered. Then aloud he said, "Let him enter."

Moments later heavy footsteps were heard and the centurion appeared. Petronius recognized him. His name was Aper.

"Noble sir," he said "here is a letter from Caesar."

Petronius extended his hand lazily and took the tablet. Casting his eyes on it he remarked casually to Eunice, "He is composing a new chapter to his *Troyad* and bids me come."

"I only have orders to deliver the letter," said Aper.

"There will be no answer to it," said Petronius. "But Aper, why don't you rest a while and empty a goblet of wine?"

"Thank you, noble sir, I will drink a goblet of wine but I cannot tarry because I am on duty."

"Why was the letter sent out by you and not by a slave as usual?"

"I know not, sir. Perhaps because I was heading in this direction on another duty."

"I know. Against the Christians?"

"Yes, sir."

"How long since has the search begun?"

"Some divisions were sent out before midday to the Trans-Tiber." He then took the goblet of wine, drank and soon left.

In the meantime, Petronius gave the sign for the singers to finish the hymn. He thought wryly, "Bronze-beard is toying with me. He first wants to terrify me by sending me a message through the soldiers. No doubt they will ask Aper how I received him. No, by Jove! You will not be amused on my account, you wicked monkey. I'm sure that you will not forget the offense; I'm sure that my end is inevitable but if you think that I shall look into your eyes imploringly and that you will see fear in my eyes, then you are grossly mistaken."

Eunice interrupted his thoughts, "Sir, Caesar writes: 'Come if you wish.' Will you consent to go?"

"Yes, I feel fine and I can even listen to his verses. Yes, I will go."

After he took his usual after-dinner walk, he ordered his litter bearers to carry him to Caesar's palace.

It was late evening; it was calm and warm outside. On the streets amid the ruins there were crowds of people rushing about, many of them drunk. The promise of food and drink, the promise of games and gifts filled many with joy. Some even danced about, not caring that they were dancing amid the ruins of a great city.

Petronius wondered about Vinitius. Why wasn't there any news from him? He was an Epicurean and an egotist but since his acquaintance with Paul of Tarsus, his dealings with Vinitius and the Christians and their ways of living, he had mellowed somewhat in his general outlook on life. A certain gentle breeze had blown from them in his direction and unbeknown to him, some seeds were sown in his soul. Yes, he had changed but he was not aware of that change. He began to think about the welfare of others, not merely of himself now. The plight of Vinitius and Ligia and all those good people who would be persecuted even though innocent affected him and he wondered about that. Of course, he always loved Vinitius. After all, he was his nephew but now he was also concerned about all the other Christians.

Petronius did not lose hope that Vinitius had anticipated the soldiers and fled with Ligia in time. He would have preferred however to be certain on this point now that he was about to face Nero. He alighted at the house of Tiberius where Caesar lodged and entered Caesar's chamber which was already filled with other Augustians. His former friends were surprised to see him. After what had happened on the previous day, they were sure that he would not be invited. But Petronius moved about with his usual freedom and casualness, self-confident and as if nothing at all bothered him. At seeing this, some who turned away from him were fearful that their attitude may have been premature.

Caesar, however, pretended not to notice him and did not return his greeting but Tigellinus approached him and said sarcastically, "Good evening, Arbiter of Elegance. Do you still maintain that the Christians did not burn Rome?"

Petronius shrugged his shoulders and patting him on the back as if he were a freedman replied easily, "You know as well as I do what to think of that."

"I don't dare rival you in wisdom."

"And you are a hundred percent right! When Caesar reads to us and asks us our opinion about it, then instead of crying out like a crow you would have to give a sensible opinion and you are not capable of that."

Tigellinus bit his lip. He was not overjoyed because Caesar decided to read part of his work on the *Troyad* that evening. And, as a matter of fact, as he always did in the past while reading his verses he turned his eyes toward Petronius inquiringly. The latter listened, raised his brows, nodded his head in places as if he approved some phrase or word. Nero himself knew that with the others it was simply showering him with praises from fear but with this man, it was only the love of poetry and that he was sincere in his criticism. If he did criticize, it was only because the verses deserved criticism and if he praised them they deserved praise. Gradually then, he began to discuss and to dispute with him about the verses. At one point when Petronius brought the fitness of a certain expression into doubt, he said, "You will see in the last book why I used it."

"Ah," thought Petronius, "then I shall be spared until then."

The others, upon hearing this conversation between the two, said to themselves, "Woe is me! Petronius in time will regain Caesar's favor and even overturn Tigellinus." But at the end of the evening when Petronius was taking his leave, Nero asked him suddenly and with a malicious face, "Why did not Vinitius come?"

Had Petronius been sure that Vinitius and Ligia were beyond the gates of the city, he would have answered, "With your permission he got married and left Rome." But, seeing Nero's strange smile, he answered, "Your invitation, divinity, did not find him at home."

"Tell him that I will be glad to see him and tell him also that I don't want him to miss the games when the Christians will perform in the arena."

These words alarmed Petronius. It seemed to him that they were directly related to Ligia. Sitting in his litter, he gave orders to be borne quickly home. This was not easy because the streets were filled with inebriated rabble who cried out hoarsely and drunkenly, "Down with the Christians! To the lions with them!"

"Common herd," muttered Petronius with contempt. "A people worthy of Caesar!" And, he began to think that a society such as this cannot endure for long. Rome indeed ruled the world but it was also its ulcer. The odor of death was rising from it as of from decaying flesh. Never before had Petronius a clearer realization of this truth than at this moment. The chariot, laureled and triumphant, which was Rome dragging behind it numerous chained nations, was going over the precipice. The life of that world-ruling city seemed to him a kind of mad dance, an orgy which must end soon. He saw now that the Christians alone had a new basis of life; but he judged that soon with the persecution coming on, even the Christians would all be killed, wiped out, and what then?

The mad dance would continue with Nero. After Nero another would take his place who might even be worse than he. For such people, for such patricians, there was no reason to find a better leader. In the future, he could see new orgies, new crimes and perhaps fouler than the ones at present. But orgies cannot last forever and thereafter some rest should come even for sleep after the exhaustion.

Thinking of all this Petronius became immensely tired. Was life worth all this? To live in uncertainty of tomorrow, with no purpose except luxury and pleasure? After all this, then what? The god of death is like the god of sleep with wings on his shoulders.

The litter stopped at his house. Petronius asked the doorman, "Has the noble Vinitius returned yet?"

"Yes sir, a moment ago."

Then, thought Petronius, he did not rescue Ligia. Casting aside his toga, he rushed inside. He saw Vinitius sitting on a stool with his head in his hands. At the sound of footsteps he raised his head. Pain and sorrow were reflected on his face.

"You were late!" said Petronius.

"Yes, they seized her around midday." A moment of silence followed.

"Did you see her?"

"Yes."

"Where is she?"

"In the Mamertine prison."

Petronius trembled at this news and looked at Vinitius questioningly.

"No." said Vinitius. "She was not thrust down to the Tullianum (dungeon beneath the Mamertine prison). I bribed the guard to relinquish his room to her. Ursus is at her door guarding her."

"Why did not Ursus defend her?"

"They sent fifty soldiers and moreover Linus forbade it."

"And Linus himself?"

"They did not take him; he is dying."

"What do you intend to do?"

"To save her or to die with her. I too believe in Christ."

Vinitius spoke with apparent calmness but there was so much despair in his voice that Petronius felt great pity for him.

"I understand," he said, " but how do you intend to save her?"

"I paid the guards quite a bit of money to shield her from indignity and also not to prevent her rescue."

"When can that happen?"

"They cannot allow that right away but later on when the prison becomes full, when the tally of prisoners becomes confused, they will let her go. But that is the last resort. Right now, you have to save her. You are a friend of Caesar. He himself gave her to me. Please go to him and save her before it is too late."

Petronius, instead of answering, ordered a slave to bring two dark mantles and two swords. Then he turned to Vinitius. "On the way I will tell you. Now, take the mantle and sword and let us go to the prison. There give the guards even a thousand pieces of gold to get her out right now. Afterward, it will be too late."

"Let us go!" said Vinitius. They both left.

"Now listen to me," said Petronius while they were walking. "I did not wish to lose time in telling you before at my house but I tell you now that as of now I am in disfavor with Caesar. My own life hangs by a thread hence I cannot do anything with Caesar's help. Worse than that! He would hear your pleas sooner than he would mine. Would I advise you to flee if it were not so? Now, get her out of prison and flee! Nothing else can be done now! Know also that Ligia is in prison not only because she is a Christian. Poppaea's vengeance is pursuing her and you. You have offended the Augusta by rejecting her, remember? She must hate Ligia because she was the one for whom you rejected the Augusta. Otherwise, how can you explain that it was Ligia they imprisoned before all others? Who could have pointed out the house in which she lived? I tell you she must have been followed. I know I wring your soul by telling you all this but you have to know that freeing her right now is imperative. Otherwise you are both lost."

"Yes, I understand," said Vinitius quietly. The streets were empty due to the late hour of the night, however they saw a drunken gladiator approaching them, lurching from side to side. As they came near him he swayed drunkenly toward them and placing his hands on the shoulders of Petronius shouted hoarsely, "To the lions with the Christians!"

"*Mirmillo* (Gladiator)," spoke Petronius quietly, "listen to good advice and go your way." But the drunk began shouting all the harder, "Yell with me or I'll break your bones!"

The Arbiter's nerves had had enough of these shouts. From the time he left the Palatine, he was stifled by them. So now, when the fist of the drunken fool was raised threateningly over his head, he lost his patience altogether.

"Friend," he said through his teeth, "you smell of foul wine and you are blocking my way." With these words he thrust his short sword in the man up to the hilt. Then, as if nothing happened, he put his arm around Vinitius and continued talking to him. "Today

Caesar told me, 'Tell Vinitius to be at the games in which the Christians will appear.' Do you understand what that means? They wish to make a spectacle of your pain. That seems certain. Perhaps that is why you or I are not imprisoned yet. Do your best to bribe Ligia out of prison. Go to Acte even. Who knows even Tigellinus may be tempted by your possessions in Sicily. Try everything."

"I will do so."

The Forum was not far away from Petronius' house, hence they arrived there soon. They recognized the walls of the prison in the paling light of dawn. Suddenly, as they turned toward the entrance to the prison they stopped.

Petronius cried out, "Praetorians. Too late!"

The prison was surrounded by a double rank of soldiers. The morning dawn shown silvery on their helmets and the metal parts of their javelins.

Vinitius grew pale, "Let us go on," he said. They halted before the officer of the guard. Petronius who was gifted with a phenomenal memory recognized and spoke to him, "But what is this, Niger? Are you commanded to guard the prison here?"

"Yes, noble Petronius. The prefect was afraid that someone will try to rescue the prisoners from inside here."

"Have you orders to admit no one?"

"No, but we were told to watch all those who visit the prison. In this way we will be able to catch other Christians."

"Then let me in!" ordered Vinitius. Turning to Petronius he clasped his hand and asked, "Please see Acte for me. I will come to see you later and find out what she has to say."

At this moment, beyond the thick walls and as if from the underground, voices were heard in song. The hymn was heard plainly. The voices rose and fell calmly as if nothing threatened them; there was even a note of gladness and triumph in those voices.

The soldiers looked at one another in amazement.

The first rosy golden gleams of the morning appeared in the sky.

CHAPTER LI

"CHRISTIANS to the lions!" This cry was heard in every part of the city. At first many believed that it was the Christians who burned the city and they looked forward to seeing them punished in the arena. The gods were angered, many claimed, therefore purifying sacrifices were in order. Offerings and sacrifices were ordered by the Senate to take place in the temples. Public prayers to Vulcan, Ceres and other gods were decreed. Roman matrons made offerings to Juno; whole processions of them went to the seashore in order to take up water and sprinkle with it the statue of the goddess. Married women prepared feasts amid the so-called night watches in honor of the gods. All Rome determined to purify itself from sin and the ire of the gods. They made all kinds of offerings in order to placate them.

Meanwhile Rome was being rebuilt. From the ashes and ruins, new and wider roads were opened and new foundations for beautiful buildings and temples were laid. First of all, a magnificent amphitheater constructed entirely of wood was put up hastily. In this the Christians were to die. Orders went out to all parts of the empire for all kinds of wild beasts. Elephants and tigers were brought in from Asia; huge crocodiles from the Nile; lions from Africa; wolves and bears from the Pyrenees; savage hounds from Spain; Molossian dogs from Epirus; bisons and huge wild bulls from Germany. Because of the number of prisoners, the games were to surpass in greatness everything that had been seen in the past. Caesar wanted to drown the memory of the fire with blood and make Rome drunk with it.

The willing people helped the soldiers in rounding up the Christians. This was not difficult because many Christians were eager to confess their faith openly and did not fear imprisonment. They willingly gave themselves up to suffer and die for their religion. The meekness with which they gave themselves up only infuriated the populace. Madness and anger seized them because many did not realize and understand the reason for this mildness and patience in suffering and dying for what they believed in. In some cases, the wildness of the people caused Christians to be torn away from the soldiers and then torn apart by them on the spot. Christian women were dragged to prison by their hair; children's heads were sometimes dashed against stones amid the howling of the mob. Victims were sought everywhere: among the ruins, in the cellars of dwellings, in cemeteries. There were bacchanalian dances and orgies in front of the prisons. The howls of delight could be heard far into the night.

The prisons began to overflow with Christians, yet more and more victims were rounded up. Pity died out; people seemed to forget to speak calmly; they only shouted like wild beasts and everywhere shouts were, "Christians to the lions!" The hot days continued and also muggy nights. The very air round about seemed to be filled with blood, crime and madness.

This overwhelming measure of cruelty was answered by an equal measure of desire for martyrdom. The confessors of Christ went to death willingly and even sought death themselves till they were restrained by the stern command of their elders in the Church. By the injunction of these superiors they began to assemble only outside the city, in excavations near the Via Appia and in vineyards belonging to the Christians who were patricians. None of these had been imprisoned as yet but it was well known on the Palatine that Flavius, Domitilla, Pomponia Graecina, Cornelius Pudens and Vinitius were Christians. Nero was sure that the people would never be convinced that Christians such as these would ever burn Rome so he deferred punishment for them until a later time. Some were of the opinion that it was Acte who protected them from prison but Petronius found out differently when he came to visit Acte himself. She could do nothing for Ligia. All she was able to offer were her tears for she herself was merely tolerated by Caesar. However she did visit her in prison, bringing her clothing and food and the request for the prison guards to treat Ligia kindly and save her from injury.

Petronius was unable to forget that if it weren't for him Ligia most likely would now be free. Also, he wanted to beat Tigellinus in this deadly game he was playing. In order to gain some kind of advantage, he went to see several dignitaries who in the past were always helpful to him. This time though no one dared to help him openly. Some promised to help for money but after receiving the money did nothing at all. So, all his efforts proved fruitless.

Seneca heard him out, but justified the coming slaughter of the Christians as being for the good of society; in other words he justified it for political reasons. Terpnos and Diodor took money from him but did nothing. Vatinius reported to Caesar his talk with Petronius. Aliturus, who was at first hostile to the Christians, took pity on them and spoke on their behalf to Nero. But Nero answered him, "Do you think that my soul is inferior to Brutus who did not spare even his own sons for the good of Rome?"

When this answer was repeated to Petronius he said that since Nero compared himself to Brutus, there was no hope for the Christians. However, he was sorry for Vinitius and he feared that his nephew would take his own life if Ligia were killed.

Meanwhile Vinitius did all he could to save Ligia. He visited the various Augustians and begged for any help whatsoever. He even offered Tigellinus all his possessions in Sicily but Tigellinus, not wanting to offend the Augusta, refused him. To go to Caesar himself would do no good; he was sure nevertheless he was about to do this when Petronius asked him, "What if he refuses you to your face and even insults Ligia in your presence. What then?"

At this the face of Vinitius took on a menacing look and he gritted his teeth. "Yes," said Petronius. "You see why I advise you against that? By your wild action you will close all paths of rescue."

However, Vinitius soon restrained himself and rubbing his forehead began saying: "No, I am a Christian. I must forgive."

"But you will forget as you momentarily forgot a moment ago. You have the right to ruin yourself but not to ruin her. Remember what the daughter of Sejanus passed through before her death."

Although Petronius spoke sincerely, he was more concerned about Vinitius than anybody else. The suffering that Vinitius felt inside was etched on his face. His grief for Ligia was unbounded.

He loved her before but now his love took on even a greater meaning, almost as if he could honor her in a religious sense, just as he would honor a saint. Now, as he thought about what she might have to go through before death, his blood began to congeal in his veins. His soul turned into one groan of despair. At times he wondered why Christ did not come down and save his adherents from this tyranny? Why does he not crumble the walls of the Palatine and let it sink into the earth? With Nero and all his evil companions? How could He not do otherwise? All this is just a dream, he thought sometimes, not really happening...and then he began hearing the roaring of lions and other animals and he knew that it was only too true...too real...and his faith in Christ began to waver a little and this fact alarmed him more perhaps than anything else.

Meanwhile the words of Petronius kept resounding within him. "Remember what the daughter of Sejanus had to pass through before her death."

CHAPTER LII

ALL efforts failed. Vinitius lowered himself to such a degree that he even begged for any kind of help from the freedmen of Nero. He offered his own villa in Antium to Rufinus who was a former husband of Poppaea. Nero got angry when he heard about this. Vinitius finally realized that he was only fooling himself that any one dared to help him.

Meanwhile days passed; the amphitheater was already finished. Tickets were distributed for the coming *ludus matutinus* (morning games) and would be prolonged for weeks on account of the many victims involved. Already there were so many Christians that all the prisons were filled.

Prison conditions were terrible. Hardly any care or medical help was given. Sanitary conditions were non-existent. Many, in fact, died in prisons from fever and neglect. Caesar and his courtiers feared that soon there would be no Christians left for the games so they determined to open the games sooner than planned originally.

Vinitius lived in constant tension and strain. He feared that Ligia would be tortured in a horrible manner and put to death. Everything that he tried proved fruitless. He became sick with worry and dread. His manner and speech became mechanical; his face showed plainly what was going on inside of him. He still could not fully understand why something could not be done to save Ligia. His wish now was that she should suffer as little as possible in her last days on earth.

He himself was sure that he would not survive her. His friends and even Petronius could hardly recognize him; he had changed so much.

Almost daily he watched and stayed with Ursus in prison. Ligia's pity for him when she saw him prompted her to urge him to take his rest at home but he refused. When he wasn't with her in prison, he paced constantly the rooms of Petronius' house and knelt often in prayer. He was now sure that only a miracle could help Ligia and he prayed for a miracle. Praying thus he thought of Peter and determined to go and see him.

With this thought in mind he went out one night to find him. He finally found him at a gathering of Christians who were praying with outstretched arms before a large crucifix. He first wanted to go to him and cry out: "Help Ligia! Save her from death." But seeing all the sorrowful faces about him he refrained from doing so. He merely sank on his knees. The prayer, "Christ have mercy, Lord have mercy" was heard everywhere. The people all around him uttered this prayer as if their hearts were breaking from sorrow and pain. They still had faith that Nero's power would be toppled and his reign with all his wickedness would be consumed by the earth and that the reign of Christ would begin momentarily.

Vinitius was sure in his heart that with these people praying in such a way and with Peter in their midst, Christ must hear them and come down in thunder and lightning with heavenly power and free them all from this evil which reigned on earth in the form of Nero and his cohorts, and send them all to eternal perdition.

Vinitius fell to the ground on his knees expecting at any moment this miracle to happen. This cry of the suffering and wretched must be heard by the all-merciful and mighty God.

Silence followed the prayers. Then a woman's voice broke in a mournful wail. Other voices were heard in supplication.

Then Peter stood up and faced the people. "Children, raise your eyes to the Lord and dry your tears." A voice was heard, "I am a poor widow. My only son was taken away from me. Please return him to me, Lord." Another voice took up the complaint, "The ruffians defiled my daughters and Christ did nothing to stop them." A third voice was heard, "I am alone with my children. If they take me, who will take care of them?" A fourth cried out, "They have taken Linus again and tortured him." Another, "When we return to our dwellings, they will be there to capture us. We have no place to go. Who will help us?" These, and similar cries sprang up on all sides begging Peter to help them. Peter, hearing these anguished cries, looked at the people sadly and with utmost compassion.

Vinitius wanted to rush over to him and add his own woes to the others but Peter spoke up, "My children, on Golgotha I saw the Lord crucified. I heard the hammer and saw the nails entering his feet and hands. I saw Him elevated on the cross. And, I cried out, 'Woe to us! You are God and You permit this? We expected Your kingdom to reign on earth. Why this?' But He, Our Lord and Our God, hung on the cross and died. He died for us all. To free us for eternal salvation. Yes, He died but He rose again from the dead on the third day. He tarried with us and then ascended into heaven. And we, with our faith fortified anew, go about strengthening and rallying the faith in others."

He then turned toward the voice of the first complaint. "Why do you complain? God Himself suffered crucifixion and death. Is this the only life which you have? Isn't there eternity waiting for you? The Lord is saying to each one of you, 'Follow me,' and He's lifting us toward Himself. But you are clutching frantically to this earth crying, 'Help me!' I am but dust in the eyes of God but I am also His Apostle, the Shepherd which He appointed to guard over you and so I say to you, death is not the only thing before you. After death you will have life everlasting. No more suffering and pain but everlasting delight and happiness awaits you."

"I then tell you, widow, whose son was taken away, that he will not die forever but will live in eternity and where you will join him in happiness.

"You, mother, whose daughters were defiled, I tell you that you will see them pure and white as the lilies of the valley. You, mothers and fathers, who have lost children, to you I say, you will regain them in heaven; your tears will be dried and your suffering turned into joy. You, who are about to be imprisoned and to die in the arena, I tell you most solemnly, you will be resurrected into glory after a few moments of suffering and pain. You, who will witness dear ones suffer, know and be sure that it must be so before the reign of God will supplant the reign of terror and evil. In the name of Christ, may you see the light and truth of my words and may your souls be strengthened."

Thus speaking, he lifted up his weary head and looked up, full of majesty and promise. To the listeners he was no longer a poor, white-haired old man. No. He now was a pillar of strength and hope who would take up the pain and suffering of each one of them and present them at the feet of his Lord and Master.

"Amen! Amen!" they all cried out.

Peter continued, "You will sow in tears but will reap in joy. Why are you fearful of the power of evil? God is with you and His power is greater than any on earth. He lives in you. Do not fear! Your tears and blood will be followed by victory. God will conquer evil. Your blood of martyrdom will be the seed of the faithful in generations to come. Do not fear!"

He spread his arms over them as if to bless and console them. They sensed that he now was talking to his Master. "Yes, Master, show me Your way. What? In this city of horror and crime you want me to establish your capital? Not in Jerusalem but here? You wish to build Your Church on the foundation of the martyrs? Here where Nero reigns, Lord? And You ask Your faithful not to weaken in spirit? You say to me that I shall rule over them until my time will come? Master, thank You! You inspire me, your faithful servant, with courage and strength in order to feed Your sheep in spirit and hope. O Lord and Master, be praised forever and ever. Your final victory will come and Your truth will prevail. Hosanna in the highest!"

The people hearing these words rose with faces changed. Timid and fearful at first, now they were full of courage and resolve. Some voices cried out, "*Pro Christo! Pro Christo!* For Christ."

Peter prayed for some time yet and then began again to console them. "This is how the Lord wants you to overcome your doubts and fears. You will go in victory in His name. Now, I bless you, my children. Go in peace and be ready for whatever may happen, be it even torture and death. Have courage!"

They gathered round about him, thanking him for the words of hope and consolation. "We are ready!" they cried, "but you, O holy one of God, guard yourself well against the beast. Your living presence is now more necessary than ever before to encourage us, to teach us. Please, guard yourself well!"

They then began to disperse encouraged and fortified in spirit.

They now had enough courage and strength to withstand the cruelty of the beast.

Nereus, the servant of Pudens, led the Apostle to his cottage. Vinitius followed at a distance and when they entered the cottage, he hurried over and without saying a word fell at Peter's feet. Peter, recognizing him and seeing his great sorrow said to him, "I know. The maiden you love is in prison. Pray for her."

"Sir, I am but a wretched worm but you knew the Lord on earth. Please beg Him for me." His voice shook in grief and anguish.

Peter was moved seeing this great suffering. He said, "My son, I will pray for her but keep in mind the words I spoke to the others. Remember that Christ Himself suffered and died on the cross."

"I know, sir, but you see, I cannot help myself. I am a soldier. Let Christ double and treble the torment against me but allow her to live and be free. I will gladly suffer but let Him spare her. She is an innocent child and Christ is mightier than Caesar. You who love her and blessed our love, please ask Christ to help her. Christ will listen to you. He loves you and He made you the prince of the Apostles, the heir apparent of His reign on earth."

Peter closed his eyes and prayed earnestly. Then turning to Vinitius he asked, "Vinitius, do you believe that Christ can save her?"

"Yes, sir. I do believe!"

"Then keep believing this always. Even if you see her in the jaws of the lion or under the sword, believe still that Christ can save her. Believe and pray and I shall also pray with you."

Then, raising his voice and looking up to heaven, he cried, "O Merciful Christ. I look upon this aching heart and console it. Merciful Christ, You prayed to the Father to turn away the cup. Turn this cup of sorrow from the lips of this servant of Yours. Amen."

Vinitius with arms raised cried out in agony, "O Christ, please take me instead of her."

The sky began to grow pale in the east.

CHAPTER LIII

VINITIUS left the Apostle and returned to the prison with renewed hope. In the depth of his soul there still was a cry of despair but he managed to stifle that cry. It was impossible, he told himself, that Peter's prayer would not be heard. "I will believe in Christ's mercy no matter what." This belief gave him strength. He had heard that strong faith can move mountains. He wished to possess that kind of faith. It now seemed to him that the greatest danger had now passed somehow. He saw, in his mind's eye, that holy man, that Apostle of the Lord, praying and beseeching Christ to have mercy on Ligia and on him. "No. Christ will not refuse him and I will not doubt!" He walked now with a better frame of mind.

At the prison however something unexpected awaited him. Usually the guards would allow him to pass their cordon without any trouble. This time, he wasn't allowed to pass. The centurion approached and said apologetically, "Pardon, noble tribune, but today we have strict orders to allow no one to pass."

"Orders?" asked Vinitius growing pale.

The soldier looked at him with pity and answered, "Yes, sir, strict orders from Caesar himself. Perhaps the reason is because of sickness spreading from the inside of the prison."

"Did you say that the orders are only for today?"

"Yes, sir, the guards will change at noon."

Vinitius was silent. He uncovered his head for the cowl seemed to him extra heavy all of a sudden. The soldier came closer and spoke in a low voice, "Calm yourself, noble tribune; Ursus is

372

guarding her inside." When he said this, he made a quick sign of the fish on the sand.

Vinitius looked at him with amazement. "And you are a Praetorian guard?"

"Yes, till I shall be there," he said pointing to the inside of the prison.

"And I too profess Christ," said Vinitius.

"Yes, I know. May His name be praised! I cannot allow you to go in but I would be glad to carry in a letter from you if you wish."

"Thank you, brother." Pressing the guard's hand, he walked off. The previous heavy feeling seemed a bit lighter now. The rising sun shone brightly and filled Vinitius with some hope. This Christian soldier was proof of Christ's power. He raised his eyes and said to himself sadly, "I cannot see her today, Lord, but I believe in Your mercy."

Petronius awaited him when he returned to his house. He greeted him with these words: "I attended a feast at the house of Tullius Senecio. Caesar was there. Poppaea came with her son of a former marriage, Rufius son of Rufius Crispinus. Unfortunately while Caesar was reciting his poetry, poor little Rufius fell asleep. Seeing him thus, Nero threw a goblet at him and hit his forehead, wounding him severely. Poppaea fainted. All of us heard Nero mutter angrily, 'I have had enough of that little brat!' You know what that means!"

"The wrath of God is pursuing Poppaea but you must have a reason for telling me this."

"I tell you this because Poppaea is now occupied with this personal tragedy of hers and may put aside her vengeance against you. I will see her tonight and will let you know."

"Thank you. This is indeed good news."

"You must bathe and rest. Your lips are blue and you are a mere shadow of your former self."

Vinitius asked, "Was there any talk about the morning games?"

"In ten days. Other prisons will be taken first. We still have some time. All is not lost yet." Petronius spoke thus although inside he did not feel optimistic at all. Since the time when Nero compared himself to Brutus in his answer to Aliturus, he felt that there wasn't much hope for Ligia. He, therefore withheld from Vinitius the bad news that Caesar and Tigellinus had decided to pick out the more beautiful girls in order to defile them before death; others would be given over to the soldiers on the day of the games.

He knew that his nephew would not outlive Ligia but to this esthete it was important that, if Vinitius were to die, he would die calmly and peacefully, not this way with his heart rent asunder by grief.

"Tonight, I will speak with the Augusta. I'll tell her this: 'Save Ligia for Vinitius and I promise you I will do my utmost to save your son,' and I really will put my best efforts to that end. With Nero, it takes but a word spoken at the right time to either save or condemn someone. Anyway, we will gain some time."

"Thank you, very much," repeated Vinitius.

"You will thank me rather by resting. By Athene! Odysseus, in the time of his greatest misfortune had time to eat and sleep. You spent all night at the prison, I suppose?"

"No," replied Vinitius. "I wanted to enter the prison this morning but I was told that the orders were given not to allow anyone to enter. Please find out for me how long this order will be in effect, will you?"

"I'll find out tonight and let you know tomorrow morning. But now, by Jove, I am going to sleep and you better do the same."

Vinitius however went to the library and wrote a letter to Ligia. He carried it himself to the prison and gave it to the centurion who returned a little later with a promise from Ligia that she would write to him also.

Vinitius had no wish to return to the house of Petronius however and sleep there. He determined to await Ligia's letter outside the prison. So, he sat down on a stone nearby and waited. The sun had risen high in the heavens; people were passing by on the way to the Forum. Hucksters called out their wares, soothsayers offered their services to the passersby. Others hurried along to hear the orators from the rostra of the Forum.

As the heat of the day increased crowds of idlers went to the porticoes of the temples. Flocks of doves flew overhead, their white feathers glistening in the sunlight. The heat, the hum of the crowds about him and mostly his own weariness caused his eyes to close. In the distance he barely heard boys playing *mora* and the measured steps of soldiers as they passed by. All this lulled him to sleep. He sighed again from great weariness and fell soundly asleep.

He began to dream. He was carrying Ligia in his arms and it was night. Pomponia was leading the way with a lantern. A voice like that of Petronius is heard from the distance. "Come back!" But he pays no attention to the call and follows Pomponia until they reach a hut in front of which Peter is awaiting them. "We are returning from the arena," he tells Peter, " but we cannot awaken her from sleep; maybe you can do that." Peter replies, "Christ Himself will awaken her!" Afterwards the images begin to change. He now is seeing Nero and Poppaea who is holding a severely bruised Rufius in her arms. Petronius is attempting to apply some salve on the bruises. He sees Tigellinus sprinkling ashes on tables filled with food and Vitellius devouring them greedily. Other Augustians are at table watching, he himself with Ligia at his side are both reclining at table. Lions walk between the tables, their tawny manes covered with blood. Ligia begs him to take her away from there. He tries mightily to do this but is unable to even move. Other visions follow, all a jumble and then darkness.

He was awakened by unusual loud shouts around him. He rubbed his eyes. The street was filled with people. Two runners with sticks paved the way for a splendid litter which is carried by four strong slaves. The runners cry out: "Make way for the noble Augustian!"

In the litter sat someone dressed in white robes and reading from a roll of papyrus. The crowds were unusually heavy and the litter bearers had trouble passing through. The occupant, impatient to proceed, put his head out and called to his slaves, "Push the wretches aside and let's go faster." Seeing Vinitius standing by, he suddenly drew back inside and raised the papyrus to his face. But in that moment, Vinitius recognized him. It was Chilo Chilonides, and suddenly many things became clear to him. He approached the litter and said, "A greeting to you, Chilo."

"Young man," answered the Greek with arrogance and impatience in his voice, so endeavoring to give his face an expression of calmness which he did not feel inside. "Greetings to you but do not detain me now. I'm hastening to my friend the noble Tigellinus."

Vinitius, grasping the edge of the litter and looking him straight in the eyes, said in a low voice, "It was you who betrayed Ligia!"

"Colossus of Memnon!" cried Chilo fearfully, but seeing no threat nor anger in the eyes of Vinitius, his alarm vanished quickly. He remembered too that he was under the special protection of Tigellinus and even Nero himself, a power before which everything else trembled, that he was surrounded by strong slaves and Vinitius was alone and unarmed with emaciated face and bent with suffering and pain.

Seeing all this, his insolence returned to him. He looked haughtily at Vinitius with eyes which were red-rimmed and hissed maliciously, "When I was dying from hunger you ordered me flogged!"

For a moment both were silent and then from Vinitius, dully, came the words, "I was wrong, Chilo."

The Greek raised his head disdainfully, and snapping his fingers in the face of Vinitius which was a sign of contempt, he ordered the litter to proceed. His final words to Vinitius were, "My friend, if you have any business with me see me some morning on the Esquiline. I talk to clients only then."

With these mocking words he was borne away. The runners kept on shouting before him, "Make way for the litter of the noble Chilo Chilonides. Make way. Make way."

CHAPTER LIV

IN her lengthy letter to Vinitius, Ligia bade farewell to him. She was aware that he wasn't allowed to visit her in prison. She was now convinced that the last time she would see him on earth would be from the arena. She begged him to find out when her turn would come. She was not afraid to die, she wrote. She and the other imprisoned Christians yearned for death as a release from suffering and the terrible conditions in prison. She would also like to see Aulus and Pomponia from the arena if they return home in time.

Her every word showed that she was ready to die and attain heaven. "Whether Christ frees me in this life or after death, He promised me through the lips of the Apostle to be your wife so I am yours now and for always." And she begged him not to despair and grieve too much over her death which would not separate them. With her firm faith and the innocence of a child she consoled Vinitius saying that she would talk to Christ and tell Him of her Vinitius who was left behind. She would beg to come back in spirit to him to say that she was happy and was waiting for him.

The whole letter was filled with great hope for the future in heaven for both of them. Her single wish as to her body after death was for Vinitius to bury her in his private cemetery as his wife so that her remains would lie next to his when he passed on.

He read every word, his heart tearing with grief. It seemed impossible to him that Ligia would be clawed to death by animals in the arena. Christ would surely take pity on her. He strongly believed this.

Returning home, he wrote again, telling Ligia that he would be outside of the prison daily until Christ Himself freed her. He told her that she must believe this; that Peter confirmed the belief that Christ could save her even from the jaws of death; that he is constantly praying for this miracle; that it will surely come.

The next day when he approached the prison Vinitius was met by the centurion who took him aside and said, "Hear me, sir. Christ has shown His mercy. This past night Caesar's freedmen came and took the maidens of the prison to defile them but Ligia had come down with a fever of which many have died so they left her alone. Last evening the fever started and she was unconscious through the night. This fever which saved her from defilement may save her from death."

Vinitius placed his hand on the shoulder of the centurion for support. The centurion continued, "Maybe now that she is sick, they will return her to you, sir."

Vinitius answered him, "That's right, soldier. Christ who protected her from rape can also protect her from death."

He sat in his usual place until evening, then he returned home where he gave orders to the servants to take Linus to one of his villas outside the city.

When Petronius found out what happened, he decided to visit Poppaea once more. His previous talk with her did not help. Now, he decided to talk to her again. He met her at the bed of her sick son. The child had a fever. The mother wailed that even if her son would get better, he may be put to death by Nero.

Even though she refused to hear about Ligia the previous time, she listened to Petronius who said to her, "You have offended this unknown divinity. You yourself, Augusta, honor the Hebrew Jehovah. The Christians say that Christ is His Son. Think now, isn't the anger and vengeance of the Father pursuing you in this matter. The life of your son may depend on how you act toward Ligia and Vinitius."

"What do you want me to do?"

"Appease the offended deities."

"How?"

"Ligia is sick. Use your influence to free her."

"Do you think I can?"

"You can do something else too. If Ligia gets better they would force her to enter the arena. Go to the temple of Vesta and ask the

Vestal Virgin to be at the Tullianum prison when Ligia is taken out. She should then command that the maiden be freed as is the custom some times. The Vestal Virgin will not deny this favor to you."

"What if Ligia dies from this fever?"

"The Christians say that their Christ is powerful but also just. It could be that your willingness alone will appease Him."

"Let him give me some sign that he will save Rufius."

Petronius shrugged his shoulders. "I didn't come here as his envoy, Augusta. I only say be at peace with all the gods, both Roman and all the others."

"I will go," she responded.

Petronius sighed in relief. "At last I've accomplished something," he thought.

Returning to Vinitius he said, "Pray to your God that He save Ligia from the fever. The Vestal Virgin will free her. This Augusta herself has promised."

Vinitius looked at Petronius with feverish eyes. "Christ will free her."

To save Rufius, Poppaea was willing to do anything. That evening she went to visit the Vestal Virgin in the temple of Vesta and left her son in the care of Sylvia, her servant. However, on the Palatine orders were already given. Hardly had Poppaea left when two of Caesar's freedmen entered the room where Sylvia was tending the sick child. They immediately attacked Sylvia and killing her took the little boy and choked him to death by a strap. The child didn't suffer much but died almost immediately. They then took the body of Rufius in order to fling it far into the sea at Ostia.

Poppaea did not find the Vestal Virgin in the temple. She and the other Vestals had been invited to the house of Vatinius. Poppaea returned hurriedly, but at the sight of the dead Sylvia and the empty bed of her son, she began to scream and wail, and continued far into the night.

The third day, however, Caesar ordered her to attend a feast. She dressed up and sat with her face immobile and pale, golden-haired, beautiful but also ominous as an angel of death.

CHAPTER LV

BEFORE the Flavius family erected the Colosseum, amphitheaters in Rome were built of wood so that during the big fire they all went up in smoke and flames; Nero ordered some to be built after the fire, among them one very large amphitheater was put up with great haste. Huge timbers were brought in by way of the sea and the Tiber. It was to surpass all others in size and shape as well as seating capacity.

This huge building was finally finished after constant work on it day and night. It was a splendid structure with immense pillars inlaid with bronze, amber, ivory, mother-of-pearl and other ornamentation.

Troughs running among the seats were filled with ice-cold water from the mountains to keep the area pleasantly cool during the heat of the day. A giant overhang called the *velarium* provided welcome shade from the rays of the sun. Between the rows of seats there were containers where incense was burned. There were also sprinklers to scatter saffron and verbena upon the people. The famous builders Severus and Celer consolidated all their skills in construction of this imposing structure, which surpassed in magnificence everything previously built.

On the day when the morning games were to begin, crowds gathered at the entrance, some even waiting all night. They listened with awe and pleasure to the roars of animals caged inside. These animals had purposely been denied food for the last two days and had been teased and maddened by bloody pieces of meat outside their reach.

Every now and then crowds outside could hear singing coming from inside, which made them wonder. Yells of "It's the Christians. It's the Christians!" were heard in different places. During the previous night many Christians were brought in, a few from each prison throughout the city. It was known that these games were to last some time and some people wondered whether all could fit in the arena at one time—there were so many of them.

The voices of the singers grew louder. Men's, women's and even children's voices could be distinguished from one another. There were so many of them that people wondered whether the animals would get tired of tearing and eating all of them. Some felt that too large a crowd of victims would spoil the spectacle.

Wagers were made regarding the gladiators who were to appear in the arena preceding the Christians. There were several kinds: some were called Samnites, others Gauls, Thracians and *retiarii*, depending on their armor and method of combat.

All these marched in with heads held high, dressed magnificently with wreaths and garlands on their heads. Although many of them would not see the end of the day, they, for the most part, felt seemingly calm and without a care in the world.

The crowds greeted each one of them in a manner which their rank and former performance demanded. "Hail Furnius. Hail Leo...Hail Maschinus...Hail Diomedes." Young girls threw them adoring looks and kisses as they walked proudly into the arena, smiling at the girls and answering them with shouts such as, "Embrace us before death embraces us!"

After the gladiators came the incitors, men with whips who would use them on the contestants in order to incite them to greater effort.

Then came wagons filled with wooden caskets. The great number of these assured the crowds that many indeed would be buried by nightfall.

Then came people dressed to resemble Charon or Mercury. Their duties were to give the fatal death blow to the wounded. They were followed by the custodians of the circus; these were to keep the crowds from unruly actions.

Next came the slaves whose assignment was only to distribute food and drink to Caesar and the dignitaries.

The entrance gates were finally opened and the crowds poured

in. There were so many people that some wondered whether the
huge building would hold them all. The yelling increased in inten-
sity; the crowds wanted the spectacle to begin, they did not want
to wait any longer.

Finally, the prefect of the city with his retinue of soldiers made
an entrance. After him came the long lines of litters carrying
senators, consuls and other personages of note. Some litters were
preceded by lictors bearing maces in bundles of rods. The assorted
litters gleamed in the sun with colorful feathers, earrings, jewels,
and the steel of the maces. From the crowds came shouts of
greeting for the various dignitaries. Small divisions of soldiers
marched in as well from time to time.

Priests of the various temples entered next followed by the
sacred virgins of Vesta.

All were awaiting the appearance of Caesar who, not wanting to
stress the people by over-long waiting and wishing to win them
over by his promptness, soon arrived in the company of the
Augusta and the Augustians.

Petronius with Vinitius in his litter was among the Augustians.
Vinitius knew that Ligia was sick and unconscious but because
entrance to the prison had been strictly forbidden during the past
few days, and as the former guards had been replaced by new ones
who were not permitted to even speak or communicate with those
who came to inquire about the prisoners, he was not absolutely
sure that she was not among the victims of the first day.

The jailers had been bribed to hide Ligia in some dark corner
and to give her at night into the hands of a confidant of Vinitius
who would take her at once to the Alban Hills. Petronius, aware of
the secret, advised Vinitius to go openly to the circus and after he
had entered to disappear in the throng and hurry to the vaults
where, to avoid possible mistake, he was to point out Ligia to the
guards personally.

The guards admitted him through a small door by which they
came out. One of these, named Cyrus, led him at once to the
Christians. On the way he said, "I don't know if you will find
whom you are seeking. We inquired about a maiden named Ligia
but no one gave us an answer. It looks as if they do not trust us."

"Are there many?"

"Yes, sir. But many had to wait until tomorrow."

"Are there any sick ones among them?"

"There were none who could not stand."

Cyrus opened the door and entered into an enormous room with a low ceiling and dark. The only light came from the grated opening which looked out on the arena.

At first Vinitius could see nothing; he heard only murmurs but when his eyes grew accustomed to the darkness, he was able to see strange figures about the room. These were Christians sewn up in the skins of beasts. Some were standing, others were kneeling in prayer. Those with long hair flowing over the skins appeared to be victims who were women. Some of them carried children in their arms who were also dressed in animal skins. The faces which were visible shown with a feverish light. They had but one thought and desire and that was to die for Christ.

Vinitius walked about asking and looking for Ligia. After searching for quite a while in that stifling enclosure, he became convinced that she was not there.

Suddenly he heard a familiar voice. Pushing through the crowd he came upon Crispus who was berating the crowd, "Repent for your sins!" he cried. "The moment is at hand. If you think that death alone will redeem you, then you are committing a new sin and you will be hurled into everlasting fire. How dare you think that eternal life awaits you if you do not repent now? Today the just and the sinners will die the same death but the Lord will pick and choose His own. The Lord showed enough mercy for you when He died on the cross for you. From now on He will only be a just judge who will avenge all wrongs and sins. If you think that you will atone for your wrong doings by the coming suffering and death, you are mistaken. The mercy of God is at an end; anger of God is nigh. You will soon stand before the judgment seat, so repent of your sins or the gates of hell will engulf you all. Woe to you all, men, women and children!"

Spreading his bony hands before him, Crispus shook with indignation and unrelenting justice even at this time of impending death. The crowd took up the cry: "Woe to us! Let us repent!"

Vinitius hearing these words of Crispus and the cry of despair from the people wished that the Apostle Peter were here to console the flock. He would speak of mercy and forgiveness. He would tell them all that the mercy of God was everlasting.

Vinitius felt much depressed. The air itself around him was suffocating and he had difficulty breathing. He was afraid of fainting. Again he began calling the name of Ligia.

A figure suddenly stood before him and a voice spoke to him, "Sir, she and Ursus were left behind. I saw her sick in bed when they were leading me out."

"Who are you?" asked Vinitius.

"1 am the quarryman in whose hut the Apostle Peter baptized you. Today I will enter the arena."

Vinitius breathed easier. On coming here, he was hoping to find Ligia but now he was thankful to Christ that she was not here.

The quarryman spoke again, "Do you remember, sir, that it was I who led you to the Apostle Peter?"

"Yes. I remember."

"The Apostle blessed me the day before I was imprisoned. I would like to look upon him at the time of my death. I will have more courage to die if I see him. If you know where he is seated in the arena, please tell me."

Vinitius spoke quietly, "He is among the people of Petronius dressed as a slave. I don't know the exact place but I will find out when I return. Look in my direction. I will turn my head toward the place where he is among the slaves of Petronius."

"Thank you very much, sir. Peace be with you!"

"May the Savior be merciful to us."

"Amen."

Vinitius left the enclosure and entered the amphitheater; he hurried over to Petronius.

"Is she there?" asked Petronius. "No. She remained in prison."

"Hear me. I thought of another thing, but while you're listening gaze nonchalantly toward Nigidia as if we are discussing her hair-do. Tigellinus and Chilo are observing us closely. Listen then: Let them put Ligia in a casket as if she were dead; the rest you can surmise yourself."

"Yes," said Vinitius.

Further conversation was interrupted by Tullius Senecio who leaned toward them and asked, "Do you know whether the Christians will be armed?"

"No, we don't," answered Petronius.

"I would prefer to see them armed; otherwise it would resemble a slaughter. But, what a magnificent amphitheater!" said Tullius.

It really was a splendid sight to behold all around them. The lower center seats glistened in the sun with white togas of the dignitaries. In the gilded podium sat Caesar wearing a diamond pendant and a golden wreath on his head. Next to him sat the beautiful but gloomy form of Poppaea. The Vestal Virgins sat in a circle around the podium and close around the podium in the lower seats sat the various dignitaries. All that constituted the power and wealth of Rome were there.

Festoons of roses, lilies, ivy and grapevines hung all around in decoration.

People talked loudly among themselves; there were catcalls, peals of laughter and some singing everywhere. The crowd began to stomp its feet showing their impatience for the games to begin. Hearing this, Caesar nodded his head toward Tigellinus to begin. The prefect of the city gave a signal with a handkerchief. The signal was answered by the crowd with a final "Ahhhh..." of consent.

Usually a spectacle was begun by hunts of wild beasts in which the barbarians from the northern regions excelled. This time, however, due to the great number of animals, this was put off for a while. It started instead with the battles of the *andabates,* i.e., men with helmets which hid their faces completely so that they could not see at all. They were to fight each other blindly.

These came at one another, slashing about with their swords. The incitors packed them together with long prongs. This spectacle was not considered highly by the dignitaries but the people in general cried derisively at the contenders, directing them with shouts such as, "Go left. Go right. Straight ahead." They laughed loudly when the opponents backed into one another. A number of pairs, holding each other's hands, fought savagely without their shields to the death of one of them. Gradually the number of combatants dwindled to one last pair, and these fought until both fell mortally wounded. Then the cry of *"Peractum est!"* (It is finished) came from the throngs. The servants rushed into the arena to carry out the bodies after which the whole arena was raked and then sprinkled with leaves and saffron.

Now began the more important contests, the battles of the gladiators. During these, the patricians made enormous bets, often losing everything they owned. Tablets were passed among them on which were written names of the favorite gladiator and alongside his name the amount wagered on him.

Some of the people, having no money of their own, put up as a wager their own freedom. These awaited the outcome with fear, praying to their gods to help their favorites to win.

The blast of the trumpet was heard and silence followed. All eyes turned to the main entrance from the underground to the arena. A man dressed as Charon approached the main door and struck it three times with a hammer as if to call to death those who were within. The door was then opened into the arena and out marched the gladiators to the center of the arena. They walked in groups denoting the type of armor and mode of battle to be used. At the sight of them, people began to applaud loudly and yell encouragement as the gladiators circled the arena. They finally paused before Caesar's podium. The trumpet blasted once more and at this the gladiators raised their right hands and eyes toward Caesar and began a sort of a sing-song shout: *"Ave, Caesar, Imperator...Morituri te salutant!"* (Greetings, Caesar Emperor. We who are about to die salute you!)

Then they separated quickly, taking their places in the arena. They were to fight in groups later but now the more well known and popular gladiators met in single combat.

From among the Gauls, who were dressed in heavy armor with large swords in hand, stepped forth one who was named Lanio. He had come out victorious in all his previous meets in the arena and was well known by all. He was gigantic in stature with a huge helmet on his head, and resembled a formidable giant bird in his armor. From among the *retiarii,* who were very agile of foot and had as their weapons a net in one hand and a three-pronged fork in the other, stepped Calendio.

The viewers began to shout their bets.

"Five hundred silver on the Gaul!"

"Five hundred on Calendio!"

"By Hercules! A thousand!"

"Two thousand!"

Meanwhile the Gaul, reaching the center of the arena, began to fall back slowly with his sword upraised and his shield at the ready. Through the opening of his helmet he measured his opponent.

Calendio, dressed only in a loincloth, circled his opponent with quick lithe steps raising his trident and singing the usual song of the *retiarii*: *"Non te peto, piscem peto. Quid me fugis Galle?"* (I seek not you, I seek a fish. Why do you flee me Gaul?)

However Lanio did not flee. He stopped, only turning each time to face his adversary who was circling him constantly. He was indeed a menacing figure of armor and strength, only awaiting the proper time to cast himself upon his opponent. The latter, always circling, now springing forward with his trident, now springing back, was constantly on the move. The trident striking the shield could be heard clearly. It seemed though that the Gaul was not worried about the trident, his main concern being the net circling above his head like a bird of prey. All eyes were upon them awaiting the outcome. The Gaul chose his moment, and suddenly rushed at his opponent thrusting with his sword; the latter with equal quickness shot past under the sword, straightened himself with raised hand and threw the net. The Gaul, turning where he stood, caught it on his shield, then both sprang apart. It was a beautiful maneuver on the part of both and the crowd applauded loudly yelling, *"Macte!"* (Well done!) The wagering increased. Caesar, who until then spoke with Rubria and paid little attention to the contest, now turned his attention to the fight.

The gladiators with precise movements went about their work as if it were not a life and death struggle but only a matter of dexterity, suppleness and skill. Twice more the Gaul escaped the menacing net. Twice more Calendio managed to evade the huge sword.

Lanio paused a moment to catch his breath but those in the crowd who bet against him urged him on. He heard them and attacked suddenly. The arm of Calendio was instantly covered with blood and he lowered his net. The Gaul summoned his strength and sprang forward again in order to give the final blow. Calendio, however, feigning uselessness of his net arm, was waiting for this moment. He sprang aside as fast as lightning, escaping the thrust of the sword, and with his trident he tripped the Gaul who fell down heavily. He tried to rise at once but in a twinkle of an eye, he was enmeshed by the fatal net. Struggling to avoid it, he became more and more entangled by his adversary. At the same time the trident pierced him time and time again to the earth. He made one last noble effort but managed to only rise on one arm. But his effort was in vain. He could no longer hold his sword and fell on his back. Calendio tore his helmet off and pinned his neck to the earth with the trident. He then turned toward Caesar to see if permission was granted for the kill.

The whole circus shook with applause and yells. To those who had bet on him, Calendio was now greater than Caesar. There was no anger nor vengeance in their hearts toward Lanio. They would spare him. At the cost of his blood they had filled their purses.

Voices around the amphitheater were divided: some wanted him killed, others wanted him spared.

Calendio looked at Caesar. His signal and the signal of the Vestal Virgins would determine the final action toward his opponent. To the misfortune of the fallen gladiator, Nero did not like him. He had bet against him once before and lost heavily to Licinius. So now, he made a thumbs down signal which meant death. The Vestal Virgins showed the same sign in support of Caesar. Calendio thereupon knelt on the breast of the Gaul and thrust a short knife into the neck of Lanio.

"Peractum est!" cried the crowd.

Lanio quivered for a moment and then digging into the sand with his heels, stretched once and lay motionless in death. The man dressed as Mercury did not have to place a heated iron to his body to see if he were still alive. His body was then carried away.

Other pairs followed them in battle and after them, whole groups fought with one another. The crowd urged them on in their bloody battles. They howled, yelled and whistled approval or disapproval. The combatants fought savagely, realizing that death awaited many of them. With tremendous strength and skill they tried mightily to prevail. Toward the end such terrible fear struck some of the novices among the gladiators that several turned to flee the place of bloody slaughter, but the whips in the hands of the incitors drove them back into the fray. Now, more and more bodies lay in their own blood on the sand. The living fought standing on the fallen bodies.

The audience was intoxicated with the blood shed by the contestants in the arena. They madly yelled their delight and pleasure.

A few barely survived the slaughter. They knelt down in the

center of the arena and with trembling hands accepted the crowns of olive wreaths as victors of the day.

The bodies were then taken away, the sand smoothed out and incense burnt in the vases around the amphitheater. Sprinklers scattered saffron and violet showers on the people. Cooling drinks, roasted food, sweet cakes, wine, olives and fruit were served. The crowd ate and drank and shouted thanks to Caesar for being so generous to them. Then after they were satisfied with food and drink, hundreds of slaves distributed baskets of assorted gifts. Little boys and girls dressed as cupids picked out the gifts from the baskets and threw them with both hands among the seats. When the lottery tickets were distributed there was such a terrible crush that many were actually hurt, some even seriously. The cause for such enthusiasm was that some lucky ticket holders could win as much as a house with a garden, a slave or costly attire, or even a wild animal which they could in turn sell back to the circus.

On numerous occasions it took the Praetorians to stop the fights over the tickets and many had to be carried out as victims of these fights.

The dignitaries and the wealthier spectators refrained from taking part in the struggle for tickets. The Augustians amused themselves watching Chilo who tried to show the others that he could also look upon the bloodshed without qualm but in this he was not successful. He wrinkled his brow, grew pale, bit his lips and squeezed his fists till the nails cut into his palms. His Greek nature and personal cowardice were unable to endure such sights. His teeth began to chatter and a trembling seized his entire body. At the end of the gladiator contests he recovered somewhat but when the others began to make fun of him, he desperately and angrily lashed back at them.

"Ha, Greek, the sight of a torn skin is beyond your strength!" cried Vatinius pulling at Chilo's beard.

Chilo bared his last two front teeth at him and retorted, "My father was not a cobbler so I can't mend it."

"Macte! Habet!" called out some in encouragement.

"It's not his fault. He has a piece of cheese instead of a heart in his chest," cried Senecio.

"It's not your fault either that you have a blister instead of a head," answered Chilo.

"Maybe you'll become a gladiator. You'll look good with a net over your head!"

"If I caught you with that net, I would have me a prize nincompoop!"

"How will it be with the Christians?" asked Festus from Liguria. "Don't you want to be a dog and bite them?"

"I wouldn't want to become your brother."

"You Meotian leper!"

"You Ligurian mule!"

"Your skin is itching. Don't ask me to scratch it."

"Scratch yourself. If you scratch a pimple on your body, you will destroy your best possession."

Thus they baited him, and he in turn defended himself venomously amid the general laughter. Caesar, clapping his hands and yelling, *"Macte!"* urged them on. After a while Petronius approached Chilo and touching him with his ivory cane said coldly, "That's fine, philosopher! But there is one thing you didn't count on. The gods created you as a pickpocket but you have become a demon. This is why you will not last."

The old man looked at him with red-rimmed eyes but this time he could not come up with a ready retort. He only muttered with an effort, "I'll last. I'll last."

The trumpets now gave a signal that the spectacle was to resume. People hurried back to their places. Gradually the noise subsided and order was slowly restored in the amphitheater.

It was time for the Christians to appear. All waited with curiosity, not knowing what to expect. They did look forward to seeing something unusual. Most still felt an antagonism toward them since they believed the accusation that the Christians burned Rome and demolished its treasures. After all, were they not the enemies of the human race? Did they not commit atrocities, murder children, poison fountains? The worst punishment would not be enough for them.

The sun rose to its highest peak. Its rays filtered through the purple shade above and spread around the circus in a crimson hue, not too unlike the color of blood.

There was something ominous in the rays emanating from the sun and filtering through into the arena. Even the sand of the arena seemed bloody in color. Terror was sensed by all, something ominous and tragic as if impending doom was awaiting all of them. The crowd felt this and waited now with mixed feelings.

Then the prefect gave the signal. At this, an old man dressed in the garb of Charon, the god of death, who had appeared previously to greet the gladiators, came out once more. Again, he hammered three times on the door of the arena. The murmur around the circus rose. "The Christians. The Christians!"

The iron grating creaked open. Cries from inside were heard; they were the yells of the scourgers or the incitors who with their whips urged the prisoners onto the arena. "To the sand. To the sand!" they cried.

In a short space of time the whole arena was filled with human beings all dressed in skins of assorted animals. Some knelt on the sand praying and singing a song which was unknown to the crowd of watchers: *"Christus regnat!,* Christ reigns, Christ conquers, Christ will take care of us," ran the song.

The spectators were amazed at hearing this. The song they heard was filled with victory not defeat; joy, not sadness, with a divine promise of things beyond their lives as Roman citizens. "Who is this Christ Who will rule and conquer?" they wondered. "What unusual courage and inspiration He gives to His followers who are about to die!"

Meanwhile another grating was opened and into the arena ran a pack of dogs, huge in size with ferocious eyes resembling wolves more than dogs. Maddened from forced hunger, they ran around bewildered at first.

The Christians huddled together as much as possible, knowing that their hour of death was near and uttering words that gave them courage: *"Pro Christo, pro Christo."*

The dogs, detecting human smell inside the animal skins and confused at the immobility of these forms before them, at first hesitated to attack them. Some reached with their front paws toward the lower loges wherein sat the spectators; others ran about madly as if chasing some unseen wild creatures.

The crowd wanted action. They began to yell and loudly imitate the sounds of animals. The whole circus was filled with shouts.

The wild dogs now began to jump closer to the immobile Christians; one, a huge wolfhound finally grabbed a kneeling woman and began to drag her backwards. At this, hundreds of the dogs jumped in slavering in their hunger and thus began the holocaust of the first Christians. Blood flowed profusely from their bodies. Here and there were still heard voices in prayer and song but soon these were muffled in the agony of death. Children's fearful voices rose up in a wail for mercy and that soon died in death.

Vinitius, as he had promised the quarryman, stood up and turned his face toward the place where Peter sat. Then he remained seated as stiff as a statue, looking with glassy eyes upon the holocaust. He feared that the quarryman could be mistaken and that Ligia could be among those Christians now in the arena, and this at first filled him with dread, but upon witnessing the martyrdom of so many who died with words of *"Pro Christo"* on their lips, he had another feeling. Christ Himself suffered and died and now thousands are dying in His name and for their faith in Him. Why should one more victim mean so much? Was it not merely one more drop of blood in the great holocaust? Yet, he could not fully give himself up to this finality. He would hope and pray to the end. "Oh Christ!" he whispered through pale, dry lips. "Your Apostle is praying for her." Then he lost all awareness of where he was. There was only the sensation that a river of blood would flow from that arena and fill the entire city. He became numb to what was going on around him. He did not hear the cries of the nearby Augustians shouting, "Look, look. Chilo fainted!" Chilo indeed had fainted dead away. His face was deathly white, his head thrown back and mouth opened wide.

Now, new victims were forced into the arena, and like their predecessors, prayed and sang. The dogs, as if already sated, refused to rush at them. Only a few attacked the newcomers. The others sat or stood aside as if gorged with the flesh and blood of the other victims.

The crowd began to cry out for the lions. "The lions. The lions."

The lions were reserved for the following day but the voices of the crowds took on such a menacing demand that Nero, to whom the applause and favor of the people meant so much, acceded to their demands.

He gave the order for the lions. The grates were opened and the lions appeared walking into the arena slowly and majestically. The dogs grouped themselves together uttering fearful, short barks and yelps.

Nero himself now gave his full attention to the lions. He observed them through a magnifying emerald. The crowd and the dignitaries began applauding at the sight of the lions. They all wondered what effect the sight of the lions would make on the Christians. These again took up the cries which comforted them in the hour of death. *"Pro Christo. Pro Christo!"*

The lions, although starved for the last two days, did not rush at their prey. The purple glow of the sand and the air evidently had an influence on them. They opened their enormous jaws in yawns, showing the spectators huge fangs. Soon the smell of blood and the flesh of the Christians began to incite them. Their movements became nervous, their nostrils drew in air hoarsely. One suddenly sprang upon the corpse of a woman whose face was mangled horribly and began licking the blood; another came up to a Christian man holding in his arms a crying and frightened child. The child trembled with fear and convulsively gripped the neck of his father who, wishing to prolong the life of the little one a bit longer, sought to pass him to others in the back of the group. But the sounds and movements incited the lion, and with one swat of his paw he killed the child and seizing the head of the father in his jaws, crushed it instantly.

The other lions now joined the first and the slaughter began once more. Women in the audience began screaming; others applauded with enthusiasm; most watched silently. It was a terrible scene; heads of victims were swallowed whole by the lions, breasts torn apart with one blow, human entrails torn out. The crunching of bones was heard even above the noise of the crowd. Some of the lions holding their victims in their jaws were running about as if to find a secluded place where they could devour their prey. Some fought among themselves emitting thunderous roars.

The crowd became agitated now by so much bloodshed. Caesar watched intently holding his magnifying glass to his eye. The face of Petronius showed disgust. As for Chilo, he had to be carried out.

Meanwhile new victims were driven into the arena.

Peter the Apostle looked on all this from on high. No one watched him; all eyes were turned toward the arena. Standing up, he blessed the victims below. With an extremely sad and tearful face he looked upon these his sheep who were shedding their blood for Christ. Some of the Christians in the arena noticed his tall figure and blessing. Their faces momentarily lit up and they smiled seeing the sign of the cross.

His heart was filled with bottomless grief and sadness and he prayed earnestly, "O Lord, Your will be done. These sheep are perishing as a testimonial of Your truth. You commanded me to feed them and I offer them to You. Heal their wounds, soften their pain, give them happiness in a much larger measure than the torments which they suffer at present." And he blessed them all and offered them to Christ as victims and as children.

Caesar wanted to surpass everything that had ever been seen in Rome to the present so he whispered orders to the prefect of the city. He in turn hurried to the dungeons of the arena to give specific instructions. The result of these orders was the entrance of all kinds of animals into the arena: tigers, panthers, bears, hyenas, jackals and many others—these last filled the arena almost completely. The different colors and shades of skin glistened in the partial sunlight let in through the overhang. Wild movements took possession of the animals, and with ferocious growls they attacked one another and fought to the death. Blood flowed everywhere in the arena; it was a veritable orgy of blood. The crowd looked upon all this in amazement and unbelief.

Finally, the effect of all this shedding of blood, human and animal, took its toll on the viewers. Women screamed, many people fainted; there were now many shouts of, "Enough. Enough."

However it was easier to let the animals into the arena than to chase them out. But a way was found. Archers appeared at different locations around the arena on the lower levels. Soon their arrows found their marks in the bodies of the animals. This pleased the crowds evidently because cheers were uttered at every good shot of the archers. All the animals that were not killed by other animals were now put to death by the arrows.

Then hundreds of slaves ran into the arena and within a short space of time they cleared and sanded anew the entire arena.

In the meantime other slaves began to burn aromatic perfumes. Young girls dressed as cupids passed along the aisles showering the people with petals of roses, lilies and other flowers.

The people talked excitedly among themselves wondering what would follow next. Then they got something which they did not expect. Caesar, who had left his loge some time before, now suddenly appeared walking to the center of the arena with his purple mantle and golden wreath. He was accompanied by twelve singers with lyres in their hands. He reached the center of the arena, then bowing to all sides, lifted his eyes and stood motionless for a while as if waiting for inspiration; then he struck the strings of the lyre and began to sing:

> O radiant son of Leto,
> Ruler of Tenedos, Chios, Chrysos,
> Art thou he who, having in his care
> The sacred city of Ilion,
> Could yield it to Argive anger,
> And suffer sacred altars,
> Which blazed unceasingly to his honor,
> To be stained with Trojan blood?
> Aged men raised trembling hands to thee,
> O thou of the far-shooting silver bow,
> Mothers from the depths of their breasts
> Raised fearful cries to thee,
> Imploring pity on their offspring.
> "Those complaints might have moved a stone,
> But to the suffering of people
> Thou, O Smintheus, wert less feeling than a stone!

The song passed gradually into an elegy, plaintive and full of pain. In the circus there was silence. After a while Caesar, himself moved, sang on:

> With the sound of thy heavenly lyre
> Thou couldst drown the wailing,
> The lament of hearts.
> At the sound of this song
> The eye today is filled with tears,
> As a flower is filled with dew,
> But who can raise from the dust and ashes
> That day of fire, disaster and ruin?
> O Smintheus, where wert thou then?

Here his voice faltered and his eyes grew moist. The Vestal

Virgins began to weep silently. The people listened in silence and finally gave out with a prolonged burst of applause.

Meanwhile from the outside of the gates could be heard the creaking sound of wagons which bore the bloody remains of the Christians to be buried in the sand pits.

The Apostle Peter seized his trembling white head with his hands and cried within himself, "O Lord, to whom have you given rule over the earth? And why do You elect this place as Your capital?"

CHAPTER LVI

THE sun was beginning to set and dusk was coming on. The day's spectacle was at an end. The crowds began to pour out of the exits into the city. Caesar and the Augustians waited until the last. Nero himself was basking in the applause and praise of those who remained behind. He was somewhat morose because, although the applause was overwhelming, he had expected more. So, despite the praise of the Augustians, the effusive shouts of the Vestal Virgins (Rubria herself rested her head on his chest as if enthralled)... despite all this, Nero was not fully content. It irritated him that Petronius did not say a word.

Finally, motioning Petronius to approach, he said to him, "Tell me!"

"I am silent," was the cool response of Petronius, "for I cannot find appropriate words. Indeed Caesar you surpassed yourself!"

"So it seemed to me, but this people, this rabble..."

"Can you expect dogs to appreciate poetry?"

"Then you yourself noticed that they did not applaud as I deserved?"

"Well, you did choose a bad moment."

"How's that?"

"When the people are full of the smell of blood, they can't listen attentively."

"Oh, those Christians!" replied Nero, clenching his fists. "They burned Rome and now they deprive me of proper applause and thanks."

Petronius noticed that his words produced an effect, the very opposite of what he intended, so to turn Nero's mind in another direction he bent toward him and whispered, "Your song is wonderful but I will make one remark: In the fourth line of the third stanza the words leave something to be desired."

Nero, blushing with shame as if caught in a disgraceful act, fearfully whispered back. "So you noticed? It is true. I will have to rewrite that. Thank the gods that no one else noticed it. And you, Petronius, do not mention this to anyone if life is dear to you."

Petronius replied as if in vexation or anger. "You may condemn me to death, O Divinity, if I am in your way, but don't try to scare me, for the gods know best whether I fear death." And, speaking thus, he looked straight into Nero's eyes who replied hurriedly, "Don't be angry. You know I love you."

"That's a bad sign," thought Petronius.

"I wanted to invite all of you to a feast today," said Nero, "but instead I'm going to close myself in and work on that damnable stanza. Perhaps Seneca or even Secundus Carinas or Acratus noticed it as well as you. But I'll get rid of them." Saying this he called Seneca over and told him to accompany Acratus and Secundus to all the provinces of Italy for provisions and money. Seneca, however, refused outright, knowing full well that such a chore was beyond his dignity.

"I am not well, Caesar," he replied, "and I have to take my cure for I am old and death is not far away."

Nero noticed his condition and relented a bit. "I don't want to endanger your health so you may remain but because I love you, I want you confined to your quarters."

Afterwards, he laughed aloud. "When I send Acratus and Carinas by themselves, it is like sending wolves to poach on sheep. Whom shall I appoint over them?"

"Me, sire," cried Domitius Afer, "put me in charge."

"No! I don't want to incite the wrath of Mercury. You would certainly fleece the sheep. I need a Stoic like Seneca or perhaps like my new philosopher friend Chilo. By the way, what happened to him?"

Chilo, who had already recovered and returned to the circus in time to hear Caesar's singing, responded eagerly, "Here I am, O radiant offspring of the sun and the moon. I was ill but your song revived me."

"I want to send you to Greece. You must know what treasure each temple there contains."

"Do so, O Zeus, and the gods will furnish such an enormous treasure for you as never before."

"Yes," said Nero. "I would send you but I do not wish to prevent you from seeing the rest of the games."

"O divinity," cried Chilo mournfully.

The Augustians began to laugh seeing the improved humor of Nero. They began to taunt the Greek. "No, Caesar, don't deprive this valiant Greek of seeing the games."

"Preserve me, sire, from the sight of these noisy geese whose brains put together would not fill a nutshell. I am writing in Greek a hymn in your honor, O firstborn son of Apollo. That is why I want to spend a few quiet days in the temple of the Muses in order to implore inspiration from them."

"No, you don't!" exclaimed Nero. "You just want to escape from the future games and I won't allow that!"

"I swear to you, sire, I'm only writing a hymn."

"Then write it at night. Beg some inspiration from Diana who, by the way, is a sister of Apollo."

Chilo hung his head but at the same time threw malicious glances on all sides.

Nero, turning to Tullius Senecio remarked in surprise, "Imagine, of all the Christians assigned for today's arena, only half of them were disposed of."

At this, old Aquillius Regulus, who knew quite a bit about circuses and games in the arena spoke up. "These spectacles in which the victims appear without arms and without skill to protect themselves usually last a long time and are less entertaining."

"Then I'll order them to have weapons!" cried Nero. Vestinus, who was very superstitious, asked the others, "Did you notice that they all seemed to see something before dying?" He raised his eyes beyond the opening of the roof to the stars which had begun to appear.

The others, however, laughed at him and his superstitions concerning what the Christians could see at the moment of death.

Meanwhile Caesar gave word to be carried out. After him followed the Vestal Virgins, senators, dignitaries and Augustians.

The night was clear and warm. In front of the amphitheater

some of the people remained in order to view the exit of Caesar and his court. Their applause was rather hushed because they were still gloomy and silent after witnessing all that shedding of blood.

Petronius and Vinitius were silent too as they were carried home together. Only when they were close to the villa did Petronius break the silence, "Have you considered what I told you?"

"Yes."

"This is very important to me now. I must liberate Ligia despite Caesar and Tigellinus. It is a struggle which I want to win even at the cost of my life. This day confirmed me in this resolve."

"May Christ reward you."

"You'll see!"

Thus speaking they got out of the litter at the entrance of Petronius' home. A figure approached them from the shadows and asked them, "Is that you, noble Vinitius?"

"Yes, it is I," said Vinitius. "What is it you wish?"

"I am Nazarius, the son of Miriam. I return from the prison and have news of Ligia."

Vinitius now recognized Nazarius and grasped his arm with an unspoken question on his lips, his face full of concern.

"She is still alive," said Nazarius. "Ursus sent me to you to tell you that in her fever she cries your name and prays for you."

Vinitius replied, "Praise Christ Who can return her to me!" Whereupon he introduced him to Petronius. Nazarius continued, "The fever saved her from defilement. Ursus and Glaucus watch over her constantly. She is still in the guards' quarters."

"Are you a Christian also?" asked Petronius. Nazarius looked at Vinitius and seeing him with his eyes raised in prayer, answered without fear, "I am."

"How is it possible for you to enter and leave the prison freely?"

"I offered myself for the work of carrying out the corpses from prison. This way I can be of service to my brethren and give them news from the city."

Petronius looked more attentively at the handsome youth before him.

"What country do you come from?"

"I am a Galilean."

"And would you like to see Ligia free?"

"Yes, even at the cost of my life."

Vinitius spoke now, "Tell the guard to place her in a coffin as if she were dead. Get some help and carry her out at night. I myself will have a litter and bearers ready and waiting. Bribe the guards heavily if you have to."

Vinitius spoke like a soldier, and some of his former energy returned.

Nazarius was glad to hear of this plan and raised his eyes in thanksgiving. "May Christ restore her health; she will be free."

"Won't you have any trouble with the guards?"

"Not at all! Especially if they carry her out as a corpse. It's true that one of them places a red-hot iron to the bodies of those taken out, but he can be bribed. He will only touch the coffin, not the body, with the hot iron."

"Can you get reliable men to help you?" asked Petronius.

"I'm sure I can."

Vinitius added, "I'll be disguised as one of them."

Petronius however opposed this strenuously. "No! The Praetorians may recognize you through your disguise and all will be lost. No. You can't go near the prison or the dungeons of the arena. Caesar, Tigellinus and all have to be convinced that she died. She can be taken outside of Rome to the Alban Hills or even to Sicily. After a week or two you will have to pretend that you are sick and call Caesar's own physician who can be persuaded to advise you to leave Rome for your health. Only then can you join Ligia."

"She is ill and won't be able to stand a long journey," said Vinitius.

"Then we will have to place her close by and give her sufficient medical care. I'm sure you know of such a place?"

"Yes. In the hills near Coriola. I will give directions to have her sent there. I'd like for Ursus to go with her."

"Sir," said Nazarius, "that man has superhuman strength. He could tear out the prison bars and follow her. All he would need is a rope to get to the bars which are high up toward the ceiling. I'll furnish him with a rope."

"By Hercules!" cried Petronius. "Let him escape any way he wishes but not right away. He would certainly be followed and they would locate Ligia that way. Don't lose her by a rash act!"

Both Vinitius and Nazarius mentally agreed to the logic of his words and said nothing.

Nazarius promised to come at dawn the next day. He wished to bribe the guards that very night but first he wanted to see his mother who worried about him. Before he took his leave, he whispered to Vinitius, "Sir, I won't tell a soul about our plan, not even my mother, but if the Apostle Peter is there, I will tell only him."

"You may speak openly here. Peter was among the people of Petronius in the circus. Anyway, I'll go along with you." They both left.

Petronius breathed a sigh of relief. He thought to himself, "I wanted the girl to die of the fever as a lesser evil but now I'm willing to offer the golden tripod to Aesculapius that she will recover and be free. You filthy Bronze-beard...you wish to make a spectacle for yourself of a lover's pain! You shameless Poppaea! First you were jealous of the girl's beauty, now you would eat her alive because your dear Rufius was murdered! You miserable Tigellinus. You want her to perish to spite me. Well, we'll see. I'll tear her away from the yapping dogs that you are and you won't know how I did it. Whenever afterwards I look at you, I will smile and say to myself: You are the fools outwitted by Petronius."

With a smile of self satisfaction he entered the dining room where he and Eunice took supper while listening to poetry, a work of Theocritus read by the lector. The weather outside was threatening with thunder and lightning but both of them were happy together.

When Vinitius returned, Petronius hurried to see him and asked, "How is everything progressing? Did Nazarius leave for the prison?"

"Yes," answered the young tribune. "He went to take care of the matter with the guards. I saw Peter who urged me to pray and have faith."

"Good! If everything goes according to plan she will be free tomorrow. Rest now a little; you look tired."

Instead of resting Vinitius went to his room, knelt down and prayed earnestly.

At the break of dawn, the man from Coriola, Niger by name, came to see him. He had everything ready: the litter and four strong men who were to carry Ligia to the safety of his dwelling.

He hadn't seen Vinitius for some time and on seeing him now was moved to pity by the sight of the tragedy marked on his face.

"My dear Marcus," he cried out. "You must be ill! I hardly recognize you!"

Vinitius told him about the whole plan. Niger was happy to know that Ligia and Vinitius were Christians for he was one also. With tears of joy he embraced Vinitius thanking Christ.

Petronius came up with Nazarius who exclaimed, "Good news!" Indeed everything seemed to be working according to plan. The guards were bribed and even Glaucus gave assurance that Ligia's fever was breaking.

Nazarius said, "We made holes in the coffin so she would be able to breathe. Our only hope is that she will not utter a sound while she is being carried out and is near the Praetorian guards. But, she is so very weak that I do not think this will happen. However, for added precaution Glaucus will have her take a sleeping potion."

Hearing all this Vinitius was stirred to his very soul.

Petronius asked, "Will there be other bodies to be carried out?"

"At least twenty will die during the night; several more will die during the day. Our plan will be to tarry a bit behind the others because the men with torches will be in front of the coffin-bearers. May God help us."

"He will!" assured Niger. "The weather seems threatening again for tonight. This will also help."

Petronius reflected a moment. "Yesterday I felt that you and I, Vinitius, should remain at home. But now, even I won't be able to remain behind at home. There should be no slip-up; everything is well planned and should succeed."

"Yes. Yes. I have to be there! I will take her out of the coffin myself."

"And, once she is in Coriola, I will guard her with my life," added Niger.

They parted. Niger, to his people; Nazarius with the money for bribing the guards.

Petronius assured Vinitius, "Everything should go as planned. Afterward you will have to fake a stricken lover whose loved one died and wear a dark toga. Don't avoid the circus, however. Let them all see you. Yes, all should go well. But are you sure of Niger?"

"Yes, he is also a Christian."

Petronius gazed at him in surprise. "By Pollux! How this sect does expand and how firmly it holds together its adherents. All the other gods, especially Roman, Greek and Egyptian, should beware. Don't hesitate to give generous offerings to this God of the Christians."

"I have offered Him my very soul!"

Petronius went to his library and Vinitius went to look from afar at the prison wherein Ligia lay sick. He stayed a while and then went to the hut of the quarryman where he was christened by Peter. This hut had an exceptional attraction for him. Here he felt that he was close to God and here he spent most of the morning in prayer. Then he dozed fitfully.

In the afternoon he was roused by the sound of trumpets which seemed to come from the direction of Nero's circus. He left the hut and went home.

Petronius was waiting for him.

"I have just returned from the Palatine," he said. "I purposely wanted to show myself there and even participated in the dice game. There will be a feast in the house of Antius tonight. I told them that we will both be there but only after midnight because I have to get some sleep. It would be well for both of us to be present there."

"Was there any news from Niger or Nazarius?"

"No. We'll both see them around midnight. It looks as if a storm is brewing. Tomorrow in the arena a crucifixion of some Christians is to take place, but perhaps tonight's rain will postpone it." Thus speaking, he placed his hand affectionately on the shoulder of his nephew. "No! You won't see her on the cross. She will be safe in Coriola. By Castor! I'd rather see her free than possess all the gems in Rome." He then left to catch a few hours sleep.

With the approach of midnight they both put on dark mantles with hoods and, with short swords at their sides, they left. Because of the storm, there were few people about in the city. Lightning flashed now and then illuminating the surrounding area and showing partially built new homes and streets. After a lengthy walk they finally came upon the group under Niger waiting for them.

"Niger," Vinitius called softly.

"Here I am," answered Niger.

"Is everything ready?"

"All ready. We have been waiting here for some time. A real hail storm is brewing. That is why we came early."

It began to rain hard and in fact hail came down with the rain. They all huddled together under the protection of a rampart overhead.

Suddenly Niger exclaimed, "I see a light yonder. There are more of them. Yes, they are the lights of the torches."

"Yes," said Petronius. "They are coming."

The lights became brighter as those holding the torches approached closer.

Niger began praying for the success of the venture.

Meanwhile the gloomy procession drew nearer and then halted close by. Petronius, Vinitius and Niger pressed up to the rampart in silence not knowing why the halt was made. But the men stopped only to cover their nostrils and mouths with cloths to ward off the stifling stench which was barely endurable at the burying grounds that were called the Putrid Pits. Then they raised the biers with the coffins and moved on. Only one coffin remained behind. Vinitius sprang toward it and after him, Petronius, Niger and the others.

But, before they reached it in the darkness the voice of Nazarius was heard full of anguish and sadness. "Sir, they took her and Ursus to the Esquiline prison. We are carrying another body. They came and took them away before midnight."

Petronius, when he returned home was as gloomy as the storm outside and did not even try to console Vinitius. He knew that to try to free Ligia from the Esquiline prison was out of the question. He guessed too that she was purposely taken there to be sure she did not escape the arena. Therefore, she was watched and guarded more than the others. He was sorry for Vinitius and Ligia but he was also irked very much by the thought that for the first time in his life he had not succeeded in what he set out to do. For the first time he was beaten in a struggle of wits.

"The goddess Fortuna has deserted me," he said to himself, "but the gods are mistaken if they think that I will settle for a life such as his." Here he glanced toward Vinitius who was looking at him with eyes wide open.

"What ails you? You must have a fever?" he asked Vinitius. The latter with a broken, halting voice like that of a sick child answered, "I still believe that Christ can restore her to me."

Above, the echoes of faraway thunder could be heard.

CHAPTER LVII

THE rain with occasional hailstorms continued for three days and nights. This was very unusual for that time of year and it caused the spectacles in the circus to be postponed.

Due to the continuous rain people began feeling an alarm for the grape crop. Lightning struck the bronze statue of Ceres on the Capitol, demolishing it. This event caused sacrifices to be offered in the temple of Jupiter. The priests of Ceres spread a report that the anger of the gods was on the city because the punishment meted out to the Christians was too slow in coming.

The crowd therefore began to insist on the resumption of the spectacles despite the bad weather, and they were delighted when the announcement was made that in three days' time, they would begin again.

Meanwhile, the weather improved and when the resumption of the games arrived, the amphitheater began filling up rather early in the day. Caesar, the Vestal Virgins and his court also put in an early appearence.

The show was to begin with Christians fighting one another, for which they were given all sorts of weapons. But the Christians disappointed the crowds because they threw down the weapons and embraced one another giving them encouragement to endure the coming torture and death. This irritated the spectators who were eager to see the spilling of blood in combat. They began to curse and shout, accusing the Christians of cowardice and hatred of the Roman people.

Finally Caesar gave orders for the gladiators to come in and kill them off, every one of them, even the children.

The bodies were carted away. Then followed spectacles which were supposed to have mythological significance, conceived by Nero himself. One was of Hercules being burned on the hill of Oeta. At first Vinitius thought that Ursus might be chosen to represent Hercules but evidently his turn had not come for another Christian had that part. Some of the other scenes were of Greek origin and Chilo, who had to be present to fulfill Caesar's orders, recognized them immediately. There were the deaths of Daedalus and Icarus. In the role of Daedalus appeared Euricius, the old man who gave Chilo the sign of the fish; the role of Icarus was taken by his son Quartus. Both were raised with hoists and hurled fiercely to the ground to their death. Young Quartus fell so near Caesar's podium that his blood splattered over the purple drapery just in front of Caesar.

Chilo did not see this because he had closed his eyes firmly; he only heard the dull thud of the fallen body. When he opened his eyes and saw the splattered blood he fainted dead away. Other scenes followed in quick succession. Young girls and women were defiled before they were killed by the gladiators who were dressed in the guise of different animals.

The crowds shamelessly applauded these creations of Caesar who now had his entire attention on the arena and the victims dying there.

Scenes depicting historical figures of Rome were also shown, such as Mucius Scaevola who was famous for holding his arm over a tripod of fire without flinching or uttering a sound. The Christian, like the real Scaevola, did not utter a groan even though the odor of his burnt flesh permeated the entire amphitheater. With his eyes raised he only murmured a prayer to his God.

At midday, there was a break for refreshments. Caesar, the Vestal Virgins and the Augustians left the circus and withdrew to an immense scarlet tent erected purposely for Caesar and his retinue. A sumptuous meal awaited them there. Most of the spectators also left the circus to roam and loll about the adjoining grounds and accept food from Caesar's slaves. There was much talk among them about the spectacle thus far and predictions of things to be seen later on.

Meanwhile the circus was being prepared for the coming scenes in the afternoon. Christian men and women and children too were pushed into the arena, each carrying his or her cross according to their ages and size. They were hurried in and ordered to place their crosses alongside the holes that were dug out in the sand, after which they lined up in front of them. These Christians were the remnants of the number which were supposed to be executed the previous time, but who were forced to wait until now.

Slaves now pounced upon them, nailing them, each one to his own cross and lifting them up into the holes. The whole circus resounded with the noise of hammers which could be heard also in Caesar's tent. Caesar himself ate and drank together with his court and the Vestals. He laughed at the fears of Chilo and whispered strange words in the ears of the priestesses of Vesta.

The preparation did not take long and soon the arena was filled with standing crosses upon which hung the tortured victims. Among these was Crispus. He was ready for martyrdom and was glad that his hour had come. His body was bare except for a girdle of ivy encircling his hips. In his eyes was the same fanatical energy and his face was as stern as always. His heart had not changed. As once before he had threatened his brothers and sisters sewn up in the skins of wild beasts with the wrath of God, so today he began to remonstrate instead of consoling them. "Thank the Redeemer," he cried. "He Himself died. Maybe a part of your sins will be remitted for this, but remember justice must be satisfied, so fear the Lord! There will be eternal punishment for evil deeds." He thundered on, "I see the heavens opening but I see too the abyss below. I do not know what awaits me even though I have believed and hated evil. I do not fear torture and death but I fear the judgment of God. Beware, all of you, for the day of wrath is at hand!"

At that moment from one of the lower rows a voice was heard, a voice both solemn and peaceful. "Not the day of wrath but the day of mercy and love; the day of salvation and happiness for I promise you that Christ will gather you in; he will comfort you and seat you at His right hand. Be confident and fear not for heaven is yours."

At these words all eyes turned toward the one who spoke; even the Christians on the crosses looked at him and were consoled by his words. The man who spoke approached closer to the barrier and blessed them all with the sign of the cross.

Crispus made an effort as if he wanted to stretch out his arm and rebuke them, but when he saw who was speaking, he whispered, "It's Paul of Tarsus! Paul the Apostle!" Paul turned to him and said, "Do not threaten them, Crispus, for this day they will be with you in paradise. Will God condemn them? He gave His Son for them. Will Christ Who died for their salvation condemn them? No! They are dying for His name! And, how is it possible for Him Who loves us so much to condemn?"

"I have hated evil all my life!" cried Crispus.

"Christ's command was to love, not hate! He gave us all a lesson of love rather than hate."

"I have sinned at the hour of my death," moaned Crispus remorsefully.

Then an attendant approached Paul asking who he was. "I am a Roman citizen," answered Paul calmly and turned again toward the arena. "Be confident," he assured Crispus, "for this day is a day of grace and salvation for you and you will die in peace with the Lord."

Crispus cried out to the other Christians, "Brethren, pray for me!"

His face softened and lost its usual sternness and he felt more at peace. He prayed fervently, the words of Paul were as a balm on his soul. Only when the crowds began to fill the circus with shouts and laughter did his brows knit in a frown of anger at these people who were disturbing his calm and peace of sweet death.

All the crosses were now raised so that they resembled a forest of trees with people hanging on the trees. On the arms of the crosses and on the heads of the martyrs fell rays of sunshine, but the arena itself was in deep shadow. This was supposed to be a spectacle of lingering death and the crowds were attuned to it. Never before had they seen such a density of crosses. The cross with Crispus on it was in the forefront.

None of the victims had died yet but many were unconscious. No one groaned; no one cried out for mercy. Some were hanging with heads inclined on one arm or dropped on the breast as if in deep sleep; some moved their lips in prayer. There was something ominous in that silence.

The crowds filed in to their former places with happy shouts but at the sight of that forest of crosses they fell silent. The nakedness of strained female forms roused no feelings. They did not make the usual bets as to who would die first. It seemed that Caesar himself was bored for he turned lazily and began to arrange the valuable necklace around his fat neck.

At that moment, Crispus, who was hanging opposite and nearest to Nero's podium, opened his eyes and looked at Nero. Seeing the emperor of the world of wickedness, his face assumed an expression so menacing that his eyes flashed a message of eternal damnation at Caesar who, noticing him now, put his magnifying glass to his eye. Both glared at one another.

Everyone was silent. Crispus made an effort as if to tear his right arm from the cross and point it toward the podium of Nero. The intake of breath made his breast rise so that his ribs were clearly visible and he cried out with a horrifying voice, "Woe to you! Woe to you, you murderer! Woe to you, murderer of your mother. Woe to you!"

The Augustians, hearing the mortal insult against this master of the world in the presence of thousands, did not dare breathe. Chilo slouched prone as if dead. Caesar trembled and dropped his magnifying glass. People all around gasped in astonishment.

The voice of Crispus rose louder and louder. "Woe to you! You murderer of your wife and brother! Woe to you Anti-Christ! The abyss is opening before you. Death is stretching out its jaws for you. The grave is awaiting you! Woe to you, you living corpse. You will die in terror and you will be damned into eternity!" Unable to tear his arm from the cross, Crispus strained his whole body, unbending in vengeance as predestination itself. His white beard trembled, his head shook, displacing the garland of roses on his head.

"Woe to you, murderer. Your hour has come!" he cried again. Again he strained forward, but his body relaxed, his head fell on his breast and he died.

In that forest of corpses, the sleep of eternity began closing the eyes of all the victims.

CHAPTER LVIII

"O CAESAR!" Chilo addressed Nero. "The seas are now very calm and tranquil. Let us travel to Greece. The glory of Apollo awaits you there; the people deify you; the gods will receive you as a guest; but here, O sire..." and he paused because his lower lip began to quiver so badly that he was unable to utter a sound.

"We will go when the games are over," Nero replied. "I know that even now some call the Christians harmless beings. If I were to go now, all the people would call them that. What are you afraid of, you mouldy fungus?"

Nero frowned at Chilo but at the same time looked questioningly at him as if expecting some answer from him about something that was bothering him too. He still felt the fear which the words of Crispus instilled in him, together with rage and shame against the public accusation.

Here, the superstitious Vestinus, who was listening to this conversation, looked around furtively and spoke in a fearful voice, "Listen, sire, to this old man. There is something strange about these Christians. Their God gives them a calm death but He may also be vengeful."

Nero said hurriedly, "I'm not the one arranging these games; Tigellinus is!"

"True, I am," said Tigellinus, "and I scoff at all the Christian gods. Vestinus is merely a superstitious blister of a man ready to burst from fright and this valiant Greek is ready to breathe his last at the sight of a hen with her feathers up in defense of her chicks."

"True," said Nero, "but from now on cut out their tongues or stuff up their mouths.... these Christians!"

" Fire will consume them, O divinity!

"Woe is me!" groaned Chilo.

Nero regained some semblance of composure due to the words of Tigellinus and said, pointing to the old Greek, "Look at this noble descendant of Achilles!"

Indeed Chilo looked terrible. The remnant of hair had turned white; his face was etched in uneasiness, fear and dread. At times he seemed only half conscious of what was going on around him. Often he gave no answers to questions asked of him; then again he felt sudden anger and became ruthlessly insolent so that even the Augustians preferred to leave him alone. Now he showed his anger at them all and cried out, "Do whatever you want but I won't attend the games any more."

Nero looked at him for a moment and turning to Tigellinus said sharply, "You will see to it that this Stoic will be near me. I want to see for myself what effect the fires have on him."

Chilo felt sudden fear despite everything. "Sire, I won't be able to see anything at night. Even in the daytime I have some difficulty observing clearly."

Caesar responded with malice, "The night will be as light as day." And, turning to the others, began discussing the chariot races which were to follow the games.

Petronius approached Chilo, touched him lightly with his ivory cane and said, "Did I not tell you that you won't last?"

Chilo managed to mutter, "I want to get drunk," and reached out with a trembling hand for a goblet of wine. His hand was shaking so badly that he was unable to bring it to his mouth. Seeing this, Vestinus took the goblet from him and helped him drink. Afterward he moved close and with curious and frightened eyes asked, "Are the furies pursuing you?"

The old man looked at him with vacant eyes and open lips, not understanding the question, but finally replied, "No, but the blackness of the night is before me."

"What do you mean, night? May the gods pity you. What do you mean night?

"Night, ghastly and impenetrable, in which something is moving toward me but I know not what it is and I am terrified."

"I'm sure there are evil spirits all around us. Do you have strange dreams?"

"No, because I cannot sleep. I never realized they would be tortured in such a way."

"Are you sorry for them?" asked Vestinus.

"Why do you shed so much blood? Did you not hear what that one said from the cross? Woe to us!"

"Yes, I heard. But they burned Rome."

"It's not true!"

"And, they are enemies of the human race!"

"Not true!"

"And poisoners of our water supply."

"Not true!"

"And murderers of children!"

"Not true!"

"How come? You yourself have given them over into the hands of Tigellinus."

"That is why the blackness of the night is surrounding me and death is near. Sometimes it seems to me that I'm already dead and all of you are too."

"No, you are wrong! It is they who are dying; we are alive. But, tell me, what do they see when they are dying?"

"They see Christ."

"He is their God. Is He a mighty God?"

But, Chilo himself asked a question which was very much on his mind, "What kind of torches are to burn in the gardens; have you heard?"

"Yes, I heard. These will be human torches. The Christians will be dressed in so-called suffering tunics, which will be steeped in pitch to which fire is set. May their God not send misfortune on the city because that is an awful way to die."

"I would rather see that than the spilling of blood. My hands tremble much now. Please tell a slave to help me drink from this goblet."

Other Augustians were also discussing the Christians. Old Domitius Afer reviled them, "There are so many of them; you would wonder if being so numerous that they won't cause an uprising. In fact there were such fears going around, but they keep on dying like sheep."

"Let them just try anything," spoke Tigellinus menacingly.

To this Petronius replied, "You are all wrong. They are armed."

"How?"

"With patience and fortitude."

"A strange way to be armed indeed!" scoffed Tigellinus.

"True, but do you still say that they die like common criminals? On the contrary, their actions tell us that the real criminals are those who condemn them to death, that is we and the whole Roman people."

"What nonsense is this?" cried Tigellinus.

"Indeed you were stupid not to see this happening before your own eyes." replied Petronius.

The others too saw some truth in the words of Petronius and they began to look at one another with astonishment and some even remarked, "True, there is something peculiar and strange in the way they die."

"I tell you," cried Vestinus. "They see their God!"

Some turned to Chilo and asked him, "Hey, old man, you know them well. Tell us what do they see."

The Greek spat out some wine on his tunic and answered, "The Resurrection! They see the Resurrection!" And he began to tremble once again, which caused the others to burst out laughing at him.

CHAPTER LIX

VINITIUS spent several nights away from home. This caused Petronius to wonder whether he had perhaps found a new plan for freeing Ligia and was working on it. He decided not to pry for fear he might spoil it. This resolve was a contradiction of his former belief in his own luck. From the time when he failed to rescue Ligia from the Mamertine prison, he had ceased to believe in his own good luck. Besides, he did not think that a new venture against the Esquiline prison would bring good results. This prison, which was built in haste and had as its foundation the cellars of houses which were burned, was not quite as formidable as the old Tullianum near the capitol but it was guarded much better.

Petronius was sure that Ligia was taken there to escape death from fever and sickness but not to escape the arena. Therefore she was well guarded.

"Evidently," he said to himself, "Caesar and Tigellinus have reserved her for some special spectacle more dreadful than the others. The efforts of Vinitius, if in fact he is still trying, will therefore come to naught."

As a matter of fact, however, Vinitius himself had lost all hope of being able to free Ligia. Christ alone could do that. His only concern was now to be able to visit her daily in prison.

He thought of the time Nazarius was able to get inside the prison as a corpsebearer. He made up his mind to try the same method in the Esquiline prison. He managed to bribe the overseer of the Putrid Pits with a huge amount of money to allow him to be admitted in disguise among those who were sent nightly to take out the corpses. The danger that Vinitius might be recognized was small. The disguise of a slave and the dark of night helped to minimize the danger. Besides, who would think that a son of a consul and a patrician could be among the corpsebearers and amid the stink of the Putrid Pits.

When evening came, he gladly put on a disguise, covered his head with a cloth steeped in turpentine and with his heart beating faster, took himself with others to the Esquiline.

There was no trouble from the guards. He had the proper pass which the guard examined by the light of the lantern. After a while the great iron doors of the prison opened and they entered.

Vinitius found himself in an extensive cellar which was illuminated by tapers and which led to numerous smaller cells filled with people. Some were lying by the walls sleeping, or perhaps dead. Some crowded around a large tub of water in the middle, out of which they drank as if tormented with fever. Others were seated on the ground, elbows on their knees, heads in their palms. Here and there children were sleeping, nestled in their mothers' arms. Groans were heard, weeping and whispered prayers. Above these noises could be heard the curses and cries of the guards.

There was a smell of death; dark figures were seen everywhere. Closer to the flickering lights, pale and terrified faces could be seen, eyes wide and lips burning with fever, hungry and cadaverous in appearance with sweating foreheads and clammy hair. In some corners the sick were moaning loudly; some of these begged for water, others begged to be led to death for they could not stand it any longer. The legs of Vinitius trembled at this sight, and the thought that Ligia was in the midst of this misery made his hair stand on end in horror. He barely stifled a cry of despair. The arena, even death itself, was much better than the conditions of this dreadful dungeon. The cry, "We want to die!" came to his ears more and more often.

Vinitius pressed his nails into his palms for he felt that he was growing weak and that he might lose consciousness. Now, he too desired to die with Ligia.

Just then he heard the overseer of the Putrid Pits inquire, "How many corpses have you here today?"

"About a dozen," answered one of the prison guards, "but there will be more before morning; many are dying by the walls."

He began to complain about mothers who conceal their dead children to keep them near as long as possible. "We have to nose them out by their smell. I would rather be a slave in some rural prison than guard these dogs rotting in here."

The overseer of the pits told him that his own job was no easier. By this time realization of his surroundings returned to Vinitius and he began to search the dungeon. At first he sought in vain; he was afraid that he would never find her alive. There were many passages to minor cells, but luckily the overseer of the pits, who was bribed, helped him. He spoke to the prison guard, "I will leave four of mine who will search everywhere for corpses." The guard readily agreed for it was less work for him and the other guards in prison. "We will have a drink together tomorrow if you do that to help us." he said gratefully.

"Very well, we'll have a drink on that tomorrow," agreed the overseer.

Four men were selected, and among them was Vinitius. He took the others to pile up the corpses on the biers.

Vinitius could now search thoroughly. At first he had no luck but coming to the fourth small cell and raising his torch overhead he thought he saw the giant form of Ursus. He came closer and whispered, "Ursus, is that you?"

"Who are you?" asked the giant.

"Don't you know me?"

"You doused your torch. How can I see you?'"

But at that moment Vinitius noticed Ligia lying on a cloak near the wall. Without saying anything further he came close to her and knelt beside her. Ursus now recognized Vinitius and knelt alongside.

"Praise be Christ but don't wake her up, sir."

Vinitius gazed at her through his tears. In spite of the darkness he could now distinguish her features; her face was very pale and her arms were thin. At this he was seized by a love so great that it was like a tearing pain, a love which shook his soul to the depths. At the same time he felt an enormous pity for her and respect and homage so that he fell on his face and pressed the hem of her cloak to his lips.

Ursus looked at Vinitius in silence. He grasped his tunic and asked, "Have you come to save her?"

Vinitius rose and struggled for a moment with his emotion. "If only I could find a way," he said despairingly.

"Only one way comes to me," said Ursus looking at the strong bars over the opening by the ceiling. "Yes," he continued, "I could break them but there are many guards outside."

"Yes, at least a hundred Praetorians."

"Then that way is out, but how did you get in?"

"I have a pass from the overseer of the Putrid Pits." Then suddenly he stopped. "By the Passion of Our Lord! I will remain here; she can take my pass, wrap her head in a cloth, cover her shoulders with a mantle and be free. Among the slaves who carry out the corpses there are several young men not full grown, hence the Praetorians will not notice her. Once she gets to the house of Petronius, she will be safe."

The Ligian dropped his head on his breast and replied sadly, "She would not consent to this, I'm sure. If you and the noble Petronius cannot get her out then who can?"

"Christ alone." said Vinitius. Then they were both silent. "Christ could save all the Christians," said Ursus, "but since He does not save them, then it is clear that the hour of torture and death has come."

He himself was resigned to death but in his simple soul, he was grieved for Ligia, the child whom he carried in his arms and whom he loved above life. Vinitius knelt again by Ligia. Through the bars above the moonlight shone a bit brighter. Ligia opened her eyes now and seeing Vinitius whispered, "I see you. I knew you would come."

He took her hand in his, pressed it to his forehead, then raised her a bit and pressed her to his breast.

"I am here, dearest. May Christ guard you and set you free, beloved!" He could say no more; his heart was torn with love and pain and he did not want her to see his pain.

"I am sick, Marcus," said Ligia. "I must die here in prison or in the arena. I prayed to see you before I died and you are here. Christ heard me."

Unable to utter a word, he pressed her closer to his breast. She continued, "I saw you through the window in the Tullianum; I knew you wanted to come to me. Now the Lord has given me a moment of consciousness so that we may say farewell to each other. I am going to Him, Marcus, but I love you and always will."

Vinitius stifled a groan and began to speak in a voice which he tried to keep calm. "No, dear Ligia, you will not die. The Apostle told me to believe and he promised you to me; he knew Christ; Christ loved him and will not refuse him. Were you to die, Peter would not have told me emphatically, 'Have confidence!' No, Ligia. Christ will have mercy. He does not want your death. He will not permit it. I swear to you by the name of the Redeemer that Peter is praying for you to live."

Silence followed. The one lamp hanging above the entrance went out but there was sufficient light coming through the bars from the moon. In the opposite corner a cry was heard for a moment from a sick child. Outside, voices of the Praetorians playing cards could be heard.

"O Marcus," said Ligia. "Christ Himself called to the Father, 'Remove this bitter cup from Me!' yet He drank from it. His Father's will be done. He Himself died on the cross for our redemption, and now thousands are being tortured and put to death for His sake, for belief in Him. Why then should He spare me? Who am I, Marcus?" She continued, "I have heard Peter say that he too will die in torture. Who am I compared to Peter? When the Praetorians first came I dreaded torture and death but I dread them no longer. This is a terrible prison but I am going to heaven. Here is Caesar, but there is the Redeemer, kind and merciful. There will be no more suffering and death. You love me, so think how happy I will be. And you, dear Marcus, will come to me there."

Here, she paused for breath after which she lifted his hand to her lips. "Marcus?" she asked.

"Yes, dearest."

"Please don't cry overmuch for me and remember that you will come to me. My life was brief but Christ gave me your soul. I'll tell Christ that even though I die and even though you looked upon my death and though you were left in grief, you did not blaspheme. It is His will, Marcus, and you do love Him. Will you then endure patiently? He will unite us. I love you and I want to be with you for all eternity."

Now, barely above a whisper, she asked, "Promise me, Marcus."

"By your sacred head I promise!"

Her face became radiant in the pale light of the moon and once more she raised his hand to her lips, "I am your wife."

Beyond the walls the soldiers raised their voices in dispute but Ligia and Vinitius forgot the prison, forgot the guards, forgot the world and, almost sensing the presence of the heavenly angels around them, began to pray.

CHAPTER LX

FOR three days, or rather three nights, nothing disturbed their peace. When the usual prison work was finished which consisted of separating the dead from the living, when the weary guards lay down in the corridors to sleep, Vinitius entered Ligia's cell and remained there till daylight. She put her head on his breast and they conversed in low voices of love and death.

Both were like people who, having sailed from land in a ship, saw the shore no more and were sinking gradually into infinity. Both were in love with Christ and with each other and were ready for eternity. Only on occasion did pain arise like a whirlwind in the heart of Vinitius. At times there were flashes of hope born of love and faith in the crucified Lord, but he was increasingly resigned to death.

In the morning when he left the prison, he gazed about him at the city as though he were dreaming. Everything seemed strange to him, distant and fleeting. Now, even torture ceased to terrify him. He, together with Ligia, was convinced that for them eternity had already begun. Their thoughts and words were of things beyond the grave. Their only worry was that Christ should not separate them and they were convinced that He would not. The souls of both were pure. Under terror of death, amid misery and suffering in that prison den, heaven had begun, for she had taken him by the hand and was leading him to the source of endless life.

Petronius was surprised to see on the face of Vinitius increasing calm, a strange serenity which he had not seen before. At times he supposed that Vinitius had found some method of rescue and he was irked that his nephew did not confide in him. Finally, unable to hold back the doubt, he asked, "Now you look different but please don't keep any secrets from me for you know that I want to help you. Have you arranged anything?"

"I have but you cannot help me. After her death I will confess that I too am a Christian and follow her."

"Then you have no hope?"

"On the contrary, I have Christ will give her to me and I shall never be separated from her again."

Petronius began to pace irritably. Disillusion was evident on his face. "Your Christ is not needed for that. Our god of death can render the same service."

Vinitius smiled sadly and said, "No, dear uncle, you do not understand me."

"No, I can't understand you any more. I remember you telling me, 'Christ can restore her to me!' Let Him restore her to you. If I cast a costly goblet into the sea, no god of ours can give it back to me; if yours is no better, I know not why I should honor him above the rest."

"But He will restore her to me."

Petronius shrugged his shoulders, "Do you know that Christians are to light up Caesar's gardens tomorrow?"

"Tomorrow?" asked Vinitius. And, in view of the near and dreadful reality, he trembled in pain. "This is the last night perhaps which I can pass with Ligia," he thought. Bidding farewell to Petronius he went hurriedly to the overseer of the Putrid Pits for his pass. But he was disappointed; the overseer would not give him the pass.

"Please, forgive me," he told Vinitius. "I have done what I could for you but I cannot risk my life and the life of my family. Tonight they are to conduct the Christians to Caesar's gardens. The prisons will be full of soldiers and officials. Should you be recognized, I and my family will be lost."

Vinitius understood that it would be of no use to insist. He had hope, however, that the soldiers who had seen him before would admit him even without a pass, so with the coming of night, he disguised himself as usual and went to the prison. But that night passes were verified with greater care than usual, and what was more, the centurion, Scaevinus, who was devoted soul and body to

Caesar, recognized him. However, surprisingly, he showed a glim-
mer of compassion. Instead of striking his spear against his shield
in the sign of alarm, he led Vinitius aside and said to him, "Return
to your house, sir. I recognize you but I do not wish you ruin, so
I'll remain silent. I cannot let you in, so go your way and the gods
send you solace."

"You can't let me in but let me stand here and look at those who
are led forth."

"My orders do not forbid that," said Scaevinus.

Vinitius stood before the gate and waited. About midnight the
prison gate was opened widely and the prisoners appeared: men,
women and children surrounded by armed guards. The night was
bright, hence it was possible to distinguish the faces of the prisoners. They marched out two abreast in a long, gloomy procession
amid stillness broken only by the clatter of weapons. In the rear of
the line Vinitius recognized Glaucus the physician, but Ligia and
Ursus were not among the condemned.

CHAPTER LXI

EVEN before dusk had fallen many people already began to flow into Caesar's gardens. The gaily attired crowd, some singing, some drunk even that early, were looking forward to the oncoming spectacle. Shouts of, *"Semaxii. Sarmentacii."* were heard everywhere, even along the Tiber and the Via Triumphalis. In Rome scenes of people burning on fiery pillars had been seen before but never had there been such great numbers of victims as now.

Caesar and Tigellinus, wishing to be finished with all the Christians and to avoid the possible spread of disease due to the gruesome conditions of the prisons, had given command to empty all dungeons so that there remained only a handful which were saved for future special scenes. So, when the crowds passed through the gates they were amazed at what they saw.

All the main and side alley ways were filled with dense groves and along the lawns, thickets, ponds and fields were crowded pillars smeared with pitch to which Christians were fastened. From the higher elevations, one could see whole rows of pillars and bodies decked with flowers, myrtle and ivy, extending into the distance. The numbers surpassed the expectations of the crowds. One might have supposed that a whole nation had been lashed to these pillars for the amusement of Rome and its Caesar. The people began to inquire among themselves: "Is it possible that all these are criminals? Even children who can barely walk? Can they have been guilty of burning Rome?" Such questioning created an uneasiness all around.

Meanwhile darkness came and the first stars twinkled in the sky.

Near each condemned person a slave stood bearing a burning torch in his hand. When the sound of trumpets was heard in various parts of the gardens, as a sign that the spectacle was to begin, each slave put his torch to the foot of a pillar. The straw, hidden under the flowers and steeped in pitch, burned at once with a bright flame which increased every instant, consuming the ivy and rising to embrace the feet of the victims. The spectators looked on in silence but the victims on the pillars gave out groans and cries of pain which resounded throughout the gardens.

Some of the victims, however, raising their voices to the starry sky, began to sing, praising Christ. People listened and their hearts were filled with terror, especially upon hearing the fearful cries of children and seeing the agonized squirming on the pillars. It did not take long for the flames to engulf them.

The main and side alley ways were alight as if in daytime. When the odor of burnt flesh filled the gardens, slaves sprinkled the area with myrtle and aloes.

Soon the fires embraced entire pillars and began to consume the victims.

At the very beginning of the terrible spectacle, Caesar appeared in a magnificent chariot driven by four white steeds. He was dressed as a charioteer in the color of the Greens, which was his and his court's chosen color for the races. After him followed other chariots filled with courtiers, senators, Augustians, temple priests and even naked bacchantes, who, in brilliant array and already somewhat drunk, held pitchers of wine and uttered drunken cries. Musicians dressed as fauns and satyrs were heard also. Matrons and maidens of Rome, some drunk and half naked were visible in chariots. Around and about ran slaves tossing ribbons and flowers.

The whole immense procession of chariots moved about amid shouts and cheers of the crowds. Caesar, having Tigellinus and Chilo on each side, drove his chariot himself. He wanted Chilo close by so that he could find amusement in his terror. Now and then he stopped his chariot to look more closely at the burning bodies on the pillars. He seemed like a terrible and powerful god, riding with his arms outstretched, holding the reins as if blessing the crowds on each side. He had a smile on his face because the crowds were ecstatic in their shouts of praise. At times he bowed to the crowds, then again, bending backward, drew in his reins and spoke to Tigellinus.

When he reached the great fountain in the center of the main alley way, he stopped, alighted and mingled with the throng. He was greeted with shouts and applause. The bacchantes, the nymphs, senators and Augustians, priests and fauns together with soldiers surrounded him in an excited circle but he, with Tigellinus on one side and Chilo on the other, walked around the fountain to where the pillars were larger and held the more important Christians. Stopping at each one, he made remarks about the victims or jeered at the old Greek whose face depicted boundless despair. Finally, he came to a lofty mast decked with myrtle and ivy. The red tongues of fire had risen only to the knees of the victim thereon. At first the face could not be seen due to the rising smoke but then a light breeze cleared it away and the face of the man was visible. His head and beard rested on his breast.

At the sight of him, Chilo suddenly squirmed like a wounded snake and from his mouth came a croaking cry of pain and despair, "Glaucus. Glaucus!"

Yes, it was indeed Glaucus on that pillar. He was still alive. His face expressed pain and was extended forward as if to look more closely for the last time at his executioner, this man below, who had betrayed and robbed him, sold his wife and children into slavery, set a murderer upon him and, when all was forgiven in the name of Christ, delivered him to death, to this death on a pillar of fire. Never had one person inflicted more dreadful and bloody wrongs on another.

Now, the victim was burning above on a pitched pillar and the executioner was standing below. The eyes of Glaucus did not leave the face of the Greek. At moments they were obscured by smoke but when the breeze gusted Chilo saw again those eyes fixed on him. He tried to flee but he had no strength to do so. His legs seemed as heavy as lead; an invisible hand riveted him to the pillar with superhuman force. He was petrified with fear. He felt that something inside him was being rent apart; a critical moment in his life had been reached, and his end was now at hand. Everything was vanishing: Caesar, the court, the crowds, and what remained was a bottomless pit, dreadful and black, awaiting him. All this time those eyes were piercing his very soul, summoning him to judgment!

Those present guessed that something unusual was taking place; laughter died on their lips at the sight of Chilo's face. A pain and fear of such immensity distorted it that it seemed the tongues of fire were burning his body. He staggered and extending his arms upward, cried out in an anguished voice, "Glaucus, Glaucus, in Christ's name forgive me!"

Everyone was silent; a shudder ran through the spectators and all eyes were lifted toward Glaucus.

The head of the martyr moved slightly and from above came distinctly but painfully the words, "I forgive!"

Chilo threw himself down on his face moaning dreadfully. He grasped some earth with both hands and sprinkled it on his head. Meanwhile, the flames shot up engulfing the breast and face of Glaucus and turned his whole upper body into a fiery holocaust.

Chilo rose after a while. His face was so changed that to the Augustians he appeared to be another person. His eyes flashed with new inner light; an aura of dignity and resolve showed on his features.

"What's the matter with him? Has he gone crazy?" asked a number of voices.

Chilo turned toward the crowd and raising his right arm called out in a loud voice, "People of Rome! I swear to you by my impending death that the Christians who are perishing are innocent. The true burner of Rome is he," and he pointed his finger at Nero.

Silence followed this cry. The courtiers of Nero and the crowd were numb with surprise at hearing this charge. Chilo continued to stand with his finger pointing at Nero.

All at once there were shouts from all directions. People moved in to get a closer look at Chilo. Shouts of, "Woe is us!" were heard more frequently. There followed accusing shouts against Nero. "Bronze-beard. Matricide. Incendiary," and other names. These came from all sides. There was much confusion everywhere. The bacchantes screamed in piercing voices and ran about trying to hide. There was movement around Chilo and this surge swept him away from the scene and bore him into the depths of the garden.

The pillars began to burn through everywhere and fall across the alley ways, filling the whole area with smoke, sparks, the smell of burnt wood and burnt flesh. The lights began to dim. The garden became darker and darker.

The crowds, alarmed, gloomy and disturbed, pressed toward the gates. News of what had happened passed from mouth to mouth increasing in horror as it passed. Some claimed that Caesar had fainted, others that he fell seriously ill and still others that he had to be carried out as if he were dead. Here and there voices were raised in sympathy of the Christians.

"If they did not burn Rome, why torture them and put them to death? Why so much blood?" The words *innoxia corpora* (innocent bodies) were repeated now more often. Women loudly expressed their pity for the children who were fed to the beasts, nailed to crosses or burned in the gardens.

Finally, pity turned into abuse of Caesar and Tigellinus. People began questioning what kind of divinity it was which gives such strength to meet torture and death. And they returned to their homes in deep thought.

Chilo wandered about in the gardens not knowing where to turn. Again he felt his former weak, old and helpless self, a sick old man. He stumbled against burnt pillars and bodies, striking ashes which sent showers of sparks after him. Finally he sat down, not knowing what to do. The gardens had become almost totally dark. The pale moon moving among the trees shone with uncertain light on the alley ways; the dark pillars lying across them and the partly burnt victims had become shapeless lumps. It seemed to the old Greek that in the moon he saw the face of Glaucus, eyes still boring into his soul and he tried to hide from them, but he could not. He turned once more toward the fountain where Glaucus breathed his last.

Then a hand touched his shoulder. He turned and saw an unknown person before him. "Who are you?" he asked.

"Paul of Tarsus."

"I am accursed. What do you want of me?"

"I want to save you," answered Paul.

Chilo supported himself against a tree. His legs bent under him and he moaned, "There is no salvation for me."

"Haven't you heard that Christ forgave the thief on the cross who felt sorry for him?"

"Do you know what I have done?"

"I saw you suffering and heard your testimony to the truth."

"O, Sir."

"And, if a servant of Christ forgave you in the hour of death, why should not Christ forgive you?"

Chilo seized his head as if bewildered. "Forgiveness? For me? Forgiveness?"

"Our God is a God of mercy!"

"For me?" repeated Chilo and he began to groan like a man who lacks strength to control pain and suffering.

"Lean on me," said Paul, "and come with me." Then taking him by the arm he went with him over to the fountain.

"Our God is a God of mercy," repeated the Apostle. "Were you to stand at the sea and cast pebbles in it, could you fill its depth with them? I tell you that the mercy of Christ is as the sea and that the sins and faults of men sink in its depths. I tell you that it is like the sky which covers mountains, lands and seas for it is everywhere and is limitless. You have suffered at the pillar of Glaucus. Christ saw you suffering. Without fear of what may happen to you on the morrow, you testified with the words, 'This is the real incendiary, this the burner of Rome!' Christ heard your words. Now listen to me. I once hated Christ and persecuted his chosen ones. I did not want Him; I did not believe in Him till He manifested Himself to me and called me. Since then, He is pure mercy for me. He has given you sorrow so that He wants to call you to Him. You hated Him but He loved you. You delivered His faithful to death but He wishes to forgive you and save you."

Heartfelt sobbing shook Chilo; his whole soul was rent to its very depths.

Paul spoke to him soothingly, "Come and I will lead you to Him. This is my mission to lead souls to Christ. I do this service in the name of Christ. You think that you are accursed but I tell you believe in Him and salvation awaits you. You think that you are hated and despised by everyone but I repeat that Christ loves you. Look at me. Before I accepted Christ I was full of malice but now His love is sufficient for me. His love is worth more than the love of father and mother, more precious than wealth and power. In Him alone is refuge. He alone will mitigate your sorrow, lessen your misery, remove your fear and raise you to Himself."

Thus speaking he led Chilo over to the fountain. Round about was silence; the gardens were empty for the slaves had removed the remnants of the pillars and the charred bodies of the martyrs.

Chilo threw himself on his knees and hiding his face in his hands remained motionless. He raised his eyes to the stars above. "O Lord," Paul prayed, "look upon this poor miserable man; look on his tears and his suffering. O God of mercy, You have shed Your blood for our sins, forgive him. By Your suffering, death and resurrection, forgive him, Lord." Then he was silent, but for a long time he gazed upon the stars and prayed.

At his feet he heard a cry, "O Christ, forgive me."

At this Paul approached the fountain and, taking some water in his hands, turned to Chilo and said, "Chilo, I baptize you in the name of the Father, the Son and the Holy Spirit. Amen," while sprinkling the water on his head.

Chilo raised his head, opened his arms and remained in that posture. The moon shone fully on his white hair and his pale sorrowful face. Moments passed. The crowing of roosters was heard in the distance but Chilo remained kneeling. At last he regained some strength, looked at Paul and said, "What am I to do before I die?"

Paul was roused from meditating on the great power of God which even such souls as that of this Greek could not resist and answered, "Have faith and bear witness to the truth."

They left the gardens together. At the entrance Paul blessed Chilo once again and they parted. Chilo insisted on this since he was sure that after what had happened Caesar's wrath would pursue him. And he was not mistaken. When he returned home, the Praetorian soldiers were there waiting for him. They took him prisoner and led him to the Palatine. Caesar had already retired to bed but Tigellinus was waiting for him. Seeing the unfortunate Greek, he greeted him calmly but ominously. "You have committed the crime of treason," he said, "and you must be punished, but tomorrow you will first testify in the arena that you were crazy with drink and that the Christians burned Rome. Your punishment will be limited to stripes and exile."

"I cannot do that," Chilo spoke calmly. Tigellinus came closer to him and with a low but vicious voice said, "What's that? You cannot? You dog of a Greek! Were you not drunk and crazy and

don't you realize what is awaiting you? Look there." And he
pointed to the opposite corner where four slaves stood holding
implements of torture.

"I cannot," Chilo whispered.

Rage seized Tigellinus but he restrained himself. "You saw how
the Christians died. Do you want to die in the same way?"

The old man raised his ashen face and for a brief moment prayed
silently and then replied, "I too am a Christian. I too believe in
Christ."

Tigellinus looked at him in amazement. "Dog, you really have
gone crazy!" And he sprang upon him, grabbed his beard with both
hands, hurled him to the floor, trampled over him foaming and
raging all the while. "You will retract! You will. You will!"

"I cannot," answered Chilo.

"Torture him!" ordered Tigellinus.

At this command the slaves seized the old man and put him on
a bench, then tying his arms and legs, they began to squeeze his
thin shanks with pincers. As they were tying him, he kissed their
hands with humility, then closed his eyes. He was still alive when
Tigellinus bent over him and asked once again, "Will you retract?"
His white lips moved slightly and from them a whisper was barely
audible. "I cannot."

Tigellinus ordered further torture and began to pace angrily, his
face distorted with hostility and hate. Finally, turning to the slaves
he ordered, "Tear out his tongue!"

CHAPTER LXII

A popular drama in the theaters of Rome was called the *Aureolus*. This was a tragedy about a crucified slave who was eaten by a hungry bear. Of course in the regular performance of this tragedy there was an actor playing the part and the story was simulated. But now, the real thing was to take place with a real victim on the cross to be crucified and eaten by a bear. It was the idea of Tigellinus to have it so. At first Caesar proclaimed that he would not be present at this spectacle but his favorite courtier talked him into changing his mind. He explained that after what had happened at the gardens it would be better for Nero to show himself to the crowds and he assured him that from this victim there will be no accusations like the ones from Crispus.

Tickets for this spectacle were distributed among the populace who were assured of a free meal after the show. It was to take place in the evening in a well lighted arena.

The time arrived for the show and the people began to appear at dusk. Tigellinus made sure that all the courtiers and Augustians would be present to prove to Caesar their full allegiance to him. Furthermore, all were curious to see Chilo.

People from Rome all knew about the incident in the gardens. They knew that Caesar was in a rage and could not sleep for several nights. He was obsessed with terrible visions and hallucinations. It was rumored that he had decided to go to Greece. Others however denied this, saying that now he would show no pity at all for Christians.

There were some too who fearfully claimed that as a result of

Chilo's accusation many grave and terrible things would befall Rome at Caesar's bidding. There were some, even among the Augustians, who tried to call a halt to all the persecutions of Christians.

"Where will all this lead, Tigellinus?" asked Barea Soranus. "You wanted to allay people's anger and convince them that the punishment was falling on the guilty. But now, the result is just the opposite!"

"True," added Antistius Vetus, "everyone is whispering that the Christians are innocent. You may have thought that you were clever, but you brought on a result which you did not count on, and truly Chilo was right when he said that you have as many brains as could fit into a nutshell."

Tigellinus turned to each one and said, "Barea Soranus, some people are whispering also that your daughter Servilia hid her Christian slaves from Caesar's justice. They also whisper the same things about your wife too, Antistius."

"That is not true!" cried Barea, greatly alarmed.

"The divorcees of Rome wish to bring ruin upon my wife whose virtue they envy," exclaimed Antistius Vetus, no less alarmed.

But others began speaking of Chilo. "What happened to him?" asked Eprius Marcellus. "He himself delivered the Christians into the hands of Tigellinus. From a beggar, he became rich. He could have lived out his days in peace, had a splendid funeral and a magnificent tomb. But no! He suddenly prefers to lose everything and destroy himself. He must really have gone crazy!"

"Not crazy, but he has become a Christian," put in Tigellinus.

"Impossible!" cried Vitellius.

Vestinus spoke up, "Didn't I say to you that you can kill Christians all you like but don't wage war against their God. See what is taking place? I myself did not burn Rome, but if Caesar gave me permission I would erect a hecatomb to the honor of this God of the Christians. And, we should do this, I repeat, because he must be powerful and we cannot fool around with him."

"And, I said something else," said Petronius. "Tigellinus laughed when I said that they were gaining strength but they are also gaining new members, new adherents all the time. By Pollux! Even a man like Chilo could not resist them. If you think that they do not increase after every spectacle, then you should all become coppersmiths or barbers for then you would be more aware of what Roman people are talking about, what is really happening in the city."

"He speaks the truth, by the sacred peplum of Diana!" cried Vestinus.

Barea, turning to Petronius asked him, "So, what do you think should be done?"

"All I'm saying is that there has been enough bloodshed," replied Petronius. Tigellinus glared at him. "Perhaps, just a little more."

"If the head you have on your neck is not good enough for you, then you better replace it by the one on your walking stick," replied Petronius with contempt.

Further conversation was interrupted by the entrance of Caesar who came in with Pythagoras. Soon the show started but the spectators were bored. They hissed, shouted uncomplimentary remarks and yelled for the bear to appear. If it weren't for the fact that they would see Chilo and the bear, many would have left.

The time for Chilo soon came. The roustabouts first placed a cross on the ground. The cross was not great in size because the scene called for the bear to have a good opportunity to attack the victim on the cross. Slaves dragged out Chilo, nailed him to the cross arms, and raised him up quickly. Before many realized what was happening, there was Chilo nailed up and all eyes were riveted toward him. The Augustians could barely recognize the thin and emaciated body hanging on the cross as that of Chilo. After the torture which Tigellinus inflicted on him, there seemed not a drop of blood left in his face. Only a dried-up streak of blood was noticeable on his white beard caused by his tongue being pulled out. His face was resigned and calm in appearance; perhaps the remembrance of the thief on the cross whom Christ had forgiven lent him confidence; perhaps also his soul spoke to the merciful God. "Lord, I bit like a venomous snake but all my life I was miserable. I was always hungry and thirsty. People trampled on me, beat me, jeered at me, and I was unhappy. Now they put me under torture and nailed me to the cross, but You O Merciful God, You will not reject me in this hour of my sorrow."

Peace entered his heart at last. No one was laughing at him as he hung on the cross. On the contrary, there was only pity for him. He seemed so defenseless, so weak, and people asked themselves how was it possible to torture and kill someone who would soon die anyway?

Among the Augustians, Vestinus was whispering in all directions. "See how they die!" Others were looking for the bear to appear, wishing the spectacle to end as soon as possible.

Finally the bear entered the arena. It swayed slowly from side to side looking around. As it spotted the cross and the naked body on it, it approached slowly. At the cross, however, it paused, sat down and began to growl as if in its animal heart, it pitied this poor old man.

Cries were heard from the slaves trying to incite the bear but the people in general were silent.

Meanwhile, Chilo raised his head slowly and for a time looked over the spectators. His eyes rested somewhere on the highest rows of the circus. His breast heaved once and his face lit up briefly as if he saw something which consoled him. Tears welled up in his eyes and fell on his beard and flowed slowly down his face, and he died.

At that same moment a loud firm voice high up amid the spectators spoke out, "Peace to the martyrs!"

Deep silence reigned in the amphitheater.

CHAPTER LXIII

AFTER the spectacle in Caesar's gardens, there weren't many Christians left in the prisons. There was still pursuit and imprisonment of the new sect but there weren't many caught and imprisoned, barely enough for the coming shows which were to follow soon. In general, people were becoming sick of this kind of spectacle and were superstitiously fearful of the effect it had on the condemned. As did Vestinus, so too numerous citizens felt a terrible omen for the future of Rome. Rumors spread like wildfire of the vengeance that would befall the city and its inhabitants from the ire of this God of the Christians. Prison typhus, which spread through the city, increased the general fear. People were dying from numerous causes. Offerings were made in the different temples to placate the gods. The most persistent rumor that could not be hushed up was that the city was burned at the command of Nero and that the Christians were innocent.

For this reason Nero and Tigellinus continued in the persecution. To calm the multitude, fresh orders were issued to distribute wheat, wine and olives. Restrictions in the building of new homes were eased; wider streets were being planned and materials in the building of homes were regulated to prevent future fires. Caesar himself attended the sessions of the Senate and counseled with the city fathers on various projects which would benefit Rome and its people. But the rights and privileges were not restored to the doomed Christians. The ruler of the world was anxious to instill in everybody's mind that the Christians were indeed guilty and their punishment just. In the Senate no voice was heard on behalf of the

437

Christians for no one wished to offend Caesar. Moreover, those who looked into the future were convinced that here was no reason for the existence of this new sect.

According to Roman belief, however, reverence for the dead extended also to the dead Christians. These bodies were permitted to be taken away and buried as was the custom. To Vinitius, this was somewhat of a solace because he could take the body of Ligia and bury it in his family tomb and then after his own death, he would rest near her.

There seemed to be no hope for rescue and so his thoughts turned to the hope of joining Ligia, but not in this world. He now lived the life of the future promise in heaven. There, he would take Ligia's hand and live in light as peaceful and boundless as the rays of dawn. He only implored Christ to spare her the torments of the arena and prayed that she would die calmly in her sleep. After that, he would be ready to die too for he could never live without her by his side.

In view of the sea of blood which had been shed, he could not hope that she alone would be spared. He had heard from Peter and Paul that they too must die as martyrs. The sight of Chilo on the cross convinced him that even a martyr's death could be serene; hence he wished it for Ligia and himself; he looked forward to a better fate in heaven away from the present evil of Nero and his persecution.

At times he had a foretaste of life beyond the grave. Sadness was giving way to the calm acceptance of God's will. He who previously struggled against the current was now resigned to the future, whatever it would bring. He knew too that Ligia was also preparing for death and her beautiful soul was longing for heaven. Truly, they were both calmly facing death, without fear, without bitterness, only with hope that they would never be separated in the future. Death was only a liberation from the terrible walls of the prison for Ligia, a liberation from the evil designs of Caesar and Tigellinus. In view of this unshaken certainty, all else seemed insignificant. After death would come to them true happiness and bliss without end.

That immense current of faith which swept away from life and bore beyond the grave thousands of those first confessors also bore Ursus away. In his heart he was never resigned to Ligia's death, but when day after day through the prison walls came news of what was happening in the arena and Caesar's gardens, when death seemed the inevitable lot of all Christians, he did not dare to pray to Christ to deprive Ligia of that privilege, to die for Christ. And, in his simple half-barbarian soul, he expected her, who was a daughter of a king, to inherit more of the happiness in heaven than perhaps others, and that she certainly would be closer to the Lamb than many others.

It is true that he had heard that before God all are equal, but down deep he was sure that the soul of a king's daughter was not the same as the first slave one might meet. He also hoped that Christ would allow him to serve her in the hereafter.

His own personal wish however was to die on a cross as the Lamb had died. But this favor seemed so great that he hardly dared to pray for it, though he knew that in Rome even the worst criminals were crucified. He thought that he would be condemned to die by the teeth of wild animals. This was his only sorrow because from the time when he had lived in the forests as a child, hunting was a natural part of his life. As he grew up, his superhuman strength made him famous among the Ligians. Even before he had grown to full manhood, he hunted wild animals, but held a great respect and liking for them. In Rome he visited the different zoos occasionally just to be near them. This brought to his mind that many times in the past he had tested his great strength by taking strong bulls by the horns and overcoming them in that manner. His fear was that if confronted by such animals in the arena, he would do something which would not be pleasing to the Crucified Christ and would be unworthy of a Christian whose duty was to die piously and patiently. But, in this he committed himself to Christ and found other more agreeable thoughts to comfort himself. His constant prayer was that he would die as a martyr for Christ.

In the meantime, in prison he performed many a menial task to alleviate the plight of his weaker brothers. Especially, he took care of Ligia and saw to it that she would be as comfortable as possible in prison. She was his queen and his devotion to her knew no bounds.

The prison guards, who at first feared his great strength since neither bars nor chains could hold him, came to like him for his mildness, gentleness and his great devotion to Ligia. They were all amazed at his good temper. He spoke to them with such certainty of the life to come after death that they all listened to him with surprise and wonder. This way they too learned something about Christianity and were themselves convinced that Christians were not such terrible scoundrels and wrongdoers as they previously thought. For them, death brought fear of the unknown and promised nothing, but this giant of a man and his Christian brethren went out to meet death with hope for the future life as if entering gates to a new kind of happiness that was awaiting them beyond the grave.

CHAPTER LXIV

SENATOR Scaevinus paid Petronius a visit one evening and had a long conversation with him. It was an unusual conversation and his complaints about Nero were so open that Petronius began to be cautious. Scaevinus complained that the world was going to the dogs and that some terrible catastrophe was bound to follow the present evil times, something worse than the burning of Rome. He spoke of the dissatisfaction even among the Augustians; that Faenius Rufus, who was second in command of the Praetorians, endured with the greatest effort the vile orders of Tigellinus; that Seneca himself, Nero's old teacher, was driven to extremes by the actions of Nero. Finally, he began to hint of the dissatisfaction of the people in general and even the Praetorian soldiers, the greatest part of whom had been won over to his side by Faenius Rufus.

"Why tell me all this?" asked Petronius.

"Out of concern for Caesar," replied Scaevinus. "I have a distant relative among the Praetorians named Scaevinus also. Through him I know what is going on among the Praetorians. Discontent is growing there. You know, Caligula was mad also and see what happened. Cassius Chaerea took care of him by assassinating him. That was a dreadful deed, I admit, but still Chaerea freed the world of a monster."

"In other words," said Petronius, "What you are saying is that Cassius Chaerea was a great man and the world needs another like him?"

Scaevinus changed the subject in a hurry and began to praise Piso, his family, his nobility of mind, his devotion to his wife and family, his intellect, his calmness and his wonderful gift of making friends.

"Caesar is childless," he continued, "and all see his successor in Piso. Many would want him to succeed in power. Faenius Rufus loves him; the house of Annaeas is devoted to him. Plautius Lateranus, Tullius Senecio, Sulpicius Asper and even Vestinus likes him very much."

"Not much comfort will Piso get from Vestinus. He is afraid of his own shadow."

"Vestinus fears dreams and spirits, it's true, but he is also a practical and courageous man and there are some who want to elevate him to the consulship. He is opposed to the further persecution of the Christians and that should concern you also."

"Not me, but Vinitius," answered Petronius. "But it is true that out of concern for Vinitius I should like to save a certain young woman but now I cannot because I have fallen out of favor with Bronze-beard."

"Perhaps not altogether. Everyone notices that he is seeking out your company more and more, especially now that he is planning that long-awaited trip to Greece where he intends to sing the songs which he composed himself. He is eager for the journey even though he wonders how he will be received by the cynical Greeks. According to him, it will be one of his greatest triumphs or, on the other hand, it may be his greatest failure. On account of this uncertainty he needs good counsel and he knows that no one can give it better than you can. This, in my opinion, is the reason why you will regain his favor."

"Lucan can do the same for him."

"Nero hates Lucan. As is his custom, he is only seeking an excuse to do away with him. Lucan therefore feels that it is necessary to act soon."

"That may all be true, I grant you. But, there's another way by which I can regain Nero's favor."

"Which is that?"

"By repeating to him all that you have told me just now."

"I didn't say anything!"

Petronius placed his hand on the arm of his friend. "You merely called Nero a mad man; you were sure that Piso will be a popular

successor to Nero and you spoke of the need for action soon. Tell
me, how do you all intend to act?"

Scaevinus grew pale and merely stared at Petronius, "You won't
repeat it, will you?"

"Of course not! You should know me better than that. But I'll
pretend that I haven't heard a thing. Only one thing I ask of you
and that is that you visit Tigellinus today also."

"Why?"

"Because, if in the future, Tigellinus would come to me and say,
'Scaevinus was with you that day,' then I can reply, 'Yes, and he
visited you the same day too.'"

Hearing this Scaevinus broke the ivory cane which he held in his
hands and said, "May the evil one take this cane. I'll do as you
wish. I'll visit Tigellinus today and later on attend the feast given
by Nerva. You will be there too, won't you? Anyway, we'll meet
again in the circus for the last remaining spectacles with the
Christians. Until then, good-bye."

When he was alone Petronius repeated the words, "After tomorrow.... Then there is no time to lose. Bronze-beard will really need
me in Greece, it is true. Perhaps it will work." And he determined
to try one last thing.

At Nerva's feast Caesar himself asked Petronius to recline near
him for he wished to talk to him about the Greek cities which he
intended to visit. He cared mostly about the Athenians and their
acceptance of him as an artist.

The other Augustians listened to this conversation with attention in order to seize the crumbs of the arbiter's opinions and quote
him later on.

Nero was saying, "It seems to me that up to now I haven't fully
lived and I feel that only in Greece I will realize the fullness of life."

"You will indeed rise to new glory and immortality," answered
Petronius.

"I hope you are right and that Apollo will not be jealous of me.
If I return in triumph, I will offer him such a hecatomb as no god
heretofore has received."

Scaevinus began to recite the line of Horace: "May the powerful
goddess of Cyprus, With the stars, Helen's brothers, And the father
of the winds, Take you by the hand on this journey."

"The ship is ready at Naples," said Caesar. "I would like to be on it soon."

Here Petronius rose and looking directly at Nero said, "Before you leave, O divinity, permit me to celebrate a wedding feast to which I would like to invite you above all others."

"What wedding feast?"

"That of Vinitius with your hostage, the daughter of the Ligian king. She is in prison right now, but as you know that as a hostage she is not subject to imprisonment. Furthermore, you yourself have given permission for this wedding and your desires, just like those of Zeus, are unchanging and I am sure that you will want her to be freed and returned to her intended."

The coolness and the confidence which accompanied these words of Petronius confused Nero who always acted in the same manner when confronted and, dropping his eyes, he stuttered, "Yes. I know. I have thought of her. I have also thought of that giant who killed Croto."

"In that case both will be free," spoke Petronius calmly.

But Tigellinus came to the aid of Nero. "She is in prison by the will of Caesar. You yourself, Petronius, have stated that his wishes and desires are unchanging."

Every one present knew the history of Ligia and Vinitius and all understood what this was all about. They fell silent, curious of the outcome.

"She is in prison against Caesar's will and only through your error and by the ignorance of the laws of all nations," Petronius said with due emphasis on the guilt of Tigellinus. "You are a very naive man, Tigellinus, if you assert that she burned Rome."

Nero by now had recovered somewhat, and his nearsighted eyes were squinting giving his face a look of malice.

"Petronius is right," said he after a while.

Tigellinus looked at him in amazement.

"Petronius is right," repeated Nero, "and tomorrow the gates of the prison will be open to her, but of the marriage feast we will speak the day after the spectacles finish."

"I have lost again," thought Petronius.

When he returned home, he was so certain that the end for Ligia had come that he sent a trusty freedman to the amphitheater to take care of the matter of delivery of her body because he wished to give it to Vinitius for burial.

CHAPTER LXV

IN Rome public displays in the evening were rare but during Nero's time they became more popular. The Augustians liked them because they were followed by feasts and drinking orgies which lasted till daylight.

Even though the people were already sated with the blood spilling, they turned out for the last of the Christian spectacles in great number. There were rumors that Caesar had something unusual and dramatic to show this time, so all were curious. They surmised that the tragedy of Vinitius would be displayed in some way and they all wondered about the form it would take. Those who had seen Ligia in the past, told others of her great beauty. The Augustians generally wondered what would be the final outcome of Ligia's future. Nero's answer to Petronius was intriguing so they contemplated whether Ligia would indeed be returned to Vinitius and in what manner. They knew that she was a hostage, hence free to worship any divinities she liked and that international law prevented her punishment for any religious beliefs.

Uncertainty and curiosity took possession of all. Caesar arrived earlier than usual which caused the people to whisper to one another that something unusual was going to take place. Proof of this was the fact that Caesar had with him his favorite bodyguard, the massive and powerful man named Cassius, whom Caesar summoned only when he wished to have a powerful guard at his side to protect him in case of any eventuality. He usually took Cassius along on his nightly expeditions to the Subura where his amusement consisted mostly in capturing young girls and tossing them on a soldier's mantle. Precautions were also taken at the amphitheater. The guards were increased and command over them was given to Subrius Flavus who was noted for his blind devotion to Caesar. Evidently Nero wanted to guard himself against an outburst of despair from Vinitius.

All eyes turned toward the place where Vinitius was sitting. He was very pale and his forehead was covered with beads of perspiration; the awful uncertainty and dread shook his whole being. Petronius himself did not know what was to occur in the arena. He did not say anything to Vinitius except to ask him if he was ready for anything. Vinitius answered in the affirmative.

For some time now he had lived a sort of half-life and was reconciled to the death of Ligia because he knew that it was a liberation into heaven. But it was a different matter to face death from a distance than from the bitter reality of seeing her in torment and agony. All sufferings which he formerly endured rose up once again in his soul. Earlier in the day he tried to enter the prison but with no success and again he tried to bribe the guards but they did not want even to listen to him.

His only hope now was that Ligia would die before her turn for the arena would come. Christ could not refuse him this last request. He had the feeling and the fear that if he should see Ligia tortured, his love for God may turn into hatred and his faith into despair. But, he tried with all his might to put aside this kind of feeling. He knew that God, if He wished, could destroy Nero and all of Rome and save Ligia. She was lying there in prison defenseless but she believed and trusted Him. He now recalled her request of him not to despair and he resolved that he would try his utmost, even up till the end, not to falter in his faith and he held onto this belief as a man falling over a precipice grasps at anything which grows on the edge in order to save himself. So too, he grasped at the thought that faith alone could save Ligia. It was all that remained to him now. Peter himself said that faith could move mountains, therefore with the remnant of inner strength he rallied and crushed the doubt that rose within him. He compressed his whole being into the conviction, "I believe!" and waited for a miracle.

However just as an overdrawn wire must break, so too this final exertion almost broke him completely. The pallor of death covered his face and he thought that he was dying. This way, he and Ligia would die together. But the great weakness did not last long and he roused himself, or rather the stamping of the impatient crowd roused him to full consciousness.

"You are ill!" Petronius cried. "I will give command to bear you home." And, without regard to what Caesar would say, he rose to support Vinitius and go out with him. His heart was filled with pity; moreover, he was irritated beyond endurance at Nero who was looking through his magnifying glass at Vinitius, studying his pain with satisfaction. No doubt, he wished to describe this pain later in his verses.

Vinitius shook his head. He might die but he could not leave. Anyway, the spectacle was about to begin for at that moment the prefect of the city waved a red flag and the gates opposite Caesar's podium opened and out of the dungeon and into the arena stepped Ursus.

Momentarily dazed by the glitter of the arena, Ursus blinked his eyes and began walking to the center, all the time looking around him to see in what manner he would die. Many of the spectators were aware that this was the man who killed the mighty Croto and they began telling one another about his strength. They had seen many a formidable individual in their time but never had they seen such muscles and such a great specimen of strength as this one who stood calmly in the center of the arena. The murmur rose to shouts and eager questions were asked. "Where do people live who can produce such a one?" Ursus gazed calmly about...at Caesar's podium...at the spectators...and wondered from where his executioners would come.

At the moment when he stepped into the arena his heart still hoped to die on the cross like Christ, but when he saw no cross in the arena, he was sure that he was unworthy of such a great favor; he was now sure that he would be torn to pieces by wild beasts. Meanwhile, he wanted to pray for the last time, so joining his hands and lifting his eyes toward the stars, he prayed.

This action of his displeased the crowds. They expected the giant to use his muscles in some manner. If he did not, the spectacle would be a failure. Here and there hisses were heard. Some began to shout for the enforcers whose task was to ply with lashes those contestants who were unwilling to fight.

Suddenly the shrill sound of trumpets was heard and at that signal, a grating opened and out into the arena rushed an enormous German aurochs, a bull of huge size, bearing on his head a tied body of a naked woman.

"Ligia! Ligia!" cried Vinitius. Then he seized his hair at the temples and writhed with pain like a man who feels a sharp lance in his body and began to repeat hoarsely, "O Christ, I believe. O Christ, a miracle!"

At that moment he was not aware that Petronius covered his head with his toga. It seemed to him that death or pain had closed his eyes. The feeling of great emptiness possessed him. Only his lips muttered the words still. "I believe."

All in the amphitheater were quiet now because something amazing was happening down in the arena. That giant Ligian who was resigned to die, when he saw his queen on the horns of the wild bull, sprang up suddenly as if touched by living fire and, bending almost in half, ran full tilt at the raging beast.

From all hearts a cry of wonder and amazement was heard and then all fell silent watching the scene before them.

Ursus sprang at the bull and seized him by the horns.

"Look!" cried Petronius, snatching the toga from the head of Vinitius, who rose and looked down on the arena with a glassy, vacant stare.

There was a great silence now, and everyone held his breath. People could not believe their eyes. Since Rome was built no one had seen such a spectacle.

The Ligian held the wild beast by the horns. His feet sank into the sand up to his ankles; his back was bent like a drawn bow; his head was almost hidden between his shoulder blades; the skin of his arms appeared ready to burst from the pressure of the bulging muscles. He had stopped the bull and held him in his tracks. Man and beast, seemingly, remained motionless, but the great struggle between the two was one in earnest. The bull's feet also sank in the sand and his dark shaggy body arched up into a gigantic sphere.

Which of the two would prevail? That was the question uppermost in the minds of the spectators. It was more important to them at this moment than their own fates, than all Rome and its mighty power over the world. In their eyes this Ligian was a demi-god worthy of honor and statues. Caesar himself was standing in his excitement. He and Tigellinus, hearing of the giant's strength, had arranged this spectacle purposely, and they said to each other jeeringly, "Let that slayer of Croto kill a bull which we shall choose for him." So they looked now in amazement at what was happening, not believing their eyes.

There were people with arms upraised, sweat covering their faces as if they too struggled mightily with the bull. The crackle of the flames in the lamps and the burning torches were the only sounds heard. The struggle below became prolonged. Man and beast continued their mighty exertions.

A dull roar, resembling a loud groan, was heard coming from the bull. His head began to turn slowly, held in the iron grip of the giant. The face, neck, arms of the Ligian turned purple; his back bent still more. It was now clear that he was rallying the remnant of his gigantic strength but he could not last much longer. Duller and duller...hoarser and hoarser...greater and greater the pain in the roar of the bull as it mingled with the whistling breath of Ursus. The head of the beast turned more and more and from the jaws crept forth a long lathered tongue.

In a moment the ears of the spectators sitting close to the arena detected the distinct crack of bones breaking, after which the huge beast fell to the ground and rolled on the earth with his neck twisted in death.

In a twinkle of an eye Ursus untied Ligia from the horns and held her in his arms, still breathing hard and very pale after the amazing exertion which he showed. His hair was stuck together with sweat, his arms and shoulders were drenched. For a moment he stood as if only half conscious, then he raised his eyes and looked at the spectators.

The amphitheater had gone wild.

The walls shook from the shouts of the crowd. Their enthusiasm was never greater. Those sitting in the upper rows clambered down for a better look. Everywhere were heard cries of clemency and mercy, some passionate and even persistent. This giant became dear to these people enamored of tests of strength; he was to them the most important man in all Rome.

Ursus understood that the crowd was favorable to him but he did not think of himself. He looked around a while, then approached Caesar's podium and holding the girl, he stretched forth his arms as if in supplication for her, as if to say, "I have done this not for me but for her. Please have mercy on her."

The spectators understood this gesture perfectly. At the sight of the unconscious girl who, in his arms, seemed but a small child, emotion seized the multitude, the nobles, senators and even Augustians. Her slender form white as alabaster, the dreadful ordeal which was spared her, and finally her beauty filled them with pity for her. The utmost devotion which they witnessed moments before by Ursus moved every heart. Some thought that it was a father begging mercy for his child. They had had enough bloodshed, torture and death. Voices all around were shouting and demanding pardon for both.

Ursus, holding Ligia, moved around the arena and with his eyes and gestures kept entreating that her life be spared.

Vinitius started up from his seat, sprang over the barrier which separated the front places from the arena, and reaching Ligia covered her naked body with his toga. Then he tore his tunic at his breast, laid bare the scars left by wounds he received in the Armenian war and stretched out his hands to the audience.

At this the enthusiasm of the crowd grew to a high pitch. They stamped and yelled louder and louder demanding mercy for both Ursus and Ligia. They were also rising up in defense of a soldier of Rome...a maiden...and their love. Thousands of spectators turned toward Caesar with flashing eyes and angry fists.

However, Caesar hesitated. He had nothing against Vinitius and the death of Ligia did not overly concern him but he preferred to see the body of the girl rent in two by the horns of the bull or torn by the claws of the beasts. His cruelty, his depraved imagination and desires found a kind of delight in such spectacles. And now, these people wanted to rob him of this pleasure. Hence anger appeared on his bloated face. Self love also would not let him yield to the wishes of the multitude but he did not dare to oppose it because inwardly he was a coward.

He looked to see if among the Augustians at least he could find the thumbs-down sign of condemnation. But Petronius held up his hand and looked directly at, even appearing to challenge, Nero. Vestinus, superstitious and fearing ghosts but not men, gave also a sign of clemency. So did Scaevinus the senator...as did Nerva, Tullius Senecio, Ostorius Scapula, Piso, Vetus, Crispinus, and, most important of all because he was held in high esteem, Thrasea...all gave the same sign of clemency.

In view of all this, Caesar took the magnifying glass from his eye with an expression of contempt. Tigellinus came up to him and said, "Don't yield, divinity, we have the Praetorians."

Nero now looked at stern Subrius Flavus, who was so devoted to him and was surprised to see him, with tears in his eyes, holding up his hand in the sign of clemency. Here, Nero looked around and noticed the angry faces and heard the angry cries of the crowd. He heard the cries of, "Bronze-beard...Matricide...Infanticide...Incendiary..." and suddenly became alarmed.

Many times in the past, the Roman people had forced their wills on a ruler, especially during the circus games. Perhaps Caligula was the only exception who sometimes resisted the will of the people but when he did, it always brought disturbances and bloodshed. All the other rulers usually gave in. Nero felt himself in a position of trying to placate the people after the big fire and so he wanted the crowd on his side. Now he understood that to oppose the people's will may cause unrest and especially loss of popularity.

Again he looked at Subrius Flavus, at Scaevinus, at the soldiers and seeing nothing but frowning brows and baleful glares fixed upon him, he finally gave the sign of clemency. The Vestal Virgins all followed suit.

At this a thunder of applause rose from every part of the amphitheater. The people were now sure of the lives of the condemned because from that moment they went under the protection of the whole Roman people and even Caesar himself would not dare to pursue them any longer with his vengeance.

CHAPTER LXVI

FOUR strong Bithynians carried Ligia carefully to the house of Petronius. Vinitius and Ursus walked at her side hurrying to get her into the hands of Petronius' own physician as quickly as possible. They walked in silence. After what had recently happened to them, they could only be silent. Vinitius himself was barely conscious; he couldn't believe it yet and had to repeat to himself that Ligia was saved, that prison and death threatened her no longer. Now he could take her away, far away from all this. Her suffering had ended and his also, as well as that of Ursus. This conviction was still unreal to Vinitius. Every now and then he bent over the litter to gaze upon that beloved face which in the moonlight he could barely distinguish as she slept peacefully. He kept repeating to himself, "Yes, it is she! Christ saved her!" He remembered that while he was carrying her from the arena, an unknown doctor came up to examine her and after the brief examination, assured him that after perhaps a lengthy convalescence she would definitely recover. At this assurance joy so filled his heart that it almost made him weak and he had to have Ursus carry Ligia the rest of the way to the waiting litter.

Ursus, meanwhile, was gazing at the stars and praying silently while they walked on hurriedly. The city was empty; only here and there they encountered some people tarrying before they returned to their homes after the spectacle. These were in an especially happy mood as were all the rest for on this night they had witnessed something to be remembered for a long time.

When they were near the house of Petronius, Ursus turned to

Vinitius and said with complete conviction, "It was the Savior Who rescued her. When I saw her on the horns of the bull, I heard an inward command: 'Defend her!' and that was the voice of Christ. The prison eroded my strength but at that moment He returned it to me and also inspired the crowd to intercede for her. His will be done!"

Vinitius answered, "May His name be glorified forever!" and he could not say more because he was overcome with emotion. He even wanted to throw himself on the ground in thanksgiving but they were almost home.

The servants and slaves, knowing what had transpired, were awaiting them with jubilation. Most of them were Christians converted by Paul of Tarsus. Their delight at the outcome of events at the circus was great. This joy spread throughout the whole house when the physician of Petronius, Theocles, corroborated the words of the doctor at the arena. Ligia would eventually recover but she needed much care and attention.

Consciousness returned to her that night. Waking in the splendid chamber lit by Corinthian lamps amid the smell of verbena and nard, she knew not where she was nor what was happening to her and around her. She remembered the moment in which she was lashed to the horns of the chained bull. Now, seeing the face of Vinitius above her, she at first supposed that she was no longer on earth. Her thoughts were confused; it seemed natural to her that she be detained somewhere on the way to heaven. Feeling no pain, however, she smiled at Vinitius and wanted to ask where they were but from her lips came only a low whisper in which he could barely discern his name.

He knelt before her and placing his hand lightly on her forehead said, "Christ saved you and returned you to me."

Her lips moved again but Vinitius could not hear what she was trying to whisper; her lids closed after a moment, her breast rose with a light sigh and she fell into a deep sleep for which the physician had been waiting and after which she would feel much better.

Vinitius remained kneeling near her, sunk in prayer. His soul melted with love so immense that he utterly forgot himself. Theocles returned often to Ligia's chamber; the golden-haired Eunice appeared a number of times but Vinitius remained kneeling before his beloved, thanking God for her delivery from death. He neither saw nor heard what was happening around him; his heart was full of gratitude and love for his God.

CHAPTER LXVII

AFTER the liberation of Ligia, Petronius, not wishing to irritate Caesar, went to the Palatine with the other Augustians. He wanted to know what the conversation would be about and at the same time to learn if Tigellinus was planning something new to destroy Ligia. Both she and Ursus had come under the protection of the people, it is true, and no one would dare harm them without raising a riot. Still Petronius, knowing the hatred directed to him by the all-powerful Praetorian prefect, considered it likely that Tigellinus would find some means of revenge against him and against Vinitius.

Nero was angry and irritated since the spectacle had ended quite differently from what he had planned. At first he did not even look toward Petronius, but the latter approached him cooly and with all his former ease as an Arbiter of Elegance, said to Caesar: "Do you know, divinity, what a wonderful inspiration came to me? Write a poem about a maiden who, at the command of the master of the world, was freed from the horns of a wild bull and given to her lover. The Greeks are sensitive and I am sure that the poem will please them."

This thought pleased Nero despite his irritation. It pleased him for a twofold reason: first as a theme for a poem, and second because in it he could glorify himself as the magnanimous lord of the earth. He gazed at Petronius for a while and then said, "Yes, perhaps you are right. But, does it behoove me to exalt my own goodness?"

"There is no need to give names. In Rome all will know who is meant and from Rome reports go out to all parts of the world."

"But, you are sure that this will please the people of Greece?"

"By Pollux! I'm sure it will!"

Petronius was satisfied, for now he felt that Nero would not allow anyone to spoil this theme. Furthermore, he was also sure that now the hands of Tigellinus would be tied from harming Vinitius and Ligia. However he did not change his plans for sending Vinitius and Ligia out of Rome as soon as Ligia's health would permit it. So, when he saw Vinitius the next day he remarked, "Take her to Sicily. As things stand now, Caesar will not forbid you. As for Tigellinus, he is ever ready to even use poison if he can get revenge on me, but I don't think that he will try anything now."

Vinitius smiled at him and said, "She was on the horns of the wild bull, still Christ saved her."

"Then honor Him with a hecatomb," replied Petronius rather irritably, "but do not beg Him to save her a second time. You know how Aeolus received Odysseus when he returned to ask a second time for a favorable wind. Deities do not like to repeat themselves."

"When her health returns I will take her to Pomponia Graecina," said Vinitius.

"Fine, especially now that Pomponia is ill. Antistius, a relative of Aulus told me so. Meanwhile things will happen here to make people forget you, and in these times the forgotten ones are the lucky ones. May the goddess Fortuna be your sun in winter and your shade in summer."

Then he left Vinitius and went to inquire of his physician as to the health of Ligia. Danger threatened her no longer. Foul air and the discomfort of prison life would have killed her but amid the most tender care and even luxury, she began to get better quickly. After two days in bed, she was permitted by the doctor to sit in the garden. Vinitius conversed with her there amid irisis and anemones. More than once, hidden in the shade of spreading trees, they spoke of past sufferings and fears. Ligia told him that Christ purposely led him through all his suffering in order to change his soul and raise it to Himself. Vinitius felt that this was true and that now there was nothing remaining in him of the old haughty patrician who knew no law but his own desires. In those memories there was nothing bitter however. It seemed to them that many years had gone by and now the dreadful past lay behind them. At the same time heavenly calmness possessed them both. A new life of immense joy had now begun for them.

In Rome, Caesar might rage and fill the world with terror but he was no longer a threat to them and their happiness; they feared neither his rage nor his malice. Once, about sunset, the roars of lions and other beasts reached their ears. Previously, these sounds filled them with dread but now they merely looked at each other and smiling raised their eyes to the evening twilight.

At times, Ligia, still very weak and unable to walk alone, fell asleep in the quiet garden. He watched over her and looking at her sleeping face reflected that she no longer resembled the great beauty whom he met at the house of Aulus. Prison and suffering had quenched some of her physical beauty. There she was as beautiful as a spring flower; now her face had become pale, her hands and body very thin and even her eyes lost some of their former luster. The golden-haired Eunice, who daily brought her flowers was, in comparison, a vision of beauty. Petronius tried in vain to find in her the former charms which he exalted and, shrugging his shoulders, began to think that perhaps she wasn't worth all that trouble and suffering on the part of Vinitius. Nevertheless, Vinitius, enchanted now with her very soul, loved her all the more and when watching her repose, felt as happy as if he were watching the greatest treasure in the world.

CHAPTER LXVIII

NEWS of the miraculous rescue of Ligia spread quickly among the scattered Christians who had escaped persecution. Some came to look upon her to whom Christ Himself had showed His special favor. First came Nazarius and Miriam with whom Peter was staying at present; after them came others. All listened with rapt attention to the words of Ursus who told them of the inner voice of Christ which prompted him to attack the bull. They all went away consoled, hoping that Christ would not let all his followers be killed off before His second coming on the day of judgment. Hope sustained their hearts for persecution had not yet ceased. Whoever was accused of being a Christian was thrown into prison by the city guards. It is true that now the victims were fewer; the majority had already died for Christ.

The Christians who had escaped thus far were scattered everywhere, especially in distant provinces. Though it was generally admitted in Rome that they were not guilty of burning Rome, they were declared as enemies of humanity and the edict against them remained in full force.

Apostle Peter finally came himself to see his beloved children in Christ. Ligia, who was now able to walk, and Vinitius went out to meet him and both fell at his feet. He greeted them with joy, especially knowing that many of his flock over which Christ gave him authority, had passed on and his noble heart grieved for them all. So, when Vinitius said to him, "Sir, because of you, the Savior returned her to me," he answered, "He saved her for you because of your strong faith and also because some of the flock will remain to build upon as on a foundation."

He reflected sorrowfully for a few moments on those thousands of his children torn by wild beasts; on those crosses with which the arena had been filled and those fiery pillars in the gardens of the beast. Vinitius and Ligia noticed how his hair had turned completely white; how his whole figure was bent and his face showed enough sadness and suffering to have passed through all those torments himself. Both Vinitius and Ligia understood that since Christ had given Himself to torture and death, no one should try to avoid it. Still their hearts bled at the sight of the sadness, suffering, toil and pain. So, Vinitius who intended to take Ligia soon to Naples where they would meet Pomponia and then go to Sicily implored him to leave Rome in their company.

But the Apostle placed his hand on the tribune's head and answered, "Within myself I hear the words of the Lord which He spoke to me on the lake of Tiberias. 'When you were young you girded yourself and walked wherever you wanted, but when you become old, you shall stretch forth your hands and another will gird you when you don't wish to go.' Therefore it is proper that I follow my flock!"

And, when they were silent, not fully understanding his remarks, he added, "My toil is nearing its end; I shall find rest and surcease only in the house of the Lord." Then he turned to them saying, "Remember me for I have loved you as a father loves his children and whatever you do in life, do it for the glory of God." Thus speaking he raised his trembling hands and blessed them. They clung to him as if knowing in advance that this would be his last blessing upon them.

They did see him once more however. A few days later Petronius brought bad news from the Palatine. It had been discovered that one of Caesar's freedmen was a Christian. On this man were found letters of the Apostles Peter, Paul, James, John and Jude. Peter's presence was already known by Tigellinus but he thought Peter perished along with the other Christians during the bloodbath in the arena or in the gardens. Now it was clear that the two leaders, Peter and Paul, were still alive in Rome. It was determined therefore to seize them at all costs, for it was hoped that with their death, the last roots of the hated sect would be plucked out.

Petronius learned from Vestinus that Caesar himself had issued orders to bring in Peter and Paul within three days. For this purpose, whole detachments of soldiers were sent out to search almost every house in the Trans-Tiber section.

When he heard this, Vinitius decided to warn the Apostle. In the evening he and Ursus put on Gallic mantles and went to the house of Miriam where Peter was staying. The house was at the very edge of the Trans-Tiber, at the foot of the Janiculum. On the way they saw houses surrounded by soldiers and others searching within them. Crowds of curious people were assembled and watching. However, Vinitius and Ursus got safely to Miriam's house before the soldiers and there they found Peter, with Paul and Timothy, Linus and a few more of the faithful.

At the news of the danger of the searching soldiers, Nazarius led them by a hidden passage to the garden gate and then to the deserted stone quarries which were a few hundred yards distant from the Janiculum gate. Ursus had to carry Linus whose bones, broken by torture, had not set as yet. Once in the quarry they felt safe and began to make plans about how to save the Apostles, especially Peter.

"Sir," said Vinitius, "let Nazarius guide you at daybreak to the Alban Hills. There I will find you and escort you to Antium where a ship is ready to take us to Naples and thence to Sicily. Blessed be the day and the hour in which you shall enter my house and bless it."

Others cried out, "Do so in Christ's name!"

"My children," answered Peter, "who knows the time and place assigned by the Lord as the end of his life?" But, he did not say that he would not leave Rome, and he began to hesitate about what he should do. Uncertainty and even fear had been creeping into his soul for some time. His flock was scattered; the evangelism, so well begun in Rome and other parts of the world, was now sputtering, especially in Rome; the whole Church was shaken by the power of the beast. Very little remained except tears, torture and death. Legions of angels had not come to aid the perishing flock. Nero, however, kept his mighty power over the Roman empire, the lord of all seas and lands. More than once the poor fisherman of the Lord stretched his hands heavenward and asked, "Lord, what must I do? How do You want me to act? How can I, a feeble old man, fight this seemingly invincible power of this evil one whom You permitted to rule on earth."

He called out in anguish from the depths of his soul, "Those sheep which You commanded me to feed are no more; the Church is decimated; there is mourning among Christians everywhere. What shall I do? Do You want me to remain here or lead the remnant of my flock away from here in order to glorify Your name somewhere safely beyond the seas?"

He believed firmly that the living truth would not perish; that it must conquer, but at moments he thought that the hour had not yet come, that it would come only when the Lord descended to the earth on the day of judgment, in glory and power, a hundred times greater than that of Nero.

It occurred to him too that if he were to leave Rome, the faithful would follow. Then he would lead them far away to the shady groves of Galilee, to the calm lake of Tiberias, to peaceful shepherds and their calm and peaceful sheep. Tears came to the eyes of the fisherman, a nostalgia for calm of the sea.

But, at the moment when he made his choice, sudden alarm and fear came upon him. How was he to leave the city in which so many martyrs' blood had sunk into the earth? Where so many of the dying had given testimony to the truth? And what would he say when the Lord and Master confronted him with the words, "They all died for the faith but you...you fled!"

Nights and days passed in anxiety and anguish of decision. The others who had been torn by lions...who were fastened on the crosses...who had been burnt in the gardens of Caesar had all fallen asleep in the Lord...after a few moments of torture. But he himself could not sleep and he felt greater tortures than were inflicted upon the others. He cried from the depths, "Lord, why did You command me to come here and found Your capital inside the den of the beast?"

For thirty-nine years after the death of his Master, he knew no rest. Staff in hand he traveled afar declaring the good news to the world. His strength was about gone when he saw again the great need to take up the struggle anew after the recent persecutions which were still continuing. On one side, was the power of earth: Caesar, the Senate, the legions holding the world in a grip of iron; on the other, one old and feeble fisherman who could barely hold his staff in his hand. How could he stand up against all that might? Christ could but not he.

All these thoughts passed through his mind when he listened to the entreaties of the faithful. They repeated their request: "Hide yourself, teacher, and lead us away from the power of the beast."

Finally, Linus bowed his tortured body before him and said, "The Savior commanded you to feed His sheep but there are no more here, or there will be no more soon. Go then to places where you will find them. In Jerusalem, in Antioch, in Ephesus and in other cities. What can you do here in Rome? If they capture you, they will raise their heads in triumph. The Lord had not predicted the length of John's days. Paul is a Roman citizen and they can't condemn him without a trial, but if the power of hell rises up against you, O teacher, those whose hearts are dejected will ask, 'Who can conquer Nero?' You are the rock on which the Church was founded. We others could die but the regency of the Church passed on to you so do not return here until the Lord crushes him who shed innocent blood."

"Witness our tears!" pleaded the others. There were tears too on the cheeks of Peter. After a while, he rose and stretching his hands over the kneeling people said, "May the name of the Lord be glorified! May His will be done!"

CHAPTER LXIX

ABOUT dawn the following day two dark figures were moving along the Via Appia toward the Campania. One of them was Nazarius, the other, the Apostle Peter who was leaving Rome and his brethren.

The sky in the east began to be tinged with yellow; silver-leafed trees, the white marble of villas and the arches of the aqueducts were taking form. The sky was gradually clearing and becoming golden hued. Then the east began to grow rosy and illuminate the Alban Hills in rays of light. The haze grew thinner allowing more and more of the open country to be seen.

The road was empty. The villagers who brought their produce to the city had not begun their trek yet. The sandals of the travelers could be heard resounding in the emptiness of the surrounding area.

Suddenly, up ahead a vision struck the eyes of the Apostle. It seemed to him that the golden circle of the sun, instead of rising in the sky, moved down from the heights and was advancing on the road toward them. Peter stopped and asked Nazarius, "Do you see the brightness up ahead approaching us?"

"I see nothing," replied Nazarius.

Peter shaded his eyes with one hand and said after a while, "Someone is coming toward us amid the gleam of the sun."

But no approaching footsteps could be heard. All was quiet around them. Nazarius however noticed that the trees were quivering in the distance as if someone was shaking them. The light too was spreading in a broad vista over the plain. He looked in amazement at the Apostle.

"Teacher, what is the matter?" he cried out in alarm.

The staff fell from Peter's hand to the ground. He stood motionless looking intently ahead of him; his mouth was open; on his face Nazarius could see surprise and rapture.

Then Peter threw himself on his knees, his arms outstretched and cried out, "O Christ! O Christ!" He prostrated himself as if kissing someone's feet.

The silence continued long. Then the words of Peter could be heard by Nazarius, with mingled sobs coming from the old fisherman, *"Quo Vadis, Domine?"* (Where are You going, Lord?)

Nazarius did not hear the answer but to Peter's ears came a sad but sweet voice saying, "When you desert my people, I am going back to Rome to be crucified a second time."

The Apostle lay on the ground, his face in the dust without motion or speech. It seemed to Nazarius that he might have fainted or even died, but he finally rose, picked up his staff with trembling hands and without a word turned back towards Rome.

The boy, seeing this, asked, *"Quo vadis, domine?"* (Where are you going, sir?)

"To Rome," answered the Apostle in a low voice. And he returned.

Paul, Linus and all the faithful received him with surprise and also with alarm because only that morning, just after his departure, soldiers surrounded Miriam's house searching for Peter. To all questions thrown at him, he could only reply, "I have seen the Lord!"

And that same evening he went to the Ostian cemetery to teach and baptize. From that time onward, he went there daily and after him went increasing numbers of the faithful. It was evident that out of every tear shed by a martyr new confessors to the faith were born and that every groan in the arena found an echo in other thousands of breasts. Caesar was immersed in blood; Rome and the whole pagan world went mad, but those who had had enough of madness, those whose lives were filled with misery and oppression, all who were weighed down...the unfortunate...the sad...all came to hear the wonderful tidings of God Who out of love for man had given Himself to be crucified and to redeem their sins.

When they found a God Whom they could love, they found something which the society of that time could not offer them and that was happiness and love.

Peter understood now that neither Caesar nor all his legions could overcome the living truth, that they could not overpower it by shedding blood and causing suffering, that now its victory was beginning. At the same time he understood why the Lord had turned him back on the road. The city of pride and corruption and crime was to be eventually His city and the capital from which would flow out upon the world the spiritual realm of God.

CHAPTER LXX

THE final hour struck for both of the Apostles. But, even at that last hour, it was given to the fisherman of the Lord to win over two souls. The soldiers Processus and Martinianus, who guarded him in the Mamertine prison, became Christians.

At the time of the capture of the two Apostles Nero was not in Rome. The sentence of death was given by Helius and Polythetes, two freedmen to whom Caesar delegated rule in his absence.

On the aged Apostle Peter, scourging before crucifixion was prescribed by law and the next day he was led forth beyond the walls of the city toward the Vatican Hill to be crucified. The soldiers were astonished at the huge crowd which accompanied them on this last journey of Peter. They did not understand however that the crowd was not drawn by curiosity but because they were confessors of the faith.

The sun had declined somewhat toward Ostia; the day was clear and calm. Because of his advanced age, Peter was not required to carry the cross; they also had not hung anything around his neck as an added burden. He walked without hindrance and the faithful could see him plainly.

At times when his white head showed itself among the iron helmets of the soldiers, weeping was heard in the crowd, but it was not prolonged because the face of Peter had in it so much calmness and was so bright with joy that all understood him to be not a victim going to destruction but rather a victor celebrating his triumph.

And so it was. The fisherman, usually humble and stooping,

467

now walked erect, taller than the soldiers and full of dignity. Never had the people seen such majesty of bearing. It was as though a monarch was passing by, attended by the military and the people. From every side voices were heard, "There is Peter going to the Lord!"

They did not think of the death that was awaiting him. They were convinced that just as the Lord's crucifixion on Golgotha redeemed the whole world, this death of Peter's was to redeem the city.

As he passed the different temples, he said to them, "You will henceforth be temples of Christ!" Looking at the people, he said to them, "Your children will be servants of Christ!" He thus advanced with the feeling that he had conquered, conscious of his service, conscious of his strength and content at the outcome.

The soldiers conducted him over the Triumphal bridge as if giving involuntary testimony to his triumph and they led him toward the circus area. The faithful from beyond the Tiber joined in and there was such a crowd now that the centurion understood that he had indeed a high priest surrounded by Christians. Momentarily, he grew alarmed because of the small number of soldiers. But there were no cries of rage or indignation amid the throng. People all around had solemn faces in conformity with the solemnity of the moment. Some believers, remembering that when the Lord died, the earth shook and the dead rose from their graves, now thought that some signs would appear at the death of the first Apostle of the Lord. Others said to themselves, "Perhaps the Lord will select this hour of Peter's death to come from heaven as He promised and judge the world." With these emotions they commended themselves to the mercy of the Redeemer.

However there was only a peaceful calmness round about. The hills seemed to be warming themselves and resting in the sun. All finally reached the place of crucifixion, between the Circus and the Vatican Hill. Soldiers began digging a hole for the cross. Others placed the cross on the ground and began making preparation for the crucifixion. The crowd, quiet and attentive, knelt round about.

The Apostle, with his head in the sun's rays and golden light, turned for the last time toward the city. At a distance the river Tiber could be seen gleaming in the sunlight; beyond was the Campus Martius. Higher up was the mausoleum of Augustus, below that the spacious baths which had just been begun by Nero, still lower Pompey's theater and beyond that were visible many porticos, temples and columns. On the far horizon the hills were covered with houses. Peter, surrounded by soldiers, looked at the city for the last time, the city of wickedness but also of power, the city of madness yet also of order...which had become the head of the world...its law...its peace...and still seemed mighty invincible and eternal. Peter spoke his thoughts to the city, "You are now redeemed and you are now mine!" No one there, neither the soldiers nor the crowd, could guess that he, Peter, was now the true ruler of this city; that many Caesars would pass away; waves of barbarians go by and ages vanish, but the old man and his successors would rule there for all time.

The sun sank further toward Ostia and became large and red. The whole western side of the sky glowed with intense brightness. The soldiers approached Peter in order to strip him of his clothing, but he, straightening up, stretched his right hand high. The executioners paused, the faithful held their breath thinking that he wanted to say something and were silent. Peter, standing up to his full height with his hand extended made the sign of the cross, blessing the city and the people in this hour of his death: *"Urbi et Orbi."* (The City and the World.)

That same evening along the Via Ostiensis, soldiers led Paul of Tarsus to a place called Aquae Salviae to have him beheaded there. Behind him also followed a crowd of the faithful, many of whom were converted by him. During the march, Paul stopped from time to time in order to greet friends and converse briefly with them. Being a Roman citizen gave him this privilege.

Beyond the gate called Trigemina, he met Plautilla, the daughter of the prefect Flavius Sabinus and seeing her youthful face covered with tears, he said to her, "Plautilla, daughter of eternal life, be at peace. Only give me your veil with which I will bind my eyes when I go to the Lord." And he went forward once again, his face shining happily as that of a laborer who, when he had toiled the whole day, is returning to the peace and quiet of his home. His thoughts like those of Peter were as calm and peaceful as the evening sky. His eyes gazed upon the plains which stretched out before him into the Alban Hills still shining in the sun.

He recalled his journeys, his toils, his struggles in which he had conquered the churches that he had founded wherever he went, and he was sure that he had finished his work and earned his rest. He felt now that the seed that he had planted would not be blown away by the wind of evil and malice. He was leaving this life with the certainty that the truth of Christ would conquer in the end. And a great feeling of peace and solace gripped his soul.

The road to the execution place was long. The evening hours were close at hand. Here and there groups of slaves were returning to their homes after a day of toil in the fields. Children playing on the road looked curiously at him, the soldiers and the crowd. But all around the vicinity, peace and calm reigned. Paul felt this peace in his heart and he thought with gladness that by his life he added notes of harmony without which the whole earth was like sounding brass or tinkling cymbals. He remembered the love which he taught the people to have for one another and the words he spoke to them: "If you possess the knowledge of all languages and all the secrets of the world, they would be nothing without love; love which is kind, enduring, which does not commit evil; which does not desire honors; which bears all things humbly, believes and hopes in things of God is patient and forgiving."

So, his life was to pass. He preached the truth as his Lord taught him.

Now, in spirit he cried out, "What power on earth can equal the power of Christ? Could Caesar and all his legions? Could all the might of the world? Never, and once more never!"

Paul walked toward his death like a true conqueror.

The detachment of soldiers left the main road at last and turned to the east on a narrow path which led to the Aquae Salviae. The centurion stopped the soldiers at the fountain. The time had come.

Paul placed Plautilla's veil on his arm, intending to bind his eyes with it but now he raised his eyes for the last time toward the light of the evening and prayed. Yes, the moment had come but ahead he saw a far brighter road, a road which led to heaven and to his reward. Inwardly, he repeated the words of one of his epistles: "I have fought the good fight. I have finished my course. I have kept the faith. Henceforth, there is waiting for me a crown of glory."

CHAPTER LXXI

IN Rome, madness raged as usual. The world-conquering city seemed almost ready to tear itself to pieces. Even before the last hour of the Apostles had struck, Piso's conspiracy was found out. Then followed the extermination of some of the most notable dignitaries of Rome. Nero, who was considered by many as a god, was really a god of death to quite a few. Mourning fell on the whole city. Terror struck the hearts of citizens, high and low. However, porticoes were still adorned with ivy and flowers, for it was not permitted to show signs of sorrow for the dead. People waking up in the morning asked themselves, "Whose turn will come next?"

Piso, head of the conspiracy against Nero, paid with his life. After him followed such outstanding personages as Seneca, Lucan, Faenius Rufus, Tullius Senecio and many others. Some were destroyed by their own wickedness, some by fear, others because they possessed vast riches or even because of their courage and bravery. Caesar himself was amazed at the vast number of those who were against him. His soldiers were holding the city everywhere as if by siege. And each day there were new sentences of death sent out to the different dignitaries.

The condemned debased themselves by writing open letters to Caesar, full of praise and even thanking him for the sentence of death and bequeathing to him part of their property. This way they hoped to save their families and part of their possessions.

It almost seemed as if Nero wanted to find out how base and abject people could be in their willingness to endure his bloody rule. Not only the conspirators were executed but also their families, relatives, friends and even mere acquaintances. There were many daily funeral processions. Some people like Pompeus, Cornelius, and Martilus were put to death merely because of lack of love for Caesar. Novius Priscus died because he was once friendly to Seneca. Rufus Crispinus was deprived of fire and water only because he had been at one time the husband of Poppaea. The great Thrasea was ruined because he dared to live virtuously. Even Poppaea herself fell victim to the momentary rage of Nero.

The Senate fawned on the terrible ruler; it raised a temple in his honor, made offerings for his divine voice, appointed priests to serve him as a divinity. Senators trembled for their lives; Augustians and the whole population trembled not knowing what the morrow would bring.

Meanwhile, from below, in fields soaked in the blood and tears of martyrs, grew the sowings of Peter, stronger and stronger every moment.

CHAPTER LXXII

VINITIUS TO PETRONIUS:

We know, dear Uncle, what is going on in Rome and what we did not know you revealed to us in your letter. When one casts a stone in water, the wave expands in an ever increasing circle...so too the news of madness and evil has also reached us here far away from Rome. On his way to Greece Carinas stopped in Sicily and plundered the temples and treasury coffers in the various towns and cities of Sicily. A house of gold is to be built in Rome and it will be built from the sweat and tears of the people in the empire. The world has not seen such a house but it also has never witnessed such injustice as under Nero. You know how grasping is Carinas. Chilo resembled him until he redeemed his life by his death. But, to the towns near us here, his men haven't come yet perhaps because there aren't many temples near us here and not much treasure.

You ask me if we are out of danger. I answer that we are forgotten and let that suffice for an answer. At this moment from the portico under which I write, I see our calm bay and on it Ursus in a boat letting down a net of fish. My wife is spinning red wool near me in the garden under the shade of almond trees. Our slaves are singing. There is calm and peace all around. Former fear and suffering is forgotten. But, it is not the Parcae, as you write, who spin out our lives so agreeably. It is Christ Who is blessing us, our beloved God and Savior.

We know tears even now and sorrow too for our religion teaches us to weep over the misfortunes of others. But, in these tears there is consolation unknown to you. Whenever the time of our life is ended, we shall find all those dear ones who perished

and who even now are dying for the faith. For us, Peter and Paul
are not really dead, they are merely reborn to glory. Other souls
see them and even when our eyes weep for them, our hearts are
gladdened, knowing how happy they are in heaven.

Oh yes, my dear Uncle, we are happy with a happiness which
nothing can destroy since death which is for you the end of everything, for us is only a passage into a better world.

And so, days and months pass us by and we are happy. Our servants and slaves believe as we do and so we love one another as
Christ taught us. Frequently, when the sun goes down or when
the moon shines over the water, Ligia and I talk over old times
which now seem like a dream to us. When I think of her being so
close to torture and death, I praise our dear Lord Who saved her
from the arena and returned her to me.

O Petronius, you do not realize what a comfort and consolation our religion can be in misfortune, how much patience and
courage it inspires before death. So come and see for yourself how
much happiness it can give even in ordinary day-to-day living.
People up to now did not know a God Whom they could love
hence they did not love one another. From this came misfortune
because as the light comes from the sun so too happiness comes
from love. Languages, philosophies did not teach this truth and it
did not exist in Greece nor in Rome; and when I say "Rome" I
mean the whole world. The dry and cold teaching of the Stoics
tempers the heart as a sword is tempered but it makes one indifferent rather than better and loving. Why do I write thus? You yourself know better than I. You knew Paul of Tarsus and conversed
with him more than once hence you must know the difference between our religion and the others. In comparison the teachings of
philosophers, Greek and Roman, and the orators are but empty
noises without much meaning. You remember the question he put
to you that if Caesar were a Christian, would not your lives be
more bearable and safer and more sure of tomorrow?

You told me once that our religion was the enemy of life but I
answer you that if from the beginning of this letter I repeated the
words "I am happy" I still could not fully express my happiness to
you. To this you may say that my happiness is Ligia. True, but I
love her immortal soul along with her physical attributes and we
both love each other in Christ Jesus. For such love there is no
more separation, no unfaithfulness, no uncertainty of the hereafter. For us beauty and youth will pass in time but love remains,
for the spirit remains.

Before my eyes were opened to the Light, I was ready to burn my own house in order to possess Ligia but I tell you that I did not really love her then. It was Christ Who taught me how to love. In Him is the source of peace and happiness. This is absolutely true. Compare your own luxury which is tinged with fear, and also your pleasures which you are not sure of tomorrow...your orgies...compare them all to the life of the Christians. But better still, come here and see for yourself. A peace is awaiting you such as you have not known for a long time, and hearts which love you very much will be waiting for you. You have a noble soul and a good one and you should be happy. Your quick mind will be able to recognize the truth and you will come to love it yourself.

To be the enemy of Christ, like Caesar and Tigellinus, that is possible but no one can really be indifferent to Him. O my Petronius, Ligia and I are hoping to see you soon. Be well and come and visit us here.

Petronius received this letter in Cumae where he had gone with other Augustians. His struggle with Tigellinus was nearing its end. Petronius knew already that he would lose and he understood why. As Caesar fell lower and lower in his role as a clown and charioteer, as he sank deeper and deeper in a sickly foul and coarse dissipation, the exquisite Arbiter of Elegance became a burden to him. Even when Petronius was silent Nero saw blame in his silence. When the Arbiter praised him, he saw ridicule. His self-love was annoyed and his envy aroused toward the brilliant patrician. Also, the wealth and works of art of Petronius had become an object of his desire. In view of the future trip to Greece Petronius was spared thus far but Tigellinus explained to Caesar that Carinas surpassed him in taste and knowledge and would be a better adviser in Greece. From that moment Petronius was lost. They did not dare to send him the sentence of death in Rome itself. Nero and Tigellinus recalled that this esthetic person, who made day out of night and was only interested in the arts and feasts, had shown amazing ability and energy when he was pro-consul in Bithynia and even later when a consul in Rome. They considered him capable of anything and it was well known that in Rome people admired him; even the Praetorian soldiers had a high regard for him. No one could foresee how Petronius might act in a given case. So, it seemed wiser to entice him out of the city and then sentence him to death.

With this object in view, he received an invitation to go to Cumae. He went even though suspecting a trap. He nevertheless showed his usual self-possessed person to the Augustians; he could perhaps gain a last victory over his archrival Tigellinus before his death.

Meanwhile the latter accused him of friendship with Senator Scaevinus who was the soul of Piso's conspiracy. The people of Petronius left in Rome were imprisoned; his house was surrounded by the Praetorian guards. When Petronius learned of this, he showed neither alarm nor concern and with a smile remarked to the Augustians whom he received in his own splendid villa in Cumae, "Bronze-beard does not like direct questions; you will see his confusion when I ask him if he was the one who gave orders to imprison my people in Rome."

Then he invited them to a feast before his last journey and he had just made preparations for it when the letter of Vinitius was handed to him. After reading the letter Petronius grew thoughtful but after a while his face regained its usual composure and that same evening he answered the letter as follows:

I rejoice at your happiness and am surprised at your concern for me. I did not realize that two lovers like you and Ligia would remember someone far away from you. Not only have you not forgotten me but you wish to persuade me to go to Sicily to share with you your bread and your Christ Who, as you wrote, had endowed happiness upon you so bountifully.

If that is true, honor Him. To my way of thinking however, Ursus had something to do with saving Ligia and the people also had a little to do with it. But, since you believe that Christ did the work, I will not contradict you. Spare no offering to Him. Prometheus also sacrificed himself for man but alas, Prometheus is an invention of the poets while truthful people said that they saw Christ with their own eyes. I agree with you that He is the most worthy of all the gods.

I do remember the question of Paul of Tarsus and I think that if Bronze-beard lived according to Christ's teaching, I would find time to visit you in Sicily and converse with you about the philosophies of Greece and Rome. Today I must give you a brief answer. I care only for two philosophers: Pyrrho and Anacreon. All the rest I could sell to you at a cheap price even throwing in all the Greek and Roman Stoics. Truth, Vinitius, dwells somewhere so high that the gods themselves cannot see it. You call to me, "Come and see for yourself...see such sights as you have never seen before." And, I answer I would, had I the necessary legs for the journey. If you think for a while, you will concede that I am right.

No, happy husband of the goddess Dawn, your religion is not for me. Am I to love the Bithynians who carry my litter, the Egyptians who heat my bath? Am I to love Bronze-beard and Tigellinus? I swear to you by the white knees of the Graces that even if I wanted to, I could not! In Rome, there are many thousands of individuals who are either crippled or who have fat knees or skinny thighs or staring eyes or too-large heads. Do you want me to love them all? Where am I to find that love since it is not in my heart? If your God wants me to love such people, why did He not, being Almighty, give them all beautiful and unmarred attributes? How can I love beauty and deformity at the same time?

One may not believe in our gods but people like Myron, Scopas and Lysippos loved them at one time. Even if I wished to go where you lead me, I cannot. But since I do not wish it, I am unable for two reasons. You believe like Paul that on the other side of the Styx you will see your Christ in beautiful Elysian fields of happiness. Let Him then tell you whether He will accept me there with my gems, my Myrrhene vase, my many books and my golden-haired Eunice. I laugh at this thought. Paul told me that one must give up wreaths of roses, feasts and luxury for the sake of Christ. It is true that He promised another kind of happiness but I answered him that I was too old for a new kind of happiness; that my eyes delight only with roses; that the smell of violets is dearer to me than the stench of a neighbor from the tenements of Subura.

These are some of the reasons why your kind of happiness is not for me. There is also another reason and this I kept for the last. It is that Thanatos, the god of death, summons me. For you, the light of life is just beginning but my sun has already set and twilight is embracing me. In other words, I must die, Carissime. It is not worthwhile to talk about this at length. It had to end thus. You, who know Bronze-beard, will be able to understand this. Tigellinus has finally won, or rather my own victories have finally come to an end. I have lived as I wished and I will die as I please.

Do not worry about this too much. No god promised me immortality, hence I cannot complain. At the same time I think that you are mistaken, dear Vinitius, in asserting that only God teaches man to die calmly. No, Rome has taught that for a long time. When the last drop of my cup is drained, then one must pass away with calmness and courage. Plato declares that virtue is music, that the life of a sage is harmony. If that be true, then I shall die as I have lived...virtuously.

I should like to bid farewell to your goddess of a wife in the words with which I greeted her once before in the house of Aulus: "Many maidens have I seen but none equal to you...never!"

If the soul of man is something more than what Pyrrho believes, mine will fly to you and Ligia and will alight at your house in the form of a butterfly or, as the Egyptians believe, in the form of a sparrow hawk. Any other way, I cannot come.

Meanwhile let Sicily replace for you the gardens of Hesperides; may the goddess of the fields, woods and fountains scatter flowers on your path and may white doves build their nests amid the columns of your house.

CHAPTER LXXIII

PETRONIUS was not mistaken. Two days later young Nerva who had always been friendly to him sent his freedman to Cumae with news of what was happening at the court of Caesar. Petronius' death was already determined. On the morning of the following day they intended to send him an order to remain in Cumae and await further orders. The next messenger was to bring him the sentence of death.

Petronius heard the news with unruffled calmness. He spoke to the freedman of Nerva, "You will take your master one of my vases. Tell him that I am most grateful and thank him very much. Now I will be able to anticipate the sentence." And, he began to laugh like a man who has suddenly come across a happy idea and rejoices in advance at its fulfillment.

That same afternoon his slaves rushed about inviting the Augustians who were staying in Cumae and all the nobles and ladies to a magnificent banquet at the villa of the Arbiter.

Petronius spent some time writing in the library; next he took a bath and dressed in magnificent robes. Brilliant and stately, he walked about the house giving the necessary orders for the night's feast. Not the least care or worry was visible in his features. The servants and slaves knew, however, that this feast was to be something special for he had given orders to reward all those who deserved it and to punish, but only lightly, those who had some punishment due them. To the musicians, he was very generous. At last, sitting in the garden and resting, he called for Eunice.

She came to him dressed in white with a sprig of myrtle in her hair, beautiful as one of the Graces. He seated her at his side and, lightly touching her temple with his hand, gazed at her with admiration, somewhat like a knowledgeable critic would gaze at a beautiful statue from the chisel of a master.

"Eunice," said he, "you should know that for some time already you have been free."

She raised calm eyes to him and shaking her head slowly replied, "I am your slave always."

"But perhaps you are not aware that this villa, all its possessions and all slaves together with the fields, herds and all belong to you."

Eunice looked at him sharply with alarm. "Why do you tell me this?" And in her eyes there was fear and her face grew pale. Petronius only smiled at her and merely said, "Yes, that's right." A moment of silence followed. A slight breeze moved the leaves of the trees around them.

Eunice still sat immobile as a statue cut from white marble.

"Eunice," said he, "I wish to die calmly." And, Eunice, looking at him with a heart-rending smile whispered, "I hear you, master."

In the early evening the guests began to appear. They all knew that the feasts at the house of Petronius were always exquisite. However, they did not realize that this feast was to be the last "symposium." Many of them were aware that the clouds of Caesar's anger were hanging over the Arbiter. But that happened so often; Petronius seemed always to scatter away such clouds by some dexterous act or a mere phrase. No one really thought that serious danger threatened. His happy face and usual smile confirmed them in this belief.

Beautiful Eunice, when she appeared for the feast, had a calm but resolute manner and in her eyes there danced a kind of radiant purpose. At the door of the large dining room, young girls with hair in golden nets placed wreaths of roses on the heads of the incoming guests, warning them at the same time, as was the custom, to step over the threshold with the right foot first. All around was the smell of violets. Lamps burned in Alexandrian glass of various colors. Grecian maidens stood at the couches; their task was to sprinkle the feet of the guests with perfume. Along the wall, the musicians were waiting for the signal to begin playing.

Splendor and opulence gleamed everywhere but it was the kind of splendor and opulence which did not offend or oppress. Joyous feelings and ease spread throughout the dining hall. The guests were sure that here neither threat nor constraint hung over their heads as they had during the feasts of Caesar. Conversation of various kinds began to buzz as bees hum around an apple tree during blossom time. There were bursts of happy laughter and applause mingled with the sound of loud kisses on white shoulders of the ladies.

The guests, while drinking wine, first poured out a few drops from their goblets in honor of the immortal gods, in order to gain their protection and ensure favor for the host. It mattered not that many of them did not believe in the gods; custom and tradition prescribed it. Petronius, reclining beside Eunice, made small talk all around concerning topics such as the latest divorces, various love affairs, the races, Spiculus who had become recently famous as a charioteer, the latest books in the shop of Atractus and Socii, and other light topics. He poured a few drops of wine only in honor of the goddess Venus, the most ancient divinity and the greatest and for him the most enduring one.

His talk was like a ray of sunshine, like a summer breeze which stirs the flowers in the garden. He finally gave the signal for the musicians to start playing. Young girls from the island of Cos, the birthplace of Eunice, began dancing to the music, displaying their rosy bodies through sheer garments. After that an Egyptian soothsayer told the guests their future by means of the movement of rainbow colors in a vessel of crystal. Other entertainments of one kind or another followed.

When they had enough of these amusements, Petronius rose a little higher on his cushions and spoke to all, "Pardon me, my friends, for asking a favor at a feast. Will each one of you accept as a gift the goblet from which you are drinking?"

All the goblets were expensive and exquisite, gleaming in gold and precious stones, hence delight and joy filled every heart of the guests. Some thanked him loudly; others claimed that Jove himself had never honored gods with such gifts in Olympus. There were some who thought that the gifts were too valuable to give away. But Petronius raised aloft his very special Myrrhene goblet which resembled a rainbow in brilliancy and was simply priceless. "This," said he, "is the one which was especially made for me in honor of the Lady from Cypress, Venus herself. The lips of no man will touch it from now on and no hand will pour from it even a few drops in honor of the gods." With this remark, he cast the precious goblet on the floor and it broke in little pieces. Seeing all around him the astonished faces of the guests he assured them, "My dear friends, do not be alarmed. Old age and weakness are sad companions in the last years of one's life. But, I will give you a good example and also good advice. You have the power not to await old age; you can depart any time you wish as I am doing now."

"What do you mean?" cried a few voices.

"I want to drink with you, hear nice music, look upon the beauty around me and then fall asleep forever. I have already taken farewell of Caesar and do you want to know what I have written him?" He took from beneath a purple cushion a paper and read as follows:

> I know, O Caesar, that you are awaiting my presence with impatience, that your heart of a friend is yearning night and day for me. I know that you are always willing to shower me with gifts, to make me prefect of the Praetorian guards and banish Tigellinus to a role of mule driver in the lands which you inherited after poisoning Domitius. Forgive me, however, for I swear to you by Hades and by the shades of your mother, your wife and your brother and Seneca too that I cannot be with you. Life is a great treasure but there are some things which I cannot endure any longer. Don't think, I beg of you, that I am offended because you killed your mother, wife, brother...that you burned Rome and sent many good and honest people to Erebus. No! Grandson of Chronos! Death is the inheritance of man and I could not expect you to refrain from murder. But to punish my ears any longer with listening to your poetry, to watch your fat belly shake and your skinny legs gyrate in Pyrrhic dances, to hear your atrocious music and your more atrocious verses, is beyond my strength and so I will die by my own hand. Rome stuffs its ears when it listens to you; the whole world laughs at you as a very mediocre clown. I can blush for you no longer and I do not wish to do so. The howls of Cerberus will be less offensive to my ears than your music for I have never been a friend of Cerberus and I need not be ashamed of his howling. Be well, but do not sing. Murder, but do not write poetry. Poison people, but do not dance. Burn all the cities you desire, but please don't play the lyre. This is the last wish and the last friendly advice to you from the Arbiter of Elegance.

The guests were terrified after hearing the letter for they knew that loss of the empire would be a lesser blow to Nero than this letter. They understood that the man who had written thus must die. Too, they were afraid that they had witnessed the reading of it.

But Petronius laughed at seeing their terrified faces and reassured them. "Be joyous and drive away your fears! No one need boast that he heard this letter. I myself will boast about it to Charon when I cross with him by boat."

He then beckoned to the Greek physician and stretched out his arm. The skilled doctor opened a vein at the bend of his arm. Blood spurted on the cushion and also a bit on Eunice, who leaning toward Petronius said to him, "Did you think that I would be parted from you even in death? I would still follow you even if the gods gave me immortality and Caesar gave me power over the earth."

Petronius smiled, raised himself a little and touched his lips to hers and said, "Come with me. You really do love me!" She stretched out her arm toward the physician and after a while her blood intermingled with his.

Then Petronius gave an order and the music resumed. Songs were sung in honor of Harmonius and followed with a song of Anacreon in which he complains about the child of Aphrodite who was found chilled and weeping, and after he was taken in, showed his ingratitude by piercing the heart of Anacreon with an arrow. Petronius and Eunice, leaning against each other, beautiful and divine, listened smiling and growing paler and paler by the minute. At the end of the song, Petronius gave orders to serve more wine and food. Then he conversed with the guests sitting close to him. Finally, he called the physician and told him to bind his arm for a while for, he said, that sleep was tormenting him and he wanted to yield himself to Hypnos before Thanatos put him to sleep forever.

After a short sleep, he awoke and had his veins opened once again. At his signal the singers and musicians started anew. Petronius and Eunice grew much paler now and when the last sound of the music ceased, he turned to his guests and said weakly, "Friends, you must admit that with us perishes...." But he could not finish; his arm with its last movement tried to embrace Eunice, his head fell on the pillow and he died.

The guests, looking at the two white forms which resembled two beautiful statues, understood well enough what Petronius wanted to say, that with them perished all that was left to their world at that time, namely poetry and beauty.

EPILOGUE

AT first the revolt of the Gallic legions under Vindex did not seem serious. Nero was barely in his thirty-first year of life and no one dared hope that the world would be freed so soon from the nightmare which was stifling it. People remembered that which occurred in the past; these revolts did not succeed in a change of government, as for instance during the reign of Tiberius. Drusus put down that revolt. "Who," said the people, "would take over Nero's reign? All the descendants of the divine Augustus have perished." Others thought that no earthling could topple this power of Nero. There were even those who bemoaned his visit to Greece because Helius and Polythetes who governed in his absence were even more tyrranical than he was.

Caesar at first was not concerned about the rebellion of the legions under Vindex; he did not want to leave Greece. Only when Helius informed him that further delay might cause the loss of his reign did he decide to return.

In Naples, however, he tarried, neglecting to heed news of growing danger. In vain did Tigellinus try to explain that former revolts of the legions had no true leader but now there was Vindex, a man descended from the ancient kings of Gaul and Aquitania, and a famous leader of men. But Nero answered, "Here, Greeks, listen to my songs and music; the Romans do not appreciate me." He said that his first duty was to the arts. However, when Vindex proclaimed him a wretched artist, he sprang up and returned to Rome. The wounds inflicted by Petronius, and healed during his stay in Greece and Naples, opened anew and he wished to wreak vengeance upon Vindex.

On the way he saw a statue cast in bronze depicting a Gallic warrior being overcome by a Roman soldier and he considered this a great omen.

His entrance into Rome surpassed all that had been witnessed before. He used the same chariot which the great Augustus used in his triumphal entrance. Part of the circus was torn down in order to widen the road. The Senate, the dignitaries and numerous people witnessed the event. They all shouted, "Hail Augustus! Hail Hercules! Hail divinity, the Olympian, the Immortal One!" Behind him slaves carried in their hands all the crowns which he won, the names of all the cities in which he had triumphed. They wore tablets with inscriptions of the names of the masters whom he had surpassed. Nero himself was overcome. "What triumph was ever greater than this one?" he yelled out. The idea that any mere mortal should dare raise a hand against such a god as he did not enter his head. He felt himself really Olympian and therefore safe. The excitement of the crowd was great. Indeed, it seemed that not only Caesar but Rome itself and all the world was going mad.

Through all this no one could foresee that the end of Nero's reign was at hand. That same night, in fact, words were written on columns and walls describing Nero's crimes, foretelling the coming vengeance and ridiculing him as an artist. The most popular saying among the people began with the words, "He sang till he roused the roosters." Alarming news made the rounds from mouth to mouth and reached enormous proportions. Alarm even seized the Augustians.

Nero, however, went on the same way as before. He only thought of the theater and music. Musical instruments, especially a new water organ occupied his attention. Childishly, he proposed to the Senate and others that he would ward off any future danger to Rome merely through his music and song. He refused to prepare the army against the coming danger. At times, he wildly proclaimed that he would pack all his musical instruments and lead his legions to the East where he would build another empire. At moments, he was moved by his own words that as a wandering minstrel he would earn his daily bread. He considered himself a great poet whose like the world had not produced before.

And so...he raged on, played, sang, changed plans, changed quotations and utterly played the clown.

Meanwhile, in the West, a dark cloud was increasing daily. A cloud of revolt was thickening fast; the measure of Nero's wickedness was filled; the insane comedy was nearing its end.

When news that Galba and all Spain had joined the uprising came to his ears, he fell into a rage. He shattered everything around him; overturned tables and issued orders which neither Helius nor Tigellinus himself dared to execute. First, to kill all Gauls residing in Rome, burn the city once again; let out all the wild beasts and then transfer the capital to Alexandria. To him, all this seemed natural, simple. But, the days of his dominion had passed and even those who shared in his former crimes began to look at him as a madman.

The death of Vindex and disagreement among the legions, however, seemed for a time to turn the tide in his favor. Again, new feasts, new triumphs and new death sentences were issued in Rome until, finally, one night a messenger rushed to the Palatine on lathered horse. He brought news that in the city itself the soldiers had raised the standard of revolt and proclaimed Galba as Caesar.

Nero was asleep when the messenger came but when he awakened he called vainly for guards. The palace was empty. Slaves were plundering everywhere. Nero wandered through the palace, filling it with cries of despair and fear. At last, his freedmen Phaon, Spirus and Epaphroditus came to his rescue. They advised him to flee at once as there was not time to lose. Even then he refused to accept the reality of the situation. "Could he," he asked, "dress up in mourning and speak to the Senate?" He thought that they would not be able to resist his pleading and eloquence. Could he use all his skills as an orator? For, no one on earth has power to resist him. Would they perhaps give him even the rule of Egypt?

The freedman warned him that if he did not hurry, the people would tear him to pieces and if he refused to go with them, then they would leave him.

Phaon offered refuge in his villa outside the Nomentanum gate. They then mounted horses and covering Nero's head so he wouldn't be recognized, they galloped off. On the streets they saw many soldiers running about and shouting in honor of Galba as new emperor. Nero now finally understood that the end for him was near. Terror and reproaches of conscience seized him. He declared that he saw darkness before him in the form of a black cloud. From that cloud came forth faces in which he saw his mother, his wife and his brother. His teeth began to chatter from fright. Still, his soul of a clown found a kind of charm in the horror of the moment. To be absolute lord of the earth and then to lose all seemed to him the height of tragedy, and true to himself he played the role of clown right to the end. He wanted to cite quotes so that future generations would remember these last moments of his. Flashes of hope rose in him from time to time...hope, vain and childish. He knew that he was going to die but at the same time, he did not want to believe it.

They found the Nomentanum gate open. Going farther they passed near Ostrianum where Peter had taught and baptized. At daybreak they reached Phaon's villa. There, the freedmen insisted that the time had come for him to die so he had a grave dug and lay on the ground so that they could take accurate measurements. At the sight of the grave, however, terror seized him. His fat face became pale and his forehead was covered with sweat. He begged them to burn his body. "What an artist is perishing!" he kept repeating in auguish.

Meanwhile Phaon's messenger arrived with the announcement that the Senate had issued a sentence of death and that he, Nero, as a parracide will die according to ancient custom.

"What is the ancient custom?" he asked.

"They will affix a large fork on your neck, flog you to death and then hurl your body into the Tiber," they answered.

"It is time then," he cried. And he repeated once more, "What an artist is perishing!"

At that moment sounds of horses' hooves were heard. That was the centurion coming with the soldiers for the head of Bronzebeard.

"Hurry!" cried the freedmen.

Nero placed a knife to his fat neck but could not bring himself to plunge it in. Suddenly, Epaphroditus pushed his hand and the knife sank in to the hilt. Nero's eyes turned in his head, terrified.

"I bring you life!" cried the centurion entering.

"Too late!" croaked Nero and added, "What loyalty is this?"

The blood began gushing forth from his heavy neck. His legs began kicking the ground and then he died.

The following day, faithful Acte wrapped his body in costly clothing and burned him on a pile filled with perfumes.

Thus Nero passed on, as a whirlwind, as a storm, as a fire, as war or death passes, but the Basilica of Peter still stands on the Vatican Hill and rules over the city and the world.

At the ancient Capenan gate stands to this day a little chapel with the worn inscription, *"Quo Vadis, Domine?"*

Historical Notes

In his justly famous novel *Quo Vadis?*, Henryk Sienkiewicz portrays a richly detailed and historically accurate picture of Rome in the time of Nero. The many names of individuals, places in and around Rome, and details of daily and political life that are found in the novel bring to life the city and its inhabitants of nineteen hundred years ago.

The setting of the novel was meticulously researched by Sienkiewicz. Before writing *Quo Vadis?*, he traveled to Italy several times to visit the museums and historic sites of ancient Rome. He was thoroughly familiar with the ancient sources of the period, especially Tacitus and Suetonius, as well as the works of contemporary scholars, in particular Fustel de Coulanges and Ernest Renan. His careful preparation has made *Quo Vadis?* an enduring masterpiece of the historical novel genre.

MAIN CHARACTERS

LIGIA, daughter of the king of the Ligians. The Ligians were a loose association of tribes which occupied the land between the Oder and Vistula rivers, or modern-day Poland. In 50A.D., the Ligians joined a confederacy of Germanic tribes in an attempt to overthrow a pro-Roman Germanic chief, Vannius. Roman policy prohibited interference in this internal squabble among the Germanic tribes, but they did demand a promise from the Ligians not to cross into Roman territory. Sienkiewicz's Ligia is the hostage who was given to the Romans as security of the Ligian pledge.

VINITIUS, MARCUS (Vinicius), son of Marcus Vinitius. His father was elected consul in 45A.D. after a distinguished military career. Marcus Vinitius, the Elder, married Nero's aunt, Julia Livilla, and was connected with court intrigue during the reign of Claudius, Nero's predecessor. The character in the novel, Marcus Vinitius, is presumably the son of this marriage and therefore a cousin of Nero.

PETRONIUS, GAIUS. Tacitus describes Petronius in his *Annals* as Nero's "Arbiter of Elegance," who was later forced to commit suicide in 66A.D. Petronius enjoyed a special friendship with Nero and was often consulted by the emperor on artistic matters. After the great fire of 64A.D., he began to lose favor with the emperor. Most scholars identify Petronius as the author of the ribald adventure story *Satyricon*.

NERO, LUCIUS DOMITIUS AHENOBARBUS, emperor of Rome, 54-68A.D. With the help of his mother, Agrippina, whom he later murdered, he became emperor at the age of seventeen. The notorious emperor of Rome was an able administrator in the first several years of his reign. His tyranny grew as he increasingly neglected matters of state to concentrate on his own personal artistic stature. Court intrigue and Nero's paranoia had increased dramatically by the time of the disastrous fire in Rome in 64A.D. Nero used the early Christians as scapegoats for the fire and initiated their bloody executions. In the last years of his reign, his fears and suspicions caused the execution (or suicide) of countless Roman aristocrats.

AULUS PLAUTIUS, consul 29A.D. During the reign of Nero, Aulus Plautius was living the quiet life of a distinguished Roman noble and military hero. He was well known as the conqueror of Britain.

POMPONIA GRAECINA, wife of Aulus Plautius. During the reign of Claudius (41-54A.D.), she was accused of being an adherent of a "foreign suspicion," which later tradition has identified as Christianity. She was acquitted in a "family" trial and given over to her husband. Throughout her life, she enjoyed a reputation for melancholy.

AUGUSTIANS, various Roman nobles in Nero's court. Nero surrounded himself with a grand and magnificent court which included many men and women from the most prestigious Roman families, as well as other clients, freedmen, slaves and assorted sycophants. The nickname Augustians was applied to his ever-present court. Famous Augustians included Petronius, Tigellinus, Seneca, and many others who also appear in Sienkiewicz's novel.

POPPAEA SABINA, Nero's second wife. Poppaea became Nero's wife in 62A.D. following his divorce and later murder of his first wife, Octavia. Nero's murder of Octavia was accompanied by the murder of other Claudian claimants to the throne. Under these circumstances, Poppaea wed Nero and brought with her a son, Rufrius Crispinus, by a previous marriage. She bore Nero a daughter, Claudia Augusta, who later died. Poppaea was killed by Nero in a fit of rage when he kicked her in the stomach.

PETER, Apostle of Jesus of Nazareth. Some historical evidence as well as centuries-old tradition place Peter in Rome at the time of the great fire in 64A.D. and subsequent persecutions. The story of the circumstances surrounding his martyrdom emerge from the very earliest of Church traditions and the location of his encounter with Christ and his execution site are venerated to this day.

PAUL, disciple of Jesus of Nazareth. Paul's proselytizing journeys were abruptly ended when he was arrested in 58A.D. in Jerusalem. He spent the next two and a half years in trials and prisons. He was finally brought to Rome in order to have his citizen's right to appeal heard by the Senate and the emperor, Nero. In 61A.D., he was acquitted and released by Nero, who at that time showed no animosity toward Christians. Tradition and legend surround the circumstances of Paul's re-arrest and martyrdom following the great fire in 64A.D.

ROME IN THE TIME OF NERO

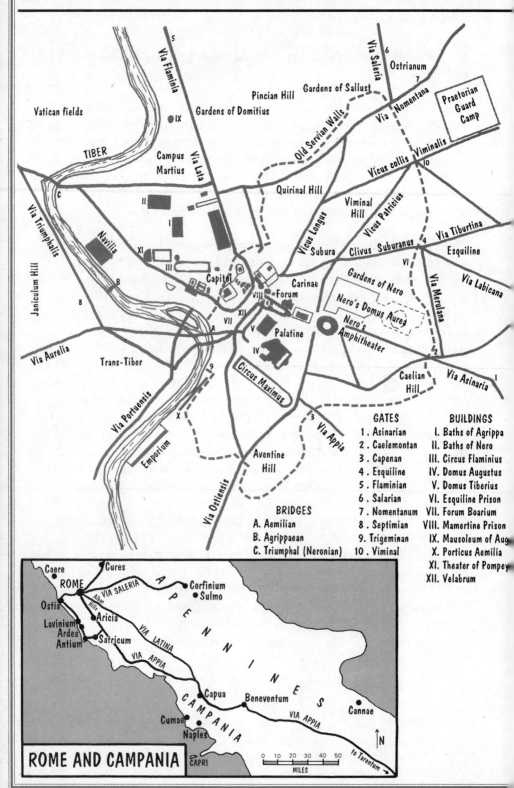

Via Flaminia · Via Saleria · 6 · Ostrianum · 7

Vatican fields · Pincian Hill · Gardens of Sallust · Via Nomentana · Praetorian Guard Camp

Gardens of Domitius · Old Servian Walls · IX

TIBER · Campus Martius · Via Lata · Quirinal Hill · Vicus collis · Viminalis · 10

Viminal Hill · Vicus Patricius · Via Tiburtina

Via Triumphalis · II · Vicus Longus · Subura · Clivus Suburanus · Esquiline · Via Labicana

Navilia · I · XI · III · Carinae · VI · Via Merulana

Janiculum Hill · Capitol · Forum · VIII · Gardens of Nero · Nero's Domus Aurea

8 · B · XII · VII · V · Palatine · Nero's Amphitheater · 2

A · IV · Caelian Hill · Via Asinaria · 1

Via Aurelia · Trans-Tiber · Circus Maximus · 3 · Via Appia

Via Portuensis · 9 · X · Aventine Hill · Emporium

Via Ostiensis

GATES
1. Asinarian
2. Caelemontan
3. Capenan
4. Esquiline
5. Flaminian
6. Salarian
7. Nomentanum
8. Septimian
9. Trigeminan
10. Viminal

BRIDGES
A. Aemilian
B. Agrippaean
C. Triumphal (Neronian)

BUILDINGS
I. Baths of Agrippa
II. Baths of Nero
III. Circus Flaminius
IV. Domus Augustus
V. Domus Tiberius
VI. Esquiline Prison
VII. Forum Boarium
VIII. Mamertine Prison
IX. Mausoleum of Aug
X. Porticus Aemilia
XI. Theater of Pompey
XII. Velabrum

ROME AND CAMPANIA

Caere · Cures · Corfinium · Sulmo
ROME · VIA SALERIA · APENNINES
Ostia · Alban Hills · Aricia
Lavinium · Ardea · Antium · Satricum · VIA LATINA · VIA APPIA
Cumae · Capua · Beneventum · Cannae
Naples · CAMPANIA · VIA APPIA · to Tarentum
CAPRI

0 10 20 30 40 50
MILES

N